Advance Praise for *The Road Ahead*

"*The Road Ahead* more than lived up to its promise—a shockingly brilliant salvo in the next wave of literature about our perpetual wars, a diverse and strange new literature which is utterly essential if we want to understand who we are as a nation, and what this era of constant war is doing to us, to our military, and to the countries where we send our men and women to kill and die."

— Phil Klay, National Book Award-winning author of *Redeployment*

"A stunning, poignant, astonishing, mournful, melancholy, brutally honest collection of stories about our wars in Iraq and Afghanistan, which makes this old soldier's heart sore. They are so well written. If you want to understand our young soldiers and the world they live in, read these stories."

— Larry Heinemann, National Book Award-winning author of *Paco's Story* and *Black Virgin Mountain*

"The writers gathered in these pages are among the finest, and the material they are working with is, by its nature, powerful and compelling. The result is stories that are by turns brutal and hilarious, dark and redemptive. Every one of them speaks to a truth we should not, cannot, turn away from."

— Mary Roach, *New York Times* bestselling author of *Grunt: The Curious Science of Humans at War*

"If war is eternal, its form alters with the times. These vivid stories are the up-to-date bulletins from the frontline of today. Injustices abound, meaning eludes us, until for moments, it doesn't. These writers deliver gut-wrecking reports of humanity at the edge of despair and offer us truths about the nature of war and the men and women struggling to survive it."

— Susan Minot, author of *Thirty Girls* and *Evening*

"These twenty-four intimate, brutal, unusual and honest portraits show us the startling effects of war, dispelling the myth that any military solution is simple. To this diverse group of writers, women and men, I say thank you for your wrenching stories. The cost of the wars in Iraq and Afghanistan is greater than we could have imagined."

— Bonnie Jo Campbell, author of *Once Upon a River* and *Mothers, Tell Your Daughters*

THE
ROAD
AHEAD

Fiction from the Forever War

EDITED BY
ADRIAN BONENBERGER
& BRIAN CASTNER

Foreword by Roxana Robinson

PEGASUS BOOKS
NEW YORK LONDON

THE ROAD AHEAD

Pegasus Books Ltd.
148 W 37th Street, 13th Floor
New York, NY 10018

Compilation copyright © 2017 by Adrian Bonenberger and Brian Castner

Foreword © 2017 by Roxana Robinson

Illustrations © 2017 Benjamin Busch

First Pegasus Books cloth edition January 2017

Interior design by Maria Fernandez

Library of Congress Cataloging-in-Publication Data is available.

ISBN: 978-1-68177-307-0

10 9 8 7 6 5 4 3 2 1

Printed in the United States of America
Distributed by W. W. Norton & Company

For all who have left home
and returned again

CONTENTS

FOREWORD

W hy not trust the body?"
That's the question, isn't it? That's the question asked
by PJ Fredrik in his dark commanding story, "The
Church." That's the question that military drill, and training, obedience and muscle memory is driving at: trust the body. That's what you need to do in the war zone.

But the body is not alone. We are something more than body, as this wonderful collection of stories shows us.

Going to war is the great expedition, a journey that changes the traveler in ways that could not have been imagined. Travel is broadening, they say, and so it is. In this case, it's deepening, too, and wounding and painful, also breathtaking and expanding. Who can say how the soul will react?

These writers can say. The writers of these stories, men and women who served in war zones, who have walked through the dust of Iraq and Afghanistan, who have spent their days breathing and feeling and living those places during the extreme weather event that is war, are here to say just how the soul will be changed.

When I began my own deployment into the war zone, that is, when I began to explore what war means to a soldier, and I began talking to veterans, I was struck by the way they would deliberately reject my assumptions. Any assumption I made, it turned out, was incorrect, which is more or less the reality between veterans and the civilian world.

I once asked a former Marine, deployed twice in Iraq, how he'd felt when he'd learned that there were no WMD. I asked with great trepidation, afraid I might be asking a question he didn't want to hear, or that I'd rouse some sleeping beast of resentment or hostility toward the great lumbering machine of the military, some hostility he didn't want to show a civilian. It could be anything, his response. I prepared myself for an IED.

Instead, he gave me a sunny smile. He said, "Roxana, there comes a time in a young man's life when he wants to go to war."

Okay. I was reminded that the way a veteran has seen the combat zone was never what I expected. If I imagined brutality, I'd find tenderness. If I expected a wounded soul I'd find mordant humor. Veterans themselves were not what I'd expected: they're greater, smarter, more damaged, more resilient, more greathearted and courageous, more frightened and grieving, more articulate and more dumbstruck, more ruthless and small-minded, more brutal and more tender.

Brutal and tender is one way to characterize these stories. From "Teresa" Fazio's silkily chilling "Little" to Benjamin Busch's hallucinatory "Into the Land of Dogs," these stories come from writers who create exquisite sentences and deep emotional engagement. War, like love, demands everything of you, as these stories show. It invades every aspect of your life, its imminence casts a long shadow before it, as shown by Michael Carson's wonderful story "War Party," which takes place entirely before deployment, and it casts a long shadow behind it, as every single one of these stories show. It's hard to mention one story without mentioning all of them, because all of them are compelling, engaging, and essential commentaries on a theme that has been a part of human history since history was first painted on smooth surfaces.

This collection is part of the intersection between the military and the literary. When I first ventured into the world of the military, I was struck by the generosity and energy of the people I met there, and these editors, Adrian Bonenberger and Brian Castner, are exemplars of that energetic generosity. With this volume they're making sure that the members of their tribe—the military—can see themselves reflected, their experience set down, their feelings made known, their thoughts made real, for the rest of the world to understand. And their own stories remind us that we can never reach the end of this terrain, never come to a full comprehension of this place.

All these stories are important: they are part of who we are, whether or not we like what we see, whether or not we've been to the war zone. They show us the most important thing a writer can tell us: this is what human beings are like.

Roxana Robinson
Cornwall, Connecticut
July 2016

LETTER FROM
THE EDITORS

Only a few years ago, it looked as if we'd closed a chapter in our nation's history, and were set to wind down two wars. Remember the time before ISIS, when we were leaving Iraq? Remember when the surge so pressed the Taliban that we could justify leaving the Afghans to fend for themselves? The authors of this anthology remember that time very well; many of them were still serving on active duty. The wars in Afghanistan and Iraq—the longest in our nation's history—are their wars. They saw what it meant to take part in the first all-volunteer war, the first war where women played such prominent and widespread ground-combat roles, and first where the heavy moral, financial, and emotional costs were borne by such a small percentage of the American people.

Many firsts, but this war yielded another superlative that receives far less attention. America has never before, by any measure, fought a war with such a well-educated force. Not only do soldiers have unprecedented technical skills, but many are also steeped in war literature, readers already well-versed in the canon from Hemingway to Herr. Tim O'Brien's *The Things They Carried* is an entrenched high school standard for the generation of men and women we sent to Iraq and Afghanistan. They knew what a war story looked like even before they put rifles over their shoulders and marched, drove, or flew to battle.

Modern life is faster, more complex, more quickly changing than ever before. So why not also the development of the veteran writers making sense of these conflicts? We should not be surprised that war literature is evolving at such an unprecedented pace. The first-draft-of-history now gives way to deep reflective fiction in only a few years; readers waited decades for the equivalent after World War II or Vietnam.

Which is to say that the stories you are about to read are more thoughtful, empathetic, generous, and fantastic than any we've ever had from veterans of a war that is still ongoing. We are all of us accelerated.

—∞—

Stories and narrative are powerful subtle things. They can smother strict history. The screaming horses of *All Quiet on the Western Front* convey the horrors of trench warfare more effectively than any stack of statistics. But this myth-making ability can be deceptive. When Americans talk about war literature, for example, what we really mean is Western war literature. How many of us have read a World War I story by a former member of the Russian Empire, let alone its Ottoman rival? How many stories can you name by Japanese, Chinese, or Siamese participants in World War II? And who gets to tell "authentic" war stories, the kind that transcend fact? Combat veterans? All veterans? Family members and friends? Citizens of the country that sent them?

Any writer who uses "veteran" to describe him or herself bears a burden of authenticity. The average reader—who, unlike us brooding war writers, occasionally puts down Caputo and Salter to enjoy celebrity chef tell-alls and vampire romance young adult novels—can mistakenly assume that when a veteran tells a war story, they are definitively saying *this is how it was,* as opposed to *this is how it was for ME,* or, in the case of many stories, *this is how I imagine it was for someone else.* Yes, we use our imaginations too; note stories in this collection like Kristen Rouse's "Pawns," about Afghan truck drivers, or Brandon Willitts's "Winter on the Rim," about a grieving widow, or Matt Hefti's "We Put a Man in a Tree," about the haunting dead.

These stories will not be the last word on the wars. Narratives evolve, and though the pace quickens, the depth and breadth of the race expands, frustrating expectations of a finish line. Nothing in this anthology is definitive. The first books from Iraq and Afghanistan were largely shoot-'em-up memoirs, war-plan nonfiction by strategists and generals, and memoirs by conflict reporters like Sebastian Junger. When the Iraq War portion of this conflict appeared to end in 2010, the fiction that appeared soon after was retrospective. That's what it felt like, at the time.

This collection, on the other hand, was written during the rise of the Islamic State and Boko Haram, Iran's emergence as a major regional power, and the resurrection of Russia as a source of funding for proxy wars. This anthology was written and edited after the invasion of Ukraine, while China built islands in the South China Sea, and while the USA expanded its footprint in Syria and Iraq. For the first time in our lives, we are beginning to realize that Forever War might be more than hyperbole. A generation raised during the Clinton boom has seen war proliferate during adulthood, profitably so, and along lines that give one reason to believe, based on factual rather than narrative history, that we have more and greater conflict to expect, rather than less.

The stories in *The Road Ahead* respond to the imaginative challenge of a world accustomed to ceaseless conflict. Some soldiers come home from war, others return again and again. Some civilians flee while others are left stuck in a perpetual violent limbo. Ask us for a solution to this conflict, or a prediction of the future, or even an explanation of how we as a country ended up here, and we present this book. It moves from particular to general, from real to surreal, from the thing as it is to the thing as it could be.

Another anthology with another perspective from editors who just shed the uniform will surely follow, by voices and from a time and context we cannot imagine today.

—⁂—

Without the work that came before it, this collection would surely not exist, and so we owe a number of debts of gratitude.

To Phil Klay, whose National Book Award–winning collection *Redeployment* not only established the short story as the preferred medium to examine these wars, but also set a mark for the rest of us to aspire to.

To the editors and contributors of *Fire and Forget*, the breakthrough anthology of war fiction to arise from Iraq and Afghanistan and an inspiration to the editors of this volume. We learned that while taking on such a challenge was probably a fool's errand, sometimes that fool's errand ends up being necessary.

To the community of veteran writers that almost universally work to support and develop each other's craft. This network takes many forms—writing workshops like Words After War, the veteran-themed reading series at the Old Stone House and Voices From War, yearly meet-ups at AWP—but the end result is clear: when we solicited stories for this anthology, our issue was one of too many options, rather than too few.

—⁂—

A final note on the process of building such an anthology. Adrian Bonenberger conceived of the idea for a new fiction collection and initiated the first call to writers, and Brian Castner served as de facto managing editor, but during the submission phase, the compilation of stories for this anthology was the work of many hands. Teresa Fazio and Aaron Gwyn served as invaluable frontline editors, doing yeoman's work on the first drafts of many of these stories. This volume would not exist without the voice and perspective of Teresa, and academic and craft expertise of Aaron. Art is a collective endeavor.

The editors, with gratitude—
Bonenberger
Castner
Fazio
Gwyn

WINTER ON THE RIM

by Brandon Willitts

After sunrise, Joyce walked into the yard to feed and water the animals. She took comfort in her morning chores. She gathered the feed and walked to the pen. The chickens roamed the yard. She called to them and scattered their feed. The goats were skittish and demanding, like cats. They waited to leave their shack in the pen until Joyce broke the layer of ice formed overnight in their water trough, and only after she'd busted through the ice would the two creatures poke their heads out to watch Joyce fill the feeding buckets with hay and alfalfa. She left the pen and latched the gate.

"You two remind me of the girls I hated in high school," Joyce said to them. "Saved from the dirtiness of the world by everyone else's work." When they craned their necks out of the shack, she yelled, "Keep it up, you two. You just might starve to death." She went inside to watch them feed.

Joyce pulled a juniper log for the woodstove and boiled water for a bath. As she undressed, she saw her reflection in the bedroom mirror. She turned to her side to measure herself in profile. She was startled by her body's starkness; the long runs and farm chores had worn her as thin as paper.

Winter had arrived too soon. Months before all of this, Joyce tried desperately to get ahead of the chores, to defend the cabin from the advancing cold. In the afternoons, after her run, she sat on the porch steps and watched the horizon. She saw her first winter coming, just in the distance, as though it sat waiting above the mouth of the Mogollon

Rim. And as the days grew shorter, winter slid a little further down the canyon walls, gathering momentum as it flowed along the valley.

She fixed her hair in a bun atop her head, turned to the steaming basin, and washed her face. As she dipped the rag in the water and wrung away the excess, she thought of how Michael took to washing her hair. His hands and fingers were calloused, but he was gentle and dedicated. He worked out any knots she had. He made such an effort to make the cabin into their home. He wanted her to be comfortable, to be happy.

After her bath, she dressed. She checked the animals, the weather. The sun shined boldly in a clear, cloudless sky. She sat in a chair next to the woodstove, wrapped herself in a blanket, and looked into the bedroom: the unmade bed, her clothes in a pile on the floor.

Two photographs hung outside the bedroom. The photographs were framed, black and white, their edges stained yellow by age. Joyce studied them. One was of Michael's grandfather in his dress blues, taken before he left for Korea. The other was of Michael, a chainsaw perched on his shoulder, leaning against a massive ponderosa pine, taken during his first season with the Forest Service.

The woodstove popped and sizzled. She shifted in her chair, remembering the day she lost him. She'd been in the goat pen when the sound of a truck pulling into the cabin's driveway propelled her out of the pen and around the side. Thinking it was Michael she rushed to the driveway. Instead she saw two men from Michael's crew, Dan and the FMO, getting out of a lime green Forest Service truck. Michael was dead. Burned up in his fire shelter. And four others were dead too somewhere in Idaho. She ran toward the woods, and sat curled against the remains of a ponderosa, sobbing uncontrollably, until the cold drove her inside.

After Michael's funeral, Joyce's mother begged her to come home, even forced her husband to drive down to Young to retrieve Joyce. But when Joyce's father arrived he never mentioned Oregon or home. The two of them sat on the porch, shared coffee, and talked about Michael. He asked about the cabin, about chopping wood, about feeding goats, and about winter in Young.

Later, she made dinner, and the two ate in peace and comfort, almost for the first time. It was the peace and comfort she'd tried to cultivate with Michael. That next morning, she made him breakfast, and when he left, he turned and kissed her on her forehead.

As she watched her father's car lurch down the gravel road, bucking with the ruts, she waved. After the final dust settled, only the sounds of his car were heard. And only after the sound of her father's car faded entirely, lost in the distance and the mountains, did she return to her cabin.

It wasn't just her mother who urged her to leave Young. No one understood her decision, perhaps least of all herself. She resisted, anyway; stood fast, stayed in the cabin. It was a choice that seemed to anchor her to the landscape. She didn't need to understand. She'd find her way. She would tend to things. If she refused to leave, she'd be as close to Michael as the earth allowed.

A truck door slammed and a voice called out her name. She jumped in her chair, startled. The blanket fell to the floor. The screen door opened and someone knocked. She watched the door.

"It's Dan," he said, knocked again. "Joyce, you home?"

"Yeah, I'm home," she called back to him. "Be right there." She went to the door. Through the tiny panes in the door, she thought Dan's figure looked hazy and distant, as though he was underwater. He was standing on the edge of the porch, looking toward the mountains. She watched a moment as he shifted his weight and leaned against the railing. He stood smoking, silent. She opened the door and walked out onto the porch. "Hey, Dan," she said.

He turned, removed his wool hat. "Hey there," he said, smiling. "How you holding up?"

"One day at a time."

"Seven of them in a week."

She smiled, walked inside. "Come in. Take off your boots."

He stubbed out his cigarette, walked inside, and removed his boots. "I didn't see you this week. I'm headed down to Payson, thought I'd drop by and see how you've been."

"I'm headed down there today too," she said. "I've got errands. You want some coffee?"

"Love some."

Dan sat on the couch. She made coffee on the stove, and then poured two cups. She handed Dan his coffee. He thanked her, and asked, "So, how are things around the homestead?"

"Fine, I guess," she said from behind her cup. "The animals eat every day, and the generator always needs fuel. Power's finally out for good. What about you?"

"Not too bad, really. The FMO has got us doing some hiring right now. We're pulling resumes and cold-calling folks. Just trying to get a feel for which ones we'd like to hire. You need any help with that generator?"

She blew into her cup, took a sip, and then said, "I got it so far, I think. But I'll let you know if I do."

Dan looked into his coffee, said, "Well, you know I'm always around if you need anything."

When Michael was alive, he spoke highly of Dan, and after Michael died, Joyce soon discovered why. In the chaotic days after Michael's death, Dan set up a collection in Young, raising enough to cover all the funeral expenses. After the funeral, Dan kept her updated on the progress of the Forest Service's investigation into Michael's death. He even helped her with Michael's will.

Dan's cup scraped across the table and broke up her thoughts. She looked toward him. "One time," he said to her leaning back into the couch, "the crew was digging line deep into the woods of the Sawtooth, for like thirteen hours, just trying to get ahead of the fire. Bone tired, dead on our feet. And the fire kept jumping the line, so we had to work faster. People were cursing and complaining, and it felt like the fire was going to get away from us. And in the middle of all of it, Michael stood up, and called out to the crew. Everyone stopped to listen, and he yelled, 'Next goddamn person who bitches about digging line with my hotshot crew will buy every single one of those engine assholes a beer for the rest of this season.' No one said a word after that, and we got ahead of it a few hours later."

They both laughed.

"I saw a different part of him."

"You mind if I grab a smoke outside?" Dan asked.

"No, go ahead."

While Dan smoked, Joyce thought back to the afternoons before fire season. If she heard the neighbor's dog bark, she knew Michael was close by. She'd walk outside to look for him. Sometimes crows flew overhead. Then she'd walk through the tall grass, and as it brushed against her pants, her boots sank deep into the mud. She'd walk toward the tree line. He'd straddle the threshold: a foot in the grass, the other in the forest. She'd watch him pick up arrowheads, a hawk's feather, a deer skull, and little bits of wood. He'd gaze intently at them, and then toss them in his pack. Lost in his thoughts, he'd finally look up. His face was tan and weathered, but he didn't look old. His shoulders were broad and his forearms were thick and ropey, like those of a man who made a living on his feet, with his hands. She'd wave and walk toward the forest. A late-afternoon sun sank slowly behind the Rim, and their shadows would grow longer in the grass. They'd walk through the woods, where he would identify the trees, and talk about how the Natives used fire to shape the land.

Dan's truck door slammed. He came back into the cabin holding a thick folder. He took off his boots and returned to the couch. Without looking at Joyce, he placed the folder on the table. "This is Michael's file," Dan said, leaning forward, his hand sliding the folder closer to Joyce. "It's the results of the Idaho investigation."

Joyce stared at the file, its red color suddenly intense. She looked up at Dan, her face hot, and nodded. "Thank you," she said. "I'll read it later."

They walked to the porch. Dan put on his wool cap and walked to his truck.

"Hey Dan," Joyce called out to him, and turned to her. "It was like the roof was torn off."

"You know where to find me if you need any help," he said.

Joyce saw what looked like relief spread across Dan's face. His shoulders relaxed slightly, less tense, and the lines in his face softened.

"I do," she said.

Inside, Joyce stared at the folder, and listened to Dan's truck idle. The clutch and shifter made a grinding noise when he changed gears. It whined as he reversed down the driveway.

Her throat was dry and tight, and her thoughts were wide and unshaped. She filled a glass with water and drank it down quickly. Her mind felt thin, like sheets of vellum. She rinsed the cups and glass and dried her wet hands on her jeans. She walked to the window and checked the animals. She sat on the couch, leaned back, and placed a pillow behind her head. She closed her eyes and soon fell into a deep afternoon sleep.

When she woke, Joyce restacked the cordwood on the porch, pulling out logs for the cabin stove. She checked the goats' feeding bucket, then filled their water trough from behind the wooden fence. She counted the chickens as she walked to the truck. She bound the gas cans with a bungee cord and loaded the trash into the truck bed.

As she turned out of the driveway, enormous clouds, the color of molten tin, floated high above the Rim. She stopped the truck and watched the clouds move undisturbed, slowly, through the sky, made denser and more menacing. After a few moments, she continued again down the gravel road, and drove the sixty miles in silence.

In Payson she dumped the trash, filled the gas cans, and bungeed them back in the truck bed. She then drove to get groceries, and inside the Safeway, Joyce grabbed a cart and pushed it toward the produce. She got ingredients for a salad, bagged the vegetables, and pulled out her list.

Joyce rolled the cart to the cereal aisle. The bright fluorescent lighting made everything look unnatural. In the cabin, the winter sun often never touched the darkest corners, and everything appeared as a light shade of blue. Suddenly, a deep loneliness tugged at her, and her hands shook. She pulled out her phone, her hands still shaking, and dialed Dan's number. It went to voicemail.

"Dan, it's Joyce," she said into the phone. "I was just in the grocery store, and I thought, well, I thought. Shit." She paused to gather her thoughts. "Sorry. So, I thought maybe you could come over and have dinner at the cabin. It might be nice to have some company. Give me a call back. I'll be in Payson for a little bit longer, but then I'm headed back up to Young. Okay." She placed the phone in her purse, and stared down the massive aisle of cereal. Her hands were now still. She glanced at her list, and pushed the cart to the next aisle.

Outside the weather had turned, dark clouds hung low over the parking lot. She loaded the groceries and started her truck. She idled and leaned her head against the steering wheel. The cold was refreshing.

The sky opened and large, heavy raindrops fell to earth. She looked up to see an older woman running frantically across the parking lot, a newspaper held over her head to shield against the rain. The woman's clothes were soaked and heavy, sagging off her frail body. A limp paper bag of groceries was cradled awkwardly against her side. The woman fumbled with her keys, dropped the paper and keys, and retrieved the keys from the wet blacktop. She clumsily loaded the wet bag of groceries into her vehicle and then drove away with a fogged windshield. Joyce stared at the abandoned newspaper, as it became nothing but grey mush.

She watched the rain pool on the street, and she wanted so much to get out of the truck and touch it. She wanted to cup it in her hands. She thought of the times, as a child, when she walked down to a stream, where she'd place her hands just below the water's surface, watching as her hands and the moving water somehow reshaped themselves to meet one another. A ring in the water was sent out that widened, making its way through Oregon's rivers, and out to the sea. The rings, she imagined as a child, would eventually return right back to the same spot where her small, delicate hands had first disrupted the water's surface, back to its beginning. The rings were tiny disruptions that circled the earth's waters, returning once again to the same small hands that gently pushed the water.

Joyce shut off the truck and cried. She placed both hands around the steering wheel, squeezed tightly, and rocked her body violently back and forth. She let out a scream. She breathed in deeply, held it, and then let it out gently. She closed her eyes and touched them with her palms, keeping them there until the rain stopped.

She drove toward Young. The truck's defrosters were broken. She wiped the windows with a rag as she drove. On the highway, the clouds parted, and she glimpsed a canyon-colored sky set back far from grey-black storm clouds. In the mountains night brought darkness. The higher she drove into the mountains, the more the rain hardened. The blacktop soon turned to dirt and gravel, and the frozen rain turned to snow. Joyce stopped the truck, shifted into four-wheel-drive, and drove on carefully. Big logging trucks, filled with the trunks of old-growth ponderosa pines were known to drive recklessly, forcing motorists into ditches, leaving them stranded through freezing nights, or worse.

The night settled around the road. She focused on the road ahead, her vision narrowed in on the falling snow, and her hands felt for any shift in the truck's grip on the ground. The high beams illuminated the large white flakes, making them appear bigger, and the blackened woods on both sides of the road formed a tunnel.

In the distance, headlights appeared, becoming bigger and brighter as she drove to meet them. For a brief moment, she saw a flash and the vehicle came to a stop. She slowed, waiting for the headlights to approach her, but they remained still, so she drove on. She could see that it was a logging truck, and as she approached, the vehicle moved forward suddenly and passed her without slowing. The snow was falling harder and covering the road. Joyce rolled down her window to look out.

She saw the blood first. She followed the trail of blood, and saw the deer. The blood was spattered in uneven lines along the snow, and the deer lay in a crumpled mess. Joyce turned on her hazard lights, grabbed a flashlight from the glove compartment, put on her jacket, and got out of the truck. She looked down the road for the logging truck, but its lights and its sound were gone. She shined her light on the dying deer: a buck.

Joyce approached the buck, and she held her light steady, listened for any sounds. She heard a faint tapping coming from the darkened woods: it was the snow falling against the bare pine branches. The buck was completely still, save its shallow breathing. Tiny bursts of yellow light flashed on the snow. The hazard lights blinked, and the outlying corners of the darkened edges of night appeared faintly yellow. The darker edges of her vision glowed but then darkened once more. She stood over the dying animal; even in the darkness, with only a small light by which to see, she saw the wild and immense power of its muscled body and the breadth of its rack.

Joyce knelt in the snow, and placed a hand on its throat. The buck was still, but Joyce felt the life quickly fading from its body. She placed both hands on the buck now. She wanted to feel the last moments of the buck's life, to know what death felt like in her hands. She clicked off her flashlight and the world was dark. She brushed away the snow collecting on its damp fur. She hoped the buck was not in pain, but knew death could never be completely painless. She stayed with the buck as it died. When she no longer felt life under her hands she cried.

The snow was falling harder, and she was still far from the cabin. She had to get out of the storm. She stood, placed the flashlight in her coat, bent at the knees, grabbed two of the buck's hooves, and dragged it away from the road. The ground was frozen. The wet snow and a gentle slope made it easier to drag. Joyce pulled the buck away from the road, then down a small embankment that led to the woods. The woods were covered with fresh snow. The buck was too heavy to pull over stumps and downed limbs, so she was forced to leave it. The snow would cover it for the night, conserving it, but soon the animals and birds and forest would reclaim it. She was breathing heavily. She tried to listen for the sounds of coyotes, but she heard only her heavy breath and the faint tapping of frozen water on the pines. She knelt to the buck a final time, placed her hands on its side, and apologized for leaving.

She climbed to the road, her feet slipping on the slope, and then walked back to her truck. She drove home. The smell of the animal was on her hands. When she pulled into the driveway, she shut off the truck and sat silently in the cab. She watched the snow blanket the land. She would shovel it away in the morning, but tonight she would watch it fall. She imagined the snow forever falling, imagining its beauty and stillness were somehow permanent. She imagined the view through a frosted and fogging windshield of the snow falling might stay forever in her mind. The silence that she experienced might somehow be the only sounds she would ever hear again.

Joyce opened the truck door, gathered the bags of groceries. She slammed the door shut with her hip. The snow crunched beneath her boots. She leaned against the railing, watched the snow, and thought of the red file sitting inside the cabin, waiting for her.

Michael's file would never tell her anything more than she already knew.

She would never be able to lie down in the woods, pull a fire shelter over her body, and wait until a deadly blaze blanketed her, cooking her alive. As the roar of a wildfire, like a jet engine, drowned out all other sounds.

She kicked her boots against the steps and walked inside. She hung up her jacket, set down the groceries, and took off her boots. The generator would be filled in the morning. She looked outside. The animals were nowhere to be seen, hunkered down in their pens, waiting out the storm.

She kept the cabin dark. She placed a log in the stove and blew on the dim coals. The fire came back to life. The room was still and the sounds of the burning log echoed in the small space. The flames grew and whipped, the pitch popped. She closed the stove. The air pulled through and whistled softly. She walked to the window to once more see the snow. It looked perfect.

The snow covered the tree line. The dark woods of winter were remade. In the woods, the ground was no longer the moist and rotting earth of autumn, nor was it the hollow and empty earth of early winter. It was something else entirely. The snow fell through the trees, hiding snags and widowmakers.

The high-desert snow fell not down but up the Mogollon Rim, as though winter was retreating away from the cabin, away from Joyce, and back atop the mouth of the Rim. She closed her eyes, placed a hand to her own pulse, and thought of the snow burying the buck. She felt her own heart beating. She looked out onto the snow-covered land. She listened as the snow fell. She listened to the sounds of the cabin. She listened for Idaho.

THERE'S ALWAYS ONE

by Kayla M. Williams

K ate closed her eyes and tried to turn off her brain, let his weight and their movement be the entirety of her world. For a minute it worked, and her mind buzzed. Then his breathing shifted, dragging her back, and a few grunts later he collapsed onto her.

She placed a hand on his chest and kissed his shoulder. "Thank you."

He rolled off of her, propped himself up on an elbow, and frowned. "I'm sorry, you didn't . . ."

Shaking her head, Kate put a finger on his lips. "No. Don't worry about it. I just have a lot on my mind." Reality was settling back in, the illusion of intimacy fading. Being alone with someone suddenly felt far worse than being alone by herself. She rose and settled a simple black dress over her slim figure, then ducked into the bathroom, glancing in a mirror while pulling her long, straight brown hair into a ponytail and wiping a bit of smudged mascara from below her green eyes.

"Don't you want to stay?"

"I can't. My dog needs to be let out." The lie slipped out, easier than hurting his feelings with the truth: she couldn't stand the thought of staying.

He got up too, pulling on a pair of discarded jeans and walking with her toward the door. "Call me?"

"Sure."

He grinned wryly. "You don't have my number."

She smiled back, pulled his head down and gently kissed his cheek before walking out. "Nope."

The clock in her car read just after midnight. Nine on the West Coast at Joint Base Lewis-McChord—her best friend Chloe would still be up. She answered immediately.

"Kate! How are you?"

Without preamble: "I picked some guy up at the bar. It was so easy— just let him think he was picking me up, made eyes at him while he told me war stories."

"Some pogue?"

"Must've been. Probably supply or something—I bet he never left the wire. You know how it is—the more they talk . . ."

Chloe laughed. "Yeah. And? How was it?"

"Meh. Am I a whore?"

Her friend's tone hardened. "No." A long pause. "After what you've been through, you deserve to do whatever you need to. Anyone who judges you can fuck off. They have no idea."

"I wish you were here."

"Oh, Kate." Chloe's empathy was palpable in the pause that followed. "I'm not allowed to fly. Why don't you come out here? When the baby comes I'll be home for a few months. My mom's taking a couple weeks, but then . . ."

"Maybe. I have to go visit our parents . . ."

"Call me anytime. I'm not sleeping much."

When she walked into her house, the cleaning lady's handmade red, white, and blue sign, "Welcome Home Kate and Paul!" seemed accusatory. She flipped it facedown on the counter. Unable to bear sliding between the freshly laundered sheets of their bed alone, she convinced herself it would be better to miss traffic by driving at night anyway, packed quickly, and left.

The highway was mostly empty except for trucks. Kate rolled the windows down and turned the radio up, singing along to bad pop music rather than thinking.

It was close to nine in the morning when she pulled up in front of Barbara's house, hours earlier than expected. She killed the engine and put her forehead on the steering wheel, wondering if just driving away was an option. It wasn't.

Walking up the sidewalk through the carefully tended lawn to the modest brick home, Kate saw the gold star flag in the window and shuddered, wondering bitterly how many of Barbara's neighbors knew what it meant without being told. She tried to push those thoughts away before ringing the bell.

"Kate! You're so early!" Barbara engulfed her in a hug. "Do you want coffee?" She led Kate through the immaculate living room to the kitchen and busied herself fixing coffees, chatting incessantly as if they wouldn't have to discuss Paul's death if she never stopped talking about other things. "Milk and sugar, right? I just got this Keurig thing; you know, you can get so many different flavors. Not just coffee, tea or hot chocolate too. Makes more sense since I live alone. Don't have to make a whole pot. Did you drive all night? Was that safe? All those big trucks on the road. And you probably still have jet lag! You must be exhausted." Finally she sat down at the table, set down their mugs, and looked straight at Kate. "I'm not sleeping much, either."

Neither of them could hold eye contact for long. Kate looked away first, sipped her coffee. "I'm so sorry for your loss, Barbara."

"Oh, honey!" Barbara's voice thickened and she swallowed hard, then took Kate's hands between her own, looking out the window and blinking fast. Kate stared down at the wood table, feeling the cool papery skin of her mother-in-law's hands. *Ex-mother-in-law? What's our relationship now?*

They spent a couple of days sharing memories, looking at old photo albums, and telling funny stories, conversations that might have approached his death suddenly veering off in other directions. The women were together, yet apart, each still feeling the outlines of her grief.

—⁊⁊—

The last morning of her stay, Kate stood alone in the living room, looking at the photos on the mantel: Paul as a chubby, diapered baby, a swim-suited toddler running through the sprinkler, a kid in a soccer uniform, a teenager in graduation robes, a young man in DCUs. He transformed in the series, body going from lanky to muscular, brown hair first growing shaggy and then cropped to military regulations, shoulders and jaw broadening—but in all of them he bore the same confident and exuberant smile that had first drawn her to him, so self-assured and fearless, unreserved. She touched the glass of the most recent picture, the two of them with Barbara at their wedding four years earlier. *If only Paul were here, he would know how to comfort us.* Kate shook her head at the absurdity of the thought and stared up at the ceiling. She wasn't ready to share her sorrow, and didn't want to add to his mother's burden.

Barbara joined her. "That's my favorite," she said, pointing at one of Paul climbing a tree. He was probably twelve or thirteen, all gangly legs and arms, looking up for the next branch to grab while sunlight broke just so through the leaves to halo his head. "I don't know why. Maybe . . . he looks like an angel, with the light—" Her voice caught in her throat and she turned away, choking off a sob. After a shuddery breath, she turned back to Kate. "Here, I thought you should have this." Barbara was holding out a folded American flag. "They would have given it to you at the funeral if you could've been there."

Kate was shaking her head. "No, no." She closed Barbara's fingers back around it. "No. I have all his other things. Put it there on the mantel with the photos." She stepped back. "I'm sorry I couldn't

come. We had a service for him over there too." The memory flooded
back: boots, helmet atop rifle, roll call with his name unanswered.
Their fellow soldiers surrounding her, squeezing her shoulder. His
men crying openly, unashamedly. "I mean, I could've come back,
but I couldn't. They tried to send me back, but I had to stay." Kate
was talking fast, trying to explain it in a way Paul's mother would
understand, remembering the controlled urgency with which she had
needed to convince her first sergeant not to make her take emergency
leave. "I couldn't leave my guys. Not then. And I had to help catch
the bad guys. For Paul." Working was the only time she'd felt calm,
going out on missions and piecing together scattered bits of intelligence. Alone at night in the CHU they'd shared had been terrible;
busyness was all that helped. Kate felt suddenly wobbly and grabbed
the mantel to steady herself.

"Did you?" There was an unusual fierceness in Barbara's voice.

"What?" Kate felt disconcerted, torn between the past and present.

"Did you catch the guys who did it?"

"No," Kate said flatly. "We killed them." Not that there had been
forensics or a trial, but she was confident the intel was good. When
a team had gone to roll them up, they'd fought back. None of them
survived. Kate wasn't sorry. Between corrupt judges and guards taking
bribes, who knew if any of them would have really been punished in
the Afghan system. Rule of law was a joke. This way she had closure.

"Good." Barbara, normally gentle, sounded cold.

Kate cringed inside. The war didn't belong here. Barbara shouldn't
relish anyone's death; it upset the order. She nodded toward her suit-
case, waiting by the front door. "I need to go—see my mom, pick up
Bear."

Barbara tried to smile. "Oh, he's such a good dog. Bring him by to
see me sometime, will you?" The smile slipped away. "Since Paul's
father passed a few years ago, you two are all that I have left, now
that . . ." Inadvertently, her hand reached out and touched Kate's belly

as she blurted out, "I just wish you and Paul had had a baby!" She turned away and crossed her arms over her chest.

"Me too." Kate reached out and touched her mother-in-law's shoulder, then stepped forward and hugged her. Barbara turned around and they clung to one another for a moment before breaking apart. "We'll come visit soon," she promised on her way out.

A few blocks away Kate pulled over and pressed the heels of her hands to her eyes while scrunching her face up, willing herself not to cry. *This isn't the time or place*, she told herself. *When is, then? Where?* another part asked back. Shaking her head fiercely, she pulled back on to the road.

—⁊⁊—

Midafternoon, she pulled up in front of her childhood home and sighed. For a moment she let herself envy Chloe's relationship with her mom, then pushed the thought away, trying to relinquish any expectations of comfort. Kate and her mother had a fraught history—this visit, too, was a duty and not a relief. *Don't expect it to suck, either—that just guarantees disaster.*

Remembering that the doorbell was broken, she knocked hard and then waited. And waited. Knocked again. Her mother looked frazzled when she finally opened the door, brushing sweaty tendrils of hair out of her eyes. "Sorry, Kate! I was cleaning out the guest room for you. It's impossible to keep on top of everything! Come in, come in!"

The breeze from the door shutting behind her set a tumbleweed of dog and cat hair adrift across the floor, settling under the table Kate set her purse on. They hugged awkwardly as Kate craned her head around, looking. "Where's Bear?"

"He's out back. You go see him; I'll make coffee."

Kate moved as quickly as she could to the back door without actually running, and flung it open. Bear must've heard her car or voice, because he was waiting, tail wagging furiously, forcing his way through as soon as the door opened a crack. "Hey, boy!" He circled Kate, bumping against her, nuzzling her hand, panting, wagging, half-jumping, and finally settling to sit on her feet and lean back against her legs while gazing up at her, his tongue lolling out. "There's a good dog," she murmured, leaning down to scratch both sides of his chin with her hands.

The black-and-brown Rottweiler mix stayed close as she walked into the kitchen and leaned against her again when she sat down.

Her mom was opening and closing cabinets, shoving things around. "I know there's coffee here somewhere. Your uncle Jim gave me some in a gift basket for Christmas. I know how much you like it . . ."

"Ma, it's okay," Kate tried to break in.

No luck. "Did you know, Jim's wife Cathy has breast cancer? And their good-for-nothing son, your cousin Jeff, he still doesn't have a job. Lives in their basement. Can you believe it? Twenty-five years old and still at home. Cathy thinks he smokes the pot."

"Mother."

The search, and the litany, went on. "I told him he should join the Army like you did, I mean, if you can do it, surely he can."

"Mom!" Sharply this time. "Tea is fine. Okay? Tea would be great."

"You didn't have to snap at me."

Kate stifled a sharp retort. "Sorry, Ma."

Her mother boiled water in silence, then set steeping cups of tea on the table before sitting down.

"How's Barbara holding up?"

"As well as can be expected."

"How are you?"

Kate quirked her mouth and blew on the scalding tea before taking a tiny sip. "As well as can be expected."

"Well," her mother sighed. "At least you didn't have any children."

Setting the tea down hard enough that it sloshed out of the cup, Kate stood abruptly. Bear jumped up, wagging his tail. She stared down at her mother, whose face had gone pale and anxious, opened her mouth to speak, then clenched it closed again. She turned stiffly and walked to the front door, picked up her purse, and walked out.

Her mother trailed after her.

"Honey?" she said.

—⁂—

Back home a few hours later, Bear ran from one room to another, tail wagging excitedly. He circled back to Kate, head cocked to one side, tail wagging more slowly. Finally finished searching the entire house, he sat at her feet and stared up at her, looked questioningly at the front door, then gave one short bark. Kate shook her head, tears welling up. Bear tilted his head, looking as if he were trying to understand, then raised a paw and scratched at her leg.

She knelt down and grabbed the thick fur on either side of his big square head, then shook her head slowly. "I'm sorry, Bear." The control finally collapsed, and she wrapped her arms around the dog and buried her face in his coat, sobbing. Bear whined and thumped his tail. Kate wept mindlessly, fingers clutching at Bear's fur. At some point her crying turned to keening, and Bear started howling. That startled her back to reality, and she went to wash her face and blow her nose.

"Come on," she said, patting the bed. "Hop up." The dog looked around. "Yeah, you. Just come on."

After one final hesitation, Bear bounded easily onto the bed and circled around before settling against her.

—⁂—

They were inseparable for the remainder of Kate's leave, going for long hikes in pleasant weather, watching *Law & Order* marathons while it rained, sleeping back-to-back at night. Kate hardly spent any time with people. She went out with friends a few times, but no one seemed to know how to act around her. Some of them wanted to hold hands over cocoa and talk about her feelings, which made her uncomfortable. They urged her to grieve, to process her emotions, to do yoga. "I know they mean well, but have they even met me?" she vented to Chloe. "I don't want to sit around singing Kumbaya and talking about my grief journey! I'd rather be back in Afghanistan than here 'engaging in self-care.' I want to do something, work, have a purpose. Not all this touchy-feely bullshit."

Others seemed to think she should already be over Paul's death and that going clubbing would be good for her, which was worse. Seeing couples made her sad. Watching single people hooking up made her sick.

"Do you want help getting rid of his things?" one of her girlfriends asked over coffee. She just shook her head, eyebrows drawn together, but then thought about it the whole drive home. Standing in their walk-in closet, she trailed her hands along his uniforms and handful of dress shirts and slacks—he was more a jeans and t-shirts guy. Kate didn't need them; maybe someone else could use them. But the thought of erasing his presence from her home—their home?—seemed wrong. She leaned into the clothes, breathing deeply but smelling only Tide, resenting his tidiness: there was nothing left that smelled of him.

Kate's father drove up to take her out to dinner one night when he stopped in Nashville on a business trip. She kept waiting for him to bring Paul up, waffling between resentment and relief that he hadn't. After hugging her goodbye, he pressed an envelope into her hand. "I'm here if you want to talk," he said, kissing her forehead, "And if there's anything I can do to help, just let me know." Safely in her living room, she opened it. Inside was a card acknowledging a donation to TAPS in Paul's memory. She sniffled and texted her thanks, telling herself she would check out their website soon. The card sat on top of her growing pile of things to take care of until newer paperwork buried it. Bills, legal documents, junk mail, and letters from her mother sat unopened. She felt paralyzed by the prospect of managing everything alone, overwhelmed by all the choices that had once been joint decisions. Everything seemed too complicated. *Can't it just be someone else's problem?*

—ⁿ—

It was a relief when block leave was over and she had to go back to work. They had to unload and clean and inventory equipment, get back into a regular training schedule. Bitching about busywork with her fellow troops was better than wallowing in her sorrow with Bear.

A couple weeks back into the routine, their First Sergeant was making announcements during morning formation. "Listen up, listen up: 2nd Brigade is getting ready to deploy, and they're short on personnel. They need volunteers. So if you didn't get enough of the suck, here's your chance."

"Are you fucking kidding, Top?" someone yelled out. Everyone laughed.

"I'll do it," Kate called. Every head in the formation turned to stare at her. Her head felt fuzzy, her chest light.

First Sergeant McKenna shook his head. "There's always one. See me after, Stevens."

She knocked on his office door after formation. "Enter," he called.

Kate stepped in and stood at parade rest. "First Sergeant, I'd like to volunteer to redeploy with 2nd Brigade."

He sighed and capped his pen. "Sit down, Sergeant Stevens." A long pause. "Do you need to be put on suicide watch?"

"Excuse me, First Sergeant?"

"Are you trying to get yourself killed? Is that why you want to go back?"

"No, First Sergeant." She took a deep breath. "You can ask my platoon sergeant. I didn't take any extra risks or anything after Paul— after Staff Sergeant Stevens was killed."

"Tell me what's going on, then."

"Nothing feels right here. Everything I see reminds me of him. I don't want to be in our house without him, but I don't want to move. There's too much to think about—too many things to keep track of. It was better when we were downrange. I was always busy, didn't have any time to sit around feeling sorry for myself. And what I did mattered: if I was good at my job, I could help keep our guys safe and destroy the enemy. I want back on mission. I was happier." She swallowed and licked her dry lips, feeling self-conscious. It was the most she'd said all at once since coming home.

The Sergeant had watched Kate's face intently during her little speech, and he stared searchingly into her eyes. He looked away first. "Staff Sergeant Stevens was a good soldier. I hope you find what you're looking for over there. I'll start the paperwork."

SMALL KILL TEAM

by Alex Horton

Our tour was almost over and I was the only one without a clean kill. The whole platoon knew it. Most of the company did too. The Sir lost count of all the firefights we were in, but we know how much ammunition we dumped into walls, bodies, and the occasional chicken coop caught in between our barrels and theirs. Our supply sergeant counted seven crates of rifle rounds expended, about 56,000 in all, and those rounds got kills for everyone in the platoon. Except for me. The notoriety was like a scarlet letter in reverse—the absence of a sin pinned to my uniform underneath my combat infantryman badge. You got the badge for taking fire and returning it. You didn't get anything for killing someone, except respect.

I thought I finally got one after we took contact during a patrol, when two insurgents were setting up a machine gun on the top of a gutted milk factory. They got a burst off before I put my sight on one of their silhouettes and pulled the trigger until my magazine was empty and the cordite streaming from Gibson's M240 machine gun burned my nostrils.

We cleared the factory and found them laid out on the rooftop. They wore black man-dresses and tennis shoes and shocked looks on their faces, mouths agape, as if they were told a terrible secret as they died. Gibson claimed the holes in their chests and necks were too big for a rifle to make. You could stick your goddamn thumb through one exit wound and not touch the sides, he said, so they must have been from his 240. "Another wicked day in the office," he said, his New England accent swirling with the heat. He took this one from me too. Gibson already had his share, drawing hash marks into his helmet band with a Sharpie after each one. He had five with a diagonal slash and faint traces of two more. He ripped a cloth ammo bandoleer off one of the fighters and held it up. Sunlight shimmered through a grouping of bullet holes. The blood had already dried in the sun, turning a faint red-orange. "Aw fuck," he said. "I can't get this past customs. Dipshit leaked all over it." Gibson flattened the vest onto the concrete floor and, with his Sharpie, traced the shape of a veiny, flaccid dick that extended from the bloodied holes now resembling testicles. "I'd love to see the face of who finds this, bro," Gibson said. "Let's bounce."

We took the stairs back down to the squad waiting in the courtyard. "Davidson, there's one thing I can't figure out about you," Gibson said behind me. "You don't have the killer instinct man. Don't you want this tour to mean anything?"

Even as a kid the kill had eluded me. It was a Thanksgiving tradition to head out toward Missoula and down a buck instead of a turkey, my dad said, because bucks could kill a man and that made the meat worth it. The only time I saw deer before that was when it was in flat and dry strips of jerky—the only thing we ate in the van on the long drive back to Lubbock. Then I turned ten and my dad said I was old enough to go out and learn the only thing my granddad passed down besides a weakness for cards. It was the hunt, and always with the same rifle. Granddad lifted a Mauser rifle from a Nazi he shot and carried it slung across his back all the way through Belgium and across the Rhine. He had one more dead kraut rifle than he did winter coats, using that line every time I asked him about the war. He moved to Montana a few years after my dad was born because it felt more like Bastogne, he said, harsh and desolate in the winter, and Bastogne was closer to what home was than Texas after that.

"Picture a buck," my father told me as we rode in Granddad's rusted out Chevy down I-90. "Now think of one your mom's dinner plates, and stick it between the top of his front legs and the bottom of his neck." He jammed his knee underneath the steering wheel to keep it straight and made a big circle with his hands over his chest. "That's the boiler room. His heart and lungs. That's the kill shot."

We found the tree stand before the sky turned a smoky pink. The ladder bars were cold and wet and the rifle sling dug into my shoulder as I climbed. It was supposed to be the first time I held the rifle, but it wasn't. I pulled it off the mantel late at night when everyone was asleep and slid my fingers down the barrel and across the trigger. It wasn't like the trigger on my Nintendo light gun, plastic and mechanical that clunked when I pressed my finger down. It was smooth and powerful, producing a sharp clink after charging the bolt, loud and promising with its potential to kill every time you pulled the iron bolt back to your chest. I knew how to cycle the rifle without a round but pretended in the stand that I had never held it.

We waited for hours in the stand. Dad grumbled and peered through binoculars. His back stiffened. "Round that big pine at eleven o'clock, 150 yards. You see him?" Melted snow clouded the telescopic sight. I saw antlers atop a massive head. I put the sight a little lower to where I thought the boiler room would be. I choked on my own heartbeat as my finger failed to make the motion I had done a hundred times before as I liberated the furniture from imaginary fascists in raids glinted by moonlight. My finger slid down and rested in the trigger well. I lied and said I couldn't see the deer, even though its breath steamed from throbbing, dark nostrils. It soon wandered away. "I'm sorry, Dad," I whispered.

"It gets easier, Son. I promise," he said. "It was hard for me too, but after your first you'll see it gets easier, just like everything else."

—⁂—

The IEDs were relentless. Big ones buried deep that we never encountered in other AOs until we were ordered to Baquba to flush out the bomb makers supplying Baghdad and northern Iraq. They were hitting our battalion daily, even off the main routes. The insurgents were using our trucks as iron maidens on wheels—a claustrophobic box where shrapnel buzzes though the air like yellow jackets trapped in a glass jar.

We had to do something different, even as our tour was ending in a month. No one wanted to be the guy who got himself killed just before going home. So our platoon filed into the fluorescent-soaked classroom on the edge of the outpost, and this guy with a pistol strapped to his thigh explained the concept of small kill teams.

He looked like CIA. We saw guys like him once in a while on post. His buddies rumbled through the compound in brand-new Silverados, the same you'd find on the farms lining I-90, except for the mounted machine guns in the back, manned by Billy Badasses growing bushy face armor under mirrored Oakley sunglasses.

"Complacency, complacency, complacency," Billy began. "It's killing you out there, gents. You've read the SIGACTs. Hell, you report the fuckers. Haj loves to use the same crater to plant an IED for the next patrol, or the intersection he sees you cross every day. But you already know that." He paced back and forth gingerly like a physics professor about to reveal a daring new theory. "But you can also use complacency just like they do. Like any other weapon system."

Billy clicked on a projector and a map of our sector was illuminated on the wall. Main roads were traced with red lines and IED strikes marked with yellow dots. The intersections we traveled most frequently were swollen with yellow grouping. It was a visual history of our dead and wounded. A dot for Johnson's arm and eye by the cement factory. One dot for all three KIA from Charlie Company coming out of the palm groves. My eyes found the single yellow dot where the platoon lost Chase outside of the school. There was only one attack because we never went back, not after that. Not after what we did to that school.

"It's about disruption," Billy continued as he hocked a glob of tobacco-brown spit into a Styrofoam cup. "Small kill teams were first used up north in Mosul, and SIGACTs involving IED strikes went down a full third. Thirty percent, men. We've found the best method is four teams of five with round-the-clock eyes on for every hotspot. Small elements, less noise. You'll need two, three days. You can last that long on the water and food you'll bring with you."

He paused a moment, standing there in front of the screen. Yellow dots projected onto his chest. "Questions?" he said.

Gibson raised his hand in front of me. "Yeah," he said. "What about drop items, dey work?" His accent provoked stifled laughs in the room.

Billy let out a howl. "Not anymore, damn it! I know some guys in Baghdad got cute and started to plant all kinds of gear on the side of the road—copper wires and AK mags mostly. But kids will pick that shit up just the same, and once you're down that road, you'll end up engaging a kid for doing nothing except being a fucking kid." His face tightened. "And embeds. Jesus. Those asswipes sit on your outpost, under your protection, eating your food, shitting in your toilets. And still they can't wait for you to smoke a a little girl in front of them. Don't earn them a Pulitzer. Roger?"

We shuffled out of the room to prep for the mission. Billy Badass stood by the projector. "Remember," he called out to us. "Disruption."

The house, we decided on an earlier patrol, had a good vantage point at the intersection of Route Blue Babe and Route Hatchet. This is what Billy Badass would call a hotspot—someplace Americans would patrol no matter how many yellow dots clustered around plant sites. A house with high rooftop walls and curtained windows overlooked the intersection, and the man who owned it—a sheepish and graying father with two kids and a wife, covered except for her milky eyes—didn't object when we asked to stay at his house. We always chose a family man who had something to lose, which was the biggest tactical advantage we had in a place like Baquba. Sergeant Matthew poked a finger at the man's chest and told him we'd come back at night with guns and rockets, and we might fire them inside, so they should stay somewhere else. And—this was stressed through our interpreter after we took a photo of his ID card and emailed it to battalion—if we came back the next night and some bad guys were waiting for us instead of an empty house, we'd find him and tape a sandbag over his head and drive past our outpost, past Route Tacoma, past the old leper colony, all the way back, we mimed with hands and solemn faces, to the last place where the women stand outside a razor wire–tipped gate to learn if they are widows or just the wives of disappeared men. Did he understand that?

"Yes, Mister," he said to Sergeant Matthew in English. "Yes yes yes, Mister."

—⁂—

We always left the main gate and took the same left toward Route Tacoma, passed by the same wide expanses of farmland, the same stretch of road where hardball pavement weaved into dirt roads, fertile ground for planting improvised bombs. The azaleas of guerilla warfare. That's where Johnson lost his right eye and arm to a blossom of molten copper darts that sliced through the lightly armored belly, tumbled through steel and bone and out toward the sky, which cooled and solidified as they fell back to earth like gleaming, elongated raindrops. We sent him a video of us burying a chunk of his forearm in a mock funeral while he recovered in Germany. "Here rests Johnson's ability to jerk off like a normal human being," Gibson barely recited before doubling over. "We'll cover for you."

We waited for nightfall at the outpost. Waiting for something to happen or not happen is the biggest preoccupation in war. Waiting for chow to arrive. Waiting for the guy in the port-a-shitter to finish jacking off with a rolled-up copy of *Club* magazine. Gibson waited for the email from home with the terms of divorce he would file on leave. After 2-3 was hit, the Stryker that Chase was driving, the platoon waited for our medic to say he was dead while Gibson looked for the finger that may still have held Chase's wedding ring before we moved toward the school. Most of the bombs you never see, so you wait until your eardrums tell you another one exploded. And then you wait to hear whose voice doesn't respond to a head count as dust masks the world, and you can barely make out the command on the radio intercomm to kill everything within one hundred meters because even the kids know where the bombs are buried and they wait for them to explode too.

Gibson and I waited for the mission at the card table at the outpost. He was short and stocky, with an angular face and narrow slits obscuring his eyes, as if he were in a constant state of waking up. He shuffled the cards under the table even though I said it was bad etiquette.

"Look around you, dude. This ain't the Vegas strip. The fuck you need etiquette for here?" Gibson bent the deck into a shuffle and dealt a round of Texas Hold 'Em.

My dad taught me card games in Montana when we weren't out on the tree stand. He said the family never had much luck, so we always had to play the man and not the cards. He taught me to watch the hands. Players would hide their widening pupils behind sunglasses, but their fingers, excitedly and clumsily grasping at chips to stack and push forward to the center, revealed cards worth playing. Steady hands were a sign of muck. A man will tell you everything with his hands, he once said.

I played Gibson long enough to know that he sat back and held his cards sideways if they were worth keeping. He peaked under his cards after the flop, rotating them down. I mucked the cards.

"Already? Pussy." He tossed his cards away and shuffled under the table for another hand. "Those shitbirds," he said as cards glided across felt faded by mildew. "They keep hitting us because we drive by the same hotspots. Wait til they try it tonight." He held a rifle made of air with an imaginary scope pointed at me. "Fuckin' baaaang. Teach these guys to be as retarded as us."

There was an unmistakable sound of boot on metal cot. Sergeant Matthew kicked every frame lined against the other side of the wall and came over to the table. "Get your shit on," he said. "SKT mission got pushed up. We're out the gate in fifteen mikes." Sergeant Matthew looked over at me while tightening his chin-strap. "Davidson," he grinned. "Get lucky on the gun and you just might lose your fuckin' cherry this time."

We could barely move in the trucks. Each man had a rucksack on his lap—extra ammunition, three days' worth of food, twelve liters of water, socks, batteries, backup batteries, poncho liners, dented iPods, paperbacks with torn covers, and porn magazines. The junior guys carried five-gallon water cans, rocket launchers, and belts of machine-gun rounds. The buckles of my ruck dug into my knees and the truck's engine whirred as we made toward Blue Babe. Everyone slept, their heads bobbing sharply as the vehicle made its turns.

We reached the infiltration point a klick from the house. The engine idled and the vehicle commander keyed up the intercom to drop the ramp and the squad spilled into the moonless street.

Gibson lugged one of the five-gallon jugs in his ruck. Sergeant Matthew motioned us to double-time. The team began to jog, and Gibson, with the water can slamming against the side of his ruck more violently, stumbled on a curb and crashed into a metal gate. He grasped at my arm to regain his footing as his machine gun sling pulled him forward.

"Infil this far out, weighed down if we get ambushed," Gibson muttered quietly. He spat into the darkness. "This is gay as fuck."

Sergeant Matthew chewed through a lock with bolt cutters and shoved us inside. The desert sun roasted concrete houses during the day, releasing heat through the night like the embers of a fading bonfire. Putrid air hung in all the rooms, and we poured water on the rooftop so we could lie without shirts as midnight prayers streamed from the minaret of a nearby mosque. We crawled on our stomachs to keep out of sight; only five of us held the house, and insurgents could storm it with suicide vests and grenades before another team could reinforce us. As Gibson would say, we weren't going to leave pretty corpses. Sergeant Matthew set up an M4 with an infrared scope pointed toward the intersection, and rockets lined the living room wall in case of an overrun. Gibson drew up a guard list and handed it to me. "No sleep for you, dickcheese," he said, and unfurled his sleeping bag to crawl inside with an iPod blaring the unmistakable beat of Dropkick Murphys through cheap earbuds.

I sat on a foldout chair and watched the intersection through a thermal scope. The procession of squeaky sedans and rumbling trucks slowed as curfew approached. After midnight prayer, roads were limited to emergency use only and anyone riding in a car could be rolled up. Most tended to keep off the road after sundown to avoid checkpoints and the trigger fingers of anxious Americans, known to spasm in moments of uncertainty, when the fog of war became cataracts. The rest of the squad lay on the floor, catching an hour or two of sleep before guard rotations came up. Sergeant Matthew was passed out face-first on a book. Gibson bunched up a uniform top to use as a pillow. The living room was sparse. A small TV sat in the corner and two lumpy couches lined a wall. The beds were hard and uncomfortable and no one slept in them; Iraqis used them only for sex and otherwise slept on thin dusty mats. Cheap cologne masked the smell of a toilet basin in the corner.

Time is no longer time when you sit and wait for something to happen, when the mind searches for a memory to override the apocalyptic tones of an IR scope, where bodies look like white phantoms gliding against black emptiness. But the streets were barren. No cars, no people, nothing to mark the presence of civilization except the constant buzz of generators whirring on rooftops. We were one hour on, four hours off, and it was nearly time for a shift change. The radio next to the chair read 0:45. Sergeant Matthew's face was still in the book.

"Yo, Sergeant," I whispered and shined a red lens light on his face. "You got guard." He inhaled deeply and rubbed his eyes. "Fuck," he said. "I'm up." He reached for his boots, and I sat back in the chair to peer through the scope. A sedan's taillights glowed at the intersection. "Hurry up, Sergeant. Eyes on a car that must've just pulled up."

Two men flickered as white-hot beams in front of the trunk. Sergeant Matthew came over with one boot on and yanked the scope from me. "Fuckin' shit," he whispered. "Get on the gun."

Sergeant Matthew edged his burly Tennessean body into the window. "I got eyes on," he said. "What'd we figure, 150 meters at the intersection?" I told him that sounded right, steadying the rifle on the window sill as I peered through my night vision monocle. My laser painted a faint green dot on one of their backs.

"I don't see weapons," I said to Sergeant Matthew, "but they're definitely grabbing shit with both hands."

"Fertilizer? Or a 155-round, maybe?" Sergeant Matthew said. "What do you think?" The infrared beam refracted on the target's shirt and spread across his boiler room. We were within the rights of ROE, I thought. Or I could explain it that way later, on the witness statement. "I'm gonna put a round through the fucker on the left, call it up on the radio," I said. I switched the safe off and held my breath, like I learned in the tree stand. I pulled the trigger.

The target fell to the ground hard, like a cartoon anvil tumbling out of a window, and the rest of the squad scrambled from their sleep and threw on vests and helmets. Gibson raced over in his shorts and slapped me on the back.

"Aw fuck yeah, finally Davidson!" he shouted. "Canoe that fucker!" The rest of the squad stood behind us, gathering equipment and chambering rounds in their rifles. Sergeant Matthew squawked into the radio to another position to light up the car with a machine gun. "Second guy, eleven o' clock," Sergeant Matthew shouted into my ringing ears. "He's booking it." I fired. He didn't drop, and scrambled over a courtyard wall. "He bounced," I shouted. The gun team opposite the inspection opened up and the car's side exploded in sparks as rounds tore through the car to kill anyone still inside. A tracer started a fire among trash in the median.

We were compromised. Sergeant Matthew called up the other teams to tell them to pack up and get ready to move out. The rest of our team stuffed their gear into rucksacks. We left the water and food behind and stepped out into the courtyard. The squad snaked its way through the neighborhood as the dogs scampered and barked among small sewage dugouts. The rest of the platoon had already arrived at the staging point to meet our trucks, the vehicles creating a box around the car for security. Their headlights pierced the darkness beyond the inter-section, where other hot spots simmered for the next patrol. Sergeant Matthew ordered us to gather up any weapons left at the scene. The car would stay. Some Iraqi unit would have to come collect the body and blow the car in place in case it had explosives. Sergeant Matthew slowly approached the car and looked for wires.

"Gibson," he said. "Search this fuck." Most of the target's body was veiled in darkness, but his face glowed red from the taillights above him. Gibson slung his rifle and stuck his hands into the dead man's jean pockets. "Hey Davidson," Sergeant Matthew said to me. "You brought your camera, right? We need to document this for battalion."

I pulled a digital camera from a pouch and made sure the target's limbs were inside the frame. The round blew a fist-sized hole through his back and out of his slender chest. I snapped five photos. Every one was too dark, only revealing the target's illuminated face and nothing else. I cupped my hands on the camera's screen to see if it was good enough. His mouth was wide open, like Granddad had described. I asked Gibson to point his flashlight at the rest of the target to get a clear shot. A bright image of the body filled my camera's viewfinder, and I snapped another photo. Gibson inched closer to the trunk to look inside.

"Aw, Jesus," he said. "You won't believe what's in here man. Fuck."

Gibson slammed the trunk and punched the taillight with a gloved fist. It was a jab at first, and then he hit it again, over and over, harder each time. Chunks of white and red plastic fell onto the target's head. "Stupid fuck. Stupid fuck," he whispered through his teeth, and he could have been talking to any three of us.

The target didn't look like a man this close up. His face was smooth and hairless and his eyes were rolled back and glinting white, like a doll's plastic eyes. I stood next to Gibson and looked in; stacked inside were bags of rice and the blood of raw lamb's meat pressed against the sides of plastic bags. Gibson lit two cigarettes and handed one to me. "Haj, man. God damned stupid as shit."

A courtyard gate rustled at the house closest to the intersection, the only house on Blue Babe with the lights still on. Gibson spun on one foot and pointed his rifle toward the gate. A woman in a headscarf emerged from the shadows, and then another, with a man following with a white sheet. Sergeant Matthew rushed over and stood in front of the gate. "Get the fuck back!" he yelled, and motioned with his arm to turn around. Two more men filed past Sergeant Matthew, ignoring his gestures. Music streamed from beyond the open door of the house.

The group laid the sheet onto the ground, and one woman picked pieces of the taillight out of the target's hair as another crossed his arms over his chest. They lifted the body onto the sheet and rolled it tight, fastening it with a green sash. Sergeant Matthew had quieted to a whisper. "You can't do that," he said to one of the women as they shuffled by, ignoring his commands. "You can't take his body. Not yet." One of the men stopped to look us over. *Ebnee,* he said. *Ebnee. Ebnee.* He made a cradling motion with his arms, then pointed at his lifeless *ebnee.*

Gibson's shoulders relaxed and he inhaled a new cigarette as the rest of the team faced away, looking for threats. The Iraqis lifted the body on their shoulders and walked back toward the house. The air chilled suddenly, like the last week of summer in Montana, where the heat felt heavy and full before cool wind swept off the mountains. Gibson tossed his cigarette onto the road. "Let's get out of here," he said. "Before more hajis hear about this shit." The Iraqis closed the gate behind them, and somebody stopped the music.

The team scrambled into the truck as I pretended to pull security, but I kept staring at the house. I wanted to go in there and tell him that his *ebnee* was my first, and it was past curfew and he shouldn't have been there, but I was still sorry and understood, because I am my father's *ebnee* too. After a moment I turned to load up in the truck and crumpled onto the bench.

Gibson came down from the hatch as we headed back to the outpost. "I don't think that one counts," he said. "But don't worry. We got time."

Battalion pulled our platoon out of that sector the next week. They were reviewing the procedures of small kill teams after our incident. We never left the wire again. The squad passed the time at the poker table, the same twenty-dollar bills endlessly shifting among players. Most of the guys went down to the phone bank to call their wives and girlfriends. I sent my dad an email as he was readying a trip to Montana when I came home. Everything was fine, just packing and cleaning, nothing to report, but the phones are broken, I lied.

I spent a lot of time on my cot, recalling the stories my dad told me from when he was young, of Granddad leading him through dense pines at Beaverhead Forest as winter settled in around the tree stand. Their own small kill team. Dad told me the Mauser which Granddad kept over the fireplace belonged to his first kill. It was a heavy instrument that traveled seven decades since it was stamped with a swastika on the bolt and assigned to a soldier bound for the Western Front. Granddad had plenty of guns, but my father was too young to hold this one, and it stayed on the mantel for several more years. It gets easier after the first one, Granddad said to him then, peering up over the flames rising through the chimney.

Granddad learned that lesson in Bastogne, when the counterattack came after the artillery barrage transformed ancient trees into foot-long shards of wooden shrapnel. The wave of starved and frostbitten Germans was coming, and after the first one it was going to get easier. That's what his sergeant told him as the machine guns began their grim chatter. He shouldn't stop killing after that, the sergeant said, because the only thing worse than the first one is the second one never coming at all.

BLEEDER

by Matthew Robinson

H ow much?" I say, one hand around her middle, one on the pistol grip of my M-4. She's soft in my hand and smells like shampoo. She giggles and leans her face in, hair brushing my ear. I have no idea what the fuck she's saying. I thumb her bottom rib, her half-shirt covering my hand, me touching skin. "Call me Sawyer."

"Sawyer," she says.

I pull her in by her bones and she giggles again. I press my barrel against her thigh, where it sticks out the bottom of her Daisy Dukes. I start to thumb my safety switch. "How much?"

She says something else in my ear. Jibber-jabber. She pushes against my rifle and there is a massive pressure in my chest, my hands go cold. We've been negotiating for what feels like an hour, her not making a lick of sense, but I can't commit money to her until my cock starts working. It's just hanging. I have a hold of my first woman since we shipped and my dick has decided to go fucking AWOL.

"You buy?" An old lady whose face is mostly forehead is at my elbow, out of nowhere. Her arms are crossed. She's tiny but severe.

"Are you the pimp?" I say.

"You buy?"

I try one last time to muster an erection, squeeze the handful of heat in my hand, but it's useless. I shake my head. The pimp walks off and the girl takes a half-step away, hair pulling free of my ear, leg off rifle. She giggles again but less than before. I let go of her slow, my fingers drag down her side, catch on her shorts, I thumb her pocket on the way. "Oh well," I say. I find a twenty in my pocket. "Whiskey?"

She smiles, pulls a stray hair out of my chin-strap. I know it's black but under the streetlight it looks gold. She lets it go. "Whiskey," she says, and she's gone.

I'm left standing in the expanse of road between the main hotel complex and the Baghdad Hotel, where I stay. There's less brass at the Baghdad, better food, a '70s-era lounge with shag carpet and mirrored walls, and a guy who sells pralines and cream ice cream cups. I only come out for guard duty and to talk to locals. So far it's the best part of this fucking deployment. The road runs along the Tigris, a shithole park takes up the space in between. The combat engineers move dirt around it during the day but right now it's quiet. City lights on the far side of the water. It's a good place to fire rockets at us from, on that other side, but there's nothing happening so I'm standing between a gaggle of hookers and a herd of kids who are inching their way closer to me.

"Go away," I say.

"Money," one says.

"Money? For what?"

"We fight."

I pull a dollar out of my pocket. The talkative kid grabs the boy next to him and they wrap arms around each other. Talker's knee buckles and they both go over, the kids around them cheer. They roll around on the pavement trying to pin the other's shoulders like they were really wrestling, but it's boring as shit so I say, "Time."

They get up and come over, both smiling. Talker was on top when I called time so I give the buck to him. They run back to the group and all the boys start yelling. It's all jibber-jabber and nobody's pairing off. "Somebody hit somebody else," I say.

Two kids grab each other and the others cheer. I look at my watch. Nothing much happens for thirty seconds and I call time. I give the kid on top a dollar. Both are smiling. I still feel the girl's hair against my ear. Smell the river in the wind.

"Somebody hit somebody else." Two boys fall down and everybody laughs. I laugh, lean against the lamppost, and look at my watch.

"Jesus." Behind me, Mills is coming out from the serpentine barriers on the hotel complex end of the street. We share a room back at the FOB. He doesn't say much, which I like, and he keeps his shit squared away. But out here he just walks around being a sad sack.

"What?" To the boys I say, "Time." They get up and I hand one a dollar. The rest of the group starts talking all at once.

"What are you doing?" Mills says.

"Nothing, I was bored. Somebody hit somebody else." Two boys hit each other and hit the ground.

"How long has this been going on?"

"For as long as man has existed." Mills doesn't laugh but I do. The kids are cheering. I look to the prostitutes, try to see the girl I gave twenty bucks to. They are at the mouth of an alleyway that fades into the unknowable. I want my goddamn whiskey. I look at my watch.

One kid catches an elbow and cries out. "Time!" I say. The boys stand up, one bleeding from his mouth. "This is why we can't have nice things." I hand the other kid the dollar and he runs off. The bleeding boy walks back to the others, pulling his shirt to his mouth, soaking up blood. As it spreads across the cloth my face flashes hot, hotter than the night air. The smell of the Tigris turns sour and the wind stalls. It comes up from the other side, a garbage gust of wind blows fresh from the alley instead.

"This is some bullshit," Mills says. To the boys, "Go away." They just look at him. "Fuck off, you don't need to fight." They look to me.

"Somebody hit somebody else." Two boys hit each other and hit the ground. I look at my watch. Fuck Mills. I scan the boys' faces and they aren't smiling. They're yelling and pawing each other and it's goddamn ruined.

From the alley behind the hookers, the kid who busted the bleeding kid's face is coming back with another, a huge boy almost the size of me, but fatter. There's pressure in my chest and I swear to god I feel my dick move. "Here we go. Somebody's ready to make some fucking money. Time!" The two fighters stand up. Neither has a mark on them but one is starting to cry. I hand a dollar to the other.

The big kid steps up. "I fight. I fight."

"Okay. Who?"

The fat kid turns to the group of boys. They all shrink back except the kid with the bloody lip—he steps forward, dropping the front of his shirt.

When they stand facing each other, it looks hilarious. David and Goliath, if they believed that sort of thing. Bleeder looking up. Fatty looking down, smiling.

"Don't fucking fight," Mills says. Nobody moves.

"Somebody hit somebody else."

"Don't—" Mills begins and Fatty grabs Bleeder around the neck in a sort of bear hug. Mills wants it stopped; he starts to raise his rifle at them because that's how we stop things. If they were Iraqi cars Fatty would be a black Mercedes, Mills would just shoot him in the hood as a warning shot. I laugh out loud at the thought of a round blowing through Fatty's grill and him slowly backing out of the fight, leaving little oil spots behind him. Mills lowers his rifle.

Fatty cranks Bleeder's neck. Bleeder winces. They fall, Fatty landing on top. Fatty hits like he knows how to hit. The other boys who cowered a few minutes ago when it was time to pick an opponent are cheering—rooting Fatty on.

From the bottom, Bleeder is fighting back. He's pounding small fists against Fatty's chest, doing no damage, but he's fighting back. Fatty lands a fist to Bleeder's mouth. His hand comes away bloody. My hand is cold around my pistol grip and my cock is at half-mast. I can't smell her shampoo but I'm almost sure I taste iron in the air.

Mills steps forward but I catch his arm. "Don't, they want to fight. Nobody's here by force."

He pulls his arm free. "They're here because you're giving away dollars and they live in a shithole."

I shrug and turn back to the fight. They've rolled onto their sides, slapping one-armed at each other. The other boys are standing over them, yelling nonsense. Fatty grabs Bleeder's hair, pulls, and slams his head into the street. I am rock hard. I smell shit and garbage and blood on the wind. My hands are still and cold and my chest loses its pressure all at once. Fatty lifts Bleeder's head again, brings it down without argument. The dull thud bounces off the buildings and cement barriers, across the broken park and down the banks of the Tigris.

"Time."

The boys are quiet. Fatty makes his way up. Bleeder is lying on the street. Fatty comes over to us, to me, his hand out, palm up. Bleeder starts checking his head for leaks. I hand Fatty a dollar. He looks down at the bill and back at me and says, "Money." He pushes his upturned palm at Mills and me, wagging it between us. "Money."

Letting his rifle hang freely from where it's clipped to his vest, pulling his hand behind him as far as it goes, Mills slaps Fatty in the side of his face. I jump at the sound, it happens so fast. Fatty falls on his ass, holding the dollar up the whole way down, like he's trying to protect something breakable. The handprint stretches from his cheekbone to his ear.

"What the fuck?" I say.

Mills stands over Fatty, who is rubbing the side of his face with his free hand, looking at me from under thick eyelids. The eyelids of gunmen with nickel-plated pistols. Of Iraqi police who used to be Republican Guard. Of men who've lived long enough and eaten well enough to be fat and old in this goddamn country. He gets up and walks slowly away, dollar in hand.

The other boys run away into the dark, leaving Bleeder sitting alone.

Mills takes a twenty out of his pocket and presses it into Bleeder's hand. He helps him up and Bleeder's off and running as soon as he's free of him. Mills just stands there, looking into the dark. He starts to wobble, takes a few steps to the edge of the street, and throws up everything he ate at dinner chow. He spits a few times, leaned out over his rifle. Wipes his mouth with his sleeve. The closest hookers walk over to him, put their hands on his bent-forward back. They talk quietly but it's all jibber-jabber. "No, thank you," he says. "I just spent the last of my cash." At the sound of *no* they leave him, and he heads off towards the Baghdad. He's soft and I fucking hate him.

"Sawyer." My girl from earlier steps out of the alley, paper bag in her hand. "Whiskey." When she comes close I breathe in her shampoo-smell and get a hand on her middle—on skin. I feel a quiet fire spark up in my chest. Through my uniform and her cutoff shorts, I press my cock against her. She presses back.

"How much?"

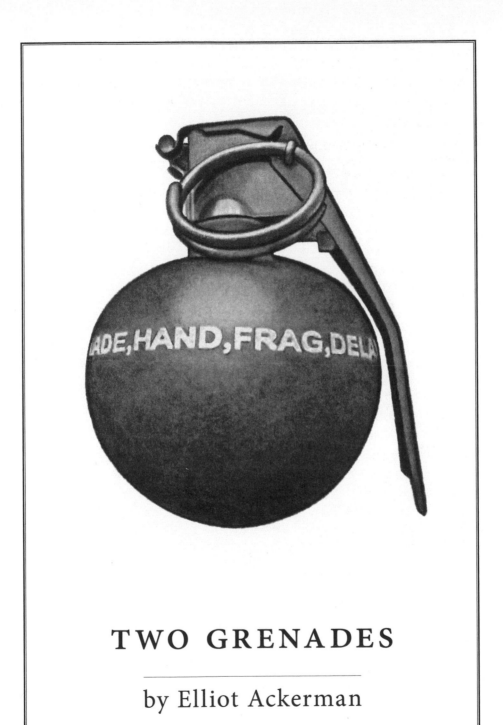

TWO GRENADES

by Elliot Ackerman

Manuel Garcia took the stairs two at a time to Raleigh Upton's room. He climbed the twelve flights, caught his breath at the door, and knocked. No one answered. There was nowhere else Upton would be at 0300. Manuel nudged the door open with his boot. Across the darkened interior there was a mound of blankets.

"Captain Upton," he said, listening.

There was nothing, just the turbines of Haditha Dam vibrating their spectral hum. They lived in the Dam.

"It's me, Sergeant Garcia," he said louder.

A rumble of half-breathed curses came from under the mound. "What the fuck time is it?"

"A little after zero three, sir. Can I come in?"

"Well, Christ, okay come in."

Upton turned on the Coleman lantern above his cot. The dim light was easy on his tired eyes. His pasty body was naked except for a pair of OD green shorts. He slid on his black shower shoes.

"Sit down, Garcia." Manuel perched himself on a camp stool behind Upton's plywood desk. "What is it?"

"I saw the patrol schedule changed."

"What do you mean?"

"The Tuesday patrol, it got canceled."

"So?"

"That's the one you promised me."

Upton crossed the room and fumbled through his desk. He found a spreadsheet and held it under the lantern. "Yeah, you're right. I'll look into it in the morning."

Upton lay back on his cot. Manuel's eyes wandered behind the Captain to a framed photo of a memorial service from a few weeks before. In it was a semi circle of empty boots and upturned rifles, each set bayoneted into the dirt, sticking up like so many candles on a birthday cake.

"We had a deal," said Manuel.

"Sorry, there's nothing I can do about it."

"Gripper's got a patrol heading out at first light. I thought I could get on it."

"C'mon, Garcia!" said Upton. "I'd have to change the manifests."

"After seven months you owe me this."

Upton didn't like to see his friend plead. It'd been a long deployment. Upton had never known Manuel to ask for anything.

"You've had a great career," he said. "You don't need to get yourself shot at to prove it."

Manuel wrapped his knuckles on Upton's desk. "Really? That's what you're going to say to me?"

"Does Gripper even have room for you?"

"They're going out shorthanded. They could use me," said Manuel.

"Where are they headed?"

"Up near the 52 and 67 checkpoints." In the bleakness of the western desert, the latitudinal northings on their maps were the only features anything could be named after.

"It ain't right, you asking me this." Upton pulled a pen from his desk and modified Gripper's manifest to include his friend.

"This might be our last patrol," said Manuel. "Most of you will go home with at least a Combat Action Ribbon. What about me? If you look at my uniform or service record, it'll be like this never happened."

"No, you don't deserve that." Upton scribbled a revision onto the manifest and handed it to Manuel. "Make sure to drop this by the ops center on your way out."

He grabbed the sheet of paper and rushed up two more levels to the top of the Dam. The air outside was crisp, and it stung almost. The warm summer nights were gone. The days were still hot, but everything was cooling. Manuel remembered the desert's otherworldly cold when they'd arrived the year before. He was glad they'd miss the winter.

A road ran along the top of the Dam, an abutment flanking its sides. Past it, spreading in one direction, were Lake Qadisiyah's black waters and in the other a drop, falling hundreds of feet down a sloping wall and into the churning Euphrates. Manuel didn't like standing on the road. He'd never learned to swim and didn't care for heights. Two Humvees were parked outside of the ops center. The stars glinted off their windshields. They would drop Gripper and him at the checkpoint.

Inside the ops center, a sleepy lance corporal sat behind a green wall of radios that were stacked in a pattern like bricks. The room was warm and filled with static. The lance corporal swiveled around in his chair. "Evening, Sergeant." His front was drizzled with potato chips and their grease spread from his chest up to his pimpled face.

"What's going on, Shaughnessy?"

"You lookin' at it."

Across the ops center Manuel's body armor, helmet, and rifle were stored in a small dusty cubby. Two grenades hung by their spoons off his body armor. The grenades' pins were secured with black electrical tape. The tape hadn't moved in seven months. It'd begun to peel.

"You heading out?" asked Shaughnessy.

"Last-minute add-on with Gripper," said Manuel. "He been in yet?"

"Not yet."

Manuel handed Shaughnessy the new manifest. He tacked it over the old one on the mission tracking board, an acetate covered map that papered one full wall of the ops center.

Manuel sat on a bench near the door with his body armor strapped on and his helmet perched on his knee. Shaughnessy came over with a pot of coffee and two Styrofoam cups. He set the cups on the bench between the two of them.

"Schedule says this is the last mission," said Shaughnessy.

"Looks that way."

"They got any more room?"

"When you add me, I think they're full up," said Manuel.

"Working in headquarters makes for a long deployment."

"You got nothing to complain about. You got yours a couple months ago," said Manuel, and he felt petty.

Shaughnessy crossed the room and pointed to a patched hole in the corrugated steel ceiling. "I'd say that rocket hit about," he opened his arms nearly as wide as they could go, "this far from my desk."

"Still, you're a lucky motherfucker."

"I guess, lucky to get mine, and lucky not to get killed getting it." He looked back up at the hole. "You think I really rate it?" he asked.

"Hey, man, a Combat Action Ribbon is a Combat Action Ribbon."

"Yeah, but do you think it counts?"

"If it could've killed you it counts."

"Too bad you weren't here that day," said Shaughnessy. "I mean too bad that you missed it all."

"That's all right, you can't chase it," he lied, and the room became awkward because he was chasing it. Shaughnessy leaned back in his chair and stared at the radio, munching potato chips. Manuel crossed the room and lay on a bench by the door. He'd get some sleep before he left.

—⁂—

The door slammed by Manuel's head. In front of him stood Gripper, his face swollen with early morning exhaustion. He crossed the room like a sleepwalker. In seven months, he'd made a hundred patrols like this.

"Hey, Gripper," said Shaughnessy.

He nodded, checking the manifest on the board with the enormous hands that were his namesake. Then he hooked his thumbs into his shoulder straps, hanging them from the body armor he wore like a second skin.

"So you worked it out, Manny?" he asked, still reviewing the manifest.

"Yeah, we're good."

"All right, the trucks are warming up outside."

Manuel snapped on his chin-strap and slung his rifle across his chest. He followed Gripper.

"Good luck!" shouted Shaughnessy.

Manuel didn't know what type of luck he hoped for.

On the road that ran across the Dam, the two Humvees coughed and sputtered, mixing warm air with cold. Their windshields vibrated and reflected a blurred night sky. Inside the cab, the Marines fogged the glass and kept wiping crusts of frost from it with their sleeves. Five of them would be dropped off between the two checkpoints: three at 52, and two at 67.

Manuel climbed into the back of the second Humvee and Gripper perched next to him. "You trying to keep an eye on me?" asked Manuel.

"I'm trying to be a good host."

"Just tell me where you need me."

"We're going to the 67," said Gripper. He banged on the roof of the cab. The Humvees lurched into gear. In the bed everything became wind and blackness. They crossed the Dam and even though Manuel couldn't see, he felt the lake and the river slip from either side of him.

They drove through the night as though the morning wasn't inevitable, but a destination on the map to be achieved. Every few kilometers, the road sunk into the wadis and then rose back onto the plain: shambles of rock and dust. When the first seam of light split the horizon, Manuel felt crushed by the desert and the road and his own smallness against them. Distant and near cyclones swirled up the dust, spooling it like squid ink across the ocean floor, but keeping speed with the convoy and at times outpacing it.

The 67 came into view. The dawn was soiled grey, overcast. At first, in the distance, the blanched mud tower looked no different than one of the cyclones that chased them, its earthen walls blending with the desert. But as they approached, Manuel could see two dark figures running down the ladder that leaned against its one side.

They pulled next to the tower. Two Marines charged up to the convoy before it could stop rolling. A light coating of dust covered their reddened, windburned faces.

"This is our stop," said Gripper as he jumped off the tailgate.

Manuel followed.

Watching from the tower above were the Iraqis, three of them. Their powder blue police uniforms had turned navy with sweat, and their eyes were dark like their sweaty shirts.

The two Marines coming off post climbed into the truck's bed.

"They give you any trouble?" Gripper asked them.

"No trouble, they're just on their own fucking program," said one of them, who also had a grenade hung on his vest, but its tape was newer, a replacement for one that'd been thrown.

"What program is that?" asked Manuel.

"They're just not in a rush, know what I mean?"

"Looks like you're in a rush to get out of here," said Manuel.

"Ain't you?" asked the second Marine who carried a flare on his vest.

"I just got here."

Gripper heaved up the tailgate, slamming it shut. The Marine with the flare pressed it into Gripper's hand. "They moved the radio to the 52. Anything happens signal with this."

The convoy lurched down the road. Manuel looked into the tower and at the Iraqis who stood in the doorway. He wondered when someone would come by to pick them up.

And then it began to rain.

Inside, the rain hit the corrugated steel roof, loud as gravel, filling the silence with something aside from conversation. The three Iraqis sat in one corner of the tower. Manuel and Gripper sat in the other, near the wood ladder, which ran from a cut in the parapet to the ground. The Iraqis didn't speak, not even to each other. Manuel stared at them, but they didn't seem to notice. Their faces were wrinkled, but appeared neither old nor young. The lines transmuted age as though they'd been born with them, like a man's fate is born into his palm. There was no hurry or patience in their expressions, merely indifference. And as Manuel watched them, that is what he couldn't understand.

"Don't they have any rifles?" he asked Gripper.

"Yes, but they prefer not to carry them."

"What if they're attacked?"

"They're only attacked when we're here."

"Well, what then?"

"We've got rifles."

"And so they just sit there?"

"More or less."

"Doesn't that bother you?" Manuel asked.

"As long as they stay out of the way, I don't care what they do."

One of the Iraqis walked in a crouch to where Manuel and Gripper sat. He pantomimed for them to move. He removed his plastic sandals and sat on the threshold with his dusty feet hanging in the storm. His cracked skin soon turned smooth in the rain.

"Do you need to do that there, Moe?" bitched Gripper.

The Iraqi, Moe, shrugged, rubbing his feet. Manuel didn't bother to ask where the name Moe came from. It was said with an irony that made him doubt it was Mo, as in Mohammed, or any other abbreviation of an eastern name. The thick black bowler cut and surly expression made it obvious that Moe's namesake, as far as Gripper was concerned, was Moe from *The Three Stooges*.

"These people wash their feet five times a day, but still wipe their asses with their left hand," said Manuel. Through the storm's grey veil, he looked down the road. It ran across the land like a warped floor in a bad house. "It cracks me up, I can't get over it."

"Makes the little fuckers endearing, don't it?" said Gripper.

"What? The feet part or the ass part?"

"Their contradictions." Gripper stepped away from the door and stood deeper inside the tower looking at the other two Iraqis who napped in the corner without apology. Manuel didn't move. He sat in the threshold watching the wet desert.

Aside from the mud tower, the checkpoint consisted of two fluorescent cones and a single spike-strip. The spike-strip was nearly invisible (hence the cones), and it lay across the pavement like a chain of sawtooth jacks. Manuel and Gripper set a rotation so one could rest while the other watched the road. Manuel offered to go first even though he needed the sleep. Gripper curled up in the tower's dank corner next to the Iraqis. The four of them lay like a pack of sodden dogs.

The day wore on and the desert flooded. Water pooled, breaking apart the cheap macadam and swallowing whole segments of the road. From time to time in the distance, a car emerged through the slashing curtains of rain, always tentative, paying great respect to the distant cones. Manuel would leave the tower's protection and search the approaching vehicle with courtesy, never forcing the occupants to stand outside with him in the rain. But all this courtesy belied his secret hope that someone in the car would shoot at him, just so he could shoot back and get his Combat Action Ribbon.

But the morning proved disappointing. Each time he left the tower to remove the spike-strip and let someone pass, it felt like a little defeat. He'd return soaked, and it was well before noon when he decided that on the whole damn stretch of road the only threat that existed was the one to his ego.

Standing in the door of the tower, Manuel kicked the bottom of Moe's feet, waking him from his nap. He crossed the mud floor, slid on his plastic sandals, and stood next to Manuel. They looked out to the road. Moe carried a plastic sheet and a single tent rod. He watched the rain, and after a moment rested his hand on Manuel's shoulder. Manuel glanced at Moe's hand. Moe smiled, revealing a mosaic of rot and gold. He looked at his watch and nodded. There were no cars coming, but he rushed down the ladder and ran into the rain to take his post.

By now, Gripper had awoken as well. "I got this shift, Manny," he said as he stretched and pulled the sleep from his joints.

"Looks like you'll have company."

On the side of the road Moe had propped his waterproof sheet up with the tent pole, protecting him from the rain while he sat in a puddle.

Manuel handed over the flare.

"Fuckin' Moe," said Gripper, watching the wet Iraqi.

Manuel leaned against the tower's mud walls and slept upright, his head slinking into his body armor like a turtle's to its shell. With sleep came anxiety. Manuel stacked his troubles one on the other and his dreams worked like cement, setting his worries into a wall he couldn't see over. He dreamed, and in it, he was home without his Combat Action Ribbon; it was years later and he was scanning a promotion list, dread pouring warmly through his guts; he couldn't find his name—he'd been passed over. He could already feel the dull shame of standing in line for early retirement, and the soul-sucking void of a regular job. He could hear his wife's chipper steps around the house, happy at first that he was around, but ceding to disappointment as she wondered why she'd married someone who'd lost his purpose before forty, and what did that say about her, and he felt a sharp lonely twist as he watched her fade away. He cried in his dreams, or for real, he couldn't tell, but he felt that tearful tension release like gas through a pinhole, slowly, with tiny whines, each one a mean little affirmation of how small he was.

—ⵗ—

Manuel awoke and looked out to the road, to the rain. Gripper and Moe sat back-to-back under the waterproof sheet. Each of them watched one direction. Neither spoke. Instead they ate, sharing the M&Ms, crackers, and peanut butter from an MRE. They passed food back and forth over their shoulders. When Moe took the last M&M and handed Gripper back the empty wrapper, Gripper elbowed him in the ribs, hard. Moe laughed, but as soon as he started he quit.

He came to his feet.

A white compact Opal wove around the cone without stopping. There was a splash of water, the spike-strip cracked like the cluck of a great steel tongue. Then everything became translucent ripples of light and dark, water and metal, barreling down the road.

Manuel saw the crash, but it was the long grinding skid of metal on asphalt that scared him. Hearing this, the other two Iraqis pressed behind him on the ladder. All three craned their necks outside. The Opal was flipped over in the road, its wheels still spinning. The twist of its undercarriage faced upward, a metallic disembowelment. Even in the rain flames licked up its side. The shrieks from inside the car sounded out of place, inanimate, as though the car, not its passengers, were calling out.

Off the road some, and away from the car, were Gripper and Moe. They both lay in the mud, not moving. Gripper's rifle had been tossed near the tower, splintered with a toothpick's ease. Manuel looked at the two Iraqis who stood next to him. They looked away. He rushed down the ladder, outside and alone.

While Manuel ran, Gripper pushed himself from the water and crawled toward Moe who was facedown in a puddle, unconscious and drowning. Manuel got there first. He fell to his knees, grabbed Moe by both shoulders and heaved his face toward the air. As he rolled him over, his joints ground against each other like crisped rice, and his mangled expression looked like the car's chassis.

Gripper continued to pull himself through the mud on his stomach. His legs hung behind him, limp and heavy as rope. Each pull became a great effort, all panting breathes and curses. He wanted to get to Moe.

Manuel called to him, "Gripper!"

He stopped, and propped himself up on his elbows, heaving. He said nothing but looked up. There was nothing to say, and he collapsed onto his side and into the mud.

The shrieks on the road were reaching a high-pitched crescendo. The flames that had lightly lapped a moment before now chewed at the inside of the car. Curiosity not compassion compelled Manuel toward the accident. Fuel, water, and blood mixed in the rain pools. Manuel pitched onto his hands and knees to look inside. The two front seats had been crushed, killing those in them. There, the fire burned hottest, marching irresistibly from hood to trunk. The shrieking became very loud now. Manuel scrambled around the car, unable to see from where. Then he looked into the rear windshield and saw her in the backseat. She punched at the glass with her palms. Manuel shouted for her to come forward and escape through the door, but he soon realized, as she had, that this would put her into the flames.

Manuel left her and ran up the road. Soon the shrieks became lower, guttural, and as he ran he wondered if she were burning. He came back with the spike-strip. The flames now consumed every part of the car. For a moment he stood motionless, afraid, and defeated. Then he heard the banging on the glass. He slid beneath the upturned rear fender and into the flames. He held a segment of the spike-strip and swung it at the back windshield, shattering the glass. He smelled burnt hair. His own? He kicked at the windshield. It came apart. He reached for the woman inside. She jumped at him, arms out, clawing, trampling his body, pinning it to the ground. There was a new burning smell, his hands tingled then his shoulders. He pushed out behind her, but his vest was caught. He kicked his feet— he was pinned. The flames lapped up his legs. He tugged again, hard, and came free. He felt the grenade come loose and roll to the ground. Despite the growling of the flames, he could hear the spoon pop off and the fuse hiss. He scrambled from beneath the car, then he felt everything lift: first above the clouds, then into the blue sky, and beyond that, to where the curve of everything trends toward darkness.

—ɯ—

The sun scooped out the clouds, every now and then warming his face. Manuel looked around for Gripper. Next to him was Moe's plastic sheet and a bundle wrapped inside it, feet coming out the end. The bundle was big, but not big enough to be Gripper. On his other side laid the woman, her wet skirts pressed tightly against her body. Her skin was sickly translucent, her stomach round and pregnant, heaving. His skin did not look like hers, it was not as badly raw. His head throbbed.

He passed out again.

There was a fluorescent light in his eyes, and then it was gone. A face blocked it and then became clear.

"Hey, sir," Manuel said. He tried to sit up.

It was Upton.

"Take it easy, Manny."

"Goddamn stupid thing I did."

"You did good work," said the Captain. "Gripper told us about it."

"He all right?" Manny's voice rose.

"He'll be okay. We already flew him out." The Captain became quiet. He then muttered, "That woman and her baby should pull through too. They were trying to get to a hospital when they rushed your checkpoint." Manny wanted Upton to leave, but he wouldn't. "You should be real proud, Manny."

"That's okay, sir."

"Real proud, regardless of that."

"Yeah, regardless." Manuel looked away.

"I'm sorry I can't get it for you," said Upton. "This whole business can be unfair, you know."

"I know you'd give it to me if you could. It's just a ribbon."

"You saved that woman."

"If we hadn't been there she wouldn't have needed saving."

"I can write a letter and try to explain things to the promotion board."

"Don't worry about it, sir, it won't help."

Upton was quiet for a while. He knew the truth of it. "They've got you scheduled to fly out in the morning," he said. "You should be happy."

"What time is it?" asked Manny.

"Just after midnight."

They sat together quietly for a bit and then Upton patted Manny on the shoulder. He walked out of the aid station and along the clean strip of road that crossed the Dam. He took the stairs back down to his room on the twelfth floor by the turbines.

Manuel sat propped up in his bed. The light was on and the room was very calm. His uniform and equipment sat in the corner, and they were still wet from the rain. Dangling on the front of his body armor was the other grenade.

He pushed himself out of bed. His head throbbed. The cool night air felt good against his naked back and fresh burns. His hospital gown flapped behind him. He shuffled stiffly over to his equipment and reached down for the grenade. The burns on his arms cracked like snakeskin, seeping at the joints. He walked toward the door bracing himself against the objects in the room as he went; the grenade held in his one hand.

Outside was quiet. The Humvees were parked on the road that crossed the Dam. Manuel could see very little, but he felt the immensity of the sloping wall to his one side and Lake Qadisiyah to the other, the spaces equally vast but one empty and the other full.

For what he was about to do, he wanted to be sitting. With difficulty, he lowered himself to the ground, pressing his back to the abutment that flanked the road. He'd begun to sweat. He thought it might be from the pain, but in truth he was afraid again. He held the grenade in his one hand. All he had wanted was his ribbon.

He pulled the pin and gripped the grenade's long smooth spoon. *No going back now.* He stared down the road. No one was around and he tossed it. It bounced toward one of the Humvees, rolled next to its tire and stopped. Manuel turned his head away. There was a hollow *crump* and the noise of a quick steel spray like a handful of pennies thrown into water.

Then everything was quiet again. Manuel took the pin, which he still grasped in his hand and plunged its sharp end into his scalp. He touched his head quickly. The new wetness mixed with his burnt skin. Then as quick as he could, he threw the pin down the side of the Dam. The Humvee had been blown up on its side, and flames climbed up its chassis. Through the flame light, a guard ran down the road and a siren went off, signaling a rocket attack.

—m—

Upton emerged on top of the Dam. His stare immediately fixed on Manuel who was half naked and bleeding outside of the aid station. He walked up to the burning Humvee and looked down onto the road where the blast had burned a wide mark like the smudge of an old eraser. Upton picked up the grenade's twisted spoon. He ran to the edge of the Dam and tossed it into the water before anyone would find that piece of evidence.

The guard ran up to him, panicked, casting his head about wildly. Upton grabbed him by the arm. "We got wounded from that rocket," and he pointed toward Manuel.

The guard ran over. "Where you hit?" he asked.

"Just take me inside," he said.

He lifted Manuel up under the armpits, his naked ass exposed to everything.

Upton stood on the road awkwardly, watching.

OPERATION SLUT

by Lauren Kay Halloran

The most unsettling feeling was a purse where her rifle should be. She fingered the beaded strap. It cut across her chest the same way as the sling of her M4. But the rifle gave her strength. This purse was dainty, inane. If she was to play this role, though, she needed the costume. She brushed her palm across the embroidered fabric. The texture reminded her of her body armor. She felt naked without the armor, though her reflection told her otherwise.

Camille didn't consider herself beautiful. Her skin was too pale—a crisp white canvas against which a smattering of freckles stood out profoundly. She hadn't inherited her mother's striking blue eyes, or the brown of her father's, but something in between: an unremarkable murky grey. Her nose was too thin and pointy, as though it belonged on a Disney princess, but without the other sharp features to match. She was too tall. Her lanky form had served her well as a long-distance runner, though not well enough to earn a college scholarship. Instead she joined the Air Force. Six years and she could get any job, the recruiter told her, plus education benefits.

She hadn't anticipated enjoying the military—certainly not to the degree that she would volunteer for a yearlong deployment to Afghanistan. That year had transformed Camille's body. She could see the effects in the mirror propped against the closet door. She was hard now. Her long sinewy muscles had tightened, and they rippled beneath the skin of her calves, thighs, and shoulders. Even her face was hard; her jaw in a perpetual clench, her eyes set deeper and rimmed with faint lines, which, rather than aging her, gave her an intense, purposeful glare. Pulling on black high heels, Camille could feel the deployment's effects as well. They lingered in the stiffness of her joints, still settling from the metal-plated pressure of the bulletproof vest that hugged Camille's slender torso in the wrong places.

Stepping back she noticed, not for the first time, that there was something else, too, something in her manner. She'd always been told she carried herself well; what she lacked in beauty she made up for in poise. Darrel had called her graceful. "Like a gazelle," he'd said, which made her laugh. Now that quality was amplified, as if she had emerged from the cocoon of body armor fully blossomed.

Camille scrutinized her appearance. The mirror showed a polished figure she didn't recognize. The black leather miniskirt curved impressively over her newly toned ass. On top she wore a blouse in a silky bright blue to enliven her eyes, with a keyhole revealing just a hint of cleavage. She'd chosen the outfit carefully. Fashion had never been her strong suit. Her look was frumpy at best, which made for a natural transition to military fatigues after high school. Five years in the Air Force—the most recent one spent in Afghanistan wearing nothing but a uniform—spoiled whatever meager sense of style she had. Chicness was key to what came next.

Camille hadn't yet returned to work. The military gave her two weeks of post-deployment "reconstitution time" to relax and decompress. She was plenty relaxed, so she used the time to plan. A quick consultation with *Cosmopolitan* in the grocery checkout line told her that her wardrobe was outdated, her makeup supply grievously inadequate. Later, a Google search for "how to look hot" delivered 1.6 billion results. It made her slightly nauseous that billions of people were so image-conscious, and more so that she was suddenly among them. She watched YouTube videos by peppy teenagers who called themselves "fashion bloggers" and studied photos of It Girls who'd become "it" in the year she'd been gone, apparently, because their names were unfamiliar. Now it was Friday night.

Time to commence Operation Slut.

—⚬—

The day before she deployed, she was in Darrel's bed, his old springy mattress creaking with every movement. The sun slanted through the blinds, warming angular streaks on Camille's bare back. It smelled like Old Spice and felt like spring. She wanted to fold herself into him, to stay there forever, to ignore the boxes that flanked the bed, labeled in Camille's loopy handwriting: "Kitchen," "Closet: 1, 2, and 3" a Camille-height stack of "Books." She'd assured her conservative Christian parents—and herself—it was the practical thing to do; no sense paying rent for a year she wasn't there, and why get a storage unit when Darrel offered his spare room? She was afraid, though. Afraid to deploy, and afraid to leave. Afraid of what would or wouldn't remain when she came home.

Darrel felt her stiffen. The mattress creaked. He rolled over and took her face in his hands and kissed her forehead. "I love you," he said. "I'll be here when you get back."

And she believed him.

—⚬—

The internet-ordained fashion gurus warned against showing too much skin, and tonight, the first night of the operation, Camille chose to highlight her legs for the simple, selfish reason that they were Darrel's favorite feature. Looking in the mirror, though, she was second-guessing herself. She could still sense his touch, her bare skin cold where his hands had been, like he'd branded her then pulled away. She shook her head to dislodge the memories, then turned to her wine glass for assistance. The malbec was so rich she could only take small sips. Half a glass and she was already tipsy—the aftermath of a year of forced sobriety. She replaced the goblet on the edge of the dresser and watched a red drop slide down the glass and onto the cheap particle board. She didn't bother wiping it up. With the exception of a purple price sticker on the corner of the mirror and Camille's makeup and blouse, the wine was the only color in the room. Everything else—the carpet, furniture, drapes, bedding, moving boxes, even the abstract geometric artwork—sulked in shades of white or brown. It looked more like a hospital than a short-term apartment. Camille hated it, but, she had to acknowledge, it was fitting. Anonymous, indiscriminate and sterile.

—⁓—

The jealousy started slowly, seeping into static-filled conversations on the morale phone. Leading questions about the guy-girl ratio. How she spent her down time, and who with. Sergeant Briggs was just a Ping-Pong partner, she assured him. Yes, she'd been hit on, but it was harmless; just guys being guys. She could take care of herself.

She didn't tell Darrel that part of her loved the attention. She had ever since joining the military. Growing up she'd been the Smart One, the Athletic One, the One-Who-Could-Always-Make-You-Laugh-With-Her-Uncanny-Joan-Rivers-Impression. She was known for things like cross country meet results, an affinity for public speaking, a name on the National Honor Society plaque. She wasn't prom queen material, and that fact never bothered her. Then came basic training. People regarded her differently than the male trainees, with a kind of intrigue, a cautious respect that quickly turned to awe when they learned that not only was she wearing the same uniform as the men, but she could perform at their level. She was charming but rough around the edges, both delicate and firm—traits more attributed to personality than gender, but when packaged in a scrawny blonde girl their effect was compelling.

Camille was a member of a vast minority, and the position carried risk, but also power. For the first time in her life, the military made her desirable. She didn't like the way the starched Air Force blues clung to her modest curves, but she noticed men admiring her—men who, she was sure, wouldn't otherwise offer a passing glance. The odds were in her favor, and the Airman dorms were an incestuous dating pool. Still, Camille only dipped her toes. She enjoyed the detached pleasure of admiring looks. She liked knowing the options were there. But her job kept her busy, and she was comfortable in her default setting as one of the guys.

Her suitemate was astounded. "I don't know how you control yourself! So many hot guys in uniform! There's like one for every night of the year!"

Camille shrugged. "I don't know. I don't really think of them that way."

"Camille." The girl's pretty face turned serious. "Are you a virgin?"

Camille laughed. "No, I'm not a virgin. I've had boyfriends. I just like relationships. And monogamy, I guess."

"I get it," her friend said. "You don't have the slut gene."

Even after she moved to Nellis Air Force Base outside Vegas, the epicenter of debauchery, Camille ignored it all in favor of work, and then Darrel.

—⚏—

She took a last generous swig from her wineglass, then dabbed on another layer of face powder to hide the alcohol flush creeping up her neck. She couldn't deny she looked good. Decidedly un-military. Her lips were painted in a pale pout. Rimmed with dark shadow, her eyes betrayed a sultriness she didn't feel. Her hair, always her best camouflage, cascaded over her shoulders in thick blonde layers. They were barely visible in her slicked-back military bun, but she was thankful now that she'd splurged on the face-framing highlights. She didn't look like herself. It was perfect.

—⁘—

In Afghanistan, as expected, gender disparity was more pronounced. Femaleness had to be wielded carefully. With the Afghans, it could shut down conversations among more traditional company, or spur interactions based solely on fascination. Among fellow soldiers it was easy to be labeled a bitch, a whore—Desert Queens, they were called—or the title Camille feared most: just a girl.

After a few weeks in country, Camille thought she'd mastered the balance. Her job performance earned the respect of her team. She would never act on or even acknowledge the attention, but she appreciated the way heads turned when she entered the military dining hall, or how, when she walked into an Afghan tribal meeting, the solitary headscarf in a sea of buzz cuts, the local men's eyes widened and they turned to whisper to each other. When she dropped off her clothes at the base laundromat, the Afghan employee always smiled and bowed graciously in a way he never did for her male counterparts. Jogging the gravel path that marked the FOB perimeter in her Air Force gym shorts, Camille felt the stares on her exposed skin, and she relished them. This reaction seemed wrong. Military briefings and her inner feminist told her she should be offended. But in the midst of the long, stressful days; the dust that clung to her arms and legs and hair and lodged between her teeth; the guns and baggy camouflage and clunky boots; these moments made her feel like a woman.

She never admitted this to Darrel. And she didn't tell him about the times she didn't feel like a woman, but like a frightened child. Such as the days she was on ECP, manning the base entry control point.

Nothing ever happened. Usually she was bored. They played poker, and the guys passed around wads of dip—she tried it once and made them laugh when she spit it out, a blob of black goo landing on her boot. Then a car would approach and Camille's heart would pound under her helmet. She'd raise her rifle and look through the sights. The guys beside her muttered things like, "Come on, motherfucker, just try something," or "I'm gonna blow your haji head off," but Camille prayed the car would slow down. It always did. The Afghan guards did a search at ECP 1 and the car wove through the HESCO barriers to ECP 2. The passengers got out. If there was a female, Camille patted her down, running her hands as gently as possible along the woman's ribs, under her breasts, across her thighs. She never made eye contact. As the car drove away, she held her breath, waiting for the explosion that meant they'd fucked up.

In the vehicle maintenance yard, the job was mostly routine. Daily convoys meant constant upkeep, and the Humvees were prone to breakdowns. Camille liked doing something she was used to, something she was good at. She liked the feel of grease on her hands and warm sand under her back, the way her muscles remembered the precise movements of each tool. Then occasionally a vehicle came in after an attack. They weren't always fixable, but they always sat there for a few days, at least. The crew gathered to admire the jagged holes in the engine block, the twisted metal that looked like it had been through a cheese grater. Camille's nose tingled with the smell of burned rubber and a substance her brain told her was charred flesh. She never cried in public. She saved her tears for the mildew-stained curtain of the shower stall or the blue paisley pillowcase she'd had Darrel ship from the box labeled "Bedding."

Camille didn't have much purpose outside the wire, except to talk to local women, but she volunteered for missions whenever she could. Getting off the tiny FOB was always refreshing in a backward way she didn't understand, as if in moving toward danger she could justify her paranoia and thereby assuage it. While the guys chatted over comms, she stared out the Humvee window, scouring the pockmarked ground for anything suspicious that could hide an IED. If she focused hard enough, her hands stopped shaking. At tribal meetings she'd scan the men from under her headscarf. An arm moved to scratch beneath a vest. Prayer beads rolled between fingers. Lips muttered indecipherable phrases. Outside, a passing vehicle rattled the thin window, and Camille felt certain something was about blow up.

Some mornings she'd wake before her alarm and stare at the plywood ceiling, listening to the melody of the FOB—crunching gravel, the rumble of Humvee engines and the whir of helicopter rotor blades, layers of harsh, grunted conversation—and try to remember what home sounded like. Nights were beautiful and terrifying. It wasn't darkness like Camille was used to in American suburbia. This was a "blackout FOB" with no outdoor lighting to mark a potential target. Generator power in the nearby city flickered off not long after the sun set, leaving just the moon marking where the black mountains met the black sky. And the stars. Camille had never seen so many stars. She gushed their beauty to Darrel—"It's like you can see galaxies!"—but she didn't tell him that, despite the stars, the darkness was consuming. Almost suffocating. Outside at night on the safety of the FOB she felt more vulnerable than she did in the hostile valley beyond the gate. She hugged her rifle, her trigger finger twitching at every movement, every noise. It took only a week to decide to never leave her room at night. She padlocked the flimsy plywood door and pushed her footlocker in front as a barricade. She cut the top off a liter water bottle in case she needed to pee.

—◊—

Maybe she miscalculated. Maybe if she'd opened up to Darrel, everything wouldn't have fallen apart. Camille convinced herself she was brusque for his sake; she didn't want to worry him. But there was more to it. Though packed with people, something about the FOB gave her a loneliness even he couldn't fill. She could confess that she was weak and needy, but then it would all flow out and she might not be able to stop. Besides, he wouldn't understand. It was best to compartmentalize. For both of them.

"It makes me uncomfortable that you're always hanging out with guys." The gruff voice on the line didn't sound like Darrel. *Probably the connection*, Camille thought, but she knew better.

"There's like five other women here, Darrel. What am I supposed to do?" She could feel her temper rising in the heat of her cheeks and the tightness of her jaw. She cupped her hand around the receiver, as if that could keep this conversation private in the crowded MWR building. "I hang out with guys at Nellis too. It's not like I'm fucking all of them."

"So just some of them then."

Camille let out an exasperated grunt, loud enough to make several soldiers turn their heads. "Where is this coming from? I've never given you a reason not to trust me."

"You're right." Darrel's normal voice was back. A sigh crackled through the phone, and Camille heaved one of her own. "Sorry. It just sucks here without you. And I worry about you." His voice shifted again. "But I mean, you're a mechanic! It's not like you're doing anything dangerous."

She slammed the phone down and stormed out of the building, not caring who stared.

—⚔—

A lot can change in a year. Darrel moved her boxes to a storage unit. Camille's parents said they were sorry, but they couldn't hide their relief—after all, she'd learned evasion from them. She was surprised how much she didn't miss him. Not his voice, anyway. Not the nightly trudge to MWR, the waiting in line for stilted conversation. Not the stress that came with knowing someone else was wrapped up in her well-being. She was free now to be lonely by herself, and to savor male attention without judgment.

Before she left Afghanistan, Camille found the cheap, furnished temporary apartment online and paid the first month's rent sight unseen. She moved in, but couldn't bring herself to unpack. The boxes were vestiges of Old Camille. The Camille who stressed over trivial things like a yelling boss or a late report. The prudish Camille who never let her hair down. The Camille who loved Darrel. She wasn't sure who she was now, only that she was changed, and empty. She needed to find a new normal, away from Afghanistan and away from Darrel.

She could do anything, as long as it was different. She thought of her old suitemate, the sparkle in her eyes when she came home after each conquest. She thought of the people she deployed with, how they seemed to cope so much better than her. While Camille was calling Darrel and pounding her stress into the treadmill, Mills was cheating on his wife. Bailey and Donahue were fucking behind the latrines. Maybe the Desert Queens were onto something.

So Camille would become a queen, she decided, in this Nevada desert. She needed sex. Not just to feel desirable. Not just to remind her that she was a woman, but that she was human and that sensations existed besides melancholy and loneliness and fear.

Tonight she'd call a cab. She'd fold her long, satin-and-leather-encased body into the back and tell the driver to take her to Fremont Street—a place she'd never been but had heard about, where it was big and loud and crowded enough to be anonymous. She would pick a bar, have a drink or two to counter her restraint, then let alcohol and music lead her to the dance floor. She would find rhythm with the sweaty writhing bodies, until one body pressed against hers. She'd let her arms wrap around him, let her lips search his neck, his ear, his lips, taste his sweat and desire. And she would let him take her somewhere for the night that was full of color and warmth.

She would fuck her way to normal.

Someday.

Camille sighed. Her reflection looked tired. Her knees ached from the heels. The wine was spreading quickly across her brain, and the shadow and mascara made her eyelids heavy. She kicked off the heels. She lifted the purse over her shoulder and draped it over the knob of a dresser drawer. The blouse fell in a dazzling blue puddle against the beige carpet.

Camille locked the door, shoved the heavy "Small appliances" box in front, and slipped naked under the cold white bed sheets. She closed her eyes and strained to hear something familiar: Humvee engines, helicopters, crunching gravel. Tonight she would fall asleep in silence. Alone. But she had plenty of time. She would try again. Maybe it would help. Maybe it wouldn't. Maybe she'd find out tomorrow.

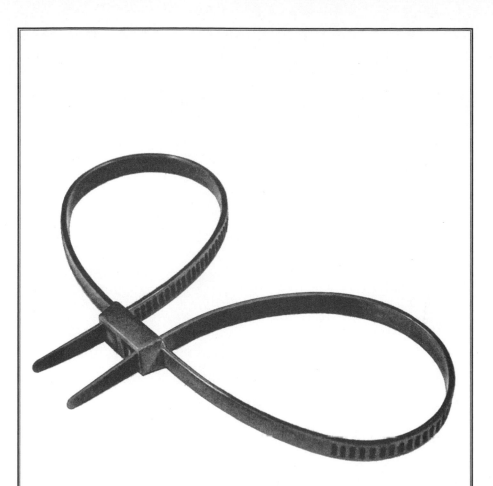

ANOTHER BROTHER'S CONVICTION

by Christopher Paul Wolfe

So a Dominican, an ex-con, and a white girl walk into an Arab-owned corner store and—

Wait. That sounds like a bad joke.

Let me try to explain it like this:

If I had to guess, 90 percent of the adult population in Bedstuy starts off its day in either an Arab- or Latino-owned corner store. And I'm part of that 90 percent.

"What's up, Akh?" I usually say to my man, Akhbar, who's *supposedly* from Iran. I say *supposedly* because everyone's story in New York is "supposedly" until it's been confirmed by an independent outside source that can upgrade it to *likely*. So yeah, Akh who, for now, is *supposedly* from Iran, owns the corner store at the end of my block and is an overly sentimental motherfucker who still feels horrible about the day the towers fell. I know this because he tells me so every morning after I say, "Yo Akh, let me get an egg and cheese on wheat toast," and then he says, "Egg and cheese! Wheat toast! Coming up!" and then I say, "Just one slice of cheese though, Akh. I want to be able to take a shit this week." And then he laughs a bit, and then I laugh a bit, because in the chaotic lifestyle of New York City, our brief exchange will be the only moment in our day when life feels like we might be living it right.

But there's something that happened on *this* day, the one I'm trying to tell you about, that made it quite different from every other one in which I'd walked into Akh's corner store. For starters, when I said,

"Yo, Akh! Let me get an egg and cheese on wheat toast," instead of saying, "Egg and cheese! Wheat toast! Coming up!" this motherfucker says "Just one slice of cheese to shit, yes?" and then waits for me to respond.

"What the fuck was that, Akh?" I say, looking at him and thinking that he'd just taken my line and rolled it into his own sort of remix to our daily routine. But I'm of the mindset that the best remixes belong on wax, not in a sacred morning ritual that's been practiced for more than five years. Akh's ad-lib meant nothing to him, but to me it was a signal, a tremor, one of those soft ripples at the center of a lake that ends as a wave at the shore, and unfortunately I had been trained to sense it, which meant that only I was left to worry about it.

Before making a move to the ATM, I look at Akh and see him smiling at me like shit is copacetic. I want to ask him why he did it, why he switched up our lines, but our moment alone is interrupted by the screeching voice of a white girl stepping in from the curb in sunglasses, a lime-green windbreaker and a Livestrong bracelet. Her aesthetic choices are a lot to take in before having a first cup of joe.

She eases up to Akh's counter and before she places her order, she stares at me like, "Who the fuck are you?" only to see me staring back at her like "Who the fuck are you?" And somehow through one of those strange unwritten rules of New York nonverbal communication, our two "Who the fuck are yous" seem to cancel each other out. So I turn toward the ATM to get my money while she stays at the front of the store doing some white girl shit that I really don't care to hear or see because between the ripple and my egg and cheese I have enough on my mind.

I enter my PIN into Akh's ATM and wait for it to access his cheap-ass, Third-World dial-up connection, which is intentionally set up to make my eyes wander around his shop for a few unintended minutes. He's hoping that I will peruse and maybe purchase a few bags of Skittles or pork rinds or some other form of salt and refined sugar that will help him push more volume, because a corner store is a volume business, not a margin business. But unfortunately for Akh, my doc at the VA told me that I have a touch of hypertension and am borderline diabetic (it runs in the family), so I continue to wait for his machine to give me my money. And it's just when it finally connects and commences to spitting out twenties that I hear the exact words no one wants to hear when they're holding a handful of money totaling in the hundreds.

"My nigga!" The Dominican. "I know you didn't just get back from where I think you just got back from. Yo Akh! Papi! Let me get a Dutch! My dude just did five years!"

Son of a bitch . . . the ripple. I just want an egg and cheese . . . on wheat toast . . . with one slice of cheese; not whatever-the-fuck this is going to be. I look over at Akh and see him standing in the large wooden frame of his countertop, his eyes steadily glancing up at the security cameras, like he's wishing that those shits were actually working. The Dominican is short and stocky and his friend, the ex-con, seems . . . well, different. He's wearing clothes about a decade too old, and when he speaks his eyes stay oriented toward the ground like he's still processing the fact that he isn't seeing a cold prison floor this morning. He's got the look of someone who's returned from—

"Five years, Akh! On Rikers!" It's the look of someone who's made it back from a place that he'd come to believe that he never would. It's the same one I had when I had just gotten back from Iraq.

"You should give us that Dutch for free, Akh. My nigga's home!" says the Dominican. Like congrats on surviving prison; here, have some lung cancer. He puts his arm around his friend, this ex-con, and says, "Damn, boy! When did they let you out?"

"I just got out last night."

"Why didn't you call? I would have came and got you."

"I don't have a phone, kid. And you don't got a car so I figured—"

"Nigga, it's been five years. How the fuck you know I don't have a car?"

"You got a car?"

"No. But damn, it's good to see you, kid. It's been five damn years!"

My eyes make their way around the room, and upon taking in each of us, I come to believe that they—the Dominican, the Arab, and the white—

Wait. Where did the white girl go? Damn, she broke out quick as hell!

Anyway, I believe that they—the listed stated earlier, less the white girl—are all in disbelief that they are making the same seldom-seen, firsthand observation of a man who has literally just walked out of prison, supposedly rehabilitated, reshaped, maybe reconditioned to be a productive, or at least less destructive, member of society. But for some reason I'm okay with it, and when I look at him I can't help but to see myself and empathize with his current state of mind. The only thing I'm wondering is: what's a motherfucker got to do in this country to earn him five years of living in a concrete box with a very limited wardrobe?

He probably sold crack, right? Or pounds of weed that he kept stacked inside his bedroom like an igloo. Wait. I should know better and be more open-minded when scrutinizing another brother's conviction. Because if I don't, then who will? Plus, if he just got out today, then I have to believe that a judge wouldn't have given him five years for weed when it's now legal in two states and medicinal in our nation's capital. How fucked up would that be? He must have done something a little bit more sinister, some straight up negligent shit that undoubtedly put his fellow man at risk, something like—I don't know—lied to the American people about chemical weapons in Iraq then sent the whole damn country into a war that lasted over a decade. Yeah! That's the type of shit that should get a motherfucker like twenty years! But if you're young enough and connected enough and a first time offender then you could probably get it down to five, right? Yeah, that's at least five years, right?

"Yo Akh . . . that Dutch man?"

I could hear Akh rummaging through a cigar box behind his countertop just before he says, "You want grape or vanilla flavor?" And I'm like Akh do you really think they care. Jesus, I could've grown the tobacco, and rolled it myself by now.

"Man, let me get vanilla. Grape is nasty as hell."

So I was wrong, but that's not important—everybody gets it wrong; just ask the ex-con—what's important is that I put my hand to my back pocket and couldn't feel my wallet. Where's my wallet? Oh, it's in my hand, along with my money. I've got to put that away.

"So you just left Staten Island, huh?" says Akh, trying to make small talk, but only straying further into ad-lib abyss.

"No, nigga. Rikers," says the Dominican.

"Same thing," says Akh, and from what I know of the borough, I actually believe he can make a strong case for a close comparison. But with having no dog in this fight, I keep my opinion to myself.

"Five years . . . on Rikers, Akh . . . is not the same thing! Five years? Damn . . ."

The Dominican sounded like it pained him to say it, like he'd served out the sentence himself. But the ex-con kept quiet, his head still aimed at the floor as if there was some weight or chain that the prison guards had forgotten to remove from his neck before he left. He was a handsome young man, about six feet tall. If he were me then he'd average at least four booty calls a day. Think about that. Four booty calls a day for 365 days over five years. I reach for my phone to do the math and remember that it's an iPhone and that the ex-con currently has no phone, which means that he might want my phone so I decide to use a more rudimentary method to get to the answer: zero, carry the two, carry the two; zero, carry the three, carry the two and . . . that's 7,300 calls. Damn that's a lot of booty calls he missed, all because he probably did some truly ignorant and tragic shit like walked up to a big nigga selling loosies on the street and choked him out for no good reason. Yeah, that's probably what he did. That's got to be worth at least five years, right? No?

Or maybe he was involved in something a bit more complex, a situation where the ability to discern between right and wrong was a little more convoluted. Maybe he was a soldier . . . Yeah, a soldier in the middle of the desert who stood guard outside a room that he saw a man enter with yellow zip-ties around his wrist and a black blindfold across his face, but how he saw the same man leave was in body bag flung onto the back of a pickup. And maybe as he watched that pickup pull away and its taillights collapse to red pinpoints in the desert night, he could feel that he'd been a part of something that he'd come to regret for the rest of his life. And maybe I knew that although I hadn't just killed a man, I sure as fuck hadn't saved him and that there was no difference between the two. I could only hope that when I got back home to my country, that my people, if ever feeling the need to scrutinize my conviction, that they would be open-minded and come to see that: as I stood guard outside that room and played my part in something I'd come to regret, I had no conviction. There was no conviction. There still is no conviction . . .

There's just Akh and the Dominican, the ex-con and his five years, and me and my egg and cheese. And somewhere, out there, in the streets of Bedstuy, there's a missing white girl.

A GIFT OF THE
SWEDISH COMMITTEE
FOR AFGHANISTAN

د افغانستان لپاره
د سویډن کمیټه

2002

FUNERAL CONVERSATION

by Nate Bethea

First Lieutenant Alan Longo, from an interview given at the Paradise Lounge Dining Facility, Contingency Operating Base Ghormah, August 30, 2009.

A car bomb detonated at the Khayr Kot Castle entry point. Two Afghan soldiers and an American died in the blast, and another American soldier was missing. We weren't sure if he was still alive, but the rules of the game stated that we'd find him regardless. My platoon received a mission: be ready to move at the FOB Ghormah pickup zone in four hours. All regular patrols cancelled. I passed the word to Sergeant Kossick, my platoon sergeant, and set about collecting all the intel that battalion had. Which wasn't much; a few satellite photos, a few PowerPoint slides showing each house in a village with a number written over each roof. I briefed the plan as we awaited our helicopters.

"They want us out there to find this guy Ellis," I said. "He's a private in Blackhorse Company that got captured. We're gonna cordon and search this entire village, then set up a blocking position afterward. If they're sneaking him through our area, we've only got so much time before he's gone for good. So, we're gonna be thorough. Pay attention to anything and everything." I told them all that I knew. Which was almost nothing. As the platoon leader, you can never let your guys know when you think the mission is bullshit. Deep down, I knew it was.

Battalion told us that we would be out for about twenty-four hours. They told us to take assault packs—basically schoolbags, not full rucksacks. We would hit a village called Adam Kalay in Ghazni province. Battalion figured the insurgents would smuggle Ellis to Pakistan through the Polish army sector in Ghazni—if he was alive, of course.

Because guess what? The Poles don't do shit. East of Highway One, the Taliban controls the entirety of Ghazni province. They've burned down all the district centers. There is no government. They've co-opted or killed anyone who might work for Karzai. People like to call it "No Man's Land," as if there were some doubt, as if it were up for grabs, but it's not. It belongs to the Taliban. They run it unopposed. We just don't like to admit that we have all these monumental US bases so close to a place we can't control. Battalion sends us out on missions to do meet-and-greets with the locals, to 'establish mutual trust and respect,' as the counter-insurgency manual says. But the locals know that we're powerless, and no Afghan will respect that.

As soon as the helicopters touched down in Ghazni, I noticed a difference: it was hotter than Ghormah. The daytime highs topped out at one hundred and fifteen degrees Fahrenheit. There were even fewer trees than in our area. No shade. Rolling hills. Distant mountains. Soil that looked like orange talc. Like southern New Mexico, except for the all the turbans and camels, and the blowing dust that's probably full of depleted uranium and hepatitis.

It was supposed to last twenty-four hours. We were out there for ten days. We walked from Adam Kalay to Shin Ghar village. We searched all the houses in both. We popped open dozens of footlockers. They were glittery tin chests with glossy red paint and acid-trip designs made out of hologram stickers. We saw every color and pattern of fake mink blanket in existence. We saw wormy, disease-infested farm animals. We saw hundreds of white Toyota Corolla station wagons that looked like they'd seen action in demolition derbies. We didn't find anything. Every time we cleared an objective, I asked for the helicopters to bring us back to FOB Ghormah. Nothing. No air available. We desperately needed water. Battalion managed to deliver a pallet of water bottles near a village called Kharbin. We searched the houses there too. Ellis wasn't around. In the open fields on the far side of Kharbin a guy rode up on a massive white horse and told us that we should leave. He looked like an Afghan Don Quixote.

The villages were warrens of mud huts and animal pens. The people had Dark Ages illnesses and disfigurations, and they spoke a Pashto that was almost incomprehensible to our interpreter, Sharif, who really sucked at Pashto, anyway. He was some kid from Kabul who wanted to make the big bucks, and here he was in the middle of hell's countryside. The villagers showed us a woman whose right eye was full of maggots. She was still alive, her eyeball eaten away, and the maggots writhed and squirmed in the socket.

We moved toward Yusuf Kalay. It was another village where battalion thought we might find Ellis. There was nothing. We walked at night, trying our damnedest to avoid having soldiers get overheated, forcing down water. It felt like a dry sauna with no exit. One hundred plus degrees every day, and we walked around in suits of armor. Each day was a new objective without resupply. I'm surprised none of my soldiers keeled over. It was probably just the fear of having to stay there that kept them from giving up.

Every single one of us stank. Every single one of us had our uniform pant legs rip, so by the end we all had our dicks hanging out. The uniforms are lowest-bidder pieces of trash, and the crotch seams blow out whenever you kneel down. Our clothes were in rags. Our hands were crackling black and our skin looked like sandpaper. Our gloves had ripped to pieces. Every bit of cut-rate military equipment was falling apart. Our uniforms took on the same color as our dehydrated piss, like a burnt sienna crayon. We conducted a traffic checkpoint outside of Yusuf Kalay and didn't catch anyone. People gave us excuses or tried to avoid us. Cars screeched to a halt, turned around, and went the other way. The children were terrified. The men made energetic gestures. We looked like monsters. We smelled like monster shit. You can imagine how weirded-out the Afghans were.

We left Yusuf Kalay by helicopter, but only to move further south, back into Ghormah district. We then flew to Dila district and did the same thing. We went to Haji Ahmanullah Kalay and searched all the houses. Nothing. Angry stares. Hateful elders. Scared kids. Excited kids. Animal shit, straw, mud bricks, gaping holes in the ground with water pumps and pipes inside the yards of Afghan compounds strewn with antique, old-timey farm instruments from the 1800s. Not a living plant in sight. Not a tree or a bush—just dirt. Long rifles. Lee-Enfields. Winchester 1895s. Martini-Henrys. Mosin Nagants. Jezails, even. Ancient jewelry. Little girls in sparkling, rhinestone-studded dresses running away from us at breakneck speed. Little boys in filthy robes running toward us asking for pens or candy. Old men in turbans, shouts in Pashto, fear, sweat, the smell of our own asses. Babies with deformities. Babies with burned feet. Anguished Afghan parents opening a diaper to show us that their little boy's penis has no hole, expecting that we can somehow fix it, as if the task organization of every US Army infantry platoon just happened to include a resident pediatric surgeon. Misery. A soldier sprained his ankle. A soldier cut his hand while opening a ration. It got infected, turned green-and-white colored, and swelled up. Blood dried on shredded, dirty uniforms, with mud caking where the blood soaked in. Running out of baby wipes, running out of toilet paper, shitting in an open field, shitting atop rocky hills, under outcroppings, in gullies, in abandoned houses, next to culverts, next to burned cars. Flies everywhere. Flies on our hands, on our faces, on our food. Mud-brick castles that Afghans call *qalats*. Qalats with towers. Qalats with towers of which one has a hole in its upstairs floor and below it is all the collected, assembled human shit from a family of forty-five people living in the compound and using the toilet on a regular basis. Offers of tea. Declined offers of tea resulting in tea nonetheless. Contempt from the elders. Denial from the elders. Nothing of value. A waste of our time.

We walked from Yusuf Kalay to another village called Nur Mohammad Khel. This time, the insurgents ambushed us. It happened in the early morning. One of my soldiers saw them before they fired. He called out, "Hey, eleven o'clock—what the fuck is that?" We all looked. In the distance: some men with a recoilless rifle. We all saw the puff of smoke from the tube when it fired, but we never heard the report. The first rounds hit within a hundred meters of us, and it knocked everyone to the ground. A thud punched the air out of my lungs. There was heat from the blast. There was dust. All the debris that the explosion kicked into the air stung my face when it hit. My ears started ringing, and everything sounded as if someone was pressing a pair of earmuffs against my head. We all screamed, "Contact front! Contact front!" We could barely see them through the dust cloud. They shot again. The next round was behind us, but only about fifty meters. We started engaging with the two-forty, just laying down heat on them, but they were probably six hundred to eight hundred meters away—just out of range. We couldn't see if we were hitting them or just making them laugh. I called up that we were in contact and needed air support. Nothing available. We ran to a nearby gulley—what the Afghans called a *wadi*—where we would be able to get a little bit of cover and concealment from them. They could see for hundreds of meters, and of course our stone-grey camouflage stood out against the orange desert like rainbow-colored hot air balloons. The next round landed right where we had been before. We didn't have much time.

From the inside of the wadi, I watched them through binoculars. They had an SPG-9 recoilless gun on a tripod set up maybe fifty meters from a qalat. They stood behind a collapsed adobe wall only about two or three feet high, like a sand castle half devoured by the ocean. They were out in the open, four of them, watching for us and aiming the barrel our way.

We couldn't range them with machine guns. If we shot, we simply gave ourselves away because of noise and tracer rounds. If we left the wadi, we stood even more exposed. If we ran up the treeless hills, we would exhaust ourselves getting there in the heat, fully vulnerable. We were too heavy and too armored to get away from them, and we couldn't sneak out and break contact. There was no artillery support. There were no drones. There was nothing to hide behind, and nowhere to go.

The only reason nobody died was a shit-hot mortarman, Private First Class Fenty, a twenty-year-old kid from Anderson, Indiana. He wasn't even a mortarman by training, but we'd taught him how to use the 60mm mortar in handheld mode. Thank God we decided to carry mortars on that mission. We had a total of twenty-eight rounds.

Fenty ran up to the edge of the wadi with the mortar tube. We consolidated ammo for him—a bunch of frenzied, dirty hands shucking mortar rounds out of their black paperboard packaging and laying them in the dirt at his feet. We were caked with muddy paste, our perspiration mixing with the dirt on our faces. Fenty popped his head up, looked one last time, and then aimed the tube. He said, "Drop the round!" One of my soldiers dropped the mortar down the tube. He held a second and then pulled the trigger. It fired. I watched.

We waited. Seconds passed. Then, impact. The round exploded in a flash and a split-second later we heard the report. He was really close—maybe ten meters ahead of them. The Taliban were down on the ground, trying to take cover. They were clowning around in the open, and now they were the ones exposed. One of them ran behind the qalat wall. The other three got up and tried to fire the recoilless gun at us. It was a matter of who shot first. Call it an Afghan standoff.

"Fenty, drop it like ten meters!" I said. "Ten meters and then fire for effect!"

He made his correction. He fired once. I looked through the binos. It nailed them. They splayed out on the ground, and within a few seconds the dust cleared enough that I could see blood spurting out of the leg of one of them as he rolled around clutching the wound. Big goopy jets of blood.

"Fire for effect, Fenty!" I said, "Fire for effect!"

One after another, the soldiers dropped rounds down the tube and he fired them, his hands still in the same place, the tube held the same direction as before. One, then another, then another, and the rounds kept hitting them, like right on top of them, like *boom*. Another round. *Boom*. Another round. *Boom*. The one behind the wall ran to help his friends, who were by this point seriously messed up. We shot more rounds. The last guy fell over. The contact stopped. My guys cheered like we were Super Bowl champions. Absolute tearful elation. It's a high that doesn't exist outside of combat. Christ, I can hardly describe it now.

I called higher on the satellite radio and told them our story. I called up our map grid and the general location of the contact, and the fact that we killed four Taliban. They wanted a battle damage assessment. BDA. We received orders to go talk to the villagers and confirm that we killed the insurgents.

"You've got to be fucking kidding me, sir," Sergeant Kossick said to me. "They want us to go talk to them now?"

"Yeah, roger," I said. "They're insane."

"Sir, let me talk to them," Sergeant Kossick said. He took the hand mic and asked for Destroyer Seven. The battalion command sergeant major. Maybe a fellow non-commissioned officer could talk some sense into the guy. Sergeant Kossick repeated the transmission a few times.

No response. He looked at me like he needed to piss but couldn't find a toilet. Finally, a warbled voice came through, a voice with all the clarity of a skipping CD player.

"This is Destroyer Seven, go ahead," it said.

"Destroyer Seven, this is Charlie Three-Seven," Sergeant Kossick said. "Just want to confirm what we're hearing from the battalion TOC, over."

"Roger, go ahead, over," the command sergeant major said.

"Yeah, roger, we just got in a firefight and killed some AAF with mortars," Sergeant Kossick said. "We don't have any CAS or any kind of air support. If we get ambushed, we're going to be hosed— and we already know they're hostile, over."

"Roger, Charlie Three-Seven," the voice said, its pitch alternating between human and chipmunk speeds. "Conduct BDA on that village, over."

"Destroyer Seven, this is Charlie Three-Seven, this is not a good idea, over," Sergeant Kossick said, trying one last time. All radio discipline went out the window.

"All right, Charlie Three-Seven, if it's too hard to lead your goddamn men, then you stay put and let me fly out there and play platoon sergeant for you," the voice said. "Conduct BDA on the village. Be a fucking NCO or I'll find one to replace you. Destroyer Seven out."

I could see the looks of panic and disgust in the eyes of my soldiers when I told them what was next. Sergeant Kossick looked nauseated. It was embarrassing enough for him without the fact that we could still get ambushed and killed. My interpreter was exhausted and scared. My guys' hearts were still pumping the animal panic blood that only comes when death is a very real possibility. Clearly, this would be the perfect time to conduct international diplomacy.

We moved in bounds. The qalats looked normal-sized until we got close, and then I started to realize that they were massive. Each wall was at least a hundred and fifty meters long. There must have been entire cities inside the gates. They might as well have had moats and drawbridges, with Afghan Rapunzels hiding in the towers.

We kept walking. It had only been thirty or forty-five minutes since the firefight. We saw divots and indentations in the dirt from where our rounds had impacted, and a purple blood spot. Their blood made me happy. It was the biggest thrill to know we had killed them first. The people in the town had since moved the bodies and all of their leftover equipment.

On the far side of the qalat stood an open field with a village well. It was the same well we see everywhere in-country: cast in shoddy concrete, falling to pieces, a fake brick pattern scraped onto it and a plaque on top reading "A Gift of the Swedish Committee for Afghanistan, 2002." Or 1992. Or 2052. Who cares. There was an adjacent graveyard. The town was having a funeral.

The men of the town were covering the bodies of the guys we'd killed with rocks and strips of cloth. The sun had already begun to dip, and their religious custom dictated that they had to bury the bodies before dark. It didn't take long for them to notice we were there. We kept walking toward them with our weapons pointed down, as if to make the automatic weapons seem kinder. And we were covered in dirt, had huge beards, everyone smelling like a dog's ass. Dicks flapping in the wind under ripped pant-legs. You could see the outrage ripple through the crowd. We walked right up on their party.

There were about fifty villagers, and they all wore either sequined hats or turbans. There were no women or girls present. Some of the boys held the burial rocks in their hands like they were ready to throw them at us. I could sense fury in the crowd. The oldest man was probably fifty, but he looked eighty. He had a long white beard, a yellow turban, sharp eyes, and old 1970s Robert Mugabe glasses. His nose was huge, comically oversized. At first glance you'd have thought that he was wearing a nose-and-mustache disguise.

"Sir," my interpreter said, "I don't want to talk to these people."

"I don't either, Sharif," I said. "We'll make it quick." He nodded.

"*Salaam alaikum,*" Sharif said. The oldest man returned the greeting.

"Look," I said to my interpreter, whose Pashto got worse when he got stressed out, "I need you to be mean. Like, talk like a bad person to these people. Say what I say just like I'm saying it."

"Okay, okay, sir," he said.

I walked closest to the crowd. I took my helmet and sunglasses off. My face probably looked grotesque—it was half-sunburned, half-pasty, and just filthy all over. I didn't recognize myself when I looked in the mirror after it was all done. The counter-insurgency classes always said that you had to take your headgear off and expose yourself to the people. It was so that they would trust you and want to be your friend. They'd be susceptible to your influence.

"I'm the commander of all of these American soldiers," I said. "My name is Lieutenant Longo."

Sharif translated.

"We're here looking for an American soldier that the Taliban captured. Have any of you seen him?" I waited for the translation. No response.

"I'll say it again, have any of you seen an American soldier who's the prisoner of the Taliban? His name is Private Ellis."

The elder spoke softly in Pashto.

"Sir," Sharif said, "he says that there are no Taliban in his village. They never come."

"I didn't think so," I said. "Those guys were just shooting off fireworks, right?"

Sharif looked at me with a dazed expression. "I don't understand, sir," he said.

"Never mind, man," I said. "Just ask him why those guys were shooting at us."

There was more chatter in Pashto.

"He says that they weren't shooting at you," Sharif said. "He said that this village is attacked by robbers, and so when they think we robbers, they start shooting."

"Oh, so this was just a big misunderstanding?" I asked, letting myself get angry. "None of you have anything against the government, right? Ask him that, Sharif." There was more chatter.

"Sir, he says that they support the government. He says that they do not understand why you are killing innocent people. He says you are welcome in this village."

"Well, shit," I said. "I sure appreciate it. Hey, no harm, no foul, right? But, no need to make tea or have us sit down. We're just looking. We don't want anything to do with you fucking people or your village." I paused. Sharif talked Pashto. I kept hearing him say *dee wayee che*, which I recognized as "He says that." Sharif was pointing the finger too. It was the only time that I wished I spoke Pashto. I don't want to study that language, that trash, but I wanted to be certain that every word I spoke was just as brutal and dirty and hostile as I intended.

"Sir, he says that these men are poor and that their children will now be starving," Sharif said. "He says, 'Americans must pay. They kill these men for no reason. They are innocent people.'"

And that was when I lost it.

"Listen to me, you fucking hajj!" I said, my finger right in the old man's face, the crowd now attentive to me alone. "Those are not innocent people. Your friends tried to kill us. You're a liar. Every last one of you shit-smelling garbage people is a liar. You tried to shoot us. But guess what? We're better shots. And in a few days your friends are going to be full of worms. Bugs are going to eat their eyes and guts out. That's their fault. That's your fault."

"Sir, I need some time to translate," Sharif said. Everything he said was too soft. I don't think he was getting my point across.

"Sharif, I'm not done," I said. "I've got something else." I was still seething.

"Okay, sir, okay, yes," Sharif said.

"Sir, we're going to walk out of this village," I said. "We're not going to pay you. No one is going to pay you. We're leaving. I ask you to leave us alone." They exchanged words again.

"He says that, unless we give money, these men's families must have revenge," Sharif said. "They will not rest until they have revenge." I could appreciate that sentiment.

"Sharif, listen to me, buddy," I said. "You need to tell him this word for word. I need you to concentrate." Sharif nodded silently.

"Can you fucking concentrate?" I snapped at him. He replied with a meek "yes, sir." I returned to the old man.

"Sir, I can't offer you any money, but I can offer you a promise," I said, slowly this time, for the benefit of the translation. "I promise you that, if you try to seek revenge, my men and I will kill everybody in this village. We'll kill your men. Your women. Your children. Your animals. We'll burn all the bodies. We'll burn down all your houses. None of you will be buried. You'll be left out for the dogs to eat. And no one will ever care. Do you understand me?"

"Sir, I cannot say that to him," Sharif said. "You cannot say that to Afghan people. It is too much, sir."

"Sharif, buddy," I said, "you either tell it to him right now, or I'm just gonna start killing them. Your choice." I didn't care how they felt. I truly meant what I said.

Sharif swallowed hard as he spoke these words. No reply from the man, but his eyes widened as Sharif continued the speech. I could tell that this disturbed him in an unbearable way.

"Sharif, ask him if he understands," I said. Sharif asked it twice—*poh sheway dee?*—and there was no response. The man ignored him. He thought we were beneath his contempt. He still had his pride.

"Poh sheway dee?" I asked with a pleading smile, hamming it up, knowing that I'd piss him off. The man gave me a hard look and, finally, spit at my feet with a look of hatred and defiance. He might as well have said, "Fuck you," because what he lacked in English vocabulary, he communicated with his eyes, green like dusty jade, with an expression that told me he wished only for my death, and soon.

And that was it. I snapped. Everything I hated about this country, its people, the war, the Army, the idiotic and insane mission, it all unleashed a fury in me that I had never entertained. I know I scared my soldiers. I certainly scared myself.

I grabbed the old man by his shoulders, tripped him with my leg and hurled him to the ground. He landed with a pathetic, hacking cough. I still had my helmet in my hand. I brought it down on his face and it thumped like an empty coconut. I shouted at the top of my lungs, *"POH SHEWAY DEE?"* I kicked him in his side. I could feel his body crunch as my foot connected. It was such a relief to hurt someone in a way that wasn't abstract or distant. My soldiers raised their weapons. I could see variations of terror and delight in their faces. *"POH SHEWAY DEE?"* I kicked him again. Bones broke, and it delighted me. The funeral crowd now stared down the barrels of thirty assault rifles and machine guns. Finally, I dropped the helmet to the ground, pulled out my Beretta, charged the slide and pointed it at him. I shouted one more time, *"POH SHEWAY DEE?"*

"Wo, wo, wo, ze poh sheway yem, ze poh sheway yem!" He shrieked at me, clutching his face. *"Ma wulah, ma wulah!"*

"He's saying, 'I understand, I understand, don't shoot,' sir," Sharif shouted at me.

"Good," I said, breathing heavily. "I'm glad we understand each other."

I flipped the safety on my Beretta. It caused the hammer to strike forward without firing a shot. The man jolted in terror at the click. He shouted in hoarse, wheezing Pashto. His broken glasses hung on his nose. He squirmed on the ground, trying and failing to get up. I had broken at least one of his ribs. There was a contusion on his forehead where my helmet struck. Ribbons of blood streaked down his face.

"What's he saying, Sharif?" I asked.

"He's saying you're a cruel man, sir," Sharif said. "He said, 'God, punish him. He is so cruel and angry. He is like an animal.'"

"You're goddamn right, I am," I said. "And he'd better remember that."

Once we returned to FOB Ghormah, we got word that they'd found Ellis's body in Wor Mamay district. Battalion stood us down, and Sharif quit out of disgust and contempt. For me. My company commander got word of what I'd done, but he just told me to be more careful. Afghans are sensitive, he said. The battalion commander was the kind of guy who might have chastised me for it, maybe even relieved me, but he never spent enough time in Khusamond to hear the legend. Crazy L-T Longo, the soldiers in my company called me. The only guy who'd stopped being nice to those people, who'd tell it for what it was. The only guy who'd go to a shura and beat the elders to death. They said it with admiration.

But, I didn't kill the old man. I told my guys to turn around and push out. Once clear of the village, we reached some high ground that kept us decently separated from them. The helicopters arrived early the next morning, and we left. The villagers could have attacked us in the night if they'd wanted to, fired a few more rounds our way, but I didn't think they'd risk it. There wasn't any need. We had already established more than enough mutual trust and respect.

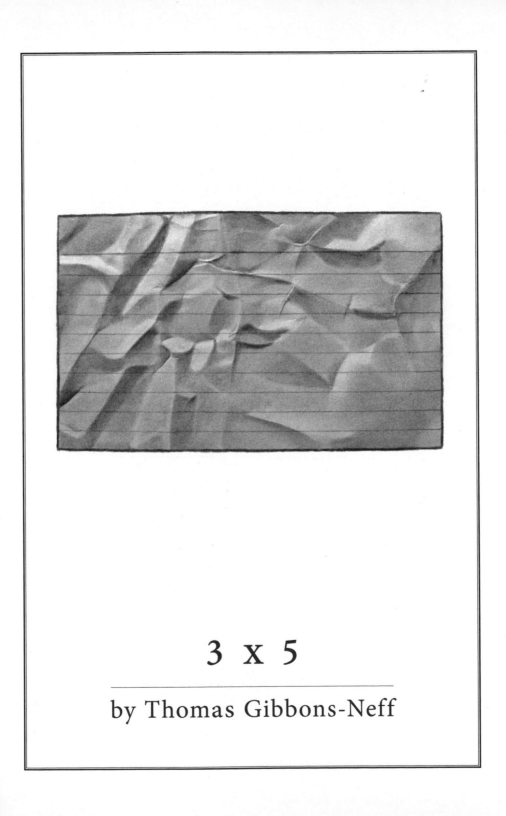

3 x 5

by Thomas Gibbons-Neff

They almost got their mail last week. The helicopter had come in low and slow; its forty-minute flight from one of the larger bases briefly interrupted by a herd of camels the pilot wanted to harass with the *thwap thwap thwap* of the rotors.

It was five feet off the ground when the airframe shuddered and snapped in half, spilling flat rate boxes and envelopes into a dying propeller wash. The crew (who were all fine) would later joke that it was the price they paid for flying a bird that once participated in the Saigon airlift.

So, nestled in between a row of sand dunes and a dying river, the outpost waited for their mail. From the air it was an oversized sandbox punctuated with a few bunkers and a cluster of radio antennae that scraped the sky like oblong blades of grass when the winds picked up or when the resupply helicopters managed to land without breaking into two. Yet, to those who lived in the dusty loam of her confines, the outpost was the same on the ground as from the sky: a barren rhombus filled with cots, a platoon of Marines, and a stray goat that a sergeant insisted on keeping even though it wouldn't stop eating people's gloves.

On one of those cots lived Alex Franklin, and today the mail had come.

He had just come back from patrol and while his eyes were drawn to the single envelope silhouetted against the olive drab fabric of his bed, he couldn't help but let out a string of expletives when he noticed that someone had moved his bottle of Texas Pete's Hot Sauce from beneath it.

Drawn to the sound of distress, a Marine on one of the posts leaned over a clump of sandbags and looked curiously down at Alex.

"No one cares that you don't like it when people touch your stuff, Franklin," he said, banging a pack of cigarettes against the stock of the machine gun his right elbow was draped over. "Besides, the mail came today so just shut up."

Alex was handsome with brown hair and proportional arms and a proportional chest and it didn't take long after he had inspected his hot sauce and opened the lone envelope to realize he had just been dumped (the date read a month prior, but that kind of time meant nothing to the outpost).

Now Alex had been dumped a fair number of times during his twenty-two years of existence, but today this was different.

Notably there was Samantha in eighth grade who did it over AOL instant messenger, and that was par for the times, but it was in an away message wedged between Blink-182 lyrics.

Oh, and Rebecca, his junior year. This was in person but she was drunk and it was after he had caught her making out with his younger brother (he was thirteen) at a prom party in his own basement. Afterward, even his dad had clapped him on the shoulder and exclaimed that she had been good *first* wife material.

Today though, today there was Sarah, and she had just dumped him with four lines on an index card.

He gagged thinking about how excited he was when he first held it fifteen seconds earlier.

Everything about the index card was upsetting, even the way it felt when he shook it against the air. It was as if the ballpoint pen she had pressed to the material had inundated the off-white surface with the weight that he felt in his stomach as he read those four lines over and over again.

It was thick, probably hemmed together from bastardized scraps of construction paper in some mill in West Virginia before being sent to Walmart or her sister's desk drawer or wherever she found it before dooming him to a life of misery.

She "had found someone else," someone who worked the dinner shift with her at Texas Roadhouse, some douche who understood what she had to deal with, and who danced with her in the middle of the dining room when that song Franklin could never remember the name of came on at the top of the hour.

And just as it dawned on him that he had been dumped by a Texas Roadhouse waitress, he subsequently recalled that people in prisoner of war camps used to write manuscripts on pieces of toilet paper and all he got was four lines on an off-brand index card.

He let out a laugh, the hollowness of which unsettled the goat.

Checkers, as the goat had come to be known, was meandering around the outpost when Alex's laugh reached his twitching goat ears. He bleated softly and stared at Alex, moving his molars rhythmically over a lost pair of mechanic gloves as he trailed off into exasperated pants.

"She's probably been fucking him this whole time," Paciello said, his dip-stained breath just inches from Franklin's ear. He didn't have to turn around to know Paciello was grinning.

"How long you been back there?"

"Since you opened it."

Paciello walked back to his cot and sat, smiling as he leaned over to take off his boots.

"Can you blame her, man?" Paciello said, lying down now, the cot's frame huffing and hawing under the pressure of his 220-pound Italian-American frame. "She's nineteen, trying to figure out what shoes to wear six times a day, and you're out here trying to keep your legs attached to your body."

Paciello was a lanky motherfucker and had worked on roofs in Connecticut most of his life. His face was pitted from the New England winters and a bad case of acne in the eleventh grade, yet for being a thirty-year-old who "actually listened to Kurt Cobain when he was alive," Paciello complained belligerently about how much he wanted to watch Seinfeld reruns on his couch. "A real couch," he would say.

Franklin would often wonder why Paciello always stressed that it was a *real* couch (as opposed to a fake one?) in his diatribes, but this place makes you stress on weird things and so he left it at that.

He knew Paciello was right, though—it was a terrible idea coming here with a nineteen-year-old girlfriend, and one index card later he knew what one of his sergeants had meant when he told him, "I don't care who the hell she is, you do not date teenagers when you're deployed."

Whoops.

In the distance a lone donkey whimpered and Franklin could hear the guy on watch keying and unkeying his radio. The short bursts of static mixed with the moan of the outpost's lone generator was the same white noise Franklin had fallen asleep to for the last hundred days, but tonight he pressed play on his iPod and let the Cranberries take over.

> *It's the same old theme since nineteen-sixteen.*
> *In your head, in your head they're still fighting*
> *Zombie.*

The stars were out and judging by where the moon hung in the sky, Franklin knew Chase would be jabbing a red lens flashlight in his eye in less than two hours muttering the same thing he did every night: "Franklin, bitch, you got watch."

Watch. Franklin tossed the word in his head and then looked at his own. He was right, less than two hours until Chase was tormenting him. Watch. Six hours of staring into the Papa Zulu sector through his night vision goggles, the dull green slowly burning his corneas, forcing him to blink constantly to stave off the headache that would come with dawn.

Watch. Six hours of thinking about Sarah and the guy from her shift at Texas Roadhouse. The guy who was a world away running his hands through her hair, kissing the matching freckles on her palms and putting up with her juvenile bullshit that Franklin thought he had put up with so well.

He sighed.

The battery on his iPod read less than 10 percent but he didn't care. It would take a day and a half to find the asshole from third platoon who had the portable charger for it, but he had just gotten dumped and he'd be damned if he wasn't going to fall asleep listening to music.

"Fuck you, Sarah," Franklin said, pulling the blanket over his face, the light of the iPod casting his cocoon in a pale glow.

—⚇—

As Alex slept, eyes moved in the dark. Eyes that were tired of the two-month-old *People* magazine that had blown to tatters, and eyes that were sick of reading their own business. Paciello had talked about it when he shuffled past him at the piss tubes and the eyes wanted to see it for themselves.

An index card? What kind of girl dumps a guy on an index card?

The eyes could see Alex sleeping and the iPod glowing and as they got closer and closer the eyes grew hands that quietly plucked the index card off the end of the cot.

—⚇—

"Franklin, bitch, you got watch," Chase said, the flashlight inches from Franklin's eye.

Franklin had been asleep for less than two hours, but already his eyelids had crusted over from the dust in the air.

"Time?"

"Zero-one-hundred," Chase said, dragging out the last syllables of "hundred" in his Florida accent. "Same time it always is."

Franklin let out a low fuck and picked up his boots, shaking each in case a scorpion had decided to crawl into the warm enclave of the toe box.

"I never do that, man," Chase said. "Life's more exciting when you put your shoes on without looking."

Chase was a year older than Franklin and made it into the military after a sideways childhood in a town just outside of Tampa. Chase called it "Itty-Bitty-Plant-City" and from what Franklin could discern, Plant City had good fishing and even better strip clubs.

Chase was short with shoulders that kept his ruck high on his back during the long patrols and the sun turned his unnaturally dark face even darker and his blonde hair even blonder, leaving only two vertical scars over his lip their naturally pinkish tone. Girls loved Chase because of his blue eyes and Franklin loved Chase because he was the best machine gunner in the company.

"Sorry about your girl," Chase said.

Franklin stopped putting on his gear and turned around.

"Who told you about that?"

Chase moved his hand to his right cargo pocket and began to tug. Alex squinted but he didn't have to, he could hear the index card grinding against the fabric of Chase's pants. He could see those eyes in the dark too, Chase's big blue eyes that were sick of reading rag mags and letters from his dad.

The eyes glowed and Alex felt the tin of violation in his gut.

As he had slept, Chase had gone to the guy on radio watch and the four posts that covered the cardinal directions with crew-served weapons and Marines who had nothing better to do than read four lines on an index card.

"The whole platoon knows?" Franklin coughed.

"The whole platoon knows," Chase said.

After he was done with the Marines doing their jobs, Chase had found the ones who weren't. He woke up the majority of second squad and had them huddle around him as he held the index card up like the Gettysburg address or Luther's 95 theses.

"And the guys asleep?"

"Woke them up."

Franklin stared at Chase, whose teeth, even in the darkness, showed a triumphant grin.

He stared at big Paciello who had rolled onto his side, silently awake and grinning a knowing grin.

He stared at the moon that was up and the rifle that was down in his hands and the dirt in his fingernails and then he remembered the last of the index card's four lines.

I'm sure you don't get it, Alex, but maybe someone else will.

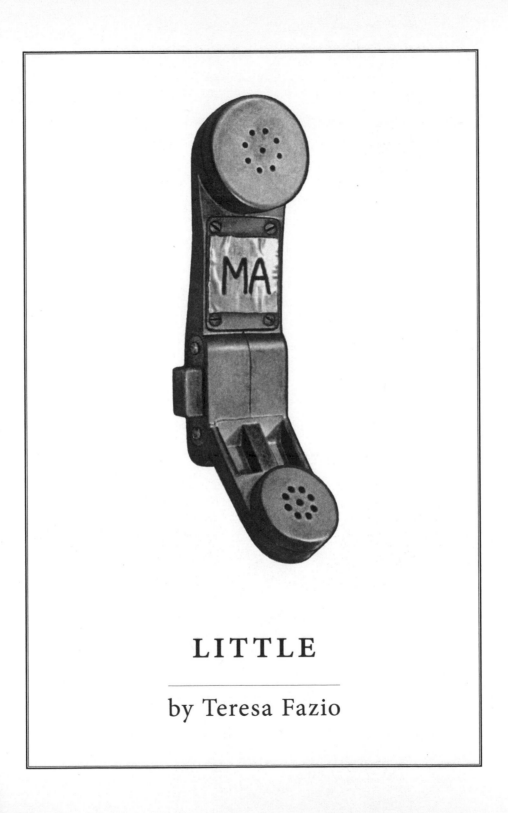

LITTLE

by Teresa Fazio

I wormed it out of Al when he joined me for cribbage, a habit since log school. I'd hung a bug zapper in my plywood-walled room, and he dealt hands punctuated by the electrocution of flies. He said the battalion XO—the Major—had put them all up to it, ordered everyone to rotate visits to my bunker to give me some human contact, some friendship or something. To cheer me up. *You have the hardest job in the battalion,* he said. I probably do. I'm the mortuary affairs officer, and not ten miles away, grunts are dying.

"What is this, some sort of check-on-the-little-lady, make sure the job isn't breaking her?" I asked, sipping my third Coke Light of the evening.

"C'mon, you know he'd say that for the rest of us too. It's a shit detail."

"Just because I have a pussy—"

"I know, I know," Al broke in. "Doesn't mean you are one." He moved his peg on the cribbage board.

—⚎—

There are perks to my billet. Two plasma-screen TVs, for instance, wangled by the major so my Marines can decompress. But I'm tired of field grades parading in for the dog-and-pony show, of stretchers, nitrile gloves, face masks that don't hide the stench. Tired of putting up a front that I'm fine while bloody scrubs swish in the washer. Once in a while I feign a deluge of paperwork and lock myself behind this plywood door, just to get an afternoon's break. I can't be friends with everyone.

But Supply's skinny second lieutenant is different from the gawkers. The day he takes his turn in the funerary rotation, he walks in all round glasses and serious eyebrows. One of those straightedge types. Instead of marveling at my platoon's MTV hookup, he looks at me, at the creased cover of *The Things They Carried*. Asks how I like it, drinks the Coke Light I offer. Looks at me again. I see the green flecks in his light-brown eyes. I rub the back of my neck, swat a stray hair from my collar, return his stare. I'm not used to second glances. But I notice the kid's corner dimple when he lets himself smile. I talk to him twice as long as any other visitor.

—m—

I call him "Little"; the other officers have christened him Chicken Little for his scrawny legs, though he's not small, a foot taller than my five-two. Afternoons, I start to look for him in the chow hall, nodding when I see him with his gunny or one of the other boot lieutenants. I know this crush is stupid, a middle-school thing, that I'm a senior captain and he's a second lieutenant and while the higher-ups are vigilant hawks against predatory male officers, no one would believe either of us if it came out that we'd hooked up. They figure him for a virgin and me for hopelessly butch. They've probably called me worse, since I went through the Corps' martial arts hazing, study Brazilian Jiu-Jitsu on the side, and now run a couple of entry-level classes for the devil dogs. During the bouts in which I cannot roll well, I roll dirty. I will let no one accuse me of being weak.

One afternoon I sidle up to the chow line behind him, sliding my tray in trace along the aluminum counter. I order red meat and white rice. He eyeballs the fish patties.

"Don't do it," I warn. "You're in a landlocked country."

"My stomach's an MRAP," he says. "Besides, I like fish."

I shrug and shake my head. Secretly adore his bravado.

That evening, my watch chief hears him heaving in a Porta John. I pour boiling water into a thermos of powdered soup, and have the sergeant bring it to Little's hooch. Little returns it the next day, clean, with a thank-you note on green waterproof paper. I tell him to come back anytime. Watch a movie, maybe. I figure—well, shit, I don't know what I figure, but I know I want to keep talking to him.

A week later, I'm teaching a nighttime martial arts course in the sand pit outside my bunker. Little stops by on his way from evening chow and asks to help, lifting his blouse to expose a green belt with white tab. Turns out he's an instructor too. I say sure. This is rare for me. I never let anyone interfere with my sense of control.

He holds a Thai pad for me to elbow and strike. I straddle him to demonstrate a mount, a kick of joy in my stomach at the contact, however public, however purportedly chaste. With a jerk of his hips he bucks me, thuds a palm to my ribs, flips me beneath him. Trying to gain some leverage, I graze his crotch with my heel, making him yelp. Next thing I know, he's got me in an arm-bar, about to dislocate my elbow. My heart beats fast as I tap his leg. He tightens his grip for a second, smirks a devilish eye-flash. "Oh, does this hurt? Ma'am?" I laugh and he lets go.

Next comes the hip toss. The Marines form a semicircle and Little looms over me, bashful as if at a fraternity formal. His eyes dart to a sharp chunk of gravel in the sand a few feet away. "Trust me," I say, nudging it aside with the toe of my boot.

Facing him, I step in, grab his right wrist with my left hand, and step back with my left foot, tracing a tiny letter C in the sand. I dig my right hip into his and hear him exhale. His body floats for a moment, hip to hip, then arcs a capital C through the air. He lands on his back, fists up and ready.

"Good break-fall," I say.

Little C, big C. Small choices snowball and slam you down on your back, blinking.

After class, I glow as he carries training pads back to my bunker. I recall one of my sergeant instructors from Officer Candidates School: a petite, muscular black woman in starched camouflage, hair slicked in an immaculate bun. She'd stood only slightly taller than the women in Munchkin Squad. She was our hard hat, the one who would run us all into the ground without chipping a manicured nail. One night we'd all stood at attention, sweat pooling even after an evening shower, and she'd savaged our platoon in a disturbingly honeyed Carolina accent.

"Lemme tell y'all something. If you a woman in the Marine Corps, you either a bitch, a dyke, or a 'ho.'" My ears had pricked. It was the most interesting ass-chewing since the other sergeant instructor had called our platoon a "friggin' abortion."

"If you always gotta be with the males," she'd continued, "and you *smiling* at them, and every time you talk to 'em you gotta touch they *arm*—" She'd whipped around. "*Then* you a 'ho.

"But if you do yo' *job*, and you treat them like they yo' *brother*, and you don't pay no attention to them 'cause *you* got a man somewhere *else* . . ."

She'd cocked an eyebrow and pointed with an index finger.

"*Then* you a bitch."

"That *last* one," she'd said, sashaying out of the squad bay and shaking her head, "I don't think I need to explain."

Walking down that concrete path with Little, carrying fighting equipment, I've staked my reputation on being a martial arts instructor, a short-haired hard-ass. I don't know what I can give him but trouble.

But after the pads are stacked in a corner of my room, he sits in a white plastic chair and fiddles with the magnetic chess set on my plywood bookshelf. My smile stretches wider and my nerves kick into high gear.

I pull two near-beers from my mini-fridge. They taste like beer, but don't feel like beer. You'd have to drink a case to imagine a buzz. But as Little gulps his, he becomes loquacious. He's spent weeks wandering warrens of twenty-foot containers, tracking contractors who go back to their air-conditioned cans at 1700. Rageful field grades yell at him nightly, claiming vehicle parts, ammo, and armor don't get downrange fast enough. He needs conversation. He makes eye contact. He relishes my attention more than he lets on in public. I only want to know more about him.

"Yeah, I'm a ham," he laughs. "Auditioned for theater in high school. *The Music Man*. Makeup, straw boater, everything. Girls all over me, saying what a perfect tenor I had. Anyway, that shit was done soon as my stepdad pulled up. Asshole." His expression darkens. It's the first real emotion I've seen in him. I incline my head his way, trying to catch his eye.

He snaps his chin up.

"Anyway," he says.

"Asshole, huh? Sounds like the audience lines to *Rocky Horror*," I say, and instantly regret it.

He lifts his can of O'Doul's to his sweating neck. "Yeah, except no 'Time Warp.'" I'm surprised he knows *Rocky Horror*, but then again—theater. I wish I could time warp so he was fewer than ten years younger than me.

When Little lowers the can, I notice the half-inch scar just under his right ear. "That fucker do that to you?" I ask.

"Nah. Cyst when I was eight," he mumbles. "Benign. And never me. Just my sister."

"Oh."

"I didn't know til later," he says, eyes pinned to the floor. "I swear, I didn't find out til later."

I can't fault him. I know this brand of powerlessness. I'm not a bad person, though my old man spent the first decade of my bird-chested life pounding into me that I was.

—⁊⁊—

So now Little comes over after martial arts class every night I'm not processing bodies. One night we pretend to watch *CSI*. Its theme song bleats, "Whooooo are you?" while a woman in a white lab coat mixes test tubes onscreen. And slowly I titrate my stories, testing his reaction. I tell him about cottage cheese and spongy white bread in an empty kitchen back home. Flung ashtrays that narrowly missed me, skittering across grimy linoleum. Mention that guy freshman year, so he knows I'm straight. And, as no doubt would delight the major, talk of my struggles with the dead. About the ultrasound of a sergeant's unborn child. The suicide note from the PFC who killed himself on Mother's Day. My buddy who I didn't know was dead until I pulled him out of a body bag. The reservist platoon bullshitting at the motor pool when they were mortared. They'd been together so long they all had the same tattoo. When my Marines marked up the outlines on their clipboards, the tattoos were all in different locations, some chests, some ankles, lotta biceps, one wise-ass on his left butt cheek. But the same tattoo.

Throughout my exorcism, Little's eyes remain steady on mine, and not with pity. I've had men look at me like that before, all little-lost-puppy-come-to-daddy-I-can-fix-you. Not this one. The set of his jaw says *no one can get in*. But I meet his hazel gaze and revise that to *please don't let anyone get in*.

During one night's martial arts training, Lance Corporal Mott, the one with zero filter between his brain and his mouth, says, "I like practicing ground-fighting with females because I feel their chests on mine."

Little points to Mott's man-boobs and says the Corps should install a red button on numbnuts like him to cut off that brain-mouth connection. But goddamned if hard biceps and solid pecs aren't just what I'm craving. After class, I ask Little if he wants to practice ground fighting in my room, where there's air-conditioning. He smiles a little wider than he needs to, says, "Sure." Adrenaline streaks through me as I slide the shard of two-by-four that locks my room door. For once, my size comes in handy; we both fit in the small open space on the fake-linoleum floor. If he comes over to watch movies, and now will do this, I know his mind orbits me too.

I sit on the floor and lean back. Damn my tight lumbar; thirty-three is no joke and I've crouched for tense eons on convoys. He mounts me, his knees astride my waist. I'm wearing PT shorts and cammie pants, and he wears his baggy-trousers-over-shorts ensemble that makes the major call him "LT HammerTime." Four folds of crumpled fabric mask his hard-on, but not well enough. I grab his lapels, break his posture, pull him down. I feel the heat from his cheeks reddening an inch from mine.

I teach him a different version of the usual front choke; the soft crook of my elbow brushes his ear as I wind my arm round his neck. Might look like a hug, were it not for his sharp exhale. Mimicking, he wraps his right bicep beside my carotid artery, compressing the other side with his forearm, driving me to the verge of unconsciousness. It becomes his go-to move in the minutes that follow, and he tries it over and over again in stiff jerks. He has not yet learned to use an opponent's energy to his advantage. I spot the choke every time, swim up out of his hold. I am never nearly as gentle with the other Marines. His body freezes when he feels me winning. He still can't relax, won't take off his glasses. "I won't hurt you," I tease. I can smell his deodorant mingled with the apricot soap I dug out of my seabag after I met him.

He grips my thighs with his own, his breath in my ear. I slide my hands slowly down his ribs and he stifles a moan. On this floor, Iraq disappears. It's only us breathing into each other.

"I want you to hold me," I whisper. Not even that I want to fuck him—though I do—but I want to wrap myself in him, like a hunter hides in a bearskin, willing the night cold to cease.

Little breathes out. He sits up and raises his wrist, snapping me from my reverie. I think he's getting ready to practice the choke again, but he looks at his watch and says, "Shit. I gotta go," and clambers to his feet. He shoulders his Camelbak; the hose slithers from the floor. He flicks the mouthpiece's lock up and down so it won't drip. His eyebrows knit, like he's gauging something. I get up from the floor more awkwardly than usual.

He reaches a trembling, browned hand and fluffs sand from my hair. I touch the side of his neck with my fingertips. He turns away when they rub his scar.

"Just trust me," I say.

He mumbles again, "I gotta go," and moves the pine lock from its place. On his way out, he looks at me over his shoulder, his eyes like a tied-up dog's. The door bangs behind him.

I worry briefly he might tell someone, but first, no one would believe him, and second, it would mean trouble for him too. Exhaustion overtakes my anxiety. I shuck my wet undershorts, slip on a clean pair, and climb onto my thin mattress. I know I'm flirting with reprimands, and worse, rumors about my reputation. But I sincerely wonder what it would take to make Little give in. How can I earn his trust?

—◊—

Gary and I had trusted each other. We'd turned fourteen the same spring, and I'd walk to his clapboard house before school, after his mom left for work. Gary was shy, and attended only shop class. He had skilled hands. The two of us fooled around in his sunny bedroom just off the kitchen, its French door latched tight. After a few weeks, he said *today's the day* and I said *okay, but don't tell anyone* as he fished a condom from under his mattress. It hurt at first, but then numbed, sort of. Romance movies had made me think it'd feel good, but it wasn't much fun. Gary grimaced for the ten seconds he took to finish.

He didn't know it was my first time too.

When I saw the blood on the sheet, I kept calm. I knew girls sometimes bled the first time.

But he thought he broke me.

He didn't believe my halting explanation, that this was normal, that it meant I'd been a virgin. Instead he rattled the French door's latch free and darted to the kitchen phone. In his panic, he called his mother. The rotary dial cranked an excruciating churn. He gripped the receiver, naked and breathless.

"Mom, you gotta come quick. We did this thing. She's bleeding. I broke her!" he yelled.

It took his mother a full two minutes to figure out what he meant. Finally, she barked a hoarse laugh. I pictured her drag on a Virginia Slim behind the DMV counter.

"Christ," she said. "She'll be fine. Go to school. Jesus."

I never went back to Gary's house. Instead, I became the shy one. But I haven't forgotten him. His face melds into a horror show of bodies as I float toward fitful sleep.

—ɯ—

Overnight, a vehicle-borne IED strikes a truck twenty miles away. My platoon and I convoy out in the early morning, trailing the Jaws of Life. When we arrive, my staff sergeant—a reservist who's an ambulance driver back home—slices open what's left of the truck like a cheap can of beans. I snap on blue nitrile gloves and do the same job I've done for months. We recover seven body bags of gristle, slop, some recognizable human parts. Might be a bad sign that I rarely gag anymore. Our convoy returns after nightfall, trailing dust clouds that leave orange puffs in a purpling sky. As I radio in to tell them we're close, my driver chews his Camelbak tip. I think of Little. Soon we're back at the gate. My Marines line up at the clearing barrel. Adrenaline leaches from my nerves, replaced by exhaustion. My lower back tightens. The heat's cooled to ninety, but I've sweated so hard I smell ammonia, and I'm thankful for that slight whiff over the coppery odor of blood.

Throughout the gut-soaked endeavor of cataloguing possessions and scissoring clothes, I hover over my buzzing Marines. I can never just turn myself off; I need to be present. My NCOs have a well-practiced routine to load the stretchers lining the bay in which we all work. I try to pitch in.

"Ma'am, let me get that," says Callas, my thin female lance corporal, motioning for an end of a body bag. Her collarbone juts from the neck of her t-shirt. No one's been hungry for a long time. They've all lost weight. People send care packages of PowerBars and whey protein powder. I have to put some meat on my Marines. They're barely older than the kid I could've had with Gary, were we less careful.

I duck into my room to collect paperwork and glimpse my rack with exhaustion and bitterness. It's been two years since I shared a rack with anyone. I hesitate to email Little; last night feels ages away. And no one from the outside can enter while my platoon processes bodies.

But as I unhook dog tags and a crucifix from what's left of a neck, my mind's eye holds an image of him standing outside our compound's barriers, watching me. I imagine him shifting from foot to foot. I want to be his heroine.

Hours later, when we've finished clumping bloodied sawdust into biohazard bags, when the stretchers lie rinsed and the bodies are boxed safely in the refrigerated shipping container, I sink into my fake-leather office chair. I reach way down under my desk, beneath a balled-up poncho liner, and pull out a plastic water bottle. Its contents look like dark piss. Its peeling label's torn to ribbons, one fringe for each night I need it. I rip another few millimeters, unscrew the top, and pour a capful. I tilt my head back a few seconds, feel the bourbon burn down my esophagus. Illegal, but it takes the edge off. I just need to close my eyes. I dig in a drawer for a nub of mint gum. Can't get caught. I rest my elbows on the steel desk and rub my temples.

The phone rings and I mutter, "Goddammit." Five fucking minutes is all I want. The tinny trill sounds again, the triple-ring that means it comes from off base, likely a combat surgical hospital. I bring the receiver to my ear and think of the tender skin on the side of Little's neck. I hope I don't break him. I don't know what I would do or whom I would call if I broke him.

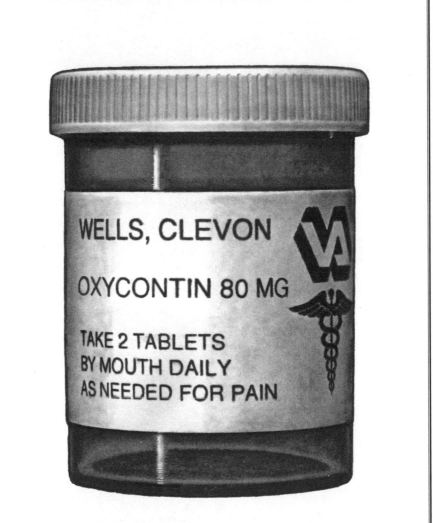

THE MORGAN HOUSE

---

by Brandon Caro

What had prompted Captain Swallow to insist that we serve dinner to the Wounded Warriors and their families at the Morgan House remains a mystery. It was perhaps spurred on by a sense of obligation to the injured soldiers, or out of spite against the command, or most likely, she thought it might be a suitable achievement to list on an eval. It was, after all, only a few weeks before the promotions board.

I had only transferred to the Defense Medical Readiness and Training institute—a non-deployable stateside command—a month or so prior and had, with the exception of Captain Swallow, not bothered to learn anyone's name. This was my last stop before being discharged; a weigh station for me to grind out the remaining months left on my contract. Though in my senses, I was still on Afghan time.

Captain Swallow had explained during a brief earlier that morning that the Morgan House was a charity service which provided housing, during their long periods of recovery and rehabilitation, to soldiers who'd been injured in combat. It was for this reason that the houses were located on the Brooke Army Medical Center Campus, a stone's throw from the Center for the Intrepid—the gargantuan physical rehabilitation facility complete with wave pool and other state-of-the-art equipment designed to help get the amputees back on their feet, so to speak.

Our cadre of roughly fourteen Army and Air Force medics and Navy corpsmen arrived around six P.M. and filed into the large house. Since there weren't enough housing units to assign one to each veteran, the families of three or four Wounded Warriors would all be quartered in one large house. The houses were spacious and brand-new, with top-of-the-line appliances and IKEA-looking furniture. All came with several flat-screen TVs in the living and family rooms, and in the bedrooms as well.

From what I could tell, there were three families staying at the house to which we were assigned, but one of the three would not be there for the dinner. Perhaps they'd been tipped off to the intrusion and opted for a night out instead.

Of the two remaining families, the matriarchs took care not to bump into one another in the common areas like the kitchen or the laundry room, which created difficulties, as these both were centrally located in the home. Watching the two of them buzz around the place, each one conspicuously avoiding eye contact with the other, I got the sense there had previously been some dispute over the occupation and use of shared resources.

Wounded Warrior Number One was a good ole boy. He and his family hailed from Appalachia or the Ozarks or the Delta or some other swath of land that had been desecrated by the Union during the war. He might have even had kinfolk in the fight; I know a lot of the Southerners did. His lover (I'm not certain the two were officially married) was an obese, homely woman with stringy orange hair that frayed out of a ponytail and stood upright in the front as though she'd been electrocuted. From what I gathered, she was called Eloise, and she ran a tight ship. But she was exhausted, that much was obvious. Between managing the two small children who tore about the house like wild boars, seeing her husband through the difficult transition of relearning to walk, of relearning everything, and maintaining acceptable boundaries with the other families at the Morgan House, she was all but run-down, and it showed on her greasy, shiny, pale-white face.

Wounded Warrior Number Two and his family were Mexican. I'm not sure if the wife could speak English or not, but she and the two small children—a boy and a girl—did their best not to make a fuss, though it was clear they felt displaced by the large presence of the first family.

I caught a glimpse of the Mexican gentleman out of my periphery as he and his clan were washing up in preparation for the dinner. As injuries go, I'd seen worse, but not much worse. This fellow, with two lower extremity amputations—one above the knee, one below, and third-degree burns down the left side of his face that caused it to droop like a smeared oil painting—had undoubtedly earned his seat at the table.

We fourteen or so medics and corpsman from DMRTI, under the direction of Captain Swallow, were divided into two groups, one for each family. The captain thought it best we bring pizza rather than prepare the meal ourselves, and for this we were grateful.

I was assigned to Wounded Warrior Number One and company, and hence began clearing the table of the clutter in order to make room for the pizza party.

"Don't touch that!" Eloise shouted.

"I'm sorry, ma'am. I was just trying to make room for . . ."

"It's fine." She corrected herself and appeared apologetic in her body language. "Just let me take care of this stuff."

She grabbed the stack of paper forms out of my hands and stowed them away in a drawer near the kitchen.

"We have plates," she said, pointing to the dishwasher. "Can you help me set the table . . ."

Just as the words were leaving her lips, one of her litter, the elder, came careening into the drop door of the dishwasher.

"No, Mommy! No!" He pleaded with her not to open the door.

I gathered that he had some fixation with the appliance that was integral to the game he'd been playing with his younger brother, because, out of nowhere, came the smaller one, screaming and kicking and begging her to keep the dishwasher door shut.

"Andrew! Jeremy! Quit it!"

She had the younger pinned down with her foot and the elder restrained in her arms.

"Ma'am, I can help with the dishes . . ."

"Yes!" she cried out, exasperated, and in her eyes I saw the full weight of her shame; her frustration and her exhaustion.

And I knew in that moment that what she truly wanted, what she needed, was precisely what we also *needed*; what we had been denied on account of this absurd exhibition inspired and brought to fruition by our great leader, Captain Swallow.

"Let's just get this over with!" she shouted.

"Right away, ma'am."

I began to retrieve the dishes from the dishwasher, aided in the effort by my coworkers. We carried out this labor of love in silence.

"No, wait!" Eloise shouted again, still not quite in control of her offspring. "You have to put down the place mats first! They're in that drawer there!"

"Yes, ma'am. We'll take care of it."

I observed the other half of the "volunteers" also disrupting the normal flow of household routine on the opposite side of the kitchen, where the dining table of Wounded Warrior Number Two was likewise being set.

The guidance of those responsible for the house's layout was logical enough to provide each family with its own dining room table, if not its own dining room. The kitchen was an open plan design with a large island in the middle. The respective dining areas radiated outward, forming a semicircle, with the kitchen as their nucleus. The separation allowed for what might have passed for normalcy amongst the families, and I surmised that they very much valued the privacy it afforded them.

"I have an idea," erupted Captain Swallow. She seemed to have materialized in the space between the two dining tables, facing the kitchen.

"Let's bring these tables together so your families can eat side-by-side! It's a celebration!"

Eloise had finally managed to subdue the two boys when she raised her head in disbelief and remarked, "Do whatever you want, this is *y'all's* idea!"

Fed up, she threw her hands into the air in defeat and disappeared into the bedroom, presumably to roust Wounded Warrior Number One.

Captain Swallow's bright, oblivious smile did not fade. Moreover, she appeared pleased with herself for uniting the estranged housemates. The family of Wounded Warrior Number Two did not put up a fight.

We corpsmen and medics, proud veterans of the wars in Iraq and Afghanistan turned wet nurses, fanned out across the large open area, grabbed hold of the two tables, and conjoined them into one long, unified Warrior Dinner Table.

The family of Wounded Warrior Number Two, having nearly finished setting their own table, scrambled out of the way, their faces bewildered. I'm not sure if they'd understood the captain's directive.

The sons of Wounded Warrior Number One resumed their rowdiness as Eloise came wheeling out of the bedroom, baby-daddy in tow, toward the table.

"Andrew and Jeremy, I ain't gonna tell you again! Quit it!"

The two boys relaxed their play, but did not halt altogether. I observed the light of the room reflected in the glossy eyes of Wounded Warrior Number One as he was rolled out to the table, a pleasant, timeless smile stretched across his face.

He was lucky in that, above the neck, he'd been spared any cosmetic damage. But he was a triple amputee, both legs above the knee, left arm above the elbow. I was puzzled somewhat, that he should have all three prosthetics—marvelous gleaming metallic appendages, the best money could buy—locked in as he was in the wheelchair and had no real need of them presently, and I could not help but allow my eyes to drift downward and really take it all in.

The legs protruded out from a pair of black Army PT shorts, and the arm from a grey Army t-shirt. He was half man, half Terminator. I figured he was just returned from some advanced physical therapy session at the CFI, and had not had time to break down his parts.

"Hey Doc, how's it goin'? You doin' all right?" The man asked.

I was not in uniform, as these were not scheduled working hours, but the large caduceus—the pair of serpents entangled on a pole, facing each other with wings jutting out from either side—emblazoned onto my left arm in dark blue ink betrayed my occupation as a technician of the military's medical community.

"Fine, sir. Thank you. How are you feeling today?"

"I ain't never been a sir, Doc. The name's Clevon and I'm doin' all right, you know what I'm sayin'?" He pulled a red prescription bottle from a pouch on the side of the chair and rattled it around in his hand.

"You're gonna ruin your appetite with those," I joked.

"Oh don't worry about that. Eloise here, she can eat enough for both of us, ain't that right honey?"

"Don't mind him." She rolled her eyes, as though she'd heard the rib a million times already. "He gets this way when he's whacked out on them pills." She paused for a moment and laughed forcibly before adding, "Which is pretty much all the goddamned time!"

She bookended the phrase with a subsequent burst of laughter. This second laugh was slightly more natural sounding than the first, though still quite contrived.

Soon the families of both Wounded Warriors were gathered round the great compound table, and Captain Swallow smiled, having achieved her goal. There was mild chatter amongst the families, though no real substantive communication between the two tribes.

It was of paramount importance that the charade *appear* successful—if for no one else than for the benefit of Captain Swallow—and for it to ride out peacefully as long as we were around to play babysitter. If they partitioned off the table and went about cutting each other's heads off the minute we departed, well that would be a matter entirely outside of our ability to control.

We got the pizza out of the duty vehicle, a tan rendered pickup, and doled it out evenly around the table. The Mexicans were bowing their heads in prayer, while the rednecks each lunged for a slice the moment one had dropped onto their plates.

"Wait a minute!" Captain Swallow hollered. "I want to make a speech! Wait!"

But there was no stopping them. The Mexicans had ended their prayers and begun their feast, and the rednecks were already clamoring for seconds, which we provided for them, then stood side-by-side at parade rest; a long row of roughs, fourteen abreast, that ran parallel to the length of the table.

Captain Swallow flitted about, nodding her head approvingly every so often or attempting small talk with the children.

The whole affair lasted a grand fifteen minutes, tops, then we were back to work, clearing the table, breaking it down into halves, and returning them to their original locations. I detected a glimmer of resignation in the captain's affect. It's possible she had believed the two families might have dined together henceforth. A failed experiment, perhaps.

"Doc, can you gimme a hand over here?" I heard Clevon grunt.

"What do you need, boss?"

"Up in that cabinet, there." He pointed to a small door above the sink. I opened it to reveal a bottle of Johnny Walker Blue Label.

"Where'd you get this?" I asked as I pulled it from the shelf and contemplated handing it off to him, before deciding ultimately against it; not on account of a sudden spell of social responsibility, but because I realized that he would not be able to unscrew the cap without assistance.

"Some fucking Soldiers' Angel, a pen pal, sent it to me." He sneered. "There's tons of crap lying around this fucking place! It's a goddamned gold mine!"

I unscrewed the cap and went milling through the other cabinets for a glass.

"Hope you don't expect me to drink alone?"

"I wouldn't dream of it."

I filled the two glasses halfway and very carefully placed one of them into Clevon's good hand, which trembled slightly after taking possession of the drink, creating small ripples on the golden brown surface of the scotch.

"To them that didn't make it back!" he yelled, and we touched glasses lightly and each threw back a glassful.

"Whoooooo!" he shouted. "That'll make you feel like a man, boy!"

I grinned, trying to suppress the acid reflux that had backed up into my esophagus.

"Say, Doc. You've been out, right?"

"Of course."

"Where at?"

"Laghman Province, Afghanistan."

"Oh yeah?" he barked, part condescending, part curious. "What was that like? Afghanistan?"

"It was hot," I answered, and he laughed and rolled his head back a moment.

Eloise breezed by us, casting a disapproving glance, rolling her eyes and rotating her head back and forth as she gathered up the children to make ready for bed.

When she'd wandered out of earshot, Clevon uttered softly, "Say, Doc. Ain't my wife a pig? I mean, look at the size of that woman, gosh!"

"I've had bigger," I replied.

"Bullshit, you have!" He burst out laughing wildly, nearly falling over in his chair. "I'll tell you what, Doc, you a funny motherfucker, you know that?"

"I've been called that before," I answered as I grabbed the glass out of his hand. "Time for round two."

As I was pouring the second drink, I noticed his good hand had found its way down to his groin, and he seemed to be groping at the area, at a shape he no longer recognized. I held the drink in front of his chest and waited as his good hand made its way back up to claim it.

"Them motherfuckin' hajis did a number on me, boy."

He allowed his head to roll forward a minute.

"You know, it's really not a good idea to mix those pills with the scotch."

"That a fact?"

"Yes, it's a fact."

He observed me quizzically a moment, then continued.

"You *really* feel that way, Doc?" He emptied the drink into his throat, slammed the glass on the table, and reached into the pocket on his chair, pulled the red prescription out and tossed it to me.

I swiveled my head side to side to get a read on the room. The last thing I needed was to go down for some amateur bullshit like this; popping pills that were not prescribed to me. I noticed most of the DMRTI folks either playing tag or hide-and-seek with the children of Wounded Warrior Number Two, or helping Eloise return things to homeostasis. There was no sign of Captain Swallow.

I peered at the literature on the bottle without opening my hands up to expose the prize.

Wells, Clevon
Oxycontin 80MG
Take Two Pills Daily As Needed for Pain

"Holy shit! They've got you on 80s? Jesus Christ!" I glanced back at him in disbelief.

"Well it didn't start out like that, but the way it is with them Oxies, you gotta keep upping the dose."

I understood the dilemma, better than most, perhaps. When I was sure the coast was clear, I opened the bottle and tapped a few of the white, disc-shaped pills into my hand, pocketing the extras and throwing back the one. I washed it down with the scotch and pulled up a chair to sit next to Clevon.

"Hey Petrino," I heard the captain call my name from far away, it sounded. "What do you think this is? We're not here to socialize, let's go!"

I began to rise when I heard Clevon's voice, shaped by a hostile, defensive tone, address the captain directly.

"Now, wait a minute, ma'am. Y'all came into *my* house and interfered with *my* family's dinner, and all for what?" He threw up his good hand in defiance. "So you could put this little fiasco together and feel good about y'all's selves."

Eloise came back into the dining area and stood next to her partner, her arms folded.

"You think it matters, y'all being here? Doing this shit?" Clevon continued. "You think it's gonna change anything? Me and Doc are bullshittin' and I'd appreciate it if you'd back off so we can bullshit some more."

Captain Swallow smarted from the lashing, but did not respond to Clevon. Instead, she redirected her resentment onto me.

"I'll see you in the morning, Petrino." And with that, she stepped off and exited the Morgan House.

"Now where were we?" Clevon said to me.

For the next several hours we told stories and laughed and drank whiskey and took more pills. It occurred to me that if I could trade places with Clevon, I would not. And as angry as I was at Captain Swallow, at DMRTI, at the military, at the hajis, at the war, at myself, in the end, I could get up and walk away. I was lucky.

After a while I sat back down in the chair and began to float up into that dreamy space, where all that mattered, all that had come and gone could be relegated to a temporary holding place, locked up and forgotten for a while.

—⁂—

When I came to, I found myself laid out on the couch with my shoes off and a blanket around me. The sky through the windows was colored an indistinguishable dark grey that did not indicate whether it was still nighttime or now early morning.

I shook instinctively from the nausea and confusion and began the extraction process. While I was tying my shoelaces, Eloise appeared before me, smiling for the first time since I'd met her.

"Thank you." She teared up mildly as she spoke. "Thank you so much, Petrino."

It was apparent that she felt silly calling me by my last name, but she did not know what else to call, and she wouldn't dare refer to me as "Doc."

"It's no bother, ma'am. I had a lovely time at your home, but I really must be getting off now. Could you tell me what time it is, please?"

"It's been so long," she continued, ignoring my request, "since someone has just actually listened to him. Someone besides me or the doctors." She smiled very genuinely at me, and I realized that if I did not leave soon, I too would be moved to tears, so I finished with my shoes and rose to my feet and embraced the woman and told her that I'd be round to say hello, and walked out into the driveway, got in my car, and drove home.

DIFFERENT KINDS
OF INFINITY

by David F. Eisler

The front door of my house leads to a grey concrete sidewalk, which leads to a small driveway split into a half circle by a large tree, then an asphalt road and the infinite possibilities of the rest of the world. I don't leave it very often anymore.

My cat, a European shorthair whose name is Ivan, often sits inside by the door, wanting to go outside. He has never been outside.

Sometimes he will scratch at the door. Sometimes he will meow, forlorn, as if he is aware of all he is missing on the other side. But I don't think he really knows that much. He's a cat. I like to tell him that, in contrast to his namesake in Tolstoy's famous story, his life has been most simple and most ordinary and therefore most pleasant. I don't think he gets the joke.

—⟐—

I don't go outside much. The farthest I normally venture is the mailbox at the end of the driveway to check the mail for new books and the occasional letter. Sometimes a letter has my name on it, and I know it's for me. Most of the mail is addressed to "Current Resident." I suppose that would be me as well.

The few minutes it takes for me to hobble to the mailbox with my cane are the worst of the day for the cat. He always thinks I'm leaving him forever, even though I always come back. The moment he catches me stepping into my sandals he comes running over, weaving in and out of my legs to deter me from going outside. I've tried to talk to him about this.

Me: I'm just going outside to check the mail.

Cat: ?

Me: I do this every day. You know I do. I always come back.

Cat: ?

Me: No, you can't come with me. You're a cat.

Cat: . . .

When I do come back, he meows and looks happy.

—∿—

I spend most of my time at home in my study looking at my books. I have many books. For every book on my shelf that I've read, there are at least three that I haven't. For years there was no reason or logic to how I'd arranged them, with some in multiple rows stacked several deep, the most recent purchases lying horizontally in piles obscuring the rows behind them, making their titles easier to identify quickly without needing to tilt my head, which hurts.

Sometimes while I'm reading one book I will scan the shelves for the next one. Sometimes the cat scans with me, though I only recently started letting him into the office. Before, he would sit at the edge of the doorway and look at me with his sad cat eyes. He likes to be around me, so I finally decided to let him in. Mostly he rests on the windowsill and looks harmlessly into the yard. His book suggestions are rarely useful.

When he was still forbidden from entering the study, he would test my resolve by slowly creeping across the line dividing the living room's wooden floor from the soft carpet of the study. He would place a single paw over the line and look up at me to see if I noticed, just like a small child forbidden by his parents to cross the shoreline on a beach. The parents tell the child not to go in the ocean because it is dangerous and the child could get hurt, a single step often the difference between safety and losing control to the ocean's unpredictable waves. But the child slowly tiptoes through the wet sand at the edge of the tide—is the tide even part of the ocean?—and waits to see if his parents will react. If my parents are silent, the child thinks, then it must be all right to put my toes in the water. And before the parents know it the child's feet are submerged. Then his legs and his arms and his whole body are splashing around while the parents wonder how their strict rules have become so easily violated. Salami tactics, it's called. I read that in one of my books.

—⁓—

I don't have as many nightmares now as I did before I got the cat. They used to be frequent. Now they are occasional. It's always the same one. I'm back over there, walking around outside on patrol before it happens, staring at a small patch of grass in the dirt the same way I did the first time. In the dream my legs are gone. When I wake up, I check to make sure they are still there. The cat always seems to know when I'm having a nightmare. He jumps on the bed and nestles next to my legs. Maybe he's protecting them.

—⁓—

Recently I decided that the amount of disorder on the shelves was no longer acceptable. The cat agreed. I cleared a large space in the center of the office, pushing the desk against the opposite wall. The cat watched, trying to figure out what I was doing. He doesn't understand the concept of reorganizing. He's a cat.

I began by moving stack after stack of books from their previous locations and placing them on the floor, forming several leaning towers. A few fell over in spectacular fashion—causing the cat to scurry away—before I discovered the inverse relationship between height and stability. I wiped each book clean of dust with a damp washcloth before placing it onto one of the many temporary piles, ensuring that the covers were no longer sticking together.

Hardcovers and old textbooks, regardless of subject, served as the foundation of each new stack, then paperback novels formed the thick spires. When the shelves were empty, I found myself standing near the center of Book City, a metropolis of knowledge, culture, and history. For a moment I imagined myself as a giant, stampeding through the leather-bound urban sprawl and knocking down skyscrapers built by the heroes of classic literature. I was in control of its destiny, the power to give and the power to destroy. I felt a guilty pleasure at the thought. But the image passed, and it was time to get back to work. The cat just stared at me.

Literary fiction would occupy the upper shelves. Beneath them philosophy mixed with the natural sciences, a vestige of my former studies in math and physics.

I looked over at the cat. He wouldn't understand any of these books. I found one about Erwin Schrödinger, who was clearly not a fan of cats. The cat hissed, perhaps sensing the subject of my thoughts. He's tough, that cat. No putting him in a box.

The first bookshelf was finished. I turned back to the city, which by now had fallen on harder times. Gone were the skyscrapers, the city center, and much of the residential areas. This is looking good, I thought. Finally, some order to the chaos.

I was just about to start stacking the second bookshelf when I heard the cat crying and scratching at the front door.

When the house is quiet and calm and the cat knows where I am, he likes to explore. He finds hiding places with good overwatch, like cardboard boxes or large paper bags that I leave around for him after the delivery guy drops off the groceries for the week. He can also spend hours on the enclosed back patio stalking squirrels and birds through the screen or chasing other imaginary creatures that he sees outside but can't reach. When he is finished he carefully crawls through the cat door and announces himself in a high-pitched meow so that I know he is back inside. I answer with my own sounds to let him know I heard him. This makes him happy, and he usually bounces around for a few minutes afterward, attacking various objects around the house and picking fights with furniture.

But lately, for some puzzling reason that I couldn't figure out, the patio didn't seem to be enough. He was spending more time near the front door, even when I wasn't about to go outside. I couldn't understand what he wanted out there. Inside he has everything he could need. Food. Shelter. Amusement. Safety. He doesn't have to worry about the horrible things on the other side of the door.

If the door were a mirror instead of a door the cat could sit and stare at his own reflection and see the world around him. Then I could place another mirror behind him and he could stare into infinity as the light waves bounce back and forth in endless reflection. He would see the other versions of himself in every mirror and wonder if they were looking back at him, from some other time or some other place. He might even wonder if any of them have ever been outside. I would tell him that an infinite number of them have, just as an equally infinite number of them have not. I like this kind of infinity, the safe kind where the only danger is getting lost in thought within the mirrors. It's the same kind of infinity as in my books. It's much better than the other kind of infinity, the one with too much uncertainty, where a single step can change everything.

The cat continued to prowl in front of the door, pausing intermittently to stare at me. For a moment I was taken back to my recurring dream, except this time he was with me as we walked. The sun was hot and the air was full of dust, but he didn't care. I looked down at him to make sure he was okay, but he just meowed and kept moving forward. We reached the patch of grass I had looked at a hundred times before that day—and countless more in my dreams since—and my hands started shaking from the tension. I braced and closed my eyes, feeling my muscles contract, waiting. But nothing happened. A voice said we should keep going, and the cat meowed at me again and nuzzled against my leg.

He was still brushing against me when I realized I was back inside the house, unsure of how much time had passed. Maybe it was the innocence in his eyes, but I began to consider letting him go outside. Just the thought of opening the door nearly brought me to my already weak knees, the fear that he might run away and leave me forever. What if something happens to him? How can I protect him?

He meowed at me again.

Maybe he was right. It's not fair to lock him in here with me, to keep him from discovering all that can happen when the door is open, the good and the bad. I took my chance, but that doesn't mean it will be the same for him. With so much uncertainty, who can predict where the waves collapse?

I walked up to the door and looked at him.

Me: Are you sure you want to do this?

Cat: ?

Me: You don't have to go out there if you don't want to.

Cat: ?

Me: Okay.

I reached for the handle. A beam of light bounced off the wall and reflected onto the floor, making a pattern I had never seen before.

The cat was skeptical. He didn't move, but stared at the empty space where the door had been. He looked up at me. Maybe he thought this was just a cruel joke.

Me: Go outside. It's okay. The world is yours to discover and explore!

Cat: !

He inched forward slowly until he was perched at the edge where the boundaries of his previous world had ended. His tail curved upward and swayed slightly from left to right. His ears pointed upright and slightly forward.

Without warning he darted out onto the sidewalk. For a moment I thought he was running away, but he stopped and turned around to look back at me with his still curious eyes. Then he lay down on the cool concrete of the walkway to the door, yawned, closed his eyes, and began to sleep.

SALT

by Colin D. Halloran

I want to go back. Need to. Back to the flames, the twisted metal and smell of blood. The sand. The constant hint of burning rubber from the burn pits. A smell distinct, but not even noticed by passersby here in the States. As they walk around me on city sidewalks, they have no idea where I am, back in the desert, back with the concertina wire, the hug of my vest, the comforting weight of an M-4 in my hands. Until one bumps into me and I'm brought home, empty-handed, into this world where chaos goes unacknowledged, where so few of us can see it. I can't stay.

So I watch the needle creep.

I push until the rising red pin is all I can see—guardrails, white lines, streetlights all blurring together on the edges of my vision. Or maybe they're tears. No, that's wishful thinking—I never cry. I want to. I just can't seem to make it happen.

I am here. Alone. Almost flying, pushing the transmission to its peak before each gear change. I like driving standard; it reinforces the illusion that I'm in control, the illusion that must have kept me alive back in the desert. But it was only ever that. No matter how much preparation, how many routes and reroutes and backup routes I knew, I wasn't controlling shit. It was out of my hands as soon as we left the wire. That's when Allah took over.

The thin red line of the needle crosses 100. I close my eyes. Cut the wheel. Relinquish all semblance of control.

—m—

One day, it was maybe May or April—early in the spring offensive—we knew we were likely to get hit. Not because of intel, really, just because we could feel it, the way you can feel when someone's watching you no matter how hard you try to sink into the shadows of a dive bar's corners. Maybe it was God's eyes watching us. But the desert lent no shadows. And we had a fucking job to do.

The thing about being a mission leader, about being the guy who drives the very first Humvee, leading all your guys like ants into hell-fire, is that you need to pretend, need to convince yourself that you have control, that the amount of preparation you put in is going to keep those guys alive. That if anyone's going to die, it's you. Because it's your tires that are going to hit the pressure plates first, your hood that will be the first to enter the kill zone. And that's okay. You didn't come all the way over here expecting to make it back.

But that day we did. I did. In spite of the intel, in spite of that feeling of eyes making the hair on the backs of our necks stand up in the desert heat that should have disallowed goose bumps, we made it back to the wire that day. It wasn't until later that I learned I shouldn't have.

The next morning's intel brief took place before the sun came up, red lens flashlights darting back and forth against the rocky ground between our tents and the TOC. My after action report had been dull the night before, nothing of real note had taken place. Some shady characters lingering roadside, but this was Afghanistan. Everyone was a little shady. If they weren't actively trying to kill you, you just kept on your way. But this time, I was wrong.

The S2 filled us in. They had intercepted some communications. There was a device. The enemy tried to blow it, stop the convoy, disable the first truck—my truck—and trap us in a crossfire. But the detonation failed. It may have been the wiring, a bad signal, or they'd buried the device too deep and the signal couldn't reach it. Either way, I was supposed to die.

They weren't targeting me, not really. The Taliban, or whoever they worked for, didn't give two shits about some kid from Upstate. Hell, they probably didn't even know what "Upstate" is. They were targeting the idea of me, or what they thought was the idea of me, of the uniform. In war you can't take death threats personally.

So I took the news I should have died and started planning the next mission. There was no time to think about it. No reason. They would get another shot at me, and that's what I needed to focus on. I planned, I executed, I repeated. Even in a place where roads were few and far between, I knew every way to get from A to B. Up hills, across deserts, along the dried-up riverbeds, through villages that couldn't possibly exist on maps. But I saw them. Navigated them. Knew them and all possible ingress and egress routes.

There was the cave I cleared along what we called "Death Valley." The smoke-stained ceiling and embers told us it had only just been vacated. The 7.62mm shells strewn around the entrance told us who we'd missed.

The next week brought a high stakes mission. So high stakes they needed me to stay behind to run QRF. Nobody knew that part of the province better, and if shit hit the fan, we had to get there fast. I was anxious, pacing the tower when the first explosion sounded. I scanned east and could see the black smoke rising. The exchange of fire rattled through the radio as I mounted up, ready to tear off base and toward the ambush. But it was over almost as suddenly as it began. My QRF stayed put, the mission went forward.

There was the MRAP I watched roll down a hill in my side mirror. Camped on the hilltop, watching headlights stream into a compound owned by a known hostile, we waited for the attack to come with sunrise. I don't know how some guys slept. We got permission to blow the downed vehicle before the attack could come. The surveillance drone footage showed men with AKs streaming out of the hill like pissed off hornets from a broken nest less than a minute after the demo team blew it and we left.

A helicopter I was on for a night insertion dodged an RPG, skipped off a mountainside, and somehow stayed airborne. I thought about middle school math class, where I'd first learned about probability and odds. When guessing on a coin flip, the impulse is to bet against what's already come up in highest frequency, but it's still fifty-fifty.

In the end, I made it out. Took that return trip I hadn't banked on. They took their shots, they tried to bring me down, and I was willing, but something got in the way.

Was it just dumb luck? Poor aim? Laziness on the part of the enemy? Or was someone watching out for me. Some higher entity, imperceptible, like the pitches only dogs can hear. Either way, it doesn't matter. I made it home. I didn't expect to, I maybe didn't even want to, but here I am. The worst place yet—I'd do anything to get back.

—⁂—

I always heard that blood tasted metallic—something about the iron. I'd seen plenty back there, smelled it, and the burned flesh that so often accompanied it. But all I can taste is salt.

There are voices, shadows, lights flashing blue and red and white. Patriotism? No, it's the middle of winter, not the Fourth of July.

Suddenly I'm five. It makes sense. The lights, bouncing off the angles of my bedroom, the salt of my tears, the figures lifting me from bed, placing me in a car, taking me away from the place my father drew his final breath.

I'm twelve. The glaring white of the sun, the blue of the sky around it, the hint of salt that hangs in the air, clinging desperately to existence after the crashing of a wave. Yes, this is the taste I know, the salt I remember so well.

I'm seventeen. The red of my cheek, the deep blue instant bruising, the taste . . . yes! The taste of my blood, trickling from my nose, from my eye where it split on impact.

I will give all of myself to this taste, here and now, this moment. The burning rubber, twisted metal, licks of flame. The salt.

BLAKE'S GIRL

by Eric Nelson

T he wood shelf jutted out of the living room wall right where Dave wanted to hang the flat-screen TV. It looked sturdy enough to hold some serious weight, but not quite secure enough for a $2,000 HD plasma television. He glanced over at his new housemate and former battle buddy from Iraq, Skeet.

"We're getting rid of this thing, man," Dave said. "I'm ripping it out." Skeet had just dumped a beat-up green duffel bag on the floor and was surveying its contents: camouflage uniforms, body armor, combat helmet. Hands on his hips, forehead creased in confused contemplation, Skeet reminded Dave of their old lieutenant in Iraq, poring over his map at a dusty intersection.

"Bro, wait," Skeet said. He took the helmet, brushed off a thin film of dust, then brought it to the shelf and set it carefully in the middle. "There. Where else are we going to stash our old gear?"

Sewn into the side of the helmet's cloth covering was a black heart-shaped patch, which had been the insignia of their regiment. To Dave, it represented a powerful contradiction. The shape signified love, but the color was dark, nihilistic, evil. Dave had always thought the symbol was badass but college was supposed to be a fresh start, the next chapter of his life. Decorating their house with all the crap they'd had to hump around the desert felt like the wrong message. Why not stick to putting up band posters and whatever else normal college students did?

"Let's just throw all this stuff away, man. Get rid of it," Dave said.

Skeet's clear blue eyes widened. Dave knew that look well: disappointment.

"Fine," Dave said. He pulled his body armor out of a plastic crate, and lifted it up onto the shelf next to Skeet's helmet. "Guess this goes here?"

"There you go, buddy!" Skeet said. Dave would have been jealous of Skeet's Chicago accent if there hadn't been so many reasons to be jealous of Skeet that there was no point to zeroing in on any particular one. The accent made him seem tough and uncomplicated, more authentic, less vulnerable. And then, the blue eyes. Guys with big muscles and deep blue eyes got blow jobs. Dave had brown eyes, and acne. All the punishing physical training he'd endured had put mass on his shoulders, but Dave didn't feel comfortable with his new army-issued body.

By midnight, trinkets bought in countryside bazaars and snapshots taken during their year in the desert lay interspersed with the military gear on the shelf. To Dave, the photographs were like fragments of a master image that had once captured the whole experience but had since been lost, leaving only these clues behind. One picture in particular made him pause, an image of Skeet, Dave, and Blake—their squad mate who was killed about two months after the photo was taken—next to a camel they'd run across while out patrolling. Dave had been thinking that Blake was more Skeet's friend than his, but there was the picture, with Blake proudly wrapping his arm around Dave and smiling for the camera, a clear sign of brotherhood and approval. Skeet and Blake had been more "squared away" (meaning confident, one to whom things came easily, in military parlance) than he was, but here was proof that he had stood with them, had been in their league.

As Dave returned the photograph to the shelf, Skeet tapped him on the back.

"Time to check out the town before the bars close," Skeet said, and adjusted his baseball cap.

Dave smashed two Vicodins with the bottom of a glass and separated the powder into lines. After a roadside bomb had gone off under Skeet's truck, and he'd limped away with a concussion and a banged-up leg, an army doc had written him a prescription for these little pills. Later, as Skeet and Dave were waiting on their flight home, they'd pop pills in a container yard filled with giant metal boxes stuffed with equipment worth tens of millions of dollars and zone out, listen to music. Following a year of excitement and danger, the opiates transformed the bleak stasis of the dust-filled container yard into something tolerable.

"I'm on point for the recon," Skeet said, crossing the street as Dave double-locked the door behind them, then rattled it to make sure it was secure. "It's in transition, a pre-gentrification phase," the rental guy had said of the neighborhood. They walked along a cracked sidewalk as the Vicodin kicked in with a rush of confidence and detachment, the same feeling of invincibility Dave had sometimes felt while out patrolling with his weapon locked and loaded. A haggard woman yelled at a drunk man leaning against a boarded-up corner store, and further on, a group of young thugs were closing some kind of deal underneath a sodium-vapor streetlamp.

"Shit man, this place reminds me of Iraq," Skeet muttered.

They found a bar around the block. Green light from a neon sign reading "Jon's Tavern" reflected off of freshly painted white concrete walls. Two men smoking near the entrance respectfully flicked their butts into a sand-filled bucket before heading back in.

Jon himself was behind the bar. He was wearing a piece of clothing that identified him as a Vietnam veteran, a well-worn denim motorcycle vest festooned with patches. His clean-shaven face harbored a gaunt, intense energy—not the bearded and overweight stereotype Dave had come to expect from biker vets.

"What can I get you kids?" Jon was asking them when Skeet noticed a black heart patch on the vest.

"No shit, buddy? You were in the Black Hearts?" Skeet asked.

"Yeah. After I was drafted I figured, what the hell, and I went airborne. What does it matter to you?" Jon said. Skeet put his arm around Dave.

"Dave here and I just got out. We were with them in Iraq," Skeet said.

"You're shitting me," Jon said.

"No, sir."

"Hey, Carl," Jon said, turning toward a beefy guy at the end of the bar, one of the smokers from outside. "These kids were in my unit. In Iraq." A wallet-chain attached to Jon's trousers knocked against the bar. "Here's one on the house, soldiers." Jon poured bourbon into three shot glasses. "Wait a minute, are you guys twenty-one?"

"Just barely," Skeet said, without hesitation. Dave kept silent—his driver's license had a big red warning on it saying he was under twenty-one until a date that was still a few months away. Jon narrowed his eyes, but then nodded and raised his glass.

"All right. Welcome home," he said, making a point of looking at them directly in the eyes before drinking. Dave managed to suppress his gag reflex as it went down his throat.

"Whoa, Jon, when did you start drinking again?" Carl said.

"Special occasion," Jon said, and turned back to the two young men. "I know a guy who's hiring. Construction. You boys looking for work?"

"Thank you, sir," Skeet replied, his Chicago accent more pronounced after the whiskey. "We're starting up at the college next week. I'm gonna do economics."

"Good for you. What about you, Dave?"

Dave started sweating as the booze hit his system. Skeet seemed to have it all planned out, as usual, but while Dave knew this was supposed to be a good time at college with Uncle Sam footing the bill, a dark cloud hovered over him, a sense of impending doom he couldn't shake.

—ɷ—

A year later, Dave and Skeet were back at Jon's. Skeet had surprised everyone by getting better grades than Dave. After all, Skeet was the one who had been busted for drunk and disorderly conduct within a week of returning from Iraq.

"Now you're the guy who was great in Iraq but can't handle life back in the rear," their lieutenant had said while lecturing Skeet in front of the platoon.

"I know I fucked up, sir," Skeet had said, but nobody'd thought he really did.

Now Skeet had cleaned up his act, and had even been elected vice president of the college's Business Club after arranging internships for several of his classmates through Jon and Carl's friends in the community. Meanwhile, after Skeet's prescription ran out, Dave had been buying pills from a retiree named Elaine who was hooked up to an oxygen tank. She counted out her extra meds slowly, one by one, with her shaky, mottled hands. Dave had been the one with the book smarts in his platoon, and he'd been able to coast through his first year of college in a haze. Lately, though, Skeet had begun worrying about him, and Skeet wasn't a worrier. He'd almost called Dave's parents after finding him passed out on the lawn one morning, and Dave wouldn't tell him where he'd been or what he was doing.

"Use your smarts for something better than being a wise-ass," had been their first sergeant's parting advice to Dave. *Good thing he can't see me now*, Dave thought.

"Hey Jon, can I get a single?" Dave asked, ordering a whiskey the way he'd heard regulars do it.

"No way. You look terrible, kid," Jon said to him, noticing the red circles around Dave's eyes. "Go home and get some sleep." Dave looked at Jon's vest and saw the black heart in the collection of patches.

"You know, I used to think that black heart was hardcore. Now it only reminds me of the bad shit."

"Lighten up. And show some discipline," Jon said as he walked to the other side of the bar and started wiping it down.

"You've got to let it go," Skeet said, also fed up with Dave's dark moods. "Whatever it is. Move on already. And you've gotta stop taking those pills."

Dave's phone buzzed in his pocket. He pulled it out and read a text message. *We're on for Friday!*

"Amy's definitely coming this weekend," Dave announced, cheered by the news. Skeet raised his eyebrows.

"Hey, Jon, her husband Blake was the guy I told you about, the one that didn't make it home," Skeet said. Jon nodded in acknowledgement while painting wet circles of cleanliness on the bar.

Dave had first seen Amy in a photograph at Blake's memorial service, a small gathering of soldiers held at a chapel built of plywood that stood in a corner of their base. Dave headed out on a patrol after and couldn't stop thinking about her as he walked through the sour-smelling streets of Iskandariyah, eyeing piles of garbage for bombs. Blake came from one of those parts of the country where people still get married before they're twenty, and it had seemed very adult and impressive that Blake had a wife. She looked great in the picture, tossing her blonde hair around, playing it up for the camera. Obviously, it had been taken before she got the bad news. Exhausted after the long patrol, everyone else feel asleep while Dave stayed up and wrote her a letter by the light of his headlamp. *Blake was a great soldier,* he wrote. *We all loved him like a brother.*

Amy wrote him back right away, saying how much it helped, reading a letter from someone who was actually there. She sent him a poem she'd written, and it made Dave's eyes water when he read it in his bunk. A tear slipped out, and he wiped it away before anyone in the busy squad tent noticed.

Two weeks after the platoon got back from Iraq, Amy came down with Blake's parents to visit the base in Kentucky. It was a sunny day.

Most of the platoon was still in a rowdy mood—this was one week after Skeet had gotten arrested for trying to steal a cop car—but Amy made the soldiers feel comfortable by patiently listening to their stories and in-jokes as she circulated around the picnic tables that had been covered with plastic tablecloths for the event. Todd, their medic, told her about a decapitated Iraqi policeman they'd found with a dog's head sewn onto his shoulders, apparently a sign of disrespect in Iskandariyah. Todd then cracked up laughing as if it were funny. Dave yanked him away before he could do any more damage, but Amy was unperturbed, taking it in like another piece of some puzzle she was putting together, her own master image of the strange place where her husband had died. Blake's mom kept crying, which made Dave extremely uncomfortable, but with Amy, it seemed like she was able to maintain a peaceful state of tranquility after all the shock, agony, and despair. Dave was humbled when Amy corrected his claim that Kentucky had been part of the Confederacy during the Civil War. It made Dave feel guilty to think it, but Blake hadn't been the deepest guy in the world, and, after getting to know her, Dave couldn't help but wonder what Amy had seen in him.

His phone buzzed again. *Can I bring Tabby?* Dave sighed, and unconsciously clenched a fist.

"She's bringing a friend," Dave said.

"Ugh, that Tabby girl?" Skeet said. Dave had forgotten about her, Amy's ostentatiously supportive friend who showed up right after Blake died and then never left. Dave and Skeet suspected that Tabby was mooching off of Blake's life insurance payout, although they couldn't be sure. *Sounds great. Can't wait to see you*, Dave responded.

"Can I ask you guys for some advice?" Dave asked.

"Are you going to listen?" Jon asked, putting down his rag and walking back over to Dave. Jon had fired Dave just ten days after hiring him earlier in the summer, but he had been fair. Dave hadn't been showing up, and Jon still paid him through the end of the week.

"Amy and I really get each other. Do you think it would be weird? I know it's probably too soon."

"Aren't you playing with fire, buddy?" Skeet said, giving Dave a knowing glance. Dave looked away while Jon folded his arms.

"You're thinking about dating your dead buddy's wife? Have some fucking respect and clean up your act," Jon said. "You're a shit show." Dave sat up straight and backed away.

"I'm fine," Dave said. "Come on, Jon. I'm depressed."

Jon shook his head. "That doesn't give you the right to be an asshole," he said. Dave thought about his planned pickup at Elaine's the next day, the dismal small talk they'd share as he stared at the floral pattern on her carpet, tapping his foot.

"All right," Dave said, and he stood up. He slammed his fist on the bar with determination and purpose. "You guys are right. I'm gonna do it!" Skeet clapped his hands.

"Thank you!" Skeet yelled as Jon walked to the other end of the bar. "He won't listen to me."

When they got back to the house, Dave dumped his baggie of pills into the toilet and hesitated before flushing it. Skeet stood in the doorway, nodding approvingly as the little white circles swirled in the bowl. Dave fought an urge to scoop them out as they slipped down the drain, one right after the other. Based on what he'd heard from other junkies hanging around Elaine's, going cold turkey was going to suck.

"You're not gonna tell her, right?" Skeet said.

"I don't know. No."

"Blake's gone. It's not going to help anyone, dragging them through it again."

"I said I wasn't going to tell her," Dave said. He tried to push his way past Skeet, but Skeet grabbed his arm.

"Do I need to be worried about you? You got rid of all that shit, right? We had our chance to blow the whistle. Now we gotta play the game." Dave wanted to hit Skeet, hating him for being so sure about everything as the comfortable, opioid dullness started slipping away. He wrenched his arm out of Skeet's grasp, went into his bedroom, and slammed the door.

—⁂—

The next day, Dave pulled his covers over his head to block out the afternoon sunshine. He waited until he heard Skeet leave the house before rising from bed and walking carefully downstairs, grabbing the banister to steady himself. Across the living room hung the shelf laden with all of the mementos from Iraq, and Dave approached it at an oblique angle, the way one approaches a pile of junk that might have a bomb in it. In a stack of mostly routine paperwork—citations, turn-in receipts he was told to keep, his jump log—Dave found what he was looking for. It was the report, not the bullshit official one telling a Hollywood tale about Blake's clean, heroic death that saved his fellow soldiers, but the original statements from Dave, Skeet, and others from the platoon who had been there. Reading through the narratives again, Dave recalled details even worse than he'd remembered: the hours of searching before they'd realized what had happened, the fucked-up Easter egg hunt for whatever pieces of Blake they could find.

He wiped his face and clutched his head; all he wanted was a few pills to stop the shakes and sweating. He lifted the heavy plates of his body armor and they clanked together with a familiar, resonant sound as he hid the report underneath them. He decided to go for a run—that had always cleared his head in the past.

Dave jogged past the seedy street gatherings, feeling good as he stretched out his legs and ran to a wooded trail around a nearby reservoir. Each footfall on the pine needles seemed to bring him one step closer to Amy. It was dark when he got back, but he couldn't fall asleep after showering and forcing down a sandwich. He imagined Amy's firm, athletic body underneath the jeans and t-shirt she'd been wearing in Kentucky. There was maybe a birthmark somewhere, and a tan line on her thigh. A serene tuft of blonde hair between her legs.

—◊—

By Friday, Dave's sweats and shakes finally began to subside. He knew that Amy had to be weary of being treated like a victim of tragedy. Dave planned a fishing trip for Saturday, hoping to do something new, something free from the pain and misery of Blake's death. Blake's death—Dave wasn't going to confront Amy with the pointless facts. Everyone in the platoon knew that Blake would have taken a bullet for him, and it had been the right thing to do, letting the hero-story stick so as not to taint others' memory of him with a conspiracy. Now, they all had to stay the course, especially Dave.

Dave was sitting on the couch when the doorbell rang. He jumped up, unconsciously fixing his hair before opening the door. When Dave saw Amy, his heart started beating faster. With the door light shining on her corn silk hair, she was even prettier than he remembered. Dave stood back and let Skeet greet her first so as not to seem too eager.

Tabby entered behind Amy. After a cautious greeting, Tabby took a seat in the corner and watched the three of them as if she'd been sent to chaperone the visit. She wasn't a bad-looking girl, Dave thought, tall and skinny, with dark hair and thick-rimmed glasses that worked with her face. Looking closer, he noticed that the glasses magnified her eyes unnaturally, and he turned away from her unblinking gaze. Amy saw the shelf.

"What is this stuff? Can I look at it?" she asked. The shelf, she was going right for it. Dave felt a flash of anxiety, but it passed when he saw that the statements were well-hidden under the plates, invisible.

"Just military gear and paperwork. Knock yourself out," Dave said, and he felt a bead of sweat forming on his forehead. Just to be safe, he covered the plates with a set of folded fatigues, pretending that his purpose was to uncover a few small chunks of cuneiform for Amy.

"These are from the ruins of Babylon," Dave said, picking one up. "Or, at least, that's what the guy told me." Dave laughed in a forced, nervous way, and out of the corner of his eye, he saw Tabby watching him. His hand started shaking, and he put the piece of clay down before anyone noticed.

"I'll get us some champagne," Skeet said, rolling his eyes at Dave's joke. "You girls drink champagne, right?" Skeet asked, trying to be charming.

"Yes, please," Tabby said. "Should I call you Skeet?" she asked.

"Yeah, that's what my army buddies call me," Skeet said as he walked into the kitchen. "Aaron, Skeet, whatever."

Amy picked up one of the photographs from the shelf. It was the one showing the three of them, Dave, Skeet, and Blake, standing next to the camel and smiling.

"I have a print of this same picture on my own little shrine at home," she said. "It makes it look like you guys were on a safari."

"Yeah, this is kind of a shrine," Dave said. He checked to see that Skeet was out of earshot and pointed at the black heart patch. "I really like this. It stands for the good stuff and the bad stuff at the same time. The love and the pain."

"It does," Amy said, into the idea. Their easy way of understanding each other relieved Dave's tremors and sweating. She picked up a rusty knife, another trinket from the bazaars, and she turned it around in her hands, looking at its pitted surface as if it held some kind of answer or revelation. Dave knew how it was. Trying to remember Iraq was like trying to remember a vivid dream that fades away before you get a chance to jot down the details. It was as if Blake died in the dream, but when they woke up he was really dead. These objects came from the dream world, the place where they left him.

—⁓—

On the way to the bar, Tabby's eyes darted around nervously. "Is this neighborhood safe?" she asked.

"Hell of a lot safer than Iraq," Dave said. Now he was being the angry vet who couldn't let go, and he wished he hadn't said it.

"We're safe with these guys," Amy said. As they walked into Jon's Tavern, Dave saw that Carl was there as usual.

"At last, some pretty girls," Carl said.

"Shut up, you," Jon said, then nodded at Amy and Tabby with deadpan seriousness. "You know what, he's right, ladies. At last. What can I get you?"

Dave heard Tabby laugh for the first time, and her posture, normally taught and attentive toward Amy, uncoiled. Skeet was being a good wingman by talking to Tabby and getting those giant eyes off of Amy.

"Are you seeing anyone?" Dave asked Amy.

"Please. I'm a mess." Music came on from the jukebox as Dave sipped his drink, feeling a gentle warmth radiating from Amy.

"You're not a mess," Dave said. Amy smiled and scooted her stool closer to his.

"Thanks for everything, this weekend, the fishing trip," she said. "I really needed to get away from home. It's almost as if . . ." she said and paused. Dave leaned closer, noticing the distance between their lips.

"Yeah?" he said, staring into her soft brown eyes. She pulled back and started crying quietly.

"As if Blake were still protecting me, being here with his two friends from Iraq," she said between sobs.

Dave looked away, embarrassed and disappointed. I'm a pale shadow, a substitute, he thought. A rivulet of sweat trickled down his back as he wondered whether Elaine was still up. Amy noticed his distracted thoughts and wiped her eyes.

"Are you okay?" Amy asked.

"Fine," Dave said curtly, and he took a sip of his drink. If he went to Elaine's, she'd probably ask him how college was going while he counted out his money, as if they had some kind of real, transgenerational friendship. Fuck Elaine, he thought as he put the glass down on the bar. He patted Amy on the shoulder in a way he thought was brotherly, supportive but not intimate.

On the TV behind the bar, a news channel showed an update from Iraq.

"Geez, you just can't get away from that place," Skeet said.

"You want me to turn it off?" Jon asked.

"Could you?" Tabby asked.

"No, leave it on, please. I like knowing what's going on over there," Amy said.

"I just don't know what to think of the war," Tabby said in a circumspect manner, cocking her head. Dave could tell that she was trying to be polite—Amy had probably asked her not to get into politics over the weekend. He remembered her saying in Kentucky how horrible it was that all of them, the poor soldiers, had to go fight over there as part of a longer anti-establishment lecture.

"If I had to go back and do it again, I would sign up, no question," Dave said, glaring at Tabby. "Whatever happens, I'm just proud I was there with the other guys."

As images of violence played out on the TV screen, Dave noticed Tabby's worried glance toward Amy, and he again wished that he had kept his mouth shut. She was just looking out for her friend. What would he do if he could go back? Maybe it would be him who died instead of Blake, and Amy could have her real husband beside her instead of his junkie friend who happened to survive. Or, maybe no one would get blown up or have his head replaced with a dog's. It could be just the pictures with camels this time around.

—⁓—

Back at the house, Amy sat down on the couch and leaned forward.

"Any champagne left?" she asked.

"I gotta turn in. See you girls in the morning. We'll leave at ten?" Dave said, heading up the stairs. Skeet noticed a tiny frown on Amy's face as she got up and walked into the kitchen. He followed Dave up the staircase and stopped him in the hallway.

"What are you doing, jackass?" Skeet whispered.

"Going to bed."

"No way, you're doing great, buddy," Skeet said. "Even you can't fuck this up."

"It's over," Dave said. "Besides, she's Blake's girl."

"He'd want her to be happy. And I've been talking to Tabby for hours. It's torture," Skeet said. Dave noticed that he wasn't sweating or shaking. It seemed like the worst of the withdrawal was over.

"I'm sorry I've been a drag," Dave said.

"You remember how fucked up I was when we got back. You were there for me."

"Alright," Dave said, smoothing out his shirt. "Here goes." He turned around and walked back down toward the living room.

At the bottom of the stairs, Dave froze. Tabby was standing by the shelf, and she had the original report on Blake's death in her hands. She flipped through a few pages, then adjusted her glasses and flipped back to the start.

Amy walked out of the kitchen holding a glass of champagne, and she smiled when she saw that Dave had come back downstairs. She looked like she did in the picture at Blake's memorial service, lighter than air. Oh boy, Dave thought, her night's about to get ruined. For him, it was like the moment of limbo after you stub your toe, when you know that you screwed up but the pain hasn't hit yet.

"What is this?" Tabby asked, waving the packet. "I think it's about Blake," she said, cocking her head and staring at Dave with her giant, questioning eyes. Then she went back to flipping through the statements as Amy peered over her shoulder.

Dave tried to stay calm as he assessed the situation. He was certain that Tabby would make a big stink about "the truth." Amy would be dragged through a new investigation into Blake's death, and it would be his fault for having kept the statements. There certainly wasn't going to be a fishing trip tomorrow. Amy might never speak to him again. Skeet was probably going to kick his ass. Dave clenched his fists and braced himself for the storm he was sure was coming.

Tabby tossed the packet aside with an air of frustration. "It's all acronyms and jargon. Tell me what it says," she said.

Dave unclenched his fists.

"Come on, Dave," Amy said, taking a sip from her glass of champagne. "It's like it's written in Babylonian. What does it say?"

PAWNS

by Kristen L. Rouse

Nasir turned up the radio. Somehow the rapid-fire Bollywood drumbeat made the dusty, jaw-rattling roads of eastern Afghanistan more tolerable. He bobbed his head in rhythm, glanced at his side mirrors to back his road-battered Hino flatbed straight against the base's wall, then reached his hand to the console, engaging the parking brake. His black turban was soaked with sweat, and he gently set it on the seat next to him, dusting away the layers of grey powder accumulated from his day of driving. He placed a clean, white skullcap, trimmed in blue and gold, atop his sweaty, bald crown. A man sang in high and nasal Urdu of sadness and despair. Nasir sat transfixed, gazing out at the familiar, rugged brown mountains until the song ended. His midday prayer was nearly two hours late, but God knew he'd been driving. God also knew that this truckload had brought Nasir to Gardez for the first time in what felt like a lifetime. Make haste, but—he thought with a wag of his head—let God make the timing right.

Nasir picked up a pitcher of water and rolled-up prayer rug from the front seat, then hopped out of his truck.

"Come to prayer," he sang to himself. "God is the most high. There is no god but God."

Nasir waved and smiled at an old man sitting cross-legged on a dust-caked Persian rug. The rug was spread beneath the shadow of the old man's ancient Bedford cargo truck, its rounded, rusty hood and grill reminding Nasir of the colorfully painted trucks that fascinated him as a boy. A rough-looking teenager sat near the old man at the edge of the rug, gazing listlessly. The boy was barely tall enough to reach his truck's pedals, Nasir thought.

The holding yard of the base at Gardez was surrounded by a wall of barriers, metal wire baskets filled with rocks and sand—an open buffer between the large base of American and Afghan soldiers and its outer wall. Trucks carrying full loads were parked in rows, waiting to be brought into the base to unload. The Americans contracted with Afghan truck companies to ship tons of cargo continuously between their bases, yet never seemed in a hurry to receive it. Nasir knew the old man from the many times they had waited together outside of bases, sometimes for hours, sometimes days. How quickly they got through the holding process seemed like a matter of luck and chance. He left this to God. When his wife Farzana would ask on the phone whether he'd be home soon, he would say simply: *"Insha'Allah."*

He walked to the back of his loaded truck. Two large, twenty-foot-long shipping containers were secured to his flatbed by chains, and he habitually tugged at the chains to check their tautness. He squatted beside the tail bumper of his truck, unrolled a green, patterned prayer rug, slipped off his worn leather sandals, then stepped onto the rug. He gently poured warm water from the plastic pitcher onto his hands and then washed it onto his face, his trimmed black-and-grey beard, his ears, his hands and arms down to the elbows, then his bare feet, rinsing away the dust of the day. He closed his eyes and exhaled, shutting out the six hours he'd spent on narrow, pitted roads since early morning. He placed his hands behind his ears and recited in a low voice, "God is the most high." He knelt and bowed, saying each prayer and verse in sequence, just as he had five times every day since he was a small boy.

He tightened the rope belt of his baggy white trousers and straightened the dark brown waistcoat he wore over his long collared shirt. His clothes were salty and wet with sweat from the glaring heat, and he felt his breath shortened by the high altitude. He stood for a moment, contemplating his prayers as he scanned the brown mountaintops in the distance. His eyes traced the familiar silhouette of ridges against the hazy blue sky and he allowed the old memories of Gardez to seep into his mind—that black-dark morning when he was last here, piled into the hulking Soviet helicopter with his platoon of young, Afghan soldiers, terrified and eager to attack the *mujahideen* base high in the mountains. He drew in his breath slowly and looked up at the cloudless blue sky, giving thanks to God that he could remember those days of death, yet still live. Nasir shook out the stiffness in his neck and shoulders, but his chest felt hard and tight. He took deep breaths as he made his way to the Persian rug.

"So good to see you *Akaa*," he said, taking the old man's frail hand in both of his. The old man beamed, broad and toothless beneath his thick white beard, holding his left hand to his chest. Nasir reached out to shake hands and greet the teenager seated next to him on the carpet, smiling and touching his hand to his heart as he wished him peace and hello. The boy offered a limp, lifeless hand. Nasir lowered himself down onto the carpet, legs crossed beneath him, next to the old man he called *akaa*, uncle.

Nasir smiled warmly and exchanged news with his friend—the old man's wives and grown sons were healthy, Nasir's two sons and two daughters were well, his wife was missing him, but happy. Nasir was pleased to see his old friend, impossible as their friendship would have been years ago. The old man was a Tajik from a village in the Panjshir valley and known as a fighter in the long-ago *mujahideen*; Nasir was Pashtun, and from a quiet, flat district of farms and orchards in Paktika. Nasir had enlisted as a young man to become an Afghan commando, trained and outfitted by the Russians to fight the American-backed *mujahideen*. Yet after these decades of turmoil among his countrymen and foreigners, and the long distances they now both traveled to make a living—they greeted each other in peace.

Nasir thought of the verse that had come to him again and again in recent years:

> *It may be that God will grant friendship between you and those who you now hold as enemies. For God has power over all things. God is forgiving, and most merciful.*

Nasir placed his hand warmly on the old man's shoulder. "How is the security line today, my friend?" Nasir asked.

"The Americans stopped the line going in. Many soldiers came out with their guns and long metal tools, searching under the trucks—more than usual," the old man explained. "Maybe there is a threat today, or maybe we will make our deliveries to the base this afternoon, *insha'Allah*," he said.

"*Insha'Allah*," Nasir repeated with a nod. He reached his fingers inside the pocket of his waistcoat, pulling out a chrome pocket watch. He folded back the worn, smooth cover to reveal a yellowing watch face with bold, scripted numbers. A tiny star and Cyrillic print arced across the bottom of the watch face: *CAENAHO B CCCP*. Made in the USSR. He'd carried it in his waistcoat pocket for decades, a touchstone of the history that shaped him, and that he'd managed to escape. He dutifully wound the watch every night after his evening prayers before he went to sleep. He rubbed his fingers slowly through his beard.

"It's two o'clock now. We may be spending the night outside, *Akaa*," Nasir said.

The old man smiled and gave a small wag of his head. "I will stay hopeful," he said, opening his mouth in a toothless grin.

Nasir smiled and took off his white skullcap for a moment to wipe the sweat from his forehead. He relaxed his shoulders and breathed deeply, reminding himself that this was in God's hands, that the timing of all things is decided by God, not men.

The old man's emerald-green eyes were watery with age, reminding Nasir of the shimmering water of the Panjshir river, a place he knew intimately in its astounding beauty—and a scene appearing in his many nightmares. Nasir's first campaign as a young soldier was in Panjshir, where hardened *mujahideen* lay in wait, dug into their mountain positions—then pounced like lions upon his division of newly trained commandos. Nasir's dreams dredged up the bodies of his comrades, thrashing them downriver, battering them onto rocks, dragging them under in the current. His sleep replayed these scenes through the darkness of night, but he wiped them away each morning before his first prayers.

Nasir remembered his first conversation with the old Tajik when they had waited at an American base in the north several years earlier. They'd exchanged memories of the green river and its valley, and the brutal battles that had turned grassland into barren waste. The old man's eyes brimmed with tears as he told Nasir that his family was thriving, and that peaceful farms had begun retaking the old battlefields. This was the first time Nasir had spoken with an old enemy as a friend. Nasir spent years feeding his rage, nursing it more than his own hungry children. Yet the word came from his mouth: *masha'Allah*. God has willed it. May all of our families stay safe and healthy for a lifetime, he found himself saying aloud, and he meant it. This was a new era, a time to dust off the soot and residues of long-ago battles. One day he had been a soldier fighting alongside the Russians, the next, one of millions of refugees piling their families onto flatbed trucks heading to Pakistan. No Afghan in those days had escaped suffering and hardship. They were pawns in a conflict that was never truly theirs.

The old man touched Nasir on the arm, stirring him from his ruminations. "Shall we have a game, my son?" the old man challenged with a grin. "The Americans are giving us time for play today," the old man said gently. Nasir was glad to retrieve the game board from his truck.

Nasir lifted himself into the passenger side of his truck to find the board, a view high enough to glimpse beyond the Hesco walls to see the top of the *qalat* that had been the Russian headquarters in the old days. He'd heard that the Americans came to Gardez early in their war, building walls and fortifications around the old base. He watched as a line of dark green Afghan army pickups and Humvees lumbered into the driveway between the base's outer gate and its inner gate, bobbling along the uneven gravel driveway, past the entry of the holding yard. He wondered whether the new Afghan soldiers held their mission in their heart like he had as a young man. He scanned the faces of this new generation of Afghan troops: they were young, but looked exhausted as old men. Nasir took a deep breath, reaching into the pocket of his waistcoat to touch the chrome watch, turning it around inside his pocket.

God does not burden a soul beyond what it can bear, he recited to himself. But he remembered the dark days when he could barely bring himself to pray. He spoke prayers of peace to God, yet never spoke aloud his wish for retribution and revenge against the faceless men who had caused the wars and destruction. He watched so many drown as he and his family struggled for air in the stifling, overflowing refugee camps. Somehow they kept breathing. Farzana had stood by him during his years lost in a heavy black cloud of anger, despair, and hashish—an old pocket watch and five prayers a day the only mark-ings of time he could account for. He couldn't lose time like that again.

Nasir returned to the carpet with a checkered wooden box in his hand. He sat down next to the teenager. The boy had dull eyes and breathed with his lips open, revealing a missing front tooth. He seemed to be one of the lost boys of these long years of war who have known no homes or parents or schools. They seemed empty, save for a bottomless capacity for mischief. The boy was about the age of Nasir's youngest son, who, *masha'Allah,* was at home with his mother and studying for school. A world away from this lost boy, thin and dirty, his face scruffy with fuzz, not yet a man's beard. Nasir thought of how Farzana would take pity. He smiled at the boy, thinking of her words. "All these lost children are our children," she would say. Nasir felt a surge of energy. He would try to draw the boy out with the game.

"Do you play *shatranj*, son?" Nasir asked the boy.

The teenager shook his head and stared down at the dusty carpet.

The old man waved his hand to dismiss the boy. "Let's have a game," he said, patting the carpet in front of him in a small cloud of dust.

Nasir opened the wooden box and dumped the thirty-two minia-ture quartz pieces onto the carpet, folding it out into a flat, checkered chessboard. He gently placed each piece onto their squares, one side an army of tan, the other dark brown. The boy looked on with what looked like a glimmer of interest.

"Watch how we move the pieces, and learn," Nasir said to the boy. "When I was your age, I was a soldier and fought against this man," Nasir explained, touching the old man on his shoulder. "Now that we're old, this is the only fight between us."

The boy's dull eyes met Nasir's for a moment, then he looked down again, saying nothing. Nasir shrugged, and the old man gave a short laugh.

"Light or dark?" Nasir asked the old man as he placed each piece on the squares.

"You seem dark today, my friend. You take light, to be less dark," the old man answered.

Nasir turned the small chessboard around on the carpet, studying it. He reached into his waistcoat and pulled out the chrome watch. He opened the cover to reveal the face. "Two minutes per move, *Akaa*. You must be quick with your cunning, my friend."

Nasir turned to the boy. "Son, pay close attention. This is where we match our skill and wit. Sixteen pieces to move, sixteen pieces to take. No chance or luck—unlike each day when we put our life's uncertainty into God's hands," Nasir said, pushing forward his first *sarbaz*, a foot soldier. "Here on the board there are only moves and consequences," he said.

The boy gazed lazily at the board and shifted his legs as he sat on the carpet. He picked at his dirty toes.

"There are rules for each piece, and there are rules in life for each one of us. As truck drivers, we are like these small pieces."

The boy rubbed the fuzz on his chin and gave a slight nod. The old man reached into the pocket of his baggy trousers and pulled out a small, rectangular tin. The old man held it out to Nasir, who politely shook his head to decline. The old man shrugged his shoulders, opened the lid, and took up a thick pinch of green *naswar* powder, which he placed in the side of his lower lip. He laid down alongside the chessboard, settling in for the game. He advanced his first *sarbaz*, then looked up and asked, "Boy, how long have you been driving your truck?"

"This is my first delivery to the Americans," he said, eyeing the old man's tobacco tin as he placed it back in his pocket.

"You have much to learn," Nasir said without looking up, and moved another *sarbaz* toward the center of the board. He missed the relaxed light-headedness he used to feel from the strong green tobacco. When he brought his family back to Afghanistan from the refugee camp in Pakistan, he promised Farzana he'd never again touch the tobacco—or hashish. He wanted to leave behind the clouded memories and habits of those dark days. Nasir watched as the old man leaned back onto the carpet and squinted his eyes as the *naswar* set in.

"We drivers can only move when the company dispatches us," Nasir said to the boy, moving his pawn a single space. "We must have our correct papers and identification to be brought in by the Americans. We must have our papers signed, we must keep them with us. Then we must wait while they load our trucks," he said.

The old man smiled a broad, toothless grin. "We must also hope that a bad crane does not flip our truck," the old man added, spitting onto the dusty gravel. The old man moved his *wazir*, the king's minister, the most powerful piece on the chessboard. "Check," he said.

Nasir rubbed his fingers along the grey and white hairs of his beard. He glanced down at the second hand of his pocket watch as it lay on the carpet. He had to make a choice. He moved his *rukh* to block the advance of the old man's *wazir*. "Sometimes we are escorted by an American convoy, and they protect us," he said.

The old man quickly moved his horseman to take Nasir's *rukh*. Nasir shrugged and wagged his head. The boy watched, index finger in his mouth, feeling the hole of his missing tooth.

"Without the Americans and their guns, we aren't protected," Nasir said. "We must always keep close watch for those who would take us," he said, nodding at the old man. The boy looked on, and Nasir thought he might finally be paying attention. This hollow boy was the opposite of his curious sons. "There are men who would kidnap us and hold us for money. There are men who would capture and burn our trucks. There are men who would cut our heads off because we move cargo for the Americans," Nasir said, drawing his hand across his throat. The boy's eyes met his.

Nasir continued, "The Americans can be trouble too. One day they slap you on the back as a friend and say words in Dari, then the next they think you're Taliban and point a rifle at you," he said.

The old man took another one of Nasir's pawns. The old man mused, "We small pieces have our value. *Insha'Allah*, we will each have our chance to make it to the other side."

The boy sat up, supporting himself with both of his hands on the carpet. He seemed stirred by a thought. He looked Nasir in the eye and said flatly, "I don't see why you try to get foot soldiers to the other side."

Nasir darkened with irritation, but breathed in and regained himself. "Foot soldiers are the key to winning, my son." Nasir explained, "We have no power as individuals, but together we are strong. We drive the trucks. We move the goods. We fire the guns. We climb the mountains. We win the objectives. When a foot soldier reaches the far side, he becomes the *wazir*. This changes everything."

As he spoke, Nasir felt a deep ache inside his chest.

The boy's eyes remained intent on Nasir. "Did your army win?" he asked.

Nasir felt a flash of anger and wanted to strike the boy. But he thought of his sons, and Farzana. Boys should be taught, not beaten, she would say. He breathed in another slow breath. "We had tanks, we had helicopter gunships and fighter jets—we had the heavy machines and artillery. We destroyed *mujahideen* bases. We killed many," he said, looking down at the board, thinking of the old man and being careful to show respect. "We won many battles, but the fighters were strong and kept coming. In the end, we did not win."

The boy said nothing, got up from the carpet, and dragged himself lazily back to his truck, his sandals scuffing up dust and gravel as he walked. Nasir caught the smell of greasy food, undoubtedly from the Americans preparing the evening meal on their base. He felt the emptiness in his own stomach. If he came home tonight, Farzana and his youngest daughter would have his favorite dinner prepared. A dish of hot stewed goat in rich, greasy spiced sauce, which he would happily sop up with freshly baked naan, along with handfuls of fresh rice pilau. He craved both his wife's cooking and her company. His favorite thing upon coming home would be to quietly eat his meal while Farzana would tell him all that has happened in his absence, all of her complaints, and all that she needed him to do now that he was home. This was his true value and worth, he thought. At home he became the *wazir*, and Farzana was like the *shah*.

The men heard the deep roar of the engines of an incoming convoy and looked up from the chess game to watch as a line of heavy armored trucks lumbered slowly along the driveway past the holding yard. Atop each truck was a heavy, shielded turret with a machine gun, and an American soldier inside, wearing helmet and goggles.

Nasir marveled that the American trucks seemed to grow larger and more sophisticated each year of the American presence. Thicker armor, bigger guns, more antennas and mysteriously shaped devices installed on the outside—to do what, he could only guess. A few of the trucks were outfitted with steel frames holding metal nets, like giant cages. These huge machines to lock inside what were surely fearful young men—women too, he'd learned. They won battles, yet they did not seem to defeat the fighters. The Americans were winning and losing at the same time, he thought.

Two Afghan flatbeds carrying armored trucks were lined up in the military convoy. Nasir recognized one of the trucks as another friend from the road. His painted cab had words in Pashto script across the front: "Road Poet." Short verses lined the wheel wells and running boards of the exquisitely painted, dust-covered truck and trailer. Nasir jogged out toward the entrance of the holding yard to exchange a wave with his friend, keeping his distance. One of the American machine gunners rotated his turret toward him. Nasir stood still in the dust just inside the holding yard, watching the convoy at a standstill.

A haze of dust blew across the convoy, clouding the mountains in the distance until they were no longer visible. He felt through the haze of his memory of Gardez those years ago, to the black morning on the helicopter pad when he and the other commandos embarked on that last mission. The smell of diesel fumes filled his nostrils and he felt the hard, tightened knot in his chest, the churning in his gut. The helicopter dropped his platoon of commandos on the wrong mountaintop, a ridge away from the *mujahideen* base called Zhawar. His was one of only eight helicopters—of the thirty-two launched that morning—not torn apart in their first minutes on the ground by *mujahideen* machine guns. Farzana would tell him to breathe when he remembered. She said to breathe, then to look at his watch and count down thirty seconds to take his breath back, to slow his racing heart. This had become his habit. He reached his fingers into the pocket of his waistcoat where he kept his pocket watch, then remembered it was still on the carpet next to the chessboard. He had exceeded the two minutes for his turn.

Nasir walked slowly back toward the carpet, breathing deeply, counting the seconds, and feeling his heart beat more slowly in rhythm. He glanced at his pocket watch beside the chessboard. The old man gummed his jaws and grinned at Nasir, easing his anxiousness. Nasir resumed his seat and saw he was in a bad position in the game. He had a choice: lose his *wazir* or allow the old man to take his remaining *rukh* and then control his side of the board. Nasir breathed and glanced at the watch, counting the seconds and weighing his options.

The boy stirred. "We have no power because of the Americans."

Nasir moved his *rukh* in a block. The old man took his *wazir,* spit onto the gravel, then looked up to answer the boy: "That may be true, son. Remember also that the Americans are only one part of our many problems."

Nasir grunted in agreement with the old man as he studied the board. He wanted to regain control of the center. The most options, the most control, came from the center. Atop the mountains over-looking Gardez, there was no center. The *mujahideen* had artillery and machine guns ready for them, hidden and set high to protect their base, with deep, elaborate tunnels packed with fighters. He and other stragglers and survivors scattered and fled the steady stream of fire like mice into the rocks. All but twenty-four of his comrades were killed. He and the other survivors holed up in the rocks, pinned down by *mujahideen* gunners for three days.

"I want to be a foot soldier," said the boy. Nasir looked up at the boy, who met his eyes. "I want to fight for Islam," the boy said.

"Son, when you are older you will see that Islam does not always take sides," Nasir said. The smell of death filled his nostrils. During those three days of hiding, he forced himself in the darkness of night to creep out, undetected, scavenging the uniforms and gear of his death-bloated comrades. The platoon's radio operator was lodged in a rocky crag, collapsed and swollen. Nasir struggled for what felt like an eternity, eyes watery with stench and grief, silently moving his comrade, reaching his hands like a thief through his clothing and pack to find a battery, then the radio and receiver. The men thought this was a miracle, giving them strength to spend silent nights stealing away like ghosts. When they reached a safe distance, Nasir pulled out the radio and, with what little was left in the battery, made contact with a nearby unit. It took them eight days to reach the unit—but the radio is what gave them hope. This is why the *Spetznaz* commander gave Nasir the watch. He had perfect timing, the Russian officer said in his accented Dari. Nasir held himself stoically until then. After the commander gave him the watch, he vomited. Before their return to their base at Gardez, he deserted.

The old man laid his hand softly on Nasir's shoulder. "It is your turn, my friend," he said gently. Nasir shook away his haze and smiled, embarrassed at his drift into dark memories. The boy turned to the old man and asked, "Where will we go if the Americans don't let us in today?"

"They will have us park outside," the old man explained. "This place," he said, sitting up and waving his arm at the holding yard's gravel lot surrounded by barriers and concertina wire, "is just where the Americans want us if one of us explodes," he explained, then spit onto the gravel.

Nasir picked up his pocket watch, holding it in his hand and counting the seconds before setting it back on the carpet. He remembered what Farzana would tell him about keeping his patience. Nasir gave the boy a fatherly smile. "I hope that doesn't happen. My wife expects me home soon."

The boy stared with cold eyes at Nasir. "Taliban would pay your family if you explode yourself," he said.

Nasir froze and felt a chill shoot through his body. Then his face flushed with anger. "Taliban would pay my family one time. I pay my family each truckload I deliver. I came back to my country ten years ago to make my family's life better, not worse. The Taliban have nothing for my family that I do not already give them," he said, growing angry.

"The Americans are infidels," the boy said.

"The Taliban are no better," Nasir said.

"God is the greatest," the boy said.

"God is the greatest," Nasir replied in a harsh tone.

"I will be a foot soldier for Islam," the boy said.

"Who has filled your head with foolishness?" Nasir asked.

"I will be a foot soldier in the jihad," the boy said.

Nasir's face flushed hot. "You don't understand what you're saying," Nasir shot back at the boy. He slammed his fist down on the small chessboard, scattering the marble pieces across the dusty carpet. The boy jumped up and trotted over toward his truck.

"Peace, peace," said the old man, tapping his hand on Nasir's sleeve. "He will learn in his own time, as we did in ours."

Nasir held his breath for a moment and kept his anger from his old friend. He inhaled slowly, then exhaled. He looked at the old man. "Forgive me, *Akaa*. Boys talking like this make my heart heavy," he said.

"My heart also," said the old man.

A young bearded Afghan soldier walked out to the two men. They stood up, reaching out hands to shake in greeting. The soldier smiled and gave greetings, holding an AK-47 over his chest instead of placing a hand over his heart. He informed the group that security was tightened, and that the only trucks coming on base that afternoon would be food deliveries. All the other trucks would have to wait outside until morning.

Nasir squatted down and began picking up the scattered pieces of the chess set, placing them carefully back into the wooden box. The old man looked over at the boy's truck and waved for him to come back over, squatting down on his haunches. The boy crept back to the carpet, squatted down beside the old man, and rubbed his hands distractedly along the dusty, multicolored pile of the carpet. Nasir tried not to show his irritation. He set the remaining pieces back into the wooden box, snapped it shut, and walked back to his truck to place it on the seat. He could hear Farzana reciting the verses to him, *God is with those who are righteous and do good.* So the orphan—oppress not. When he returned, the old man and the boy were talking loudly, almost in argument.

"I have food, I think," the boy said.

"Boy, is it food or not?" the old man asked.

"I think it is food," the boy said. "I can't read my paper."

The old man turned his head and spit the green wad of *naswar* out onto the gravel.

Nasir reached his hand out to the boy. "Let me see your paper," he said. The boy reached into his pocket and pulled out a grubby paper, haphazardly folded into quarters. Nasir opened the paper and squinted.

"You are carrying potato chips and sweets," Nasir told the boy. "Are you ready to go in?"

The boy gave a lethargic wag to his head.

Nasir caught the attention of the Afghan soldier. "Can the boy make his delivery to the base?" he asked.

"Yes, come," said the soldier, waving his arm toward the holding yard entrance and the drive that led into the base's main gate.

Nasir looked the boy in the face, but the boy didn't meet his eyes. Nasir said, "Be calm. They will look through your clothes, all of your things, your entire truck, to make sure you do not have a bomb. Do you have anything that might confuse the Americans? You want to avoid this," Nasir said. He remembered the times the Americans found things on his truck that confused them—the portable radio, a small propane stove—things the Americans not only took from him, but that made them treat him like an enemy.

The boy kept his gaze down and shook his head. "No."

"Show them everything in your pockets, your cell phone, your money, so they don't accuse you. Remember to be calm. They have rules for us that you must learn."

Without acknowledging Nasir any further, the boy got back in his truck and started the engine. Nasir now felt bad for him, making a delivery for the first time. His company should have explained more to him, or chosen a smarter boy.

Nasir turned to the old man. "We will continue our game outside, I hope," he said. The old man smiled and nodded, then began lifting up an end of the carpet to fold it. Nasir pulled up the other side of the carpet, shaking the dusty carpet into squares, then quarters, and placed it in the old man's truck. The dust made an immense cloud over them.

Afghan soldiers waved Nasir and the other trucks out of the yard and through the narrow barriers funneling toward the outer gate of the base. Nasir followed just behind the old man's truck, and they eased out into the dusty, crowded throng of trucks parked outside the base's outer barriers. Young boys straggled, and local men from the nearby village hocked kebabs, sweets, and naan to the waiting drivers. Nasir looked out at the mountains in the distance. He watched in his side mirrors as a handful of young, dirty-faced boys circled his truck, looking for something of value to steal from it. Like wild dogs, he thought. He touched the pocket of his waistcoat, but he knew in that moment what he would find.

Nasir's pocket watch was gone. His heart dropped. Then, like a flash flood, rage surged through his entire body, making his head and face hot, his limbs taut and charged. He threw open the door of his truck, jumped out onto the hard caked dusty ground, and ran after the filthy boys. He bellowed and swatted, chasing them to the back of his truck and down into the dust pit of a dried creek bed, his face hot with fury. He caught one small, thin wisp of a boy by the scruff of his collar and swatted him hard against his forehead. The child went limp, and

Nasir threw him into the dust. Nasir's arms shook, his legs twitched. His heart raced in a torrent, and he lost his breath. Nasir touched his empty waistcoat pocket, removed his skullcap to wipe the sweat from his head, and breathed as deeply as he could, slowing down his thoughts to count the seconds to calm himself. *God does not burden a soul beyond what he can bear.* He repeated the scripture in a low voice, but his breath and heart and mind raced with panic.

Nasir bent down over the child and turned him over, holding his fingers against the child's neck to feel his pulse. He could see the boy taking shallow breaths. He thought of his own children, and the rage he'd unleashed upon his family over the years. Nasir let out a shout of combined grief and relief, then convulsed, sobbing. Tears streamed from his eyes. In a moment, the boy stirred again, jumped up, and ran off toward a village in the distance. Nasir squatted in the swirl of dust, sobbing.

The old man approached. "It is time for prayers, my son," he said, pressing his warm hand on Nasir's shoulder. He gave a silent nod and wiped his tears. Nasir stood slowly, patted the dust off his clothing, and walked back to his truck to get his pitcher of water and rolled-up prayer rug. He would wait in turn for his next move.

HADJI KHAN

by David James

T he stars shone bright and multitudinous in the northern sky on a cool summer night above Kaysar Khel, a dark noiseless village on the eastern edge of the Zirwa valley, where rugged peaks rose endlessly and inhospitably into Pakistan. Two men walked surely but silently through the dusty streets, hoping to avoid the attention of dogs and children who would spread news of their arrival. The first, a tall man of not more than twenty with wisps of sparse beard, carried a rifle over his shoulder and wore a light brown pakol hat over his short black hair. The second man, older, taller, and unarmed, had a long thick black beard and an abundant white turban that folded around his neck and over his right shoulder. His thinness did nothing to diminish his imposing physical bearing and proud demeanor. The younger man spied a house with a red gate and glanced back with a slight nod. The older man knocked lightly on the corrugated iron gate, which opened with a considerable creak revealing an old man with a white beard and gray checkered turban who smiled and greeted the visitors holding his hand to his heart: "*A-salaam-alekum*, my son. Please come in."

"*Wali-kum-salaam*, uncle. Let us enter quickly without notice."

The old man, whose name was Gul Mohammed, led the men into his central room, where they shook hands and greeted the old man's six sons, then sat down upon wide flat cushions. The older guest looked around the room at each man deliberately before speaking: "Uncle, cousins, thank you for taking such care and risk to receive us in secret.

You all know by now what has happened and the consequences for all of us. This is Mateen, my most trusted bodyguard, and you should treat him as family. I owe him a debt on my life." Mateen stared at the floor in front of him, but inside he was beaming with pride to be shown such respect by Hadji Khan in front of his kin. Mateen had no living relations: his older brother was killed in a missile strike the previous spring, his parents had died while he was a young boy, and his sister had died in childbirth. Hadji Khan had been a second father to him as well as his mentor for the last three years. Hadji Khan continued: "Tomorrow, we will call a meeting of the tribal elders so they can hear what I have to say and decide whether to join our cause. It is important that my name not be used so that news of my presence is not heard by the wrong ears."

At this point, Hadji Khan stopped short as the door opened and two young girls entered the room carrying trays. The first girl was older, perhaps sixteen, and wore a blue dress covered with silver and red circles and crescents. Her head was covered with a light hijab made up of fabric from the dress and her tray contained bowls of goat and potato soup and flat bread. The second girl, barely a teenager, wore an orange and red striped dress fringed with sequined patterns and no head covering. She carried a tray with a large teapot, glasses, and some sugared pastry, and she caught a momentary glimpse of the visitors as she set her tray on the floor mat. None of the men spoke or moved until the girls had exited the room again.

The old man spoke: "Let us feast together and tell stories, and later we might discuss more serious matters."

After the two girls had closed the door behind them, they lingered and listened to the men in the other room through a crack in the door. The older girl, whose name was Farishta, said to her sister: "Niazmina, though we are not allowed to be involved in affairs outside the house, we should try to understand what the men are doing."

This is something her mother had once told her before she died of a sudden bacterial infection four years ago, leaving Farishta to manage the household. As they listened, they heard their brothers passing on local news about theirs and other villages, followed by Hadji Khan's report about Pakistan and the state of the current fighting season. Afterward, he recounted stories concerning ambushes, Americans, rockets, bombs, and other warlike things. Neither girl had ever heard anything of the type; Farishta thought about how men waste time on such silly things, while Niazmina thought about how brave her uncle must be and how handsome that young boy with him was. When one of the men got up they scurried silently to their room and went to bed, though they remained awake most of the night, stimulated by what they had overheard.

The next day four of the cousins were tasked with making the rounds and spreading the word of an important jirga to be held in three days' time. Meanwhile, Hadji Khan and Mateen rested and did not leave the compound. Hadji Khan walked circles around the courtyard sorting through his many thoughts. He reviewed his plans as he had many times already. He thought about this war, wondering if it was possible for him or anyone to live without war; it was all he had known for as long as he remembered and gave his life a genuine sense of purpose. His thoughts drifted to Mateen and his upcoming marriage to Farishta. He knew Mateen wanted to prove his bravery in battle, but was it perhaps better for this young couple and future family to grow old in peace? His thoughts turned reluctantly to his own family. His first wife, Hala, was strong and beautiful, and had given him two sons and a daughter; she became jealous when he took a second wife, Gulalai, but they soon became close companions. He tried as well to recall the face of his youngest daughter, Laila, his only child with Gulalai. Hadji Khan abruptly stopped and looked up at the sky, knowing that he must continue his mission without them, and that he would again see them one day.

Mateen often sat with his own contemplations under the shade of a fig tree as he watched Hadji Khan's inscrutable pacing. The young man was thinking about the girl who had brought them food last night and how he wished he had stolen a glance at her face; he had learned that they were to be married in autumn after the Eid festival and was immediately overcome with an anxious anticipation. He tried to imagine if his marriage would change anything regarding his responsibilities to Hadji Khan and the war.

Inside the house, a rift had developed between the two sisters. Niazmina was jealous of her sister's engagement and angry that her sister did not appreciate such a lucky union, while Farishta was incensed that her father was selling her like an animal. She had run the household for three years and had once been promised the chance to go to school. She was getting older and would soon be shackled to a housebound life she did not want with a stranger she did not know.

Like this, three days passed and the day of the jirga arrived at last.

—◆—

A procession of old and middle-aged men from all over the Zirwa valley filled the space in front of the Kaysar Khel mosque. No women were present. Some men were fat, but many were lean and rugged from decades of hard work and hard seasons; some wore orange henna in their beards and hair, which stained their hands and fingernails. Some wore pakol hats, some sindhi caps, some turbans. One man in a black turban, Mullah Abdullah, sat front and center; he served as the religious leader of the Shin Khel clan of the Ahmadzai tribe, themselves part of the larger *Wazir* tribe. Though such things were not spoken of, it was known to all that he alone would truly decide the course of action to be taken at the meeting.

After a large crowd had assembled and most had taken their seats either cross-legged on mats or crouched in a squat, Hadji Khan appeared in the back and slowly made his way to the front, walking neither slow nor fast, looking neither right nor left, until he stopped and faced the assembly in front of Mullah Abdullah. Mateen took his place behind his leader, while Gul Mohammed and his sons sat on the far side of the crowd as mere spectators. Hadji Khan looked out over the crowd and began to speak: "Mullah Abdullah, village elders, *Waziri* brothers, I am Hadji Khan of the Nasradin clan. I moved here as a boy to live with my uncle, Gul Mohammed, after my parents died in the war. I fought with our clan against the Russians, where I was wounded three times. We protected our land and our women and defeated the infidels. When the Americans came we could not fight for long on our own and I took twenty-five men and joined Jalaluddin Haqqani. For ten years I led attacks on the new infidels and their supplies. I am the lone survivor from among those twenty-six men, but in these years, however, our numbers have multiplied. I rose to become Haqqani's most successful commander, and we counted over fifty thousand experienced fighters. The Americans did not recognize friend from foe and did not trust their own Pashtun allies. On one mission, I used a false identity to enter an American base and speak directly with their CIA officers, giving them false intelligence and promises. I used my knowledge to carry out an operation which allowed two martyrs to enter the base and kill seven Americans and ten of their Afghan soldiers.

"I called this jirga today because the time is overdue for restarting operations to push the infidels out of our tribal land. Many of you have supported the Americans and taken their money for building contracts, supplies, and information, but you can gain penance for these actions. Inshallah, many of your sons will join us and share in the glory and honor of jihad."

Hadji Khan finished his speech and looked over the silent crowd, waiting to see who would be the first to speak. The lull was brief as a large old man stood to address Hadji Khan and other elders. He was sitting in the first row wearing a gray turban and a white shalwar under a brown vest, and he held his hand over his heart as he began: "Honorable Hadji Khan, peace be upon you. We all know of your famed deeds and it is known that you are a great mujahid who has brought esteem to his people. I and many of our brothers are uncertain, however, why you have returned here after living so long in Pakistan and having so much success with Haqqani. Are you here merely on a temporary mission or will you be staying long-term and bringing your family to join you?"

Hadji Khan maintained a stoic gaze and responded with no hesitation: "This is my home, where I will remain until the day Allah takes me. My wives and four children and five other relatives were murdered six months ago when one of the American buzzing flies they call drones fired a missile into my house in Wana trying to kill me. I no longer work for the Haqqani network as I believe it was Jalaluddin Haqqani's son, Sirajuddin, who used the Pakistan Intelligence Service as intermediaries to pass my location to the Americans for the assassination attempt. I had become very close to old Haqqani over the years and he was like a father to me. I was his most successful and most trusted commander, and I had the loyalty of many of the soldiers. Sirajuddin, his only surviving son and successor, most likely saw me as a threat to his future power base and conspired to have me killed. My and my family's murder by the Americans would also make me into a martyr he could use to further his cause. Afterward, I went into hiding and was eventually able to cross the mountains to reach my uncle's house. It is here where the Americans are, and it is here where I will stay until we have forced them out of our land."

Undercurrents of debate spread throughout the crowd after Hadji Khan finished his speech. Hadji Khan, mimicked by Mateen behind him, stared out over the crowd waiting with potent resolve. At last, another man from the second row stood. The eldest of all the participants, his long white beard and weather-beaten countenance gave him the dignified appearance of a centenarian even if his true age was lost to time: "Hadji Khan, we are pleased and honored by your presence and sorry for the sad circumstances which brought about your return to your people. You have made a strong case for action, which almost makes me wish I was a younger man. Nevertheless, in my years I have seen many things, including many wars and many leaders. The wisdom that my age has given me tells me that in the end everything is the part of the same cycle, merely repeated in different variations as Allah wills them. I have lost countless relatives to wars with foreigners or other tribes, and seen enough suffering to know that this world is only a grotesque shadow of what is to come in the next. The words of the Prophet, peace be upon him, preach peace as well as war, and the real struggle is maintaining peace rather than prolonging the vicious cycle of violence and retribution. I have shared tea with many Americans who have come through my village. There are men among them who actually want to do good, though, like in our own tribe, some of them are misguided. Many of you have seen the new clinic they built which has helped many women and children, and the two new boys' schools in our valley have also been a blessing and helped our children learn the words of the Prophet for themselves. Regrettably, we all know the story of the girls' school burnt down in Kaysar Khel last year the day before it was to open. This is a disgrace to us as much as to the Americans, and I fear many of you here think more about the past than the future. The Americans do not want to stay here forever, and attacking them will only cause more destruction to our land and our people. If we leave them in peace, they will give us money to help us build the things we need, and then they will go."

After the elder had finished and sat down again, Hadji Khan held his hand over his heart and nodded respectfully, but made no immediate reply. The murmuring and whispers from before now grew into a louder and spirited discussion among friends and neighbors. Gul Mohammed found his thoughts wandering in the last speech to his two daughters, but most of all the elder, Farishta. She had always been curious about the world and asked her brothers about their lessons whenever they returned from the madrasa. Gul Mohammed remembered how he had promised her that he would allow her to go to school and how happy she had been; after it was burnt down, she seethed inconsolably for days. He would have been willing to work with the Americans to build another girls' school if that was what was necessary to make his daughter happy again, but then he thought about Hadji Khan and how he would never allow that to happen. He had made an honorable match for Farishta with Mateen, who would become a powerful man by Hadji Khan's side. She was only a woman after all, yet these thoughts still troubled Gul Mohammed as his attention drifted back to the meeting. The crowd had become obstreperous and some men were ready to clobber each other over diverging viewpoints. Finally, after whispers with the men beside him, Mullah Abdullah prepared to speak. The crowd, anxious to hear their tribal leader's guidance, instantly became hushed when he stood: "Hadji Khan, no one doubts your skill as a commander nor your bravery and cunning. Some here profit from the Americans but most of us would have them leave immediately, as their continued presence is an insult to our land and our women and hence to us all. We have all endured senseless meetings and tea with the Americans when they appear in our villages; they are young and their faces are always different, but they always display the same attitude reflecting their strength. You would have us send our young men to make war against the infidels, but our young men are inexperienced in these things and we cannot contend against the Americans. We will take their money and oppose them in more subtle ways until they flee, and thus will our land and our families be protected."

Hadji Khan peered with perspicacity into the eyes of Mullah Abdullah. He had anticipated this outcome, and with a quick nod toward the back of the crowd, he signaled a young boy who then disappeared around the corner. Distant vehicle engines reverberated through the gathered assembly, causing nervous discombobulation. Hilux trucks rumbled through the streets, stirring up a thick dust cloud that drifted heavily over the crowd. Eight trucks came into view, each one topped with a large caliber machine gun and loaded with half a dozen or more men outfitted in white robes and checkered headscarves, brown chest rigs holding magazine clips, and AK-47s and RPGs. When the trucks had come to a stop, the men dismounted and stood silently and seriously.

Hadji Khan once again addressed Mullah Abdullah and the others: "Honorable Mullah, your patience and hope that the Americans will leave us in peace and go back to their country is more than we can hope for. We have this opportunity to show our strength in waging jihad, defending our homes and our women, and, God willing, establishing an independent state of Waziristan, where strong and experienced leaders will be needed to protect our people. Seventy-five of my most loyal and well-trained men who fought under Haqqani have followed me for months in the mountains, preparing for battle. The young men of the tribe who join us will earn honor and glory and become mujahideen. Some will become martyrs, but we do not fear death like the Americans. Their weakness is their arrogance, which makes them think that they are invincible with their armor and their planes, and that they know the best way to win wars and build nations. When we begin to inflict losses on the infidels they will become afraid to leave their bases, word will spread to more of my former soldiers, and our numbers will grow. The Americans have just arrived here and do not know our land or our ways, and can be led easily to defeat."

Mateen once more beamed with pride listening to his leader, and became so eager for the upcoming campaign that he forgot about his excitement for his marriage, which had occupied his thoughts for most of the jirga. Despite feeling indignant at such an unexpected display of force and insolence, Mullah Abdullah's considerable ambition had been aroused at the mention of an independent Waziristan and its need for leaders. Though he did not trust this upstart commander, he stood up again, looked Hadji Khan in the eyes, and gave a slow nod of consent.

—m—

It had been a busy day on Forward Operating Base Murphy, which sat on the western edge of the Zirwa valley, enclosed by four dirt walls topped with concertina wire, and made up entirely of a central concrete building, some plywood barracks, and guard towers. Charlie Company of the 1-305th Airborne Infantry Battalion had taken control of this FOB two months ago from a company of the 12th Jungle Infantry Division. There had been very little significant enemy activity since the handover: just a few rocket attacks, all landing well outside the walls, and no roadside bombs or direct enemy contact. On this day, two of Charlie Company's platoons patrolled local villages to the north and south, and the commander had gone on foot with the artillery officer and a rifle squad to the weekly shura meeting with village elders in the town center just half a kilometer outside the fort's gate. Both platoon leaders reported the same pattern they had noticed in every village since they arrived: strong tea and unproductive conversation with a few old men, unkempt children waiting for American largesse from the soldiers, and a conspicuous lack of women. This particular patrol was also marked by an unusual absence of fighting-aged men in the villages. Captain McMullan, Charlie Company's commander, had had a more interesting dialogue with an unexpected visitor—an influential tribal leader named Abdullah.

Later that evening, Captain McMullan discussed the next day's plans with the company officers and non-commissioned officers assembled in the Tactical Operations Center, which was little more than a low rectangular room with rough concrete walls, maps, and several computers: "Okay, guys, tomorrow's patrol has been approved. Third Platoon, you're escorting me to Kaysar Khel, a village about twenty clicks east across the wadi. We've never been that way, but the previous commander told me they suspected it was Taliban-friendly, though besides a minor firefight at the start of their deployment they never found evidence of weapon caches. Today, I had a good discussion with the local mullah who said they fully support the Afghan government and want to keep the Taliban out of the villages. He said that the people want a girls' school and that Kaysar Khel was the place to do it. The last unit contracted one out that was burnt down, but the mullah assured me it won't happen again as the people have all rejected the Taliban. Anyway, it's a good chance for us to start using our project development funds. Everybody knows the deal with the counter-insurgency doctrine from those classes we did, and our lives will be easier over the next ten months if we get off to a good start winning some local hearts and minds. Any questions?"

Third Platoon's leader, Lieutenant Howard, the company's youngest officer fresh out of training, raised his hand to open the question-and-answer session: "Yeah, sir. What is your assessment of the IED threat?"

"Good question, Mike. The last unit reported a sharp drop in roadside bombs since last year and there hasn't been one in this area for over six months. Obviously, tell your gunners and drivers to keep their eyes peeled, but this is what we've trained for, and we're going to push on."

Lieutenant Tomsky, the company's artillery officer, spoke up next: "Will we be supported by any fixed-wing or rotary-wing aircraft?"

"There will be Apache helicopters on station for our movement to and from the village, so we should be covered, Dan. Anything else?"

Sergeant First Class Hawke, Third Platoon's senior enlisted man, chimed up somewhat curtly with a tone implying that he had better things to do at the moment: "What time did you say we're rolling out tomorrow, sir?"

"We're leaving the gate no later than 0700, Sergeant."

"Thank you, sir."

The meeting thus concluded, the participants scattered their separate ways. Some lingered to discuss the plan while others chatted and joked. Lieutenant Howard addressed Sergeant First Class Hawke as they walked out of the building together: "Let's make sure all of our heavy gunners do a full cleaning and inspection of their weapons tonight, Sergeant. Actually, that goes for the whole platoon. Nobody goes to bed before checking their weapons and their gear. Things could get interesting tomorrow on this new route."

"I got it, sir. Squad leaders have already taken care of it."

Lieutenant Howard felt unpleasantly redundant, but he was just doing what he was taught to do as a leader. He had only been in charge of the platoon for three months before deploying—just enough time to do the last full training rotation with the men. He was a muscular ex-rugby player from West Point who was excited to enter the fray so soon after finishing Ranger School and being assigned to the 1-305th; he mentally calculated having enough time to do a second deployment with this unit in a couple years, probably as an executive officer, the company's second-in-command. As they approached the barracks, Lieutenant Howard attempted lighthearted conversation to ease the tension: "Look at all those stars, Sergeant. You ever seen so many that bright? Too many city lights where I'm from, I guess."

"We don't have many city lights in Wyoming, and this ain't my first rodeo, sir."

They entered the building and made preparations; after Lieutenant Howard made the rounds, he disappeared into his room, cranked up the air-conditioning, and turned on his Xbox for a stress-relieving game of Madden Football before racking out for the night.

Lieutenant Tomsky, still hanging around listening to the discussion, accompanied Captain McMullan everywhere and considered it his job to know as much as, or even more, than the commander about intelligence, troop movements and locations, air support capabilities, and the general situation in their area of operations. Eventually, he lost interest in the conversation when it broke down into sophomoric jokes between various platoon leaders and senior NCOs, and he snuck off to his quarters in an adjacent hallway; it was small enough to be a closet, but big enough for a bed and a shelf full of books. He privately considered himself an outsider within the Army ranks, especially after seeing firsthand during his first deployment the innumerable hypocrisies and inanities of Army leadership and bureaucracy, and the absurdities and abuses of war. Nevertheless, life on this deployment was not intolerable for Lieutenant Tomsky, and he planned to use as much of his limited private time as possible to work his way through the formidable bookshelf above him.

Captain McMullan fired off a long series of emails and presentation slides, and then left the TOC after all the others. Before doing anything else, he knocked on the door to the first sergeant's room. The first sergeant had deployed to Afghanistan twice, though one would be forgiven for thinking that he, too, had fought the Russians after listening to his stories and his braggadocio. In fact, for all his bluster, the first sergeant was a first-rate leader, but he had long harbored secret thoughts about retirement. He played a subtle combination of domineering his subordinates while licking the boots of his superiors, but he knew there was no way he could stand being promoted and serving as what he considered a glorified lapdog to some ambitious colonel. His aim was to take a job as a civilian contractor with a private company like DynCorp or KBR, where he could get paid six figures for pulling a security job much easier than his current one. This would likely keep him deployed even more in the future, but being in a war zone gave him more sense of purpose and vitality than anything he had ever done at home.

"Hey, First Sergeant, you want to play Call of Duty?"

"Let's do this, sir. But I only got half an hour. Gotta Skype with Carol later. The internet is finally working faster than ever after I convinced Sergeant Hernandez it was in his best interest to raise the bandwidth in the command hallway."

"Nice work. Let's get started then!"

Captain McMullan feigned excitement about the bandwidth, but he would not be calling anyone on Skype. He had gone through a divorce after returning from his first deployment three years ago to discover his wife had been cheating on him. They had dated since high school and got married immediately after he graduated West Point, but the stress and loneliness of the deployment was too much for her. Captain McMullan suppressed his anger and pain, believing it made him weak, and instead threw himself headlong into his job. Leading a company of soldiers was more difficult and thankless than he could have imagined, however, and he gradually began to feel overwhelmed by things out of his control: soldiers' disciplinary problems, senseless demands from his boss, responsibility to mentor the company's junior officers, loneliness, and a sense of constantly failing in one of his many duties.

For the next hour, anyway, all of these issues were blissfully far from his mind as he and the first sergeant battled for head-to-head supremacy in a violent virtual video game world, one not dissimilar from the real world but with neither the perturbation nor preoccupation that had muddied the waters of an otherwise orderly life.

—m—

The next morning at 0600 Staff Sergeant Cooper, the company's artillery sergeant, walked to the TOC to start his daily twelve-hour shift of monitoring company operations. It was a job no one wanted, which went to him only because the first sergeant hated him and did not let him go on patrols. Staff Sergeant Cooper, affable, gregarious, and clever, spent his days chatting up all comers, disparaging junior soldiers who happened to walk in for some reason, and teasing senior officers and NCOs for any shortcoming, real or perceived. Like his counterpart, Lieutenant Tomsky, his position left him with little accountability, and it was only bad luck that he had somehow earned the first sergeant's disfavor after arriving to the company for reasons unknown and probably arbitrary.

At 0735, the convoy left the gate for the patrol to Kaysar Khel. The first sergeant berated every NCO before leaving because of the tardiness of the departure, until it was finally discovered that the company armorer, who was also the gunner on the first sergeant's vehicle, was fixing one of the heavy machine guns of Third Platoon that had not been properly checked the night before. After the convoy left and the ample dust that had been stirred up was quickly borne away by a stiff wind, quiet calm returned to the FOB.

At 0830, Lieutenant Howard radioed back with the convoy's current location and status: they had traveled only ten kilometers.

At 0857, Captain McMullan called in another more urgent report: "Charlie TOC, this is Charlie Six, we have one vehicle incapacitated by an IED, and are currently taking enemy fire from two sides. Have Second Platoon get ready to roll out to our location, break . . . And send those Apaches down here, over."

"Roger that, Charlie Six, wilco, over."

The TOC bustled with activity. After passing the information up to the battalion headquarters, an update came immediately, which Staff Sergeant Cooper dutifully relayed to the convoy: "Charlie Six, this is Charlie TOC, over."

"Go ahead."

"The Apaches were just diverted to Khost province to support troops in enemy contact; they say at least thirty minutes before they can reach your location."

"Roger that, Charlie TOC . . . stand by for further updates."

Staff Sergeant Cooper waited on the other end, his heart pounding violently as he imagined what it must be like during a desert ambush. His last deployment was Iraq, where he was involved in plenty of firefights, but always in cities and urban environment. Out here it was different, and he could not imagine how enemy insurgents could openly attack on flat ground with no cover. The wait for the company commander's response dragged on at least fifteen minutes. Outside, he heard the engines of Second Platoon's vehicles rumbling as they raced east out of the FOB. Finally, the radio crackled again: "Charlie TOC, Charlie Six, we've suppressed the enemy and stopped taking fire. Estimated twenty enemy killed. We're going to need a medevac helicopter, ASAP. Prepare to receive report, over."

"Send it."

"Our first vehicle, 2-6, hit the IED. We have five friendly KIA. In addition, we have four WIA that need immediate evacuation. Line 1: Grid WB 3261 0965. Line 2 . . ."

Staff Sergeant Cooper took down the report while sending it simultaneously to battalion HQ, his hand shaking noticeably the whole time as he tried to speculate who was killed. Undoubtedly Lieutenant Howard was one because his vehicle hit the roadside bomb. If he remembered correctly, Specialist Jackson was the driver and radio operator, and Private First Class Rodriguez was the gunner. There must have been, Khaled, a local interpreter, but he could not guess the final ill-fated passenger. As for the wounded soldiers, he hypothesized that they must have been other gunners since the thick armor prevented small arms fire from penetrating inside the vehicles—this over-burdened the engines and axles, causing constant breakdowns, yet proved useful when caught unawares in an ambush kill zone.

Forty-five minutes passed without significant updates. Lieutenant Tomsky directed the attack helicopters by radio, but there were no apparent enemy targets near the wadi so they unloaded Hellfire missiles on a suspicious grove of trees and left to refuel. The medevac bird then arrived and picked up the nine casualties, and, soon thereafter, the convoy was ready to clean up the site and return to the base.

Eight hours later, an urgent signal intercept was forwarded directly from the CIA: they had monitored a phone call near Kaysar Khel in which the speaker mentioned an attack with many dead Americans; there was also a passing reference to five martyrs; finally, there was a request to send more brothers from Pakistan to help them continue jihad. The speaker was believed to be someone known as Hadji Khan, reportedly a senior leader in the Haqqani network. The information was passed down the chain of command until it eventually reached Captain McMullan, who was simultaneously informed by the higher-ups that a five-hundred-pound bomb would be dropped on the site of the phone call in the next ten minutes, and that Charlie Company would be responsible for conducting a damage assessment patrol at dawn.

—⁂—

Hadji Khan sent his coterie back to their mountain hideouts to regroup and prepare for the next attack, while he himself decided to stay one final night at Gul Mohammed's abode; a longer stay would be too dangerous now that he had spectacularly inaugurated a new fighting season against the Americans. Four of the cousins had gone with Hadji Khan to witness the successful ambush, with three deciding to join their uncle as mujahideen. After a lavish feast of goat and potato stew with flat bread and sugary pastries prepared and delivered by Farishta and Niazmina, Hadji Khan withdrew out of doors to bask alone in his success. Even Mateen was instructed to stay inside with the others.

After twenty minutes, Hadji Khan perceived a drop in temperature and turned unhurriedly toward the house. Sand carried by the wind recalled his memory of the Arabian Desert, where he had made the hajj to Mecca eight years earlier. That long pilgrimage was sponsored by Jalaluddin Haqqani as an honor to Hadji Khan after his second successful campaign season. Though he rarely smiled these days, Hadji Khan felt himself fully content and in fulfillment of his destiny. His senses were reawakened by the faint but distinct buzz of an aircraft far overhead, by no means an unfamiliar sound, but one which sent ominous chills through Hadji Khan as he now started to run past the fig tree toward the door. Before reaching the house, however, he was thrown backward by an enormous earthshaking impact.

The bomb had missed Gul Mohammed's compound by fifty meters and landed closer to the neighboring residence of a certain Iqbal, with whom Gul Mohammed maintained a lengthy feud over the disputed ownership of a well equidistant from both properties. This patriarchal hostility had not stopped their children from playing together by the river when they were young and remaining friends as adults. Iqbal's compound was now completely demolished, and the powerful force of the impact collapsed the roof and most of the walls of Gul Mohammed's house as well.

Hadji Khan felt and heard nothing but a profound ringing in his ears as he regained the bit of dwindling consciousness. His eyes cracked open and for a brief instant he saw nothing but sand and dust, until a gust of wind carried it away revealing a wealth of stars shining down from the cloudless empyrean. He had witnessed this night sky his entire life, thinking nothing more than how it reflected Allah's ineffable greatness. The approach of certain death focuses a man's thoughts: for Hadji Khan, the sky timelessly distilled the sum of his life's accomplishments recollected and judged in his final fleeting moments. He decided that soon he would be a martyr and find his rightful eternal peace after a life dedicated to holy war. His head turned toward the rubble, his eyes drooped, and his final gaze settled upon a crooked doorframe blown wide open with colorful folds of fabric of blue and silver, red and orange fluttering in the wind.

BROWN BIRD

by Shannon Huffman Polson

It started the day the bird hit the window. Tina was just finishing her report, hands resting on her new ergonomic keyboard from IT: new accounts, monthly revenue—for the staff meeting in ten minutes. Arvo Pärt seeped from the computer speakers, the music she had listened to ever since her friend Molly had introduced it to her on deployment. She liked it for its connection to Molly, and for its disconnection from everything else, its faith in something better. She adjusted the cover on the lamp she used to avoid the overhead fluorescent lights, unconsciously straightened the box of tissue paper on her desk, and exhaled with the deep fatigue she hadn't been able to shake since she'd come back. She straightened her shoulders, willing herself to draw strength from the life she had so carefully constructed around her, hoping it might hold her up. Ten months after leaving her uniform behind for good, a strict attention to order and organization had kept her intact. Looking over her spreadsheet on the monitor, she moved her left hand to rest on the one thing out of place on her desk, a smooth, flat oval stone her father had found for her on their last trip to the cabin, the place where all her happy memories lived. She'd worn the stone smooth over fifteen years, though she knew where she could still find the rough places.

She felt Steve's presence before she saw him stop at her door on his way down the hall. "See you at the meeting, soldier?" he said. He was always so nice, though she didn't like being called soldier by someone who had never been one himself. "Division's coming today."

"I know. I'll be just a minute," she said, only glancing up. She placed the stone up against the lamp, hit enter on the last cell of the spreadsheet, and the numbers turned over and over and stopped.

The bird hit just after that.

She knew without looking which one it was. The female house finch she'd been watching on the bird feeder all month, the one hanging next to the benches and the boulder and the neat rows of barberry and Japanese mountain grass lining the clean cement sidewalks. The male came too but only on occasion. This was the female.

Tina stood up from her computer with a jerk, knocking the stainless steel coffee cup onto the floor. She stepped over the pooling coffee and started to run, down the hall and out the glass doors beside the reception desk where a new receptionist sat. Once outside Tina slowed down, the fresh air reassuring. She'd be all right, the bird. Maybe she didn't hit hard. It was a cool morning. A few minutes to recover, and she'd fly away.

Just below her office window Tina found the bird. She was lying on her side on the carefully manicured wood chips, beak opening and closing in time with the brown and white flecked chest moving in small determined gasps. Her small dark eyes blinked. Tina knelt in grass still wet from the morning sprinklers, ignoring the wetness spreading across the knees of her grey wool slacks.

She picked up the little brown body—so soft! So warm!—and held it in her palm, the tiny feathered face looking up at her. The bird's head seemed strangely loose.

"Shhhhh, shhhhhh." Her finger stroked the flight feathers.

The tiny beak opened and closed more slowly and Tina watched, hoping her eyes might somehow impart life. The bird was just stunned. She'd be okay.

Then the small chest stopped moving, and the beak too.

Tina waited. The life-brightness faded from the small eye in an instant, as though it had never been there at all, the reflection receding into the soft feathers.

—m—

It is true that Tina did not remember her meeting. Steve would ask her later when she returned, silk blouse and wool pants wet and face and hands smeared with mud, if she needed help. There was a new group for vets he would be happy to refer her to. She looked at him and thought of the bird and thought of Molly lying on that open dusty desert road with her eyes open but not seeing, mustard colored dust on her face, her skin, and the dark blood too reaching out from under her body onto the road. The dust made Molly more a part of the ground than the smile she had worn the moment before they'd hit the IED.

Tina knew that Steve could never see what it was she saw, and she said no thank you, she was fine. She put the rock in her pocket and she walked out while the new receptionist stared and she didn't come back.

Outside, Tina looked around for the trees, for the forest, but her new building was in the middle of the campus. She saw only benches and the sometime Japanese maple. She held the bird in her hand and she walked along the winding concrete sidewalks, past blocks D and J and S. It wasn't far. She stepped off the path, cut through the lawn directly toward the woods, her heels punching into the wet grass.

She reached the woods. Doug fir and aspen and alder with a thick undergrowth of salal and new ferns uncoiling into the spring. Against the campus of Spectrum Incorporated, the ordinary woods looked wild as a jungle. Her steps quickened, her lungs bringing in new wilder air. She did not slow but walked straight in. Her blouse snagged against the barbed leaf of an Oregon grape but she pressed on until she found a small clearing.

Tina knelt among the leaves. She set the bird to the side. The dirt was wet and consolidated from the rain. She broke a branch from a snag and stabbed at the dirt, opening space. An ant climbed onto the leaves where the bird lay, and she swiped at it with the stick. She kept digging. The hole was ten inches, eighteen inches. The ant came back.

"Dammit!" she screamed. She picked up the ant between her thumb and index finger and crushed it, wiping its body against a stump. She kept digging.

Twenty-four inches. Her digging slowed, and Tina looked at the tiny bird.

She pulled off new leaves from the spring salal and lay them on the bottom of the hole. She made a bed of small sticks placed next to one another. Then another layer of salal. She lay the tiny brown flecked body on the leaves, and covered it with another layer of leaves, and then added a handful of dirt, and then another. To add dirt by the handful took time but she did not hurry. She added dirt until the hole was full. Then she patted it down and added more. She spread the old leaves back out and over the ground. She stood up and away and lay twigs across the leaves until she could not herself see that she had been there. She looked at the clearing wild and disturbed and returned to wild and she said, "Now rest. Now, you can rest."

—⁂—

Once she had left, and taken her stone, she got in her car and she drove out past the manicured streets past the school the post office the mall until she steered her car onto the highway to drive. The leaving, the shedding of the structures she had so carefully constructed, filled her with both relief and a sense of danger and this feeling grew inside of her but she did not pay it any mind. After ten minutes she'd left behind the carved underpasses and muraled concrete highway walls and mowed ditches. The highway took her toward the mountains and she felt the swell of trees on either side, the darkness of tree and trunk standing like friends, like she had found a place she could try to trust, though this freedom did not guarantee her safety. She let her foot relax on the gas pedal and set the cruise control, her body curving into the seat while her eyes breathed in deep green on either side.

Darkness settled with reluctance, she thought, though she had not kept track of time. She grimaced at the fuel low light, its harsh insistent brightness. She'd always filled the car at half a tank, never let the fuel go down so far. Her chest constricted. She reminded herself to take deep breaths. This was something that never went away, the unbearable tension, the rubberband-taut awareness.

A sign appeared in the headlights as Tina forced in breath against the tightness in her chest. She let the car move toward the exit lane. Turned left across the overpass toward the bright station sign. She filled her car at the pump, then pulled up to the glaring lights of the store, turned her car off, and walked inside. She pulled down a Diet Coke, picked up a granola bar.

When you clear a room, you line up outside the door. One person enters weapon first . . . she remembered the training lanes, the strangely high voice of the instructor.

"Miss, miss?" The man behind the counter looked at her from underneath a tightly wrapped black turban. His voice was high, the way the instructor's had been. "Cash or charge?"

She looked up with a start. Her hand lay on the box of granola bars and she realized with embarrassment that she had been staring straight ahead.

"Yes," she heard her voice say.

"Charge!" he'd said. Not the instructor, no. It was not the instructor, it was the sergeant leading the patrol, it was the sound of the bomb, it was all the sounds together and they would not be disentangled from the sticky aural web.

She brought the granola bar to the counter and pulled out her purse. The man did not look at her again but scanned each item. "Three dollars and sebety-sik cent," he said.

Tina looked up at him as she handed four worn singles from her purse.

The day she had seen the woman, spoken with her, seen her dark eyes intent with a particular kind of terror, tried to protect her from what surrounded them, the sergeant screaming, his own brutal fear forcing its way out through anger in his wild eyes. The barrel of his M16 bobbed up and down. Tina felt the world narrow until she stood alone with the woman in a cloud of dust, the sergeant's screams echoing outside. It was just the woman's deep brown eyes, the eyes looking out of and through the dust. Tina had pointed the woman back inside of her house, and thought if she looked at the woman hard enough she might save her still.

One word, one movement, meant life, or death. What did life mean then anyway? How hard life tried to make it through, push through the fear and all that lay ruined.

Tina put away her purse and began to walk toward the door.

"Miss? Miss?" the man's voice again.

"Miss, change, tenty-fur cent."

She looked back at the man and met his eyes without recognition, her own eyes wide and raw still seeing things beyond him, and she turned away and walked through the glass doors, glass smudged and dirty, back to her car and she turned the key and began to drive.

The story of the woman; that had been Molly's story, not hers. But they shared all their stories. The stories made up who they had become and one could not be separated from another. A thing had happened, they had been in this thing and how they had come into it was not the same way that they would leave it. They went into this thing and thought maybe they would do something good and instead this thing had changed them and one day, one moment, you suddenly knew that you had been changed, though you hadn't felt it happen.

She set her cruise control one mile per hour below the speed limit and held the steering wheel with her knee as she opened the Diet Coke in the darkness, listened to the slow escape of gas into the air. Until then she had driven in silence, the thoughts of her own head too loud to hear anything else. Now she pushed the CD into the player. She took a long swig of carbonated brown water into her mouth, felt it force its way into her throat. Her CD spun, the inner mechanics of the player grinding but the music won and strains of Arvo Pärt began to play.

Arvo Pärt had disappeared himself once, she remembered. He had delivered these large and complex masterpieces, and then gone away for eight years. No one knew where he had been. When he reemerged his music was more spare, ethereal. No one understood him. Truth might come only after time, and in a quiet way. But in this music she heard a faith in something else she wanted to find. Whatever it was, it was beautiful, more beautiful than she thought she would be able to see. She wanted it. She yearned for it.

What did Pärt find in those years away? Why did he go? Had he known what he was seeking? Did it change things?

She turned off the interstate onto a two-lane state highway, watching the darkness in front of her, the small spot of moving asphalt lit by her headlights shiny in a steady rain. Her cruise control blinked off. The country road was darker, and in the darkness the forests on each side pressed in, or rather grew until she knew she'd been absorbed with a growing sense of mixed relief and fear. Far ahead a light appeared and grew, lights of an oncoming car.

Tina tightened the cap back onto her Diet Coke and placed it in the seat next to her. Her right foot pushed smoothly down, accelerating, watching the light growing into two lights, so bright. She put both hands on the wheel, gripping firmly but not hard. The lights grew larger, exposed another row above them. It was late for a semi to be on this highway. She watched the lights now instead of the road, imagined the shape of the crew cab, and . . . did she allow her car to drift, or did she turn? A strange calm came over her, the mechanical rhythm of the wipers cleaning water from the windshield, the lights large now, blinding, immense

The scream of the horn sounded the reflections of her own headlights in the shiny grill the cab wrenching away.

She turned too but did not remember, must have jerked the wheel, must have pulled herself and car away, but she did not remember, and her lights shone lonely on rainy blackness that also did not remember, the mad swerve of red taillights receding in her rear view mirror. She did not stop until she saw only darkness on all sides again.

Just ahead there would be a pull-off. The bridge over the gorge. The place they had always stopped when she was a little girl. The place you could feel the spray of the waterfall rising from the gash in rocks below.

The sign emerged from the darkness. She pressed her brakes, pulled onto the roadside.

Rain fell heavily now. Tina turned off the car to feel the darkness, hear the hard drops of rain drumming on the roof. She opened her door, the sound of the rain less loud but as insistent on the asphalt and magnified in the trees around her. She walked to the edge of the bridge, the form of the thigh-high railing made of stone just visible through the wet and dark. Tina pushed herself up onto the wall, letting her feet hang over the edge toward the waterfall she could not see but only hear. The water roared, spray mixed with rain far below in the blackness. Water soaked through her pants, plastered her hair, ran down her neck, her blouse clung to her body.

Tina put her hands on the cold wet stone. She listened to the road, looked into the darkness, felt the cold and wet. She leaned forward, closing her eyes and lifting her face toward the darkness and heard the roaring grow, began to feel it inside of her. If you listened too long to the roar, it would overcome you, she thought. She arched her back, lifting her face to the rain and the darkness. Her center of gravity shifted, the slightest shift she felt all the way through her body and for an instant she thought she would fall, thought she would let herself fall. She recoiled, as though she'd been punched, felt her eyes open in the blackness with terror bathed in relief at her own fear. She pulled her legs up from over the edge, pulled them in close to her and did not notice that she was crying until she felt her body shaking from the sobs, took in a hard breath and tasted the wet cold of rain and coughed and cried until she was done and she sat with her arms holding her legs bent against her and lay her head on her knees and felt the rain hitting the side of her neck and her face until it was numbing and then it soothed her and in the darkness the rhythm became a song.

No, she said, aloud. No. It is enough.

She did not know how long she sat there. It had taken no time to be soaked through, and the bigness of the sound and feel of water falling from dark mountain and dark sky filled up what she perceived so that when she got up and climbed into her car and saw it had only been twenty minutes she was surprised it had not been much longer. As she turned the key, the car convulsed with a lurch toward life. Tina let the engine run until the rhythm smoothed, then backed up and turned again onto the highway. She pulled the stone from her pocket, felt its smoothness, and set it on the small ledge in front of the speedometer, where she could see its shape by its absence, blocking out the instrument lights behind it.

She pulled back onto the state highway and drove.

Twenty miles later she turned off the highway onto a country road. She slowed her speed, and opened the granola bar wrapper, eating the bar in tiny bites like a child, or an animal. The rain stopped and she saw the glint of moon against the torn edge of cloud and stars coming through. The trees thinned as the road climbed and then leveled out again, her headlights picking up the sharp shadows of bushes accustomed to the dry side of the mountains. She drove into the darkness, only the lights illuminating static shapes without color.

She wouldn't be able to drive past the gate. It had been years—fifteen, was it? Even then the road had been impassable. She drove by feel, she thought, after so long. Some knowledge never left you. The time it took from highway to gate—she did not know the minutes—close to an hour—but it was a time she knew inside of her, her body holding time like a vessel. After fifteen years the trees and small plants by the side of the road were not the same. How could they be? But it was the same ground she had known so well for so long. There must be larkspur in that darkness now, the first few blooms of arnica. It's dirt that tells you who you are, her father had once said, picking up that red brown dirt and letting it crumble through his fingers. The soil. The earth. It tells you where you came from.

For all she had expected the feel of the road in her body to guide her, the gate materialized suddenly in the dark. She kicked the brake pedal in, felt the seat belt against her body as the car came to a stop. She stepped out of the car, still in her heels. Ridiculous to be wearing heels. She pulled them off and threw them into the foot well of the passenger seat, then pulled out her gym bag from the backseat and changed into the t-shirt, lycra pants, and tennis shoes she would have worn to run after work.

Tina felt the air against her wrists and neck, cool air slightly warmed from what the sun had left lingering in the hard dirt. She reached in and picked up her stone and let it sit against her palm.

She climbed over the old cattle gate, hearing the jostle of chain on metal. Her feet felt for the ground on the other side in the dark. A thorn stabbed at her ankle and she winced. Her home ground still had thorns.

The clouds began to pull apart and starlight, ever brighter as her eyes adjusted, showed a faint path. There was no going back. She was committed now, just her in this dark and this desert. Fear came, and desire, too. A rush of longing for the openness, a terror of what it might reveal.

"'Fraidy cat, 'fraidy cat!" Her sister's voice called from the cabin from twenty years before, her father in from shooting squirrels with the rifle he kept above the door. "Tina's 'fraid of the dark!'

"Am not!"

"Are too!"

"Charge!"

"I thought I could save her."

The woman had been lying in the street the next day they came through on patrol. Her black hair caked with dust. The blood had dried black.

You couldn't have saved her, there's nothing you could have done, she'd said, Molly's head on her shoulder. You did everything you could. This place—there's nothing more you could have done.

Too much, it's too much, too many, Molly said.

How much can one soul hold before it breaks?

The stars, there were so many. Out this far, clouds torn away, you could see galaxies, worlds, other dimensions. Everybody should spend time looking into the night sky, Tina thought. Everybody should see these worlds. How many there are. How beautiful they might be.

The dark no longer seemed so deep. It softened, still. There are so many worlds.

The cabin loomed out of the starlit path, its small shape magnified by lack of light.

"Hello," Tina said quietly.

The cabin did not answer. A small animal scurried off of the porch, unseen.

She would not go in, not right away. The night was not cold. She sat on the steps of the small porch. There would be dust inside. It would take time to get it to a place where she could live. She had had enough of dust. The porch would be enough just now, in that quiet night.

The owl spoke from a tree so close Tina imagined she could feel its breath.

"Whoo hoo," it said.

"Whoo hoo," Tina said back.

"Whoo hoo," it said again.

The stars showed just enough on the porch to see the bench against the outside wall of the cabin and the old lantern, the one her father had taught her to trim. She reached over, let her fingers follow the curves of glass and metal. It was not smooth; the dirt and dust from years of wind had gathered in its creases and the metal was dented, rusted. Tina rubbed the grit between her fingers, felt the cut of it.

She would clean and clean, it could be done. In a week she could have that little cabin cleaned, the broken things fixed. It would be fine. There would be so much dust, but here it could be cleaned. Here she could sweep, and make it go away.

The mix of fear and deepest yearning changed, became anticipation and understanding. Her chest let go of a portion of the tension it held and she felt how much that tightness had become a part of her those past two years. She could give the things she carried over to this quiet place. This night, the sky, the land, was big enough to take her stories. Her sounds, the sounds could spin out into space. But rest might never fully come. Rest required letting go. It was the dust, you see. What she could not let go was that fine dust across an eye that had been bright, the way the dust could claim a thing.

She stepped onto the dirt and then she screamed, a deep and animal scream from somewhere far away and deep inside, and as she screamed she felt herself alive. The stars soaked in her scream. The night lay quiet.

"Thank you," she whispered to the night. She let herself feel each breath that came, the way her chest expanded and released, the strain and relaxation of muscle tissue bone, and standing on the dirt and feeling every breath she thought that maybe some things lost could be recovered, some things forgotten learned again.

The dark began to thicken all around her. She got up and tried the cabin door. It opened, and she went in.

WAR PARTY

by Michael Carson

W e agreed that if Blonde Hair drank one whiskey shot an hour he couldn't get a DUI. And we held to this policy for the first hour, only fudging the interval by fifteen minutes in the second. By the third, we debated whether pairing the whiskey with cocaine diminished or increased one's BAC. At some point during the fourth hour, the three of us consumed a liter of Canadian Club and three bottles of champagne and had difficulty telling the difference between lanes on the road much less hours in the day.

"Only drunks drink that shit straight," Blonde Hair told Black Hair as he tore the foil off another champagne bottle with one hand and steadied the steering wheel with the other.

"I have to get to the party," I told Black Hair. My face felt flush. I kept checking my cheeks and forehead for fever.

"We should keep to one shot an hour," Black Hair said. "I don't want to be stuck overnight in Jersey."

They were hippies I think. Or libertarians. Something. I had met them before, and they had told me their names. But I had forgotten them. The people I had come up with left in middle of the night, sick and tired of New York. Dan had broken a chair at the first apartment. Stacey had been bored. She never liked being far from home. Will's nose started bleeding. I stayed on with these two, friends of Will, or his cousins, until we blacked out at an apartment in Battery Park. We woke up around seven overlooking a giant hole where two towers had been, and left quickly, taking with us all the unopened champagne we could grab and a liquor bottle from the kitchen counter. I don't know who lived there.

"We need cigarettes," said Blonde Hair. His hair was not nearly as long and natty as his friend's, but stringy and unwashed. He had it cut recently though, just around the ears. Black Hair's neck was a mess of unkempt greasy curls. They spun endlessly around on themselves, and he periodically rubbed his hand through the unctuous wave as if he had fleas.

Blonde Hair spun the wheel expertly. I admired his dexterity, the way in which his hands passed over one another, long fine fingers with perfectly sheared cuticles. Around the roaring semis we maneuvered effortlessly, falling in and out of each lane as if the entire highway's movement were synchronized. We must have been inches, centimeters away from their massive spinning wheels and yet we never touched. I felt like a juggler's ball.

"Well, yes, of course," I agreed. "We need cigarettes. But after the cigarettes we need to get to the party."

"I can't drive any faster," argued Blonde Hair. "You see, if I drive any faster, I'll be drunk."

"One shot an hour," Black Hair said. "You can just tell them you had one shot an hour. They'll understand."

"The cops are fascists here. Union fascists."

The sun beat down lazily on the window, and I dozed. The car was like a cradle, the lane changes long desultory rocks—first one side, then another, back and forth, forth and back.

"You can't be in a union and be fascist," said Black Hair.

"Well, of course you can. Unions *are* fascist. Read a book."

"Fuck books."

I interrupted.

"Do I look sick? I think I look sick."

Black Hair glanced back at me. His lips were thick and his chin drooped—a basset hound with a basset hound's sad dull eyes. I touched my cheeks again. My fingers grew warm. The champagne was very dry, and each time I put the glass to my lips my throat constricted. We were out of whiskey though, so I tried again and again and hoped for the best.

"You're not sick. You are definitely not sick. I know sick people."

Above me strips of headliner fluttered down like confetti. It took all my willpower not to pull at them. Blonde Hair or some previous owner had stapled the sagging roof fabric up and it ballooned down in three distinct parachutes. The fourth balloon had popped during the trip and long strips tore away in the wind, whipping against the seat, into my lips and out the window. If I pulled my head off the window and my back off the sticky leather, my hair would rub against this soft material.

"Why are we stopping?" I asked.

"Cigarettes. We need cigarettes. Cigarettes will help your fever."

I laughed.

"Why are you laughing?" Black Hair asked.

The green Oldsmobile had pulled into a rest stop and parked between two white trucks. Black Hair and Blonde Hair stumbled out of the doors into the sun toward the service plaza.

"Get me a water," I yelled through the open window. "I'm sick."

"Yeah, yeah, yeah," one of them shouted back.

I felt very alone. The semis glided by, screaming down and up the turnpike, tearing me this way then that way, my torso from my head and my head from my torso. There were so many vehicles, so many shapes and sizes. I rubbed my cheeks again and tasted water in the air.

After about five minutes or maybe twenty, my bladder tightened. I did not listen, focusing instead on everything else, the sun, the sound of my breathing.

They did not come back. The cars and trucks screamed at me.

My bladder tightened again, loudly.

I pushed at the door, brushing the confetti aside, moving toward the golden arches, remarking on the two white trucks, the wide-open sky an indifferent blue.

—⁓—

I could not find the green Oldsmobile. The sun had grown larger by the time I left the restroom, and was now obscured by a fog, a heavy orange incandescence. I walked back toward the white trucks but there were no white trucks. There were other cars, but no trucks. I turned around and went left and then right, the fenders and bumpers brushing against my knees. After many different color cars, I found a green Oldsmobile.

Someone had fixed the headliner. Fabric no longer hung down in my face.

"Excuse me," said a man in the front seat. The man had a long skinny jaw, two lines that ran all the way down into his neck. His lips moved after the words came into my ears. He had very little hair, and what hair he did have was brown. His eyes were wide as the blue sky.

"I have to get to a party," I said.

"Are you all right, son?" he asked

"I'm sick," I told him. I felt he would understand. "I'm leaving tomorrow. I'm going to war."

The woman in the seat next to him, her eyes rolling lightly, said something to the man. She held another version of her, a miniature thing with the same eyes, nose, and hair. The thing fingered her chin.

"Where are you from, son?" said the man, loudly, too loudly. "Did you say you were in the military? Are you all right?"

"I'm not in the Army yet. I'm going to the Army tomorrow. I start tomorrow. Tonight's my party," I explained patiently, slowly, trying to keep my tongue from the words.

"I think you need to go somewhere else," said the woman, and I turned to her. Her lips had tiny ruts in them where words gurgled.

"We can take you," said the other one. "Where do you need to go?"

"My party. My war party," I said.

I looked down at my hands. They had become very heavy, almost as heavy as the warmness in my cheeks. The little thing in her lap gave me an eyeball full of empty liquid. It rolled around and around and I shifted and squirmed so it would not know me.

"Here," the lines that were a man said, "lie down. We can take you where you need to go."

"I need to talk to you outside," said the other one, her split lips red as the ends of her nails. The little thing's small hand had risen up into her hair. It ran like my hand might have run, caressing downy cheeks. I wanted to put my warm cheeks there next to those warm cheeks and fall asleep underneath all that hair.

"The least we can do," came through the air, into my head with all my other thoughts.

Through the windshield, I watched them move their hands and mouths. She pointed at the building, and then her thumb at the car. Her eyes rolled and rolled. The little thing grabbed at her hand.

I shifted my feet against the seat, and wondered if they had cigarettes. They did not look like the kind of people who had cigarettes. There were only stuffed animals next to my feet. I would push them and they would stay clinging to my foot. They would not roll away. They had eyes and mouths and ears stitched to their bodies.

Through the windshield, the man kept on nodding his head, as if to say, yes, I understand, of course I understand, but we have a certain responsibility. We have to do something.

"No you don't," I said to the stuffed animals.

My forehead grew warmer, dangerously warm. I was contagious.

Opening the door, I fell out onto the ground, spilling out like water, and the words they shouted at me made no sense. I picked myself up and ran. The bumpers scraped against my knees. Tennessee, New Jersey, Maryland, and Connecticut cut at my jeans, but I did not care. I was not afraid.

A green 1996 Oldsmobile pulled up next to me as the cars disappeared. Black Hair hung out the window, the champagne bottle's rim peaking over the edge. His eyes were very sad.

"What the fuck, man? Let's go. We got cigarettes."

The confetti swayed first this way and that, tickling the back of my neck.

Black Hair apologized when he remembered the water.

"I forgot," he said, earnestly.

I did not like being away from my friends, from the people I knew, because other people in the world would become sincere for no reason, blindly and dangerously. I lived in fear that someone would hold me accountable for what I said or did or expect me to hold them accountable for what they said or did.

They offered me a joint as a consolation. The tires squealed in the waxy asphalt and I coughed terribly. It poured out my nose.

"I need some sleep," said Blonde Hair, his delicate fingers cresting over the spinning wheel. "I know my limits."

I could feel the motor pulsing against my forehead, churning air in one side and out the other, below as above, within as without.

"Road trips are great," said Black Hair, his hair shinier and moving ever so lightly in the terrible breeze.

"It's not a road trip if you're going home."

"It's on the road. It's a road trip."

"I need to pull over. I need some sleep, maybe."

"No," I shouted over the wind. "I need to get to the party."

I was running high, spinning like a top.

"I have a party tonight. My parents spent a bunch of money. I only get one party. You can't pull over. We can't pull over again."

"I'm really tired."

I waited for more but that's all Blonde Hair said.

"You can come to the party too. You can both come to the party."

"Will they have food?" asked Blonde Hair.

"Of course, they'll have food. It's a going-away party."

He stared down at the empty pint in his lap.

"Where you going?" asked Black Hair suddenly.

"The Army."

"There's Army everywhere. I mean there's like five thousand fucking bases. Global War on Terror means we all signed up for the war. Everyone. You, me. We're all in. Whether we like it or not."

He had a point. I could see his point.

"You have a point," I said, blowing smoke at the strips of felt.

"Can we at least get some more whiskey?" he asked, as if I had a choice in the matter.

"Yeah, I think it's been an hour," said Blonde Hair.

"Sure," I said. "You're doing me the favor. I don't see why not. I don't see how another stop can hurt."

By the time we were back on the road, the sky had darkened. A storm had blown in from Pennsylvania. Thick drops slapped against the windshield—first a few, then a thousand. You could barely hear the music. I could only hear parts of what Black Hair was telling me. It came to me brokenly from the bottom of a well.

"I don't believe in war . . . you can kill now but why not later? . . . Why not ever? . . . I respect what you do but I don't see how it makes the world a better place . . . it's just bad juju in my opinion."

"Thank you," I yelled over the roaring air. "I respect you too."

I don't know if he heard me. The conversation broke off when a massive semi with the letter *M* on the side swung sharply into our lane, spraying gallons of water up through the wheel well and onto our windows. It was like driving through the ocean, through a lake, into the sky, as if someone had just pulled a bag over the car. Blonde Hair yanked the wheel to the left and then back to the right, pulling us into the other lane and what I knew would be my death, the hard smacking, the crumpled plastic, the naked impact I had dreamed of for many years, and yet there was nothing there, just more wet air. The tires squealed, spun water, and again caught pavement just before we hit 90 degrees. We straightened out, never slowing for a moment.

"You son of a bitch," I whispered. "You son of a bitch."

Black Hair crawled into the backseat with me. There was something wild in his eyes. He turned toward the rear window, the pint still firmly in his hand, close to me. I could smell its cherry scent and his greasy hair. My hands shook uncontrollably. They danced about my leg until I grabbed the seat belt firmly, pressing it against my fingers until they hurt.

"Jesus Christ. You see that?" Black Hair asked, his eyes far away from mine. "Holy shit, look at the pileup. It's a massacre back there. It's a fucking genocide."

With each passing second the Oldsmobile moved down and away from the giant truck another car slammed into the wall the Oldsmobile had erected, dividing us and them, shifting the monstrous wet squealing dinosaur a little further down the highway toward us. But it would never catch up. It could never catch up with it going as slow as it was. The entire I-95 corridor could slam into that truck and we would still be only further away.

It was unfair. We were taking their movement, the velocity of their collision to propel ourselves forward. But we did not make this world. The cars to the left and the right of us were doing the same. We had so much power, so much energy. And they were nothing at all. Yet this was exactly how it needed to happen. It couldn't happen any other way than this. This was how they died and this is how we lived.

"Fuck," said Black Hair, his breath hot with whiskey, closer to my own face than I liked. My hands had not stopped shaking.

"I need to get out of here," I said. "I need to go away."

"We are getting out of here. Don't you see?"

And we were. We were flying. My cheeks were no longer warm. Blonde Hair didn't look back or speak to us. He briefly adjusted the rearview mirror, lit a cigarette by pulling his face close to the lighter, leaned back, and let out a blast of smoke. The small gap of open window sucked the smoke out.

"Hey, look at that," Black Hair said, pointing with the half-filled pint, as he collapsed back against the other back passenger door, greasy hair hanging over his ears.

I yanked a felt strip out of the way. The sky was clearing up in front of us, and if you looked hard, if you had the sensitivity to see, you could just make out a spectrum of orange, purple, violet and a pale lovely pink rising up between the pulsing brains of cloud and last crimson sinews of sun.

THE CHURCH

by PJ Frederik

The water deployed in an unrelenting pulse, its steady undulations lulling me into a vertical daze. I had been standing under the showerhead for at least an hour, maybe two. Showers were supposed to be kept under five minutes, presumably so soldiers wouldn't jerk off. I had flagrantly violated the letter of that law but kept the spirit intact.

Pale and pruned and pathetic, yet nothing untoward—just well-scrubbed is all. After church, after I'd soap-soaked my boots, I claimed sanctuary in this shower. Since then I had been scouring my skin and steaming my sinuses to be rid of the alkaline tang of blood.

The soap in my hand was billed as manly, with sandpaper embeds to strip off dead skin. At some point in that wasteful rinse I'd developed a routine, driving scratchy soap over and around my body like a slot car on a Möbius track. Shoulder-pit-belly-groin-thigh, thigh-belly-pit-shoulder, my left and right switching at the top and bottom of each lap.

These left-right-left soap-exchanges affirmed functioning process, assured me that nerve impulses still coursed as intended without getting lost along the way. The lack of twitches or other errata convinced me that my body worked, freeing the conscious mind to step back from the controls as the gritty soap chafed along its pink ribbon course.

Why not trust the body? It's an impressive machine with capacity and precision. The hands alone are a masterpiece and we're blessed with two, each sprouting four fingers and a thumb. The thumbs boast double-joints and fingers curl around three, these amalgams of bone and muscle holding endless possible action. Alone, hands caress, stroke, slap, strike, hit, hold, cradle, comfort. Given a tool, hands can write, rape, shoot, stab, suture, arouse. My hands have covered pistol grips, torn flesh, softer skin, my own stiff need. They are complicit in the best and worst of what I am.

Only complicit, never culpable. My hands are pawns, patsies, just following orders. I ditched the soap and wiped away the lather, taking a hand and holding it in the other. I rolled them around, feeling left with right and right with left. It seemed wrong to interrogate something so familiar and personal, to question the allegiance of my own flesh and blood.

I had to give it thought. The church left me no choice.

—⁓—

The night of the church was routine. I was wearing the same uniform, sitting at the same computer, next to the same soldiers. It was all the same until an interpreter gave a sharp knock on the plywood door. I opened it to find him with a cell in his left hand, his right hiding the mouthpiece.

"My brother is at church. There are men with guns there."

His voice was excited but confused, as if undecided whether to anticipate horror or thrill.

"He called me and I have him on the phone. There are many hostages."

We notified the ops center, the ops center alerted the quick-reaction element, and the quick-reaction guys rolled out. The interpreter muted his phone's mic and put it on speaker. One guy had a radio to update quick-reaction but the rest of us just sat around, listening as the interpreter made sense of what we were hearing.

"It sounds like one guy is talking on the phone asking for prisoners to be released."

"Now some people are begging the men with guns not to kill them."

"People are reciting prayers. The men with guns are calling them unbelievers."

"They are yelling at the police outside to stay away or they'll blow everyone up."

"One of the men with guns says he will start shooting people."

The periods of speech and silence alternated for ten minutes until we heard shouting, foreign voices rising to talk over each other. The interpreter tried to follow but lost himself in a meaning that grew self-evident.

It was a few gunshots at first, then a rising chorus of begging, screaming, and crying. The crescendo arrived with the sound of 30-round clips emptied on full auto. We listened as his brother started to say something into the phone. A few syllables came across before the cheap speaker crackled and the line cut out.

The church was close enough for us to hear the boom. We said nothing. There was nothing to say, nothing we could do. Everyone knew what'd gone down. No one had to say to the interpreter, "Your brother's dead." It wasn't yet clear if he had been shot or blown up or both, but that's not an important distinction in the grand scheme.

A minute went by before a soldier radioed the quick-reaction team to not expect hostages, that they were heading into a mass-casualty instead. One-by-one, others in the room drifted away to eat. The interpreter found a chair in the corner and cried. The colonel caught me as I made to leave.

"Head over there and see what you can find."

"Sir," I nodded. The attackers were dead, the medics would evac the wounded, and it then became my job to gather evidence and make sense of the carnage. This task was called "sensitive site exploitation," but it was little more than scrounging table-scrap-data to sate our systems' hunger. Occasionally we made a match and identified a bomber or bomb-maker. Usually we didn't.

—m—

Our convoy snaked through the dark neighborhood between the base and the church, the slow ratchet of the turret-gunners' swivel lending the procession an arrhythmic snare. We were quiet otherwise: no iPod-fed music over the internal radios, no bullshitting or wise-cracking. We drove with funereal solemnity, en route to meet the freshly dead.

The church was quiet. Elsewhere the injured were getting better or worse, but in the nave the only sound was the crunch of debris underfoot. A dozen quick-reaction soldiers milled about, bearing witness and pulling security; the local police stood to the side, waiting for their turn to do nothing. I started to take photos. There was a lot to document. Bodies lay on, between, and splayed across the rows of splintered pews. Bloodied bits of flesh clung to the walls, trapped in ball-bearing pockmarks. This wasn't my first massacre, but here was more than the usual cordwood stack. This horror had *dimension*.

The victims fell as you'd expect. Still husbands lay crumpled over still wives. A few children were wedged beneath parents who'd failed to shield. One pew bore a fat baby turtled on its back, pudgy limbs reaching up to some god.

This charnel panorama filled my memory card quick. I switched from RAW to JPEG and deleted some duplicates. A soldier waved me over to the altar, his face a study in emphatic indifference. The soldier nodded down, encouraging my eyes to follow the barrel of his rifle. It pointed to a lump that lay away and apart from most of the carnage: a lonely hand, clutching a detonator.

I'd long since learned that movies are mostly shit. Reality usually underwhelms. Real bombs are often dusty clouds of flying metal, not billowing fireballs. The body doesn't dramatically convulse from striking bullets so much as absorb them like half-assed kicks. But this bomber's severed hand was cinematic and wholly manifest, right down to frayed wires and the detonator's cherry-red clit.

It was a concise visual and I wanted it. I turned a plastic bag inside-out and snatched the appendage up, sealing the baggie around the evidence. The sharp-eyed soldier watched as I pocketed the hand. I gave him a nod in appreciation and he went back to staring away. I walked off after patting to check that the hand in my cargo pocket was secure.

Some other guys found the bombers' heads. That was easy work, if slightly ghoulish. A bomber's head corks off after the lateral blast snaps the spine, largely sparing it from disfiguring damage. I took photos of the heads where they lay, close-ups for facial analysis, and grabbed the biometric capture kit—with an annoyingly broken fingerprint screen—to record retinal signatures. For the lab at Main I swabbed some DNA-bearing goop from the jangle of ligaments and veins that had been a neck.

I wasn't bullish on getting hits in the retinal, facial, or DNA databases. The classic fingerprint is still the most reliable biometric, and for that we needed more fingers. These fingers were probably on hands, hands which were likely connected to arms, but not always. Sometimes a hand is just a hand, like the death-vise paw in my pocket. All told, we had three bombers' heads but only one hand, which meant someone had to find the five others sprinkled amongst civilian bits.

Our job was about done when more local soldiers arrived with body bags. The task of scraping up the dead fell to these poor guys, who'd then hand off the jumble to the local morgue techs charged with sorting commingled limbs. We left that macabre muddle and returned to base. The hand in my pocket wasn't particularly heavy, but as anyone who has carried dead weight knows, it's surprising. The hand bounced with every step I took from the truck to the plywood shack, tugging at my side like a toddler denied attention.

The office was empty; the dorm fridge in the corner wasn't. I was exhausted and didn't feel like running the fingerprints so I threw out three pudding cups to make room. I Sharpie'd a blunt DO NOT EAT on the bag and tucked the hand into the corner.

No one ate it before the next day when I ran the prints. The search turned up nothing, ditto facial recognition and retinal queries. I needed more exploitable info, additional data that might bring some clarity. Fingerprints on the last five hands were the last hope to salvage a postmortem *who* which might give us a *why*. The dead were dead but I was alive and had a job. And I was curious. Those hands had pulled triggers, slit throats, and depressed detonators in final obedience. Why? Why didn't they save themselves?

No choice but to wait until the morgue got things sorted. The DO NOT EAT hand had outlived its dead usefulness but I didn't really know how to get rid of it. Out of an abundance of apathy I pocketed the hand and walked to where I could throw it over the wall behind the motor pool, where none would see and fewer would care.

I stared over the concrete barrier with its concertina strands bundled along the top. There was a light breeze that morning and shredded shopping bags fluttered between the coils. I held the hand. It was fridge-cold and clammy and I wanted to be rid of it. Settling into a pitcher's stance, I wound up to arc it clean over, but as I went to release my own hand tensed in sudden spasm. Its trajectory skewed, the bomber's dead weight sailed low and into the wire, stabbing-still in the razor tangle.

The birds found it quick but made slow work. A couple times a day I'd sneak out back for a smoke and to watch the hand get picked clean. It had caught upright, its palm waving toward the base. With each passing day it seemed to wave less—the pecks were taking their toll. By midweek only bones and gristle were left. I didn't see when the table scraps lost their purchase and tumbled over the wall. It was just gone.

—⁓—

The morgue called a week later after they'd put our humpty-dumpty-jihadis back together again. They apologized for the delay, explaining that the city was undergoing a sectarian cleanse and most days they had a line of bodies out of the door. I didn't get why they felt the need to explain until we drove over.

If a few hours of cooling power had retarded a week's worth of decomp I sure couldn't tell—the fetid stench was totalizing. My bile did a jig but I kept it together in that back room. I'd learned that the secret was to forget there was a smell, to let go of it all. If you didn't try to ignore it, if you zen'd-the-fuck-out and just fell away from the enveloping rot, you could outstep the realization that your every breath sucked in bits of mass murderer. Exhale used-up you, inhale putrefied killer.

On a dirty blue tarp they'd laid out the bombers in anatomical array. The two morgue techs stood back with arms folded, talking to one another and watching us, confident their work would pass muster. The younger one would occasionally laugh at something the other guy said. I imagined they made jokes like, "The fastest way to an terrorist's heart is through the rib cage," but probably they just mocked our knock-kneed soldier as he puked in the corner.

I took a few situating pictures then got down to business. I nicknamed the bodies alpha, bravo, and charlie and noted whether a hand was R or L before numbering the fingers, pinkie (1) through thumb (5). AL1—alpha corpse, left hand, pinkie finger. BR5—bravo corpse, right hand, thumb. And so on. After I'd labeled the back of each digit I fetched a plastic baggie from my pocket and a pair of tin snips from my pack. It would have been easier if we'd repaired the portable biometric kit, but the workaround was simple enough. I was just happy to have a complete set of limited-edition terrorist hands, complete with my own Sharpie'd certificates of authenticity.

Focusing on the fingers, I caught a cutting rhythm. I was almost done when my eyes wandered into an empty chest cavity and found a dazzling range of hues. The expected crimson, dull salmon, and shades of gray familiar to any butcher were all there, but from ruptured organs an assortment of colorful secrets tumbled out like piñata sweets. Pearly rivulets of Meyer lemon fat dripped down from a rib, sprinkled with bits of kale-smoothie-green bile. Blue raspberry arteries, long since drained, dangled from muscles the color of candy hearts. Rearranged and sugar-glazed, it'd probably pass for a fruit tart in a baker's window.

Skittles. Taste the rainbow.

Bile stirred. I turned back to the task at hand. A few fingers more and I was done, almost filling the bag. As I got up to go, I double-wrapped the evidence and gave a smile to the morgue techs. The older one held out a finger to pause my leaving, and shared a conspiratorial nod with his partner.

They then grabbed a double-armed torso and held it between them, swaying the rib-cage-on-up back and forth like a grotesque revue. The older one hummed out *da-dum-da* on repeat as he kicked-out one of his pointed legs, then the other. I laughed, the morgue techs laughed, and the soldier in the corner puked afresh.

I uploaded the prints back at base. It took me an hour in the plywood shack with a USB scanner and more detached digits to learn we had nothing, no matches. I laughed. It had been a complete waste of time. I'd refrigerated a hand and snipped off twenty fingers and five thumbs and spent hours steaming in miasmic rot for nothing. The laughing came on stronger, manic peals that left me bent over in pain.

Gasping for air, I stumbled outside and fell into the wall, sliding down until I sat on the ground with my back against the building. I dialed it back to an anxious giggle and scrounged for a cigarette. Every movement my hands made was clumsy and arthritic: a spasm here, a jerking clench there. Getting the cigarette to my lips wasn't bad, but lighting it took a dozen tries.

I dropped the lighter as soon as I saw flame, worried I might burn my face. One hand would tremble, then the other, then both, then stillness before another spasm. I gave up trying and let my hands fall to the side as I burned to the cherry. The nicotine helped; I felt some control return. The shakes seemed to go away. I crushed the butt in the gravel and walked back inside.

I put the fingers and thumbs back in their bag, put that bag inside another, and added a third before it went in the trash. Dinner was good that night.

—⁂—

I have a girlfriend now. She's smart enough not to ask much, to listen when I need to talk, and to shut me up when I don't. I told her about most things—about the war, my family, me—in the weeks after I said "I love you." The honesty seems good for us.

The night at the church was over a year ago. The dead are buried, the fingers long gone, but I haven't told her about it. It's not that I don't want to, or that I don't think she'll understand. I just can't lie. Not to her. If I start to tell her about the church I have to tell her about the morgue, and if I'm talking about the morgue I have to tell her about the bodies, about how soft the skin looked. I'd have to tell her how delicate it felt, the flaps and strips of epidermal evulsion, about how the skin, pulled tight, had the taut strength of a canvas tent, but was little more than shredded silk when loosed.

I would have to tell her that all bodies are the same. I would have to tell her that the chubby corpse slumped over a pew, the terrorist bits rotting on a blue tarp, and the naked girl in my bed are no different. Whether frozen in the rictus of death or gasping in ecstasy, a body is a body is a body. When she lays beside me I'm back at the morgue, piecing together what-ifs. Hers are comforting curves that remind me what flesh has to offer: thighs for my palm to follow, hair to be bunched and tugged, hands to hold and knead and trust.

My finger traces lazy circles around her navel, with every touch and tickle confirming that her body is complete, her skin without tear. I try to forget but I know too much, know what lies beneath.

Remembering that subcutaneous surprise, my pulse races in charnel anticipation. It begins this way, now. Soon my nails will be digging in, riding the fine line between rough and hurt. She'll hiss when my scratch becomes a cut, shake her head, *No!* when my fingers are too tight around her throat. My hands will obey because they know it's not the time.

I have a girlfriend now. We know the rainbow she's hiding inside.

WE PUT A MAN IN A TREE

by Matthew J. Hefti

W e are all ghosts.

We all vie for attention in different ways, but one thing is common among us: we cannot speak unless we ask questions.

Nadir is seven. She wears a white nightgown with a darkened red tummy. Elegant, like the flag of Japan.

Ray is eighty-two. Three grey hairs are combed over his splotchy forehead. He never stops smiling with gritted teeth. No one came and saw him in the home.

We all carry scars. We all have burdens. We are all bitter and unforgiving.

I, for my part, am heavy laden. I'm the one stuck in this kit, in this thirty-seven pounds of body armor, ammunition, and pogey bait. My eye pro is cocked halfway on my face, shards still stuck in what's left of my bad eye. My helmet strap is still cinched too tight. But the worst part is this: I can never close my good eye.

We are all seen in the light of our last moment. We swallow families, and we eat lives, and we crush dreams, and we eat the fire that lived in the stomachs of our youth; because for those things to live, we need answers. But not one of us has the answers. We have only the questions.

JJ, our protagonist, was a war veteran. He got out after a relatively long and regular career in the infantry. Four tours, two each to Iraq and Afghanistan, each relatively undistinguished, despite what his medal citations say.

We have always existed for him. That's part of what's so sad.

—⁂—

Tonight we chase him. When he has nowhere else to go, JJ stands at the foot of a tree at the end of the forest sniveling and whimpering, "What have I done?"

Blood covers his blue and white striped button up. The backs of his hands are covered in slick, cold blood. His right elbow is particularly bloody. By the time he is three branches up, his finger pads are as chewed and bloody as his knuckles.

Spatters of glistening red reflect the shimmer of the moon in his greying beard. We mock him. We call out, "Did you think it could be that easy?" and "Did you think we were gone for good?"

—⁂—

Earlier tonight, he sat at the Wichita Brewing Company at a high table near the bar with some guys from his new church. The chairman of the board of elders, a nice enough guy, cracked a lewd joke. He said, "Bet you heard a lot of that in the army."

JJ smiled and sipped his beer. He was often uncomfortable around people he didn't know well, and since leaving the service, he was plagued by doubts that he'd ever know anyone well again. The new terrain was unrecognizable. His girls had left. One in college. One watching kids at a home for the disadvantaged. Another an attorney who cut him off with a restraining order. His wife began pursuing her career for the first time in fifteen years. Dental hygienistry. JJ had just moved for the sixth time since getting out. He had been following his girls and wife around, trying to patch things up. Roots were impossible.

He left the men at the table to go to what he now thought of as the pisser, what he once knew as the latrine. We pestered him as he washed his hands. It was Grandpa Ray who asked the questions, always with that loony smile on his face. "How long can you keep faking this?"

and "What are you doing with your life?" and "Do you even like these people?"

JJ wiped paper towel over his beard. "Good Lord," he said. "It's like I'm having an identity crisis every time I look in the mirror."

—⁂—

It's always easier for us when he's alone.

Take, for example, how he treated those kids of his when he was younger. He'd walk up those creaking stairs from his basement study, lay eyes on those girls cuddled on the couch under the same blanket— nothing but blond hair and blue eyes peering back at him, giggles muffled underneath the fabric. While the two youngest were mimeographs of their mother, the oldest was a mirror: eyebrows, nose, teeth, questions, cynicism, and not a small bit of despair. And she was only eight at the time. We knew she'd be the first to cut him off.

He would drop to his knees in front of them and stare, tears welling in his eyes. He would say things like, "You itty bitties. You three little old biddies will love each other, want to kill each other, grow old together, and drive your husbands batty together. And I won't get to see any of it."

Yet it was as if, for those moments, he was living in the future. The problem was, of course, we didn't know if he liked how that future looked or not. We doubted ourselves back then, but in retrospect, it seems as if he knew all along that we'd win. It was almost as if he welcomed it.

Even after he got out, he was fine for a while. He had his own schedule. He did whatever he wanted, and what he wanted to do was what he did for a living back then. A little writing, a little editing, some extra schooling. He still had those three teenage itty bitties, of course, who still kissed him on his now thickly bearded cheek in front of their friends. He had that lithe and driven wife, who would still take showers with him, purposefully rub her nipples against his arm, and laugh when he reached down to touch her. The two would have a few drinks and smoke a little weed on the weekends, and they never laughed so much together.

But, of course, we saw him all the time. We saw him when he took showers alone. We saw him when he took six hours to do something that should have taken two. We saw him sit in his car for ten minutes in every parking lot before he'd take three deep breaths and plunge into the store like it was the cold ocean. It was evident to anyone who looked closely that his seams were quaking.

We didn't understand him, but then again, we have all lost our capacity to empathize. We decided to wait and watch. Surely, we thought, he will at some point have his legs hacked out from under him. It happens to everyone.

The wait has been long. We didn't mind until now. After all, a quick bloody battle is better than no battle, but a slow bloody battle is best.

But now, we have grown too hungry.

Without answers, we all have someone for whom we want to be a long and enduring portrait of guilt.

—⁂—

When he left the bathroom, X stopped him. X was a kid at his new church, maybe twenty-one years old.

X is what he called himself with no hint of irony. It was a name that fit his face and the sparse goatee he liked to stroke. The free black hair on his head that tumbled to his shoulders.

X was drunk, and he patted JJ's chest. It took JJ a moment to recognize the belligerent youth, but when he did, he invited him to the table.

"After I empty the snake," said X, pointing to the pisser.

Later, he swaggered up. Although uncouth, he was chummy. He said hello to everyone, shook everyone's hands, got some more names wrong, but then he said them aloud so as not to forget in the future.

The rest of the men left because it was awkward on account of how X was so wasted. They patted on their bellies, and they said things like, "Moderation in all things."

We all hissed. How dreadfully boring of them.

When only JJ and X remained, the kid spilled his guts. He told JJ how much he admired him, his unassuming manner, his ability to command respect, and then he started apologizing.

He said, "I just can't shake it. I feel so guilty all the time."

"First of all," JJ said. "I'm nothing to look up to. I'm nothing more than a drifter who can't command the respect of his own family."

"Yeah, but people are scared of you, dude."

"Scared? I stock shelves at a Home Depot. What's there to be scared of?" JJ frowned, as if this was a revelation.

"Like, I feel guilty now because I was drunk in front of all those church people, and I'm drunk in front of you. And you're probably all like, 'Yeah, this drunk kid is weird. Really weird.' Right? But I ask you this, Mr. J—can I call you Mr. J?"

"Call me JJ, please."

"How about Sergeant J? I should do that. Thank you for your service. Let me buy you a beer."

"That's not really necessary."

He ordered two beers.

"Sergeant J—JJ, I'm sorry. I'm really sorry to be wasted in front of you. It's like, I know I have to be better, but I'm so bored. And I know, I'm weird."

"Stop apologizing to me," JJ said, growing a bit exasperated, even annoyed. "And how are you weird? You seem like every other twenty-one-year-old kid I've ever known."

"Twenty-two," X said. "And I don't feel I can tell you." He looked down into his beer for a long time. "But then again," he said. "I feel you'd understand. The thing is, I still have my V-card. That's why I'm weird. I'm twenty-two and still have my V-card."

Over and over the kid apologized, and JJ said, "Stop it. That's great. I stand in awe of you. You really don't have to apologize. I've been there."

We jumped in, of course, and asked, "How is he not weird?" and "How can you really say you've been there?" and "What exactly was he insinuating when he said you'd understand?" and "Did he really just say that to you?"

The next thing JJ said was, "But like, you've at least gotten a blow job, right?"

"Oh yeah," the kid said. "Yeah, of course. I've done stuff. And it's not like I haven't had the opportunity to do more. Trust me, I have. I've had lots of opportunities. But I'm dealing with a lot of guilt here."

"Sure, I get that. You should be proud of your discipline." JJ said this last line with a raised eyebrow, as if he didn't believe it himself.

X said, "It's like, all I'm trying to figure out is how to have fun, be a good guy, and not be wasted all the time."

JJ cracked a smile. "Dude. I've spent the better part of two decades trying to figure that out. Trust me; I don't judge."

"You might not judge, but you also won't help." The kid put his head down on the table. "Oh, what am I doing?" he moaned.

"Let me give you a ride home."

We could all tell by the way he said it that JJ didn't really want the kid to accept the offer. Pro forma is what that was.

"Yeah. That's a good idea," X said into his arm.

JJ sighed. "Up and at 'em. Let's go." He left enough cash on the table for both of them.

"I was supposed to go home with a buddy." X stumbled over to a table near the wood burning oven, and he bent over to talk to a pale kid with sharp features and red hair.

We call him Ginger.

JJ went over to the bartender as he waited. Without equivocation, the bartender said, "They are not okay to drive."

JJ walked over and told X that he'd give rides to both of them. "You hear that, Ginger? I'm sober. I'll give you both a ride."

The kid nodded. "Sure, pops."

In the parking lot, JJ pointed toward his own beat up minivan, in which he had been sleeping more nights than he would have liked. Ginger kept walking.

"Hey, what are you doing?" JJ shouted. "You can't drive. Let me help you."

By then, Ginger was in the driver's seat of his Pontiac Firebird. X was trying to get to the passenger door, and he almost made it. He got the door open, but Ginger squealed back, not bothering to stop for X, who tumbled to the ground.

JJ ran up. "Are you hurt?" He pulled out his phone. "Did you get his license plate? What kind of car was it? At least give me that."

X was hurt, but not badly. "I don't know, man. I can't tell any of those white trash cars apart."

We asked JJ, "Are you sure you really want to call the cops?" and "Aren't you secretly glad he doesn't know what kind of car it was?" and "Isn't it enough that you tried?"

JJ slipped his phone back into his pocket. He put his hand on the back of X's neck, a fraternal gesture. "You're coming with me."

X gave him directions to the place, which was all the way on the other side of town. "I'm sorry it's so far," X said.

"It's okay, bud. I really don't mind."

For the whole drive, the kid talked about joining the military. "I think I want to go spec ops. I can almost pass the swimming test. What do you think?"

"What do I think about what?"

"I dunno. Anything. What do you think about what I'm doing with my life? I mean, I'm like in my twenties. I don't have college, and I don't have a girlfriend. All I have is a job that sucks."

"And a V-card," JJ said.

"I knew I shouldn't have told you." The kid flipped down the visor and looked into the mirror.

"Can I talk you out of all this?"

"So I know I'm not supposed to ask this," X said. "But like, since we're talking about all this—and I really do know I'm not supposed to ask this, so know that I know that—but have you ever killed anyone?"

We don't know why JJ chose to answer the question that time. Maybe he wanted to look cool. We debated it for a while and determined it was the same paternal instinct that had driven him to give the kid a ride home. Perhaps he thought he was imparting wisdom.

"Yes."

"For real?"

"Yes, I've killed someone. Someones."

"Oh shit," the kid said. "Oh, I'm sorry," he said. "I'm really really sorry. I shouldn't be swearing like that in front of the guy from church. Pardon my French."

We don't know if X was listening to him, but JJ began saying stuff like, "You're forgiven," and "Don't be so hard on yourself," and "Please stop apologizing," and "You really don't want to kill anyone. I promise it's not that special."

We don't really know if that's all he said. We weren't really listening either. We knew better.

"But did you like it?" X asked. "Do you miss it?"

We all thought these were very penetrating questions, necessary even. We would have asked them ourselves if we would have thought they would do more harm than good.

"Yes. I liked it. Yes. I miss it."

"So then why'd you leave?"

"Maybe I only like—or liked it in retrospect, because we don't know the good things in our lives until we experience something worse. Then we're reminded of how good we had it then, back then when then was the present and now was the future. Perhaps I didn't like it after all. But I do miss it." JJ lit a cigarette and cracked the window.

"Shit. You smoke? The church guy smokes?"

"It's a difficult thing to sort out. It's more complicated than most people think, this choosing to fight in a war."

"Well, tell me why. Tell me what it's like. Tell me how it feels. Tell me what you do every day, or what you did, anyway. Like, was it fucking significant for you?"

"Yes," we cried out, not as an answer, but as the prelude to a leading question. "Yes, because aren't you anything *but* significant now?" and "Do you affect *anyone* anymore?"

"Was it significant?" JJ asked himself. At this point, with nothing to show for any of his time since he had left the army, and with the news from overseas getting bloodier and more depressing every day, he had no answer. "I don't know," he said truthfully. "At the time I thought it was significant. It still *feels* like it was significant."

"So then why'd you leave? What does anyone want besides that?"

"Because I don't *think* it was significant. I guess I just felt something that was something like disillusionment. And back then, it wouldn't have mattered what anyone said. I could not be talked out of leaving."

"Kind of like for me now?" X said as he flipped the visor back up.

"Yeah, I guess," JJ whispered. He put his cigarette out in an empty pop can.

He pulled over across the street from where X was staying.

"Now, I want you to call me anytime," JJ said. "If you need a ride, if you need to get bailed out, if you need anything at all, give me a shout."

"Yeah, yeah, yeah."

"Don't yeah, yeah, yeah me. Just do it. Now, everyone needs help sometimes, and I'm reaching out to help. Don't be so dismissive."

For the first time that night we could see a darker side showing through. For the first time in a long time, we saw a commanding presence that was not in line with this passive middle-aged vet we had been following around, this shelf stocker, this loner, this sad sad man.

Then Ginger, who had run over X not twenty minutes before—pulled up and rolled one wheel onto the lawn across the street. A girl—we presumed it was his girlfriend, although she was a bit young to be riding in cars with men—stumbled out of the car and onto the dewy grass.

JJ turned to X. "You're staying at this kid's place? You kidding me?" He started across the street at an angle. As he headed straight for the Pontiac, we followed with questions. "Don't you think you should stand up straighter?" and "Don't you think you should pin back your shoulder blades?" and "Did you ever think of clenching your fists in a time like this?"

JJ opened the driver's side door, but he let Ginger pour out of the low-riding seat on his own. JJ picked up his wobbling form from the street. He got in his face, and he told him to never do that again.

"Whatever, old man."

JJ grit his teeth and growled, "You better never pull some shit like that again, especially when you have a sober person ready to drive."

"What sober person? You?" The kid laughed. "Bitch, please. You're as fucked up as anyone."

The kid's profanity sounded like a scared affectation. JJ poked Ginger in the chest. "I was ready to drive. I told you I could drive."

"And who the fuck says I have to listen to you?"

"I was sober," JJ said. "Sober as a judge." He poked again.

We whispered in his ear, "Doesn't 'sober as a judge' imply that you have the power to sentence and execute?" and "How does he plead?"

"Are you sorry?" JJ asked.

"Whatever."

"Are you sorry?"

The kid stumbled back two steps after getting thumped in the chest again.

"Isn't he soft?" we asked. "Isn't he just a soft, dumb kid?" and "Don't you think you should teach him?" and "Who better to teach him than someone who knows how it feels?"

"Don't you know that you could have killed someone?" JJ asked Ginger, who put his hands up in protest. "Why are your hands up like that?" JJ bent his neck over so his lips tickled the soft hair on Ginger's ears. "One bad choice, and you could kill someone."

We circled around behind Ginger. "Can you guarantee he gets it, even now?" and "Can you be sure he won't leave here as soon as you do and add another ghost to our company?"

"You are soft, aren't you?" JJ asked. He hit the kid with a closed fist and knocked him down. "You're going to kill someone if you keep that shit up." He dropped to his knees and straddled the boy.

"Isn't it funny that even his face is soft?" we asked. "Isn't this moment significant?" and "Isn't it seminal?" We all lay on our backs on the ground next to Ginger. We leered up at the bearded man, who seemed to be foaming at the mouth. "Isn't stopping these kids from making the worst decisions of their lives the most significant thing you could do?"

He dropped an elbow into the center of the mush that had been Ginger's face. X puked at the curb. JJ kept hitting the kid. We think his elbow had gone all the way through Ginger's pasty face and was, by this point, smashing against the asphalt. He smashed his own elbow into what looked like the mangled haunch of a butchered beast.

When X finally got around to pulling JJ off, he was still screaming, "Don't you realize that you could have killed someone?"

When he stood, he looked down at his hands. He looked up at X with a look of resignation. "Don't follow me," he said. "Trust me. You do not want to follow me." He ran toward the woods on the far side of the street.

—⁓—

Tonight we give chase.

He runs through the trees, twigs whipping at his face and out-stretched arms. He runs into a tall fence line comprised of wide cedar boards. There is nowhere for him to go but up. JJ stands at the base of a tree near the fence. He dry heaves from the exertion. He wails, "What have I done?"

The backs of his hands are covered in blood, and he has a hard time climbing. His right arm feels particularly odd and weak. His elbow, too, seems bloody, and there is a clinging mass of tissue there that won't drop away, though he shakes it repeatedly, trying for just that thing.

We throw rocks at him. We pepper him with questions and granite. Salt him with queries and quartz. Then we discuss how to bring him down. "Should we throw you a ladder?" we call.

He shakes his head.

"Do you want to come down here so we can talk?" and "Didn't that feel awesome back there?"

He shakes his head again.

"Do you want us to take care of this?"

"I need to take care of this," he whispers to himself. "I have to figure this out."

"What if we throw you a rope?" and "Would you come down then?"

He doesn't shake his head no, but he doesn't say yes either.

"Don't you want to come down?" we call as we pick up more rocks to cause more damage, to make everything harder, to make him appreciate us and what we have to offer. We throw him a rope. Its fibers catch in the crotch of two narrow branches.

He takes his time, not moving for it immediately. We once again debate our tactics. We whisper among ourselves. "Do you want us to try again?" we shout. "Or do you want us to just leave it there?"

He stares off into the distance.

"Do we need to hit you right in the face with it?" and "Won't you come down from that tree?" and "Isn't it lonely up there?"

"One more day," he says. "All I have to do is keep waiting it out."

He seems as if he is about to drift to sleep. He has learned how to grow comfortable almost anywhere, and we fear he may rest.

As his head begins to nod, little Nadir gets an impish look on her face, filled with the kind of cruelty only little children can muster. Just when it seems he will get a moment to contemplate his dreams, she throws one last rock. It hits him in the ear.

"Don't you know you can't hold on forever?"

At this, we stop. That is the question with which we wish to leave him.

We watch him apprise us, contemplate us. He looks into my open eye. He pulls the rope. We hold our breath as he works a clove hitch around the branch above his head. He pulls down, as if to test its ability to hold him. Again, we panic as he begins to take his first wobbly step off the branch, as he wraps his foot in the slack to hold himself as he climbs down.

This is not what we had in mind.

We pick up more stones. Jagged, heavy rocks of all shapes and sizes and capacities for inflicting suffering. We throw them with all our might. He weathers only the first few. When he can feel the coppery taste of his old familiar wounds seeping into his mouth, when we make ourselves larger and louder than we've ever been before, when the blood covers his eyes; that is, when he has lost his sight completely, he scampers back onto the branch. He wipes his eyes with a futility we recognize.

He still cannot see. He reaches out like a drunk, sightless and waving for the rope. He whimpers in agony. We all hold our breath, giddy, as a crumpled shadow of hopelessness flickers so fast you wouldn't have seen it if you didn't know to look for it. We marvel as this fleeting glimpse of despair soon melts into placidity, contentedness, and then finally something that looks like a gruesome facsimile of joy.

This moment is where we live. This moment is where we follow, eat, and destroy. This is the moment where we feed ourselves, we ghosts. And these acts of the will—

He draws all the hanging line to his chest. With a burst of industriousness, he tosses the end over the clove hitch on the branch above his head. He catches it, repeats, until it is snaked around the branch.

Apparitions, these acts of the will. Apparitions.

He is no longer in a hurry as he forms it into the shape of a snake slithering through the empty desert that is his life. He sighs as he squeezes a bite into the snake with his broken fist. The snake has soon coiled itself around its own body, and all that's left is a loop of a tail and a small frayed end. There is not much left for him to hold onto. The frayed end goes into the loop, and it is here that he seems to give pause.

For if that final rock was the stimulus, if any one of the thousands of rocks in any one life is the stimulus, we always have that moment after to work, to prod, to ask.

The only questions left, however, are the ones no one else is around to ask. We salivate, anticipating the moment when he lets himself down from the tree to be devoured in the light of his last moment.

But we ask no more questions. We watch him work his raw fingers as one loop pulls the other tight. The moment is so close we can taste it, but we are tense, not wanting to break the spell. We have been there before and we have learned our lessons. This slipknot could slip either way.

In that moment in which he gives pause, he has a whole repository of memories and human connections to help him determine his next move. And who knows what that bank may hold? He has a frozen moment of inaction in which all the possibilities in all of time and space present themselves for inspection, a whole lifetime of questions to contemplate.

Why don't you choose another way down? Why don't you choose to smile? Why don't you choose to go down to the bus stop and catch a ride home? Why don't you choose to talk to someone on that bus? Why don't you extend an invitation? Or better yet, why don't you ask her story? Why don't you learn? Why don't you choose to value the lives you touch, the people you know, and the people you're sure to meet? Why don't you choose to give of yourself? Why don't you think of the good you could do rather than the bad you've already done? Why don't you choose to be goofy, sing as you walk down the street, or say hi to everyone you see? Why don't you call your daughters? Why don't you go for a midnight stroll at the park? Why don't you choose to skip rocks on the river, swing fast and swing high, and think about how someday your arms won't be empty anymore? Why don't you choose to think of your grandkids, who one day will cling to your giant hands on the same swing and say, "Bigger," just as your daughters once did. Bigger? Bigger? Bigger? Again? Why don't you choose to climb the monkey bars and yell "Wheeeee!" as you ride down the slide? Why don't you choose to read what you want to read, work where you want to work, and be who you want to be? Why don't you think of grace? Why don't you realize that to be is to choose the present, and why don't you choose to be? Why don't you choose to release your guilt, that is, your past? Why don't you choose to change your escape route—that is, your future? Why don't you choose to fix your eyes on what's happening now? To just be? Why don't you choose to just exist? If not for you, then for us?

Why don't you choose to make love the verb of the year?

But, of course, we would never ask those questions. It is not in our nature.

INTO THE LAND OF DOGS

by Benjamin Busch

He escaped the day they brought him to the recovery ward. He sidled down a hall and out a door. No one thought to ask where he was going. The floor was crowded with men cocooned in bandages or studying the space where their legs should have been, waiting for them to reappear. He saw faces change under "Welcome Home" signs, a kind of metamorphosis. Parents, lovers, and children passed by trying not to look at what they saw, trying to wash their way through all the damage to a time before it happened. They wanted everything back and he could see them furrowed with wishes, eyes wet. He didn't want to be introduced to anyone. Didn't ever want to hear his name called or meet one more person who wasn't from a helicopter.

Outside, the warm night surrounded him with ingratitude, quiet families calling in their cats. He slid through them in the dark, forgetting what neighborhoods were like when you lived in them, everyone inside, lights glowing through curtains. Torch lit F-16s and prop grinding C-130s lifted and landed on runways a few miles away at Lackland, practicing for war or returning with wounded. Texas was like the flat provinces of Afghanistan, its routes laid through dust like Highway 1 between Kandahar and Kabul. Similar enough that he may have never left. How would he know? San Antonio before he deployed or after or in between. They said he was home, but no one had proved it. They said his pilot's head was missing. They said the other pilot was executed. They said he was there. Then they stopped asking him questions and put him on a plane where he slept until they told him to get out.

He stayed clear of sprawl, but some passages were webbed by suburbs, and he had to move the way the deer and coyotes did, using drainage ditches, parks, and patches of vacancies to cut through mankind. He kept moving. He could hear traffic sometimes, music playing and people talking, a city or town bedding down to sleep as he walked the shore of a river. Engines and water made the sound of static, like radio transmissions. He hadn't been that close to a city in years. He crept further into the wastelands. He sometimes had visions of people in the heat, circling like he was, entire families or patrols. He wasn't sure, when he saw them, if they were real, their liquid bodies boiling out of the ground. That must be how he would appear to anyone else, an imaginary man flickering like a thin black flame. It might be all he was. Others had tried to get away. He found piles of bones left where they had burned off.

—⁂—

He still carried his evasion chart, but it was inaccurate, an ancient draft. He was sorry he hadn't been navigating. Sorry he hadn't paid attention in the brief. They had just become routine sorties, these routes, nine years of random flights arcing over a filthy land of snakes, dirt, and dogs. Standing in an angry edge of Afghanistan, he had no point of reference. Even looking up at the sun seemed useless. They'd been flying for hours, the day late, banking to cross back. No sightings and half their fuel left. It burned on the ground, tanks ripped open, rotors gouging a ditch, throwing off pieces that spun away like ax blades.

He'd been lucky. The survivor. His mother had begun calling him that before he deployed. "They'll say you survived me," she would say from her bed. The war was his way to flee from her terminal care. That was long ago. It might have been long ago. His piled days were unnumbered, places blending, sinking or adrift on a vast mirage between earth and atmosphere. He felt small and slow, moving in limped steps. He thought he was on the border of their battlespace, near its invisible line, walking west toward the center of nothing owned by Marines or Special Forces and by neither. He would have to find an outpost, maybe in a day or two if he could make it that long. He wanted to wait for dark and run under cover of night, but he had to get away from the wreck immediately. It seemed counterintuitive. A rescue would be sent after they failed to report in. His last known location was the crash site, but every Afghan with a rifle in the valley would be heading toward it now, trying to get there before the Sparrow Hawk mission, descending quickly from the ridges to make videos, rip out the radios, and strip the dead. Whoever fired the rocket would be watching him with Soviet or American binoculars. He had to move predictably until night, then change course. His wounds could be dressed later, the blood already drying. He wasn't even sure how much of it was his. All blood looks the same. This was the easy side of tragedy and he walked, stunned, away from the falling sun as if the day was like any other.

The dark came first as mountain shadow, then as night. Dogs barked, the terrain porous with dens and he wondered if they had any fear of men here in the unmarked wild. They followed him as an expanding multitude, the sound of their panting amplified in his mind. A pickup loaded with militia arrived at sunset and swept the valley in bobs and jerks with its single working headlight. The boulders and scree kept it handicapped and he stayed low, turning north away from the echo of engine into the wide dry plain.

—∞—

He couldn't recall his medevac from Kandahar to the hospital. It reminded him of where his mother had been, the same, how he'd left her there and never returned. He was drawing a map on his evasion chart, the only thing he'd kept from the crash, overlaying his present on his past, then confusing one for the other. He marked his route, corrected topography, added missing cities, covered provinces with the roads of states, his homeland the same as enemy territory. There was only Afghanistan now, everywhere else drawn into it. The scale was 1:200,000, far too small to depict a single standing man. He was invisible on maps of land, like birds. On cloudy nights he could see the orange glow of villages lit up with business or burning, people shopping and soldiers kicking open doors, new tribes forming in suburban neighborhoods, armies hungry and having less and less to defend, fewer homes to go home to. More world abandoned. He stayed outdoors, the open safer than rooms, his civilization destroyed the moment he fell to earth.

He found skeletons and empty houses in the roadless wilds. Mining, logging, and railroad towns emptied as if by evacuation. Some were like lost temples with chambers of votive objects and myth, all the priests gone. These religions were small, the labor of a single family or an elder. Pioneers and fugitives. It was their hope to never be missing from anywhere, to avoid capture or rescue, to never be found. He began to believe as they had.

Inside a house built into the ground, the sacred was revealed to him. Its interior was lit by squinting windows cut into the walls near the ceiling. The floor was a grid of curling linoleum squares the color of moss and he stepped in their centers to keep them from shattering. It was labyrinthian, more hallway than living space, finally opening into a large room in back. No furniture, utensils, clothing, or trash. He stood astonished. The walls were covered with puzzles that had been completed and glued together, farms and wilderness, glaciers, deserts, forests, and prairies, hundreds of them, floor to ceiling, small as napkins or large as tabletops, fit together like blocks of cut stone. It gave him vertigo, a sense of spinning, rising and falling with the staggered horizon lines. He ran his hand along the glossy images, the smooth pieces like snakeskin or fish scales. Water had found its way through the roof in a corner and the puzzles had peeled away in its path, the fields and alps unzipped, a dark fissure ripped in the world. He picked a piece that dangled, a corner of it mountain, the rest sky. If he kept it, this portrait of the earth would be forever incomplete, the hundred thousand shards assembled in vain, missing the one. It was an effort of such concentration, one landscape at a time, someone sitting for all these hours searching piles to restore order, recreate views cut apart, the windows too high on the walls to see anything but night or day outside. It was an evasion chart from ground level, the open land free of cities, bombs, and soldiers, barns and cottages closed, pastures empty, no contrails or fires, the leaves on trees perfectly still. He wanted, for a moment, to burn it, to sit in the center and watch it all go blank, the jigsaw seams charred and cracking apart. But he turned, slipped the piece of puzzle into his backpack, and crept out, his toes carefully finding the middle of each tile again.

—⁓—

The helo didn't fall all at once. It shuddered and dropped, his ammunition belt rippling weightless for a moment as he floated in the fuselage, heat billowing from the cockpit, one pilot blown apart and the other on fire. He could hear both of their voices in his helmet though he was sure that one of them was already dead. He clawed the walls, his gloves slick with hydraulic fluid, the bay packed gray with smoke and by the time he caught some netting, the bird had leveled, a lieutenant's hand on the stick, driving it down as he burned.

—⁓—

He lay with the insects in the shade of a rock and watched the road and building for hours. There were stores like it every thirty miles, empty since the uranium mines closed a decade before. They used depleted uranium in ammunition. Dead metal. His focus shifted from the wide horizon to the sandy soil inches from his eyes, ants suddenly incredible in size. When the sun got overhead he stood up and approached from the rear. He hoped for the usual finds: matches or lighters, toilet paper, canned goods, bottles of anything. The deserted roadside shops often left plenty behind, just locked the doors and drove south with the last of the miners and trucks, carrying off little more than the alcohol and cigarettes.

The door in back had been pried open and he curled around the tossed refrigerators to get inside. He felt something like excitement, an archeologist's thrill in entering a tomb. He let his guard down. The floor was bare wood, a dirty oval of footsteps worn around the shelves in the center of the room. Old tins of tuna fish were stacked on a shelf marked "cat food" above swollen cans of clam chowder. Desiccated fruits and vegetables shrank dark and hard in bins by the door. He walked as if he were looking at relics in a museum, trying to see them as ordinary. No bottled water or soda. He made his way to the counter still looking back at the shelves, turned, and a boy stood up.

The youth was malnourished, lank, with angry eyes and a mouthful of something he wasn't chewing. He was dark tan, the edges of his ears scabbed from sunburns. His hair was blonde, likely Pashtun or from seed left by Greek, British, or Soviet armies, a desert child from anywhere. A fly smacked against the window. He looked past the boy at the cracked pouches of condoms, mousetraps, and corroded batteries. There was a faded photograph of a man, shirtless and thin, leaning on a truck holding a baby with one arm and a rifle with the other. Far behind them, a woman was digging with a shovel.

"Salaam!"

It was strange to hear his own voice and he expected to wake up. The boy rolled his eyes to the window, then turned his head, spat a stone the size of a small chicken egg into his hand, and made a sound as if it were still in his mouth. There was too much story here. He suddenly felt light, his senses returning. He noticed the boy's pockets bulged. A looter. He watched the boy's hands. He could hear an old truck in the distance. It had lost its muffler and was running rough, chugging and growling down the road. The boy's eyes stayed hard. He put the rock back in his mouth and gurgled a word that sounded like "run."

The space behind the store was all bad real estate. No cover and long bare miles to dull wax-sloped hills. The grass was wiry, low, and dry. He was already running hard when he heard the engine cut off, his pack swinging like an infant latched to his shoulders and his boots chiseling the gravel. He didn't look back, just fell forward, his legs trying to keep up with his panic. He made it about a hundred yards before he slowed to a trudge. He could feel the bones in his legs, heavy, stiff, and grinding at each joint. His pack lurched with a smack and he fell too fast to put his hands out. He thought he'd been pushed down and he grabbed a stone and scrambled to stand only to find himself alone. He heard the second shot. It burst through his right arm and spun him around. A man was standing behind the store reloading.

Blood streamed down his arm and he clutched the hot wound. He was running again, his legs hollow with adrenaline. The sun was high and he leaped as if dodging trees, making it hard for the man to aim. A bullet popped near his head, a brief hole through the air, another skipping on the dust past him like a stone on water. He'd been roaming through this territory as if it were ungoverned frontier, back and forth following the ranges and badlands, eluding all the hard men living thin and policing their claims. Now he understood. They shot foreigners and trespassers, likely shot each other. It was tribal here and they considered everyone to be invaders.

He ran until the store fell behind a hill, then turned and headed west, the sun in his eyes. His pulse thumped in his ears and he could barely hear any other sounds. He stumbled like a drunk, the cobbled ground loose and uneven. His hand stayed clamped to the hole in his arm and the blood had clotted into a paste. His mouth was drying down into his throat but the water jug in his pack had been shot through. Far ahead he saw the glass and metal glint of a junkyard, a crumpled island of old machinery littering a low mesa. He checked the horizon behind him, listened, and then hurried on with the last of his strength, climbing the pile to a van at the top.

—⁂—

As his helicopter struck the ground, its wheels bent and he pitched forward toward the open gun door. The blades chopped at rocks and splintered as the bird tilted, a blast of sawed stone blowing in. It smelled like too many things. Fuels and lubricants, smoke and exhaust, blood and plastic, gunpowder. He'd been sprayed with hydraulic fluid and dust stuck to him. His helmet was still on and through the sound of the engine rattling apart, he heard a voice coughing his name. The cockpit was bright now, its windows facing the sun, and he made his way over the punctured floor strewn with straps and bullets. CWO Stevens on the left was headless and disemboweled, his body opened and absurd. But Lieutenant Conrad was alive, wet with puss, his arms split open to the red muscle. Conrad looked him in the eye. They paused. The pilot nodded *No.* They had joked about being captured, what they would say before executions. Conrad wanted to say, "I will never shop here again." His eyes moved slowly down to the pistol strapped on his gunner's leg, then back up to his eyes, lifted his chin once and coughed into his mic. The words were slurred, his throat boiled, but they had an understanding. The pistol was light, like it was made of wood, everything still buoyant with terror. Conrad looked away, stared out the window at the sun.

—⁂—

The van moved sometimes. He was sure of it. Most of the wrecks shifted at night, the scrape of metal coming from different directions throughout the junkyard, and he thought the van was tilting more than it had been when he moved into it a week ago. It sat on a pile of crushed cars, springy with tires. He preferred being up high. The dogs lived on the ground level and he could hear them scampering around in the dark, chasing rats and dragging death and old garbage back from somewhere. The morning would reveal their work, piles of meager shit that other dogs had found no reason to eat and scratch marks here and there. He didn't see the dogs during the day. They hid in the catacomb of station wagons, smashed buses, and wreckage, but as he explored the expanse of ruin he could hear them snore as if the entire scrapyard was a single den, the rise and fall of piled cars caused by the breathing of thousands of sleeping animals. He also knew he was being watched. Dogs had watched him since the crash. He found a hand scythe in the bed of a truck and carried it with his good arm, picking through the trunks of cars and piles of parts in the early morning and late afternoon light. He stayed in the van when the sun was highest and during the night. He hadn't seen the pickup, but he'd heard it far away a few times.

His arm itched. He remembered that this meant healing rather than infection. A bottle of alcohol had kept it clean, but he was running out. He'd been fired on plenty of times, but he hadn't been hit with a bullet until he ran from the boy. He couldn't make sense of the boy.

A barrel of rainwater kept him alive. He scooped a layer of oil off the top and screened the water through a thick cotton shirt he found in a dump truck. There was no food and he'd been hungry for days. He had to brace for another week of recovery before braving the desert again. He could see it shimmer and lift, a horizon without a surface between him and the mountains. The water was getting low and rusty in the barrel and there were still no signs of rain. He would have to move again sooner than he wanted to, trap some dogs, make a fire, and cook them while the rest watched from the dark spaces in the cars. He worried about making smoke. The dogs thrived. They must have found a spring, maybe old rainwater held cupped in a million dents at the bottom of the piles. He imagined the metal caverns, musty with dog breath, licked clean, all the creatures sick with fuel on their tongues and sustained by rot and cannibalism.

He crouched in the van, the side door wide open, and felt like he was back in the helicopter. It was strange to be at this height but completely still, hovering without the vibration of blades swirling over his head and the sound of the air being cut open. No dust blown away beneath him and no machine gun to lean on. He could see far down the track that tow trucks and cranes had once used to haul the wrecks in and stack them. There was a scar pressed into the roof above him from the magnet but somehow the van had not been crushed. It perched on top of the heap overlooking the alcove where the crane had circled dropping cars in place. He was thinking about bait.

He had a bloody rag from his arm and a pair of socks that stank from two weeks' wear. There was some water. He gathered plenty of fine wire brake cables, a hammer, some tent stakes and crimpers and fashioned a snare. It was the one skill he thought of least value when he took the survival course and had not studied it with any seriousness, focusing instead on maps and how to start fires. His lack of attention cost him almost two days of tinkering, looping, and knotting wire the wrong way. After many elaborate mistakes, he was embarrassed to discover the clean simplicity of a snare's design. In the late afternoon, he climbed down to the surface.

It was like descending into a canyon and the ground was already in shadow when he got to it. He felt exposed there at the end of the long dirt passage, trapped as he pounded stakes and set snares. He made a square of four trip lines and placed a shallow glass headlight of water in the center with his soiled offerings. The alcove darkened as he worked and he began to rush, dropping things and pausing more often to listen, holding his breath. He finished and scrambled back up, cutting himself on a gouged Toyota hood he could have avoided if he had moved with any care at all. Back in the van he could still see the sun low in the sky. It was as if he had found a membrane separating time and that he could hide in daylight while the other world, a mere twenty feet away, was dark with dusk. He dressed the wound on his hand as the sun set.

A sharp bark straightened him. He had fallen asleep and forgotten to close the door. Now it would creak and slam if he pulled it shut. He was in view. He peered out. It was quiet again and he sensed dogs staring up at him in the dark, seeing him weak. The crescent moon was slight, the land black as the sky. His eyes were pulled so wide they hurt. A shrill yelp broke from below, its echo sounding as if it had come from inside the van. A dog began to whine, probably caught in his snare. It became mad with fear, shrieking incessantly, and wild barking spread throughout the junkyard, a land of dogs all drawn to the peril of one. Another wail rose up and he could hear the pant and paws rushing down the track toward him. The violence began in an instant, the ground below muscular with the snarl and savagery of animals tearing each other apart. He slammed the door, locked it and gasped, drowned out by the shriek of dogs being eaten alive.

He thought of his pilots and searched his chart for the spot. An officer had pointed to it after a flight brought him in and they asked short questions from a long list. Some of the questions sounded the same, but the words were rearranged. He was their only survivor. One of the pilots was missing his head. The officer kept asking the questions without frustration, even after he had stopped answering.

—⚌—

Blood was sprayed on the plexiglass, one man decapitated and splayed on his seat. His head lay strapped in its helmet between his own feet, eyes bright. The other pilot was broiled, uniform and skin melting from his arms, one hand still locked to the stick. He shook, his scorched throat coughing words. He was giving instructions.

"Do you know if he shot himself or if he was executed?"

What could he say to anyone? How could he answer, as a witness would, about what it was like to fall all the way down? He had been thinking through the short questions ever since, staring at desert, at streams bleeding through canyons, at treetops swaying in wind, stepping like a hunter through empty houses and brush. He was animal now and what could he tell them about evasion charts except that they were to keep him away from everyone? He had carried the Warrant Officer's head that night, buried it in its helmet under stones somewhere out there, safe from dogs and the Taliban. He didn't tell them that. And he didn't tell them that he shot the other pilot.

He looked at the blood on his uniform. It was almost black on his boots and arms. He wanted to tell the officer that the pilot was calm while he burned, the other ripped open, shreds of him on all the instruments, his intestines spilled over his legs and sucked out of the hole the rocket had made. His body was torn in ways blood couldn't imagine. Everyone was murdered in Afghanistan. No one was buried complete. He wanted to say that the dead pilot was from Maine, somewhere along the coast, and that he could remember him talking about ocean. He wanted to say that the pilot's head spoke to him in the desert as he carried it away and that he could still hear the other man coughing his name.

—∞—

He found belongings left along trails from the south, clothing and water bottles. Refugees running from war and from soldiers like him. He ran the same routes they did. There were bodies too, but he didn't stop to bury them. They hadn't been found, some of them for many years, picked over by vultures, pieces dragged away by dogs. He knew he was in a good area when he found a skeleton. The only safe people to be around were dead and if he found them, he was where no one was looking. He followed the charred slopes south for a while, against the direction the flames had moved. The pattern of ash was called the "burn mosaic." He liked that term. A map of the fire. The graveyard of coal-black stumps went on for miles. They seemed to move at night, tilt and straighten like exhausted guards, an army waiting for dawn to scar the next green-treed ridge with war. It was in the mountains that he found the bones of a man burned by wildfires or napalm. He lay like a god-king surrounded by his possessions in the outline of a tent; pans, knives, batteries, and canned goods rusting in the ash. The man wore dog tags, a veteran who hadn't made it back, died in his sleep like the rest of them, smothered by smoke. But he hadn't been captured. No one but nature had taken him alive. All of this was mean, gritty sleep. Out here on the fringe, you could still escape occupied territory. People could live in caves and shacks, gnawing on wilderness in between the storms, laying low as herders and patrols passed by, their names on no lists, just men and women broken away from expectations, severed from nations, following the pollen and the seed.

He found a house sitting like litter at the base of the ashen valley, saved by solitude. From the hill the home appeared untouched. No outbuildings burned. No doors swung open. A house and some sheds at the end of the line, someone's failed settlement. He had been moving at night and staying on high ground during the day. Not all the way on top of anything since the van. He would find a slope in the darkness, climb to its crest and survey the pitch for any lights or fires, then drop down ten or twenty yards and circle for cover in rocks or shrubs that would conceal him from view in daylight. He was always fascinated by what the land actually looked like lit up, a grand illusion. Moving at night he just imagined it. He had never been to this part of the country on ground level and nothing looked familiar despite years of searching this place from above. Maybe it had been somewhere else. Was it here he'd been flying over? No. Not here exactly. He watched the house all day, his eyes dry with fear of blinking, missing the moment when someone would open a door or pass by a window.

A dog crossed the road in a series of diagonals. It stopped every once in a while, looking, raising its head to taste the air, then padding on. The day was long with staring. He fell asleep, waking near dusk, afraid to move. He lifted his head and a vulture lurched away from him, hissing as if it had been stabbed in the neck. It came at him flapping hard, losing feathers, its long wings sweeping the dirt and beating at the air to push its body up. It leapt forward onto him, its weak spiked feet pressing into his chest with unexpected weight. He grabbed a wing and grappled for a grip on the other, threw the thick bird on its back, and rolled onto it. He punched at it, teeth clenched, the vulture scratching at his stomach with its dull talons and throwing its beak at his eyes. It was all violence, close quarters, and he drew himself up, jerking his knees onto the wings where they met its body, choking the bird with both hands. It took a long time to die, its short neck hard with muscle. Finally, it spat a yellow stew of rotten meat and wheezed, air finding a way through despite the tight grip of his hands. He was yelling at it, in English, demanding that it stop struggling, blurting out questions. It died in a series of convulsions, the tips of its wings shivering.

He heard the last words he said, clearly. "Who sent you?"

He realized his mistake too late. The vulture had wanted anything but to attack him. It had been graceless in its retreat, terrified that its long search for the dead had led to something living, drawn into a trap by a rival posing as prey. It must have hopped down from the large rock near his feet, to wait for him to stop breathing. But to get at the open sky when he awoke, it would have to fly over him, bounding onto his chest to get away.

He lay frozen, horrified, blood pulsing in his eyes and ears, shocked at how easily he had been found and approached while he slept. Hunger was shutting his body down. He had to move to stay awake. He could hear the vulture still hissing in his head, its harsh alarm to the predatory world that something had been found alive. Like his pilot coughing words. He'd been yelling too. He tried to write down what he'd said but it was already difficult to recall. "Who sent you?" He was sick with paranoia, certain that all eyes were on the hill now, whatever eyes there were. Someone would come for him.

—⁓—

He ran from the wreck into the split rock valley, a pack over a shoulder and his other arm cradling a helmet with a head in it. The eyes were still open, staring up, lips parted over the teeth. The shock kept him in a suspended state, running in daylight as if he couldn't be seen toward an end where everything that had happened could be reversed, the head he held restored to a body. He felt hollowed out by acids. Men called out from the heights and his pursuit began. The sun was at his back, his shadow getting long and monstrous as it broke on stones ahead of him, dark pieces of him shedding off and returning to a core.

At dark he stopped. There was a pickup truck adrift in waves of stone, its headlight visible and then gone as it pitched and turned. He felt his vest for the infrared strobe, but it was missing. The rescue wouldn't have any way to tell him from anyone else. They came though. He heard them, a cargo with two escorts flying fast and low over a mountain and then circling the wreck. He could see the door gun flicker, the attack helicopters open up on someone. He was far away, miles, driven by the pickup to keep moving. The birds began to turn in widening circles. He sifted the objects in his bag for a signal. They'd be bingo on fuel soon at this range and have to turn back without finding him. After thirty minutes on station, they did. They would drop troops in the valley the next morning to sweep for his body and the head.

—⁓—

He wanted to approach the house with the last light, but now he felt exposed again and would wait until night. A dead field surrounded the home, sparse pine replaced with fence posts, and he would have to cross in the open. It felt dangerous even in the dark. He stumbled on several barbed strands that had dipped between posts, and the scrapes on his stomach from the vulture kept him bent over. They began to burn and he worried about tetanus. He needed to find some alcohol and proper bandages. He would also need to cook the bird as soon as possible. He carried it by the feet, swung over a shoulder, its wings spread open and head thumping on the back of his leg.

He entered the house at sunrise and she sat facing him. He couldn't tell how long she'd been dead. The air was dry and the window was hot with sun. Her body had hardened, skin tightening around the bones, and she looked alert, her head held up so it didn't rest against the back of the chair. The book she'd been reading was open on her lap, a children's picture book, her right hand on the top corner with a page pinched between her thumb and a finger. *Goodnight Moon.* Americans had donated thousands of books for Afghan children. He remembered the green and red images from his own childhood, but not the exact wording. She'd stopped on: "Goodnight stars," "Goodnight air." He heard his mother's voice. They were colorless pages, the night sky grey and the land a white silhouette, roadless, treeless dunes or snow on hills. He looked around. There was no other evidence of a child. The house was full of stuffed furniture, more chairs and couches than anyone could fill, thick carpet on the floors and everything looked soft, reds and oranges faded by sunlight. Even the walls were covered by something that had the feeling of cloth. It was as if he was inside her body, all its organs dry, sponges waiting for water to swell back into the space. He crept through the room, moving, he realized, as if he were a thief, hunched and making no sound but that of his knees cracking.

He turned a corner and paused at the door to a bedroom. It felt like a milkweed pod had cracked open to reveal a room with white crocheted curtains and a large bed covered with a green knitted blanket. There was a dent on one side of the bed and a doll laid on the other. Three mirrors stood floor to ceiling on each wall away from the window, also framed with curtains, and they made the room appear to branch into narrow downy corridors. He did not enter. Beds made him uneasy. They looked like the last place you went. His reflections in the mirrors were suspicious versions of himself. The hollows of his eyes were deepening with terminal exhaustion. He watched himself as he took a few steps, legs stiffened and jaw clamped. It wasn't clear if he was still favoring his left knee from the crash, still careful on his ankles, or if he had aged. Either way he had the appearance of a man who needed repair.

Back in the living room he stood trying to make sure he was awake. He could have dreamed this, could be dreaming it. The struggle with the vulture had opened the bullet wound on his arm and blood formed drops on his fingers. His path through the house was marked by red spots on the rug. A blood trail was the worst kind to leave. Any tracker could follow that. A dog would. The man in the pickup with his sallow son. He moved again, willing himself past the woman to find a kitchen. He needed water and he had lost enough blood for the room to brighten.

In a cabinet he found a bottle of isopropyl alcohol and a towel that hadn't been chewed or sprinkled with mouse droppings. He dabbed at the bullet wound and vulture scratches, wincing at the sting. How much blood did he have left? He'd been dripping it out since the crash, across the valley, ocean, desert, mountains, and plains. All the way here. He had been writing about blood on his map for years or days. The corner where Nimroz Province began was blackened by it. Blood tries to save everyone. He could feel it trying to put a scab on him, rusting on his arm, armor forming one color thick and cracking in his palm. He had never thought about blood cracking.

How long had it been? He'd lost track. He was only making a few miles a day, slowed by caution, superstition, and fatigue. The rescue bird must have found the helo by now. He expected disappointment. He had come to rely on its constancy, a comfort from the labor of carrying possibilities. He went through the motions anyway, by habit, laying out the evasion chart and marking his way through territory outside Kandahar. He kept hearing the rasp of the truck. It seemed to be keeping its distance. He wasn't sure if it was there, what part of his mind heard it. It kept him from any true rest, afraid of the sound of engines real or otherwise. Men with rifles. Groundlings.

The land got large as he stumbled across it. He imagined that it grew in front of him, and he began to think that he had been walking in circles. The earth was spinning, orbiting the light. The sun moved too. His route was necessarily serpentine, the tilted terrain shrugging him one way or another. He was learning just how different maps and land were, his simple acceptance of symbols wearing away as he travelled. He had lost trust in depiction. No, that wasn't it. Representation. There had been such certainty in the air, all the hills, forests, dunes, and towns clearly identified and named. He worried that he was just wandering. He thought he knew where the outpost was. His mother's letter was all he had. An address blurred by winters and springs working on the ink. He recognized the name from briefings or classrooms or radio traffic or childhood. A name like it. His name. He wasn't even sure he was reading it right, the words and numbers bled into blue shapes. How long had it been since anyone had written his name? His mother sent it to him with her new address when she moved so that he could find her when he returned. She wanted to die at home. Somewhere far out west. It wasn't in her handwriting. She never wrote again. The letter arrived in the war and he carried it tucked in his chart. He thought of her telling him he couldn't find his ass with both hands. He remembered strands of her hair everywhere when the chemotherapy began.

—⚭—

All helo missions returned to the place they started. The barracks was comfortable enough, but he slept in the bird out on the tarmac. He left his room empty but for a box that kept his mail. Cards from a kindergarten class in Virginia that wrote to him: "Dear Soldier, You are brave. Thank you for protecting us." They drew flowers and tanks and eagles that looked like parrots and flags with too few stars. There was the letter from his mother telling him she had moved. She was sorry she couldn't take all his things with her. He tried to remember what he had saved from his first nineteen years, but he couldn't recall anything important. Their house was old, roof bent like a saddle and the hay barn collapsed. It was not a place anyone would buy. His room was probably still as he had left it, comics in the closet, plastic soldiers in a box under the bed, and a metal globe in the corner, names rusting off nations. He wondered if she had kept his copy of *Goodnight Moon.*

—⚭—

He saw the Afghans from high above their fields, herds, and villages, the thump of the blades on his helo shaking dust down onto their beds and babies from the roofs of their huts. He wondered how he would know who he was looking for from so high. He only felt calm in the air. Some of the men in his unit stopped talking about going home after the first bird went down in the mountains. He was one of them. He wondered if the war was still being fought, patrols still chasing tracers, soldiers getting cards from kindergarten classes.

He spread his map on the ground and studied it. It had been a long time since he had seen it in its entirety, the outline of a country cut by a frayed grid. The fold lines were rubbed bare and each square was now covered with layers of notes. The colors of contour lines, rivers and roads were consumed by language written in various inks, faded and smudged. Some had been written in the dark and was illegible, large childish letters trailing off an edge. The only rule was that nothing was written across a fold.

He felt no urge to return to a world of rooms, no need inside him to belong anywhere with a single view. He didn't consider himself homeless. A home wasn't what he wanted anymore. He was dead reckoning, a term he liked to say to himself. "Dead reckoning." He had thought a good bit on what it meant. Every meaning it could take on. His crash stayed in the present. There was no way out of the war but back up, airborne, the ground broken and troubled, people held to it by force. He moved again. Night came and he lay watching a wasted town by a dry lake. If no lights went on, he would explore at sunrise. Goodnight stars. Goodnight air.

—⁓—

He sat in the gravel beside an abandoned library, books thrown through its windows, shattered glass blown onto the ground in their paths with the reference cards that had once marked their order. Every book had been tossed, the effort of some kind of rage. He sat there not reading, picking through pieces of a smashed plastic globe. The Taliban outlawed reading. They didn't use maps either. They followed the paths of stories. It was hot, the sun bright, and he was in the shadow of the empty building. Most of the town had been burned or bombed years ago, the library upwind, full of paper, preserved. The street was straight, dropping out of sight into the valley. He had traced the road from the highway, an arrow directing passers to a town that was gone. A sign. The street ended at a ridge and smoke rose beyond it. Black smoke that came from oil. He couldn't guess the distance. Too far to get to and close enough to see. It rose in a slow coil, heat twisting over the fire. He fell asleep.

The dogs woke him. It was night and he was stiff, still propped against the library, a plastic fragment of the earth in his hand. They had encircled him at a distance and began yelping and howling, pacing as he stirred. He drew his feet back and pushed himself up the wall until he stood. They moved like coyotes, but looked larger, dark-shaped descendants of abandoned pets born with no memory of man as master. They could smell his wounds, sense his fright. Now he was certain they were from the war. The same dogs. He backed into the building, climbed the shelves, and lay on the dust. He floated there near the ceiling, dark filling the room and the outside all dirt and dogs for a thousand miles.

In the morning they were gone. Vanished. He looked at the ridge. Smoke still rose far away. Tires, he thought. Maybe trash. His heli-copter, crashed and burning, the dead crew cooking in their harnesses. He may have just come from it or circled all the way back. Fires didn't light themselves out here in the barrens. He could hear an engine on the road. Someone was coming. The Afghans. The boy. He would have to move on, out into the blank badlands. Far off he could see the grey shapes of mountains. He held up the piece of puzzle he'd carried with him, matching it to a distant peak. He could make it if he kept moving. He wasn't looking for anyplace on earth. He was searching for a way back into the sky.

DEATH OF TIME

by Maurice Emerson Decaul

TESTIMONY OF SAFIA H.

Purity

Fire choked his house. A bandit at night, it came to steal what was most dear. Fire sneaked around corners and laid blankets of ash and rubble over faces. Someone danced in flames, locked in a death tango. Fire walked from sky to house and into courtyards and into the leader. Flames leapfrogged from room to room smashing windows like delinquent boys. The Outsiders pointed machines at the sky in defiance of fire but their dragon smoke was timid and ineffectual. Fire consumed them like a haboob consuming a city. Fire played with them like children playing in mud. Fire played with them like girls making snow angels in snow. Fire played with them like people dancing at a dance party. It licked them the way horny strangers lick each other's faces. Fire fucked them hard and sweet like a couple on the verge. Fire lifted up a rock and found them hiding like scorpions. Fire fingered their assholes and came in their mouths. Fire painted the snow with them. Fire spun them in circles until they were dizzy and fell over. Fire dug holes and threw them in. Fire made new words come out of their mouths. Fire whistled to them. Fire made up songs and sang to them. Fire dressed like a demon and frightened them. Fire invented a new language and cursed them. Fire was a like a spider casting a web. Fire took them for a walk and showed them their sins. Fire stared them down. Fire walked into them. Fire knocked them down. Fire laughed at them and called them stupid. Fire pissed on their faces. Fire shot them when they ran. Fire hunted them. Fire invaded their bodies. Fire tongued them. Fire groped their cocks. Fire got rough with them and tied them up. Fire fucked them quickly and lost interest. Fire squatted above them and shat on their corpses.

I

The day the Outsiders showed up, I was on my way home with a chicken for dinner. Sporting beards extending past their throats to their suprasternal notches, they had shown up wearing black from top to bottom.

Black shirts, black pants, and black head wraps.

Some wore cartridge belts strapped across their chests. Some wore green bandanas. Others let loose their hair which varied in color and texture from blond curls to straight dark browns.

They were uniformly dirty.

Filthy from long months in the field. They smelled bad but were in good spirits, having overrun the last government checkpoints, killing some soldiers and parading the captured like slaves in a coffle, through the streets of my town.

Some of them rode atop battle tanks, hair, blond and brown and black, like fire tinged wheat on the wind.

Most of them carried a weapon known as the Machine. I knew the Machine because my father and brothers had kept several in their homes for self-protection. My brothers and father had taken their Machines which they named after their wives with them when they went to fight the Outsiders. It had been two weeks since my mother and younger sister Maryam, who was twelve, and I had heard from them.

Later when the sun reached apogee they honked the horns of their dusty trucks. Using stolen bullhorns they called the residents to town center. Some of them went house to house knocking then entering, leaving with men and boys who were older than twelve. They spoke in accents unfamiliar to me, some more guttural than others. These were the leaders.

They used loudspeakers to call everyone out to town center and when most everyone had shown up and pledged loyalty their leader addressed the crowd. He was short, ramrod slim after months in the field. He looked fatigued and in need of a bath to wash months of muck from his bullet colored hair. He looked too young. He was loquacious to a fault and went on and on about obedience to laws and stressed to us the importance of abiding by god's path on earth.

There would be no further sex outside of marriage or adultery no alcohol drinking or smoking no theft or banditry no games or music and no poetry since poets and poetry competed with god for attention he said.

Women would now be under their guardianship at all times and women even as young as me would have to be completely covered in public. They threatened punishment for waywardness: public flogging, stoning, amputation, execution by crucifixion, or other methods up to and including firing squad, immolation, drowning, or beheading would be introduced.

As they eulogized I weaved through the crowd searching for my mother and sister.

My mother had sent me to buy provision for dinner. I had bought a chicken, some rice, and bread. These foodstuffs were expensive and hard to come by during the siege but a few vendors courageous or foolish, set up market for a few hours before morning shelling. Morning shelling was more of a nuisance. The Outsiders were wildly inaccurate. On occasion they would land a shell in the market or on a roadway or hospital but most shells landed without incident.

During an earlier trip to market I came across a car which had suffered a hit from a shell. Inside were the remains of a person, flesh from fingers melted to the staring wheel, lips pulled back to reveal paper white teeth, one molar with a gold filling, cloud white bone, freed from the tyranny of flesh and skin. When I first saw this, I vomited but later, hardened by the war, I ran past without thought.

I pushed through the crowd of fearful women trying to find my mother and my sister Maryam but I would not hear my mother's voice again until days later when I, along with other women, were sold by the Outsiders.

II

The first order of business for the new regime was to make a show of its hard-won authority. They had besieged our town for months, shelling the town center, skirmishing with government soldiers and losing many of their own. With new authority to lord over the people, they made a public show of killing the captive soldiers whom they had driven into town, bound like slaves in a coffle. The government soldiers were herded to town center and a few unlucky ones were chosen to be punished publicly. Several dozen government soldiers were hung, crucified, beheaded, or thrown from buildings. A few were tied down and ground to paste with battle tanks.

The lucky ones were shot.

We were made to witness. We stood hushed. The rest of the soldiers were made to dispose of the bodies of their comrades and were themselves disposed of like rubbish some days later.

The stink of burnt flesh and hair lingered for weeks on the wind as the last of the government soldiers were immolated.

After the government soldiers were slaughtered, they turned their attention to the remaining men and boys over twelve. The men and boys were systematically sorted into groups of ten and shot in the street. The killing lasted less than an hour and their blood thickened to a raspberry jelly, clogging drain pipes before discoloring newly fallen snow.

Next were nursing babies and children under seven who had their heads dashed against stones.

None of the townspeople said or did anything out of fear.

The Outsiders, after their bacchanalia of killing, sorted us by age, beauty, and pregnancy status. The most beautiful young women who were childbearing age but not already pregnant, were most valuable. Women with child waited for midwives to evacuate their wombs to make room for new fetuses. Young girls under childbearing age were sold as house servants. Young boys under twelve were kept aside and handed out as ammunition bearers and could rise beyond their station and become them. Mature women were often seen as not valuable and sold off far from their regions. I was fourteen, pure and suitable for childbearing.

I was bought by a leader who bought three other women that day.

The leader, who was now my owner and would become my husband, tied me to three other women and beat us into a vehicle. We travelled with four other vehicles, each vehicle driven by an Outsider armed with a Machine. We drove quickly and other vehicles on the street parted. During the trip, none of us dared talk. I had never seen this part of the country and though my condition was awful, for a fleeting moment I caught glimpse of a white bird disappearing sideways in a gust of snow.

I began to cry.

Then I felt the blow. A slow burning pain at my temple and thought I had been shot.

Another girl heard me crying and hit me with her forehead. The older girl uttered something unintelligible to me and hit me twice more when I didn't answer.

I was stunned and ashamed. I quieted my crying and averted my eyes.

We drove for a long time until reaching his home. His home was atop a hill which afforded unobstructed views of the valley for miles. Switchbacks, icy roads, and sheer drops made turning around impossible.

We were unloaded into the house and taken to our rooms where matures stripped us. My room was windowless and small. I could cross it in a dozen strides and standing on my bed, I could touch the ceiling. On my bed, I found linens and near the linens were three thin, dull black dresses. A black sweater and head covering, a few pair of underwear, socks, and a pair of hard, flat, black rubber shoes. A small bureau faced the bed. My room was lit by fluorescent light, which could not be switched off.

My new household was structured around the schedule of the leader. He was high ranking. Instead of black, he wore cream and carried a briefcase instead of a Machine. He always had his briefcase with him when he came to rape me. His rapes were always rushed. He often seemed preoccupied and showed little interest in what he was doing. I submitted. After raping me he always insisted on watching me clean before leaving.

He never spoke to me. No one ever spoke to me and I went long periods of time during which the only people I saw were him and the midwife who visited with pills.

I began losing track of days but most days were the same. When he was home, he raped. I ate. I shat and pissed. And I tried to sleep.

Sometimes the matures would take me outside for air. The sun was now an enemy. My skin burned. Even though my skin is brown, bruises showed. I started to develop a rash on my elbow and bruises below my eyes deepened from blue to purple.

Twice I had been with child and each time the midwife had evacuated my womb. I bled and out of desperation I threw myself from off my bed to prevent another fetus from rooting.

III

I felt the presence of dead soldiers in my room. They were a lot less concerned with me than I was with them.

The soldiers looked frightened. Some did not know they were dead. Others were in search of water to douse their burns. Some were whole and beautiful. I was attracted to them. Once I reached out to touch one of them and as my fingers touched one's shoulder he turned to ash and fell at my feet. Ash floated from floor to ceiling filling every corner of my room. I could not breathe without inhaling ash. Ash entered my nose and mouth. Ash entered my body through pores and eyes. Ash landed on my lips and I licked it in. Ash entered my body. I felt myself floating in a cloud of ash like a skin diver in a lagoon. Ash held me up. Ash circulated like blood. Ash let me see the last moments of this man's life.

He had been burned. I could feel burning in my muscles as he excavated ground. I felt snow wet clay under my feet as he stepped in his hole. I could see them standing above, confident and cruel. Several of them pissed on him. Others spat and struck him with their Machines. A group of them fought over who would douse him with fuel.

I felt warmth between my legs.

I had felt him piss fear out.

I felt diesel wet my thighs. I smelled acetone and charcoal lighter fluid. He prayed. I heard them laughing and farting and being confident. I felt cold flames envelop his body and my body contorted like his.

Goose bumps rose on my skin. I saw him as a child with other children throwing snowballs.

I felt warm in his mother's womb.

I saw him as a sailor on a ship falling overboard. I felt the cold hug of the sea and swallowed salt water.

I woke on the floor wet and cold from sweat and pee. The room smelled of rot. The leader hovered above me.

The leader had come to rape as was his habit but before he did, he told me he planned to award me as a gift to a student who had earned fame in battle.

I offered no emotion but I was scared of being sold.

He reassured me that my new owner would treat me kindly. He said I would not be asked to do work which was beyond my ability. He tried to console me, saying that he and my new owner would be equal partners in my ownership and since this was the case, he would still sleep with me, though not at the same time as my new owner. I betrayed no emotion when he kissed me. Regular beatings had taught me to submit.

After he raped me, he ordered the matures to wash and care for me. He ordered them to move me to another room where lights could be switched off. He ordered them to feed me more. He ordered them to sew new clothes. He ordered the midwife to ensure my womb was empty.

IV

The matures who were emaciated and ill-treated resented having to care for me. They made me think of my mother. The last time I thought I heard my mother's voice was the day when women from our town had been sorted and sold. I fantasized, about my father and brothers dying terribly. My mother, would have become a slave somewhere, ill-treated and malnourished. Maryam was still too young to be touched.

But they were not my mother. The matures submitted. A regime of beatings had trained them.

They clothed me. They locked me in and fed me food. They whispered whore through the door. They spoke to me but their words were vile and venomous. They taunted, called me stupid and ugly. Called me corpse and bitch.

Once in a fit of rage, I tried to strike one of them. Another time, with rage, I turned to them and spewed venom. I said I was not sorry they were old and unwanted and witches. Enraged, they clawed my back, leaving scars.

They fattened me up and exercised me. They took me outside. They switched out the lights and boxed me behind my ears. The spit in my food and pushed me down stairs. They walked into me with force.

They took me outside and locked the door. The Outsiders who were there noticed. I feared they might rape me but none dared touch me in their leader's home.

The night the leader returned from the field, he let himself into my room. He had been gone so long I had allowed myself to dream he had died terribly.

He let himself in and turned on lights. He took up the whole room and I felt small and vulnerable.

He was filthy having been in the field for weeks. He stunk of shit and piss and cum and stale cigarettes and blood. He reached for me, but startled by his appearance, I hit him in the face.

He was lean from weeks in the field. Strong and fast and vicious.

He caught me by my hair and threw me to the ground. I bit and spit. I clawed his face and back and left scars.

He was mean after being in the field for weeks. The war continued to harden him.

I flailed at him but he was too strong and fast. I had never fought him this way. I had always submitted. I had never fought anyone this way but I was tired.

Tired of him raping me. Tired of the midwife and her pills. I was tired of the matures and the Outsiders with Machines. I had grown tired of the sun and moon and wanted to eat them and shit them out.

I bit his cock and he held me down by my throat, squeezing my breath like water from a wet sponge. I cried when he raped me and he blamed me for it.

He blamed the matures too. He called them terrible names and called me flawed and ugly and reckless.

After he raped me, he instructed the matures to remove me to the white room. He instructed them to feed me less and to take away my clothes. He told me he had changed his mind about divorcing me. He no longer trusted I would be kind and docile to my new owner. He said he would not allow me to dishonor him. He said he would make a gift of one of the other women instead.

The matures obeyed. They took me back to the white room. They stripped me and took away my linens. One mature whispered whore into my ear. Another boxed my breasts. They spat at me and locked me in.

I was cold and scared, I drew myself into a ball. I looked up to find the matures returned. They had grown in height but not in age. They took up the whole room. They feigned care, reaching down to stroke my sore breasts.

They whispered wicked things:

No one loves you.

Bitch.

Kill yourself.

Whore.

Kill yourself.

Witch.

Kill yourself.

Ugly.

Kill yourself.

Corpse.

Kill yourself.

Stupid.

Kill yourself.

V

I woke naked, and cold.

Government planes had bombed us in the night. The buzzing of their engines had been deliberate and confident. They bombed us all night until they thought everyone was dead.

I struggled.

It hurt to breathe so I breathed deliberately. Skin around my torso had begun to turn blue. I walked through the rooms of the house. Small fires still burned. Many of the Outsiders were burned. A mature, who had treated me terribly, noticed me and reached out a hand in supplication. I picked up a slab of stone and dropped it on her head.

I found another mature who had breathed in fire. I stripped her body and dressed myself. I moved rubble and found her shoes. My chest hurt tremendously and I could scarcely breathe.

I listened for bombs and heard forest birds. A few birds landed near and begun tearing open the dead. I threw rocks and books. I cried them off. I sang a song to myself.

Snow fell and I was cold and hungry. I thought about running but I could hardly breathe. For a half second I mistook smoke for bodies.

I sat in the house the rest of the night and listened for bombs but heard dogs. I thought I heard voices but it was wind. I guarded my broken rib and breathed deliberately. I made plans to walk off the mountain and follow the road.

I looked up and saw the moon.

I knew it was treacherous to move off the mountain at night, so I gathered what I could: a blanket, cans of food, and a Machine. I stoked a fire, sat near it for warmth.

When the sun came up I was cold and in misery from fever. I tried to stand but fell. I used the Machine as a cane and began to get up. The forest was loud with crows and beaten wind. I heard hoarse voices calling to me like lost phantoms. I looked over my shoulder and saw a squad of government soldiers. They put me in a helicopter and flew me here. They are confident the war will end soon. They say this but I say nothing.

AMERICAN FAPPER

by Adrian Bonenberger

Me and Chuck came up together. Deployed young to Iraq, where we learned everything they don't teach you about war in training, then to Afghanistan, where we learned everything about war we'd missed in Iraq. Then, back to Iraq, where we'd made names for ourselves as a sniper team—I was the shooter, he was the spotter. After word got around that we knew our business they sent us on deeper missions. We saw "peaceful" countries as part of ad hoc Task Forces. The kind of operations you don't read about in newspapers until months or years afterward, with guys from Delta Force and the CIA. Missions where you almost might have been on another planet, for all anyone knew.

When the only friendly faces you see for months are American, those faces mean something different from what they did before. Too, America takes on a significance that it hadn't. You learn that some places on earth are nothing like Philadelphia, where I'm from. And while Chuck grew up in the Deep South, called himself a "good-ol' boy," I remember many times when his broad, ruddy face widened, his eyebrows arching at some unexpected new vision, like the time we found a group of children butchering a camel with machetes in a courtyard, or the two-sided ambush by Sudanese Bedouin we'd scraped through outside Halayeb, the southernmost tip of Egypt, driving in a pickup truck alongside a convoy of Egyptian soldiers. After, we'd climbed out of the cab and examined the doors, which were so riddled with bullet holes they'd looked like cheese graters—yet neither of us had been hit or even grazed. A miracle. Moments like those, Chuck's deep drawl made more opaque from the wad of chewing tobacco in his cheek, he'd whistle, low, and say something like, "Never seen that be-foar," voicing his thoughts so I didn't have to say mine.

In America, we'd been about as different as they come, but over there, those differences were insignificant when placed against the extraordinary spectacles to which we'd become the audience.

Our first deployment together was back in 2005, when Ramadi went sour. That's where we gelled as a team, when he got me through my first big ordeal as a sniper, as a soldier. We were providing overwatch for a convoy of tanks. You wouldn't think tanks needed a couple guys with rifles to protect them, but insurgency plays out on the margins— and Iraqi fighters were crafty. It was summer, and hot so the air made everything slick. We were lying on a factory roof scanning for insurgents in places we'd have gone if we were in their position. A thousand meters out, on a low, desert hill, we spotted two black-hooded beebs by a beaten-up dirtbike. They were waiting for the convoy, one bent over a detonating device fiddling with the trigger, the other holding a thick pair of field binoculars. The tanks rumbled and squeaked along the road like a World War II movie.

Higher cleared us to engage. I nailed the triggerman immediately but hesitated for a clean shot on the lookout, who ducked as I fired, one of the only times I aimed and missed. The tanks were approaching an intersection and Chuck was yelling at them over the radio to stop. The lookout activated the IED as I cleared the rifle's chamber for another round. Unobserved, purely by chance, the bomb caught the lead tank full on and flipped it up and over like a toy, spinning high into the air. Its turret popped off, something human fell out, and then everything was bouncing over the earth. I'd never felt a blast like that before. It shook everything.

—⁂—

After Chuck died, I couldn't shoot worth shit. For snipers, that's a problem. I'd be out on mission staring down terrorists through a high-tech scope and instead of opening fire, I'd watch them dig bombs into the road. I always found an excuse why there wasn't a shot, and people started to notice.

Up to that point I'd been one of the best snipers the SEALs had. My thing was always hitting my targets and putting them down, no matter the distance or difficulty. If I pulled the trigger, the cunt on the other end was either dying, or getting hurt so bad they'd wish they had. During the bad time when I wasn't shooting, my stellar record gave me latitude with superiors, made the SEALs think twice about switching me off.

That's the military. You earn your stripes, you make your bones, you prove yourself, and they won't just throw you away. Still, it got to where they were talking about putting me behind a desk or sending me stateside to train other snipers. Grounding me. And once you're off the line, it's hell getting back.

—☈—

My father never served. When I was younger I watched *Full Metal Jacket* and after, asked why he didn't join, and he said Vietnam was already over by the time he was old enough to fight. Later on, I figured out that the timing didn't quite work out—he *could've* joined, and seen action, so he must've had some other reason.

Paradoxically, the only skill my father had was shooting, and unsurprisingly, he loved it. He was short, bow-legged, and what you'd call "barrel-chested," barely resembling me except his eyes were grey too. He was taciturn and aloof, but sometimes when he drank or felt low he would tell me that grey eyes were the sign of a marksman. He worked part-time and managed to make ends meet, but there was a stubborn core that prevented him from seeing himself subordinated to anyone. There was a kind of dam inside my father, a stoppage that kept him from taking risks or going beyond himself. If you didn't know any better, you'd say he was calm and collected.

So money was always tight. My father couldn't afford to buy a television, and starting when I was young, maybe five or six, he'd take me hunting. He taught me the proper way to take aimed shots, to squeeze the trigger during a long deliberate exhale, not knowing the precise moment the rifle would fire, teaching me that expectation ruins accuracy. After, he'd put me to work disassembling and cleaning his rifle, shotguns, and pistols. It's not that he was a gun nut—quite the contrary. He tried to share the one thing he loved with me, and I suppose I felt lucky. Many people had it worse. I wasn't particularly popular then, and didn't have many friends, so physical labor helped keep me busy.

—⁂—

When I go home now, people love my war stories. Guys I barely knew in high school ask about how many terrorists I killed (fifty-seven), and all about the Navy SEALs. For some reason people are interested in mundane biographical details about SEALs that weren't relevant or significant before, like how I'm six feet one with light blond hair and grey eyes, or how I have long arms and narrow shoulders, and bent, powerful legs. I can climb a twenty-five-foot rope in five seconds. I've died underwater before, part of S.C.U.B.A. training. I'm a fast runner, and I can do more push-ups or pull-ups than you'd think.

In high school I hated class and homework but I was good at sports. The humanities were my worst subjects. Usually I'd read a book and just not understand what was going on. Freshman year I almost failed English. Math and science were strong subjects for me, but the humanities really tripped me up. It seemed like I was the only kid in class who couldn't figure out what was happening in a book, no matter how hard I tried. My advisor tried to help, and said something I'll never forget: that reading was about what *called out* to you. A great book showed you something true about yourself. It helped, some, to hear that. Even so, in English I'd think I understood a book or a story, saw something true in it, but then in class I'd raise my hand and it'd turn out that I was wrong.

—⁕—

Right before freshman year, an important event helped define my adolescence. Our neighbors, an elderly couple, died. The estate sold their house to Mr. and Mrs. Erik Ruhr and their daughter, Angela. Angela Ruhr was a senior, and her curly blond hair demanded and received the attention of all who regarded it. She was a terrific athlete, and had the kind of body every high school boy coveted. Her father was a banking executive.

By happy coincidence, her second-story bedroom room was adjacent to mine. Most nights she remembered to pull the blinds shut. There were weekends, especially the summer after her graduation, where she did not remember . . . I was able to observe her, on dates with one boy or another, drinking, smoking cigarettes, and, on several occasions, having enthusiastic sex. Her parents spent a good deal of time away on vacation or for professional reasons, and often left Angela to her own devices.

I did not have a girlfriend and developed what in retrospect I can admit was an obsession with Angela's sexual habits. Quite apart from the objective fact that watching an attractive woman have sex is engaging (pornographic films and strip clubs attest to this), my own life then was drab and boring by comparison, and static.

One morning that July I walked out back. Dad was gone, and there was nothing to do around the house. The weather was comfortable. I could smell the cut grass and fully bloomed trees. Insects buzzed. The air was still, not yet humid, blasted with life and fecundity. I looked up to find Angela watching from her back porch. She pointed her index finger and pretended to shoot me, like it was a pistol, then smiled, waved, and walked inside. I raised my hand, which is to say, I did nothing.

As an introvert, I honed extraordinary powers of patience and endurance those July and August evenings waiting by my window for Angela to return from dates with boys from my high school, as well as those from other high schools. I did not film or record these sexual acts, and understood that my observing them was intrusive. But I could not stop, nor could I furnish a reasonable explanation to myself for doing so beyond fascination.

Unlike Angela's parents, it seemed like my father was always home. We lived in closer quarters than the Ruhrs. My father was no banking executive, and privacy was difficult to come by. One had to be furtive. So in addition to powers of patience, I also developed methods for gratifying my sexual urges without arousing the suspicions of those around me. Nevertheless, my father seemed to have a sixth sense for my masturbation, and while he never caught me in the act, he seemed especially intrusive during those times when I would have preferred to be alone, banging on my locked door, calling out about dinner, asking what I was up to. Achieving climax involved a delicate triangulation of the following variables: Angela's sexual life, my father's intrusiveness, and my ability both to secure my privacy in physical terms as well as psychologically to feel comfortable and safe. Practically speaking, this was quite difficult. For what it's worth, I do believe that this all helped me cultivate the skills that ultimately led to my success as a sniper.

After high school most people went to college. Angela attended Duke. I didn't have the grades or interest. In 2002, war was the only thing that "called out" to me after high school. Putting my father's hypothesis about grey eyes to the test, I joined the Navy SEALs and the rest, as they say, is history.

Occasionally I wonder where Angela Ruhr ended up. She never appeared on social media—not everyone does. For a while I checked Facebook and Twitter, as I checked MySpace and Friendster when those were active. I'd Google her name—you'd think one of the friends we had in common would bring her up—nothing. After leaving for college, it's like she dropped off the face of the earth.

—⁓—

Sniping comes down to (1) patience, (2) procedures that if you do them right it will give you the same result, and (3) luck, because even the best sniper can miss shots at greater distances. After Ramadi and the tank I had the most trouble reconciling myself with (3), but Chuck helped get me past that anxiety. He pointed out—and I can't disagree with him—that you miss 100 percent of the shots you don't take.

Now, when there's a shot, I don't hesitate. I don't think about whether or not I'll be ready to fire. Whether the bullet might pull left or right. What the shot "means"—its significance, my surroundings, the architectural composition of the neighborhood and likely historical ramifications of that architecture, as well as my embeddedness in the consequences that will spiderweb out unpredictably into the future like cracks in a window punctured by 7.62 caliber bullets. Now, I bed down and take the shot.

I like to think of myself as a scientist, tending to the various parts of my laboratory. Twisting dials, pulling levers. That's all there is to it, it's simple. When the conditions align, I make the shot. No hesitation, and to hell with luck, like Chuck said. When everything is done scientifically and objectively, according to routine, that's all you can do. I've made the shot about seventy-five times, taken targets down, fifty-nine of them permanently.

As I mentioned earlier, Chuck and I couldn't have been more different. We were partners on five consecutive deployments. He'd get emotional on mission. When I made my longest shot (over 1.5 kilometers, through a building, RPG gunner) he jumped and yelled. The war meant something to him that I never understood. I joined because I wanted to learn about my family, and I thought I might have a talent for shooting targets at long distances. Chuck had joined, I think, because he hated Muslims. When I dropped the RPG gunner, for example, after jumping to his feet he, yelled, "Fuck you, haji," then swung his hips in a circle while playing the air guitar, like David Lee Roth in "Jump," smiling down at me and nodding to a beat I couldn't hear. I was impressed with the shot as well. There had been a stiff cross-breeze, burning with dust, and thinking about it afterward, I was surprised it hit target.

Me and Chuck were together so long our luck became one person's luck instead of two, which is to say, it ran out.

Chuck looked out for me in more ways than one. In addition to guaranteeing our safety on mission, he could talk our superiors into giving us autonomy. Our lieutenant who didn't care for me—reminded me a bit of my father, always checking up on my room, always around when I wanted to be alone, never a kind word. Chuck understood how to deal with guys like that.

—⁂—

Another thing that happened to me at war was I started getting off on the more difficult shots at night. Sexually. We'd be on a mission, waiting for the target to appear or for some variable in the environment to change and I'd know Chuck was out there keeping watch—it made me feel really comfortable, knowing we were the ones with the power to kill. I'd see the target as a white blob, engaged in all kinds of personal and intimate acts, and it reminded me—there was no helping it—of Angela, of my childhood window. Except nobody could interrupt us, the only thing that would break the spell would be the crack of my rifle spitting out someone's judgment. In that darkness, I figured out how to stimulate myself. At least, until Chuck bought the farm, at which point, it didn't.

—⁂—

Here's what happened. As spotter, it was Chuck's job to pull security and help maintain our situational awareness. One mission in Iraq he was covering our six from the roof while I pulled overwatch on an Al Qaeda organizer. One of Zarqawi's acolytes, this guy wasn't holding the drill, as it were, wasn't using the calipers himself, but he was definitely green lighting the monsters who were. We were waiting for him to come home, and he did, and right when I had my shot and started to squeeze the trigger Chuck said "abort, abort" over the radio.

He'd seen the target's security detail one rooftop over from ours and was assessing the situation, probably thinking there was no way to do the mission. All of that was irrelevant because I'd been thinking about Angela and getting ready for the shot. Physically I couldn't control it, even if I'd wanted to. I let myself go, and took the shot, and capped the poor bastard.

Chuck nailed the first couple ragheads but (and I don't even know where it came from, we were taking fire from all over) someone shot him dead through his helmet, bang. I bustled him over my shoulders and ran, as Chuck's blood poured over my shoulders and arms and pants, dousing everything. I made it back through a mysterious blur of jumping and firing without shooting at anything, and at some point a helicopter was landing and grabbing me and Chuck—Chuck's body. Then it was over.

Nobody asked how the mission had gone down, and I didn't tell, I just slowly went to shit as a sniper, unable to shoot, unable to gratify myself as my sexual frustration built.

—⁂—

I was back in rotation the next day. They assigned me a few spotters but none of them worked out. In the military, you bond with someone or you don't, and I'd gotten too content with Chuck—I'd stopped being flexible enough to adapt. My habits, with which Chuck was familiar, grated on the other spotters. Didn't matter that I had a solid reputation, everyone with experience has a way of doing things and I couldn't seem to find anyone who gelled with my particular needs. One spotter would get too close, always set up next to me. Another was too far, I couldn't tell if I was safe or not. Missions went badly and sometimes not at all, sometimes targets would escape without getting shot. This went on for a couple weeks.

One evening I was going half crazy lying in my room, thinking that something had to give, when a distinctive rapping at my door brought me to attention—the lieutenant. I popped out of bed, anxious and on edge.

"Sir?" I said, but flat, so he understood that I didn't really care. He was in full battle rattle, helmet, body armor, rifle, all of it, which meant something dangerous was imminent.

"Just got back from a recon—we're heading out tonight. Got a target. Come with me to CHOPs for briefing."

I didn't understand at first. All the spotters were out, or, all the spotters who might still work with me.

"I'm going to be your spotter. Heard you have constipation when it comes to getting your shot off. I'm the laxative."

He was tall, and older—twenty-nine or thirty. He'd been a soldier like myself at some point, and done the whole green to gold officer transition at Georgetown. Got an undergraduate degree in business— not exactly the "tactical" type, more comfortable signing paperwork than spending a night outside staring at targets. I was surprised he'd decided to join me and said so.

"Don't worry if this idea is good or not, it's happening. Come with me, I'm not going to say it a third time."

I did as instructed, pulling on my boots and body armor. The lieu-tenant was already walking down the hall, toward "operations," the office where high-level briefings occurred. I hurried to catch up. We pulled even as he reached the door, and he turned before opening it.

"The target is special. It's a female. Can't afford to have you fuck this one up. Got it?"

I nodded. I'd done females before, older women who were acting as go-betweens for AQ leaders, pulling important financial strings. Didn't bother me, really. If the generals and admirals in the head-shed wanted some lady taken out, that meant the target deserved it. The lieutenant, though, he bothered me, with his cheerful eyes and empty, authoritative manner, like he knew the score.

—ɯ—

Objective Redskins was the name higher assigned, in keeping with their convention of designating targets with the names of football teams. It seemed appropriate: Redskins were what Army scouts killed on the prairie and in the American Southwest to stop settlers from losing their scalps. Savage people, in a lawless land. Removing *Redskins* would allow this particular city, and Iraq in general, to evolve into a place like Phoenix, or Des Moines. Or Philadelphia.

At the briefing, we reviewed the hide site our scouts had selected. It didn't look promising—even under normal conditions, it looked like a tough shot. Corner building, angled fire, two-floor differential from four hundred meters away—but there was no other option. I would've rather taken a longer shot from an equal elevation and clear line of sight, but *Redskins* had selected quarters masked by two tall, intervening factories. Unlike Angela, *Redskins* had thought about who might be observing. I kept snapping in and out of the actual brief, instead scanning the photos, memorizing the physical details of the area.

"Medevac plan is—primary, create improvised Helicopter Landing Zone on the roof marked using flares and smoke. Alternate will be in the courtyard to south of hide sight, marking same as for primary." The lieutenant hurried through the briefing in a monotone, shifting from foot to foot and frequently sneaking his eyes to the right, affecting the speech patterns of a seasoned combat veteran, like he had the whole thing figured out. He didn't fool me, I could tell he'd never been in the shit. Nobody ever tagged a rooftop as primary evacuation, that was movie-time cowboy crap. What it really meant was that a bureaucrat was coming out with me—that the mission was my last chance to make good. I picked up the packet to review the details, not wanting to get anything wrong, and left to finish prepping.

"See you in three hours outside your hooch," the lieutenant said as I left. "Zero one hundred hours, we link up with our infil. Don't be late."

—⁂—

I rezeroed my rifle and double-checked the equipment. I was still jittery, full of pent-up fury that bounced my legs when I sat, and propelled me down empty hallways when I stood. I hit the gym briefly, but that just got my heart rate up. With nothing left to do but wait for a half hour, I decided to loiter, see if I could endure nothing. Took my stuff outside my quarters and waited.

Outside, the night reminded me of childhood Halloween—chilly and dark, with a vivid moon, yellow in the squat Iraqi sky. Smells sharpened in the autumn air, and I felt the tainted Euphrates reeking like an ache, from the back of my skull down to my throbbing pelvis. Dogs barked desperately off to the East in Sadr City. Somewhere outside the wire, a man yelled in Arabic. The call to prayer wasn't playing, but I knew it would, again, soon.

The lieutenant found me there. I grabbed my rifle and pack and we linked up with a group of Army infantrymen heading out to our sector in Strykers—whisper-quiet armored vehicles. We rode in their red-lit troop compartments for hours, doing false inserts around the city, setting up snap traffic checkpoints with the infantry, pretending that our purpose was tactical, quotidian. When we finally reached the drop point it was early morning. Our infiltration went off without a hitch. We exited the back of a slow-rolling Stryker as we passed an alley three hundred meters away from the apartment building that held our hide location, and humped it the rest of the way, dogs barking at the vehicles, at us, at each other.

Usually, the topographical setup of a fight is worse on the ground than on the maps they use during briefs. The hill where you want to put a sniper or machine gun ends up being a mountain. An open space through which one is supposed to shoot is actually an apple orchard, or a children's playground. Sometimes, though, if intel is sparse, you catch a break, and the setup is better than you feared. As it turned out, the room where I'd take my shot wasn't as bad as it looked in the mission brief—very doable, with a great egress route for after. I took a moment to marvel at how the lieutenant and I were, shortly, to transform this humble apartment, guarded by a cheap metal door, into a workshop. The concrete walls were weak and chipped, the furniture shabby but maintained in a way that reminded me of my own impoverished upbringing. I felt a momentary surge of welcome familiarity.

The lieutenant answered my first concern by settling in at the far end of the apartment's living room, about twenty feet away. He wouldn't be bothering me by breathing over my shoulder. As I arranged furniture so I could take up a good position in the prone looking out the window, I noticed that my body was still jumpy. I was on edge, and focusing on the variables wasn't helping like normal.

For this mission, I'd brought a Jellico .303, that long-range rifle produced by the reliable manufacturers at Winchester. The lieutenant was on the thermals, and in addition had a Leopold scope that could zoom up to x25 magnification. We kept the target's rooms under observation from early morning until the sun came up, then waited several hours for the sun to slouch across the sky. Shooting from the West, we needed the sun to line up. At 1400 the light was perfect, so I returned to my scope and waited, scanning the target's bedroom and living room windows.

It all reminded me of a movie I'd watched once, set in the 1970s. A police officer was tracking some serial killer in San Francisco. I couldn't remember the details. The serial killer had threatened—a newspaper?—to kill someone—a homosexual?—and had taken up a position on a roof. I think the policeman—also a sniper?—was trying to outmaneuver the serial killer. Everything was in sepia, that washed-out quality you get with older movies. The soundtrack was really arresting, peppy, funky. But I couldn't remember, in Iraq, watching for *Redskins*, how it had all turned out.

At 1450 the target appeared briefly by the bedroom window, too quickly for me to acquire a good shot. *Redskins* had her arms around a young adolescent boy of twelve or thirteen, and kissed him repeatedly on the forehead before shooing him out, closing the door behind him. She placed her hands on her hips, and looked out the window, her face open to the daylight. I had her, and prepared to fire.

The lieutenant whistled, low. "Hey. You seeing this?"

"What?" I looked up.

"Look at this chick. She's blazing. Packet did *not* do her justice."

I brought myself back to the scope, and evaluated. Sure enough, *Objective Redskins* was a very attractive woman. The photo in the packet had been unexceptional—and while this was the same long, narrow face and nose, the moves were all different, her bearing refined, regal. The human potential of *Redskins* unnerved me. Our target was an arrogant killer, an evil sadist who unquestionably deserved death. She was also a sexy mother.

"What do you recommend, sir," I said. "That's the target, I'm sure. Mission is to take it down."

Glancing at the target through his spotting scope, the lieutenant abruptly leaned forward and grabbed it with both hands, bringing his eyes up to the near end. "Holy shit, take a look. You're not going to believe this."

I already knew what I'd see, and my scalp and forehead started to sweat. Under my crosshairs *Objective Redskins* was removing articles of her clothing. Below her burka and headscarf lay a shapely body, clad only in lacy red panties and a bra. She was beautiful. In my peripheral vision, I noted that the lieutenant had unbuckled his pants and thrust his right hand into them, all the while observing through the scope that he held with his left. I returned to *Redskins*, who was practically nude. Of its own volition, my manhood stirred.

"Sir, this isn't a call we get to make. You saw the photos in the packet—this human has done things, *horrible* things, and our mission, again, is to *take her down*."

The lieutenant wasn't paying attention. I couldn't shoot without him, I needed his approval to fire, and moreover he was *there* to help me shoot, and that's exactly what I wanted to do, take the shot, get it over with. Instead, he was masturbating furiously in the corner while an insurgent commander was defenseless, easy for the taking. I waited while *Redskins* went to her closet and took out various types of clothing, putting them up against her body in front of a mirror.

After a little while he stopped. "This isn't doing it for me." He sat up, his pants still unbuckled. "I'm bored, fuck this shit. You gonna shoot or what?"

I maintained my composure, careful not to roll my eyes or otherwise indicate my disgust for him, for this whole scene, and took aim again. When I returned to the scope, though, *Redskins* had another surprise.

A beatific smile on her face, she was leaning back on her bed, swaying. She placed her hand down her panties, and began stimulating herself. I shifted uncomfortably as my crotch stiffened, trying to dispel the exquisite, painful urge. My prone position made it impossible to avoid arousing myself with even the slightest gesture. Carefully, I brought the crosshairs to her chest, a few clicks down from her left armpit. My finger drifted to the trigger.

"You paying attention? Do it! Take the goddamned shot!"

Taking the shot now, as much as I wanted to, was clearly not what was called for. "Sir, you're going to want to take a look at this," I said.

"This better be good," he said, then, "Jackpot, total game changer!" His face back on the scope and hand back in his pants, he rendered his decision: "Hold fire."

I gritted my teeth, rocking back and forth, like an animal, powerless to prevent myself from rubbing myself with my legs. *Redskins'* knees were delicately circling as her feet and heels hung in the air, bouncing lightly, and I'd unconsciously synchronized my movements with her own. Then it happened—I finished, at almost the same time as the lieutenant. A great calm washed over me, calm like I hadn't felt since before Chuck's death. My facial tic vanished, and my arms stopped shaking. My legs stopped their macabre rattle.

After a long minute, still looking through his scope, the lieutenant spoke. "You ever listen to Rachmaninov? Second Piano Concerto?"

I had not (though I have since) and said so.

"Ayn Rand said it's the only piece of music a man needs to know," he said. "You have a girl back home?"

I did, but I was thinking about Angela. "No, sir," I said, then, "Yes, actually. I'm sorry. Yes, I do."

"Asian girl, right?"

"Roger, sir," I said.

He nodded sagely, then left the scope, lay back against the wall, and took out a pack of cigarettes. "Seems like your type, the quiet ones always get yellow fever. Want one?"

I declined his offer, and he lit up, wiping his wrist on the concrete floor. "Man that's messy as fuck," he said to himself, then launched into a story about how he'd gone hunting for elk in Wyoming on vacation once, with his dad and grandfather. Naturally, the lieutenant was the protagonist, and naturally, they'd bagged a massive beast, a record-setter. It sounded like bullshit to me, but sometimes that's how people talk in war. I kept checking the room, and spoke up when he finished the story.

"Sir, should I shoot? She's still at it."

The lieutenant dragged on his cigarette, pretentious in profile. "Sure, knock her down. I mean might want to let her finish first."

He was right. The mission wasn't personal. I just wanted to wrap it up and return to base. I returned to my rifle with a clear head, and open eyes.

One of the things they teach you to do in sniper training, which is reinforced through patrolling, is always to maintain situational awareness. The lieutenant was facing the door, rifle by his side, and I wasn't worried about us being discovered. My process for acquiring *Redskins* was to confirm that she was still in the bedroom, in her bed (she was), then to quickly scan the area for anything that might have changed during our little chat. I was about to take and make a relatively simple four-hundred meter shot, and didn't want anything to intrude on our escape, especially given what had happened to Chuck. I scanned the roof of her building, the surrounding area, and the window of her living room.

I hadn't gone home for Chuck's funeral yet. I hadn't met his parents, watched them weep loudly by his grave. I hadn't seen my father's dull grey pupils dilate when I brought home his first television—sunken-cheeked, weakened by old age and feeble with the first signs of dementia, he wasn't hunting anymore, though the weapons still hung carefully in his garage. I hadn't finished helping the cable people set things up for the television and the internet, hadn't stood in the backyard looking at the Ruhrs' porch, then gone into the kitchen to grip the sink and squeeze my face shut. I was just a sniper, with a target who was going to die better than most people—painless, after a moment of physical ecstasy.

That's when I saw the son, face plastered against the wall, hand in his boyish pants, staring through what must have been a peephole. Watching his *mother*. My face filled with blood. Shuddering with surprise and rage, I brought the sights up to him, then, swiftly, over to her. As she built to her climax, I pressed my cheek hard against the rifle's buttstock, and calculated the space between us. What effect the wind would have, the angle of deflection. How her window would change the bullet's direction. The area's architecture—quarters built for workers, single-file hallways, wide boulevards, simple egress. I breathed in, and focused on the shot's mathematics, and squeezed my index finger oh, so gently, feeling the narrow metal against my finger, knowing that at some point, the rifle would jerk in my hand. I began my slow exhale.

THE WILD HUNT

by Brian Castner

M ickey never saw the one that got him.

He was on point, and when the shooting started it came from all sides. He was strung out, separated, pinched off, his squad somewhere below and behind him on the path, and the Taliban were close, so close he could smell them, a funky mix of sweat and shit even stronger than the powder tang off his rifle. He shot at them through the trees and they shot back and somehow he never got hit until the moment the whole mountainside erupted under his feet.

Mickey was on his back. He looked down at his legs and saw two red smears in their place. The arms and scalps and organs of things that had been Taliban only a second before lay all about him. A pink mist hung in the air. Rock and timber fell amongst and through it but the haze remained. It was a mist of blood, a mist of him and them. It took shape and he looked it in the eye. The wails of the dying echoed across the valley. Mickey felt frozen in panic and when he finally took a breath he inhaled the pink mist and it coated the back of his throat. He coughed and spit red phlegm, wiped his mouth with the back of his hand, and saw that he was drenched in the stuff. The pink mist loomed, and when he took another breath, Mickey sucked it all the way into his lungs.

Then pain and adrenaline suddenly flooded his body and he felt like he was going to jizz his pants.

"Sergeant Gabe, I'm hit!" he screamed into the mic on his left shoulder.

Silence from the radio and shouts and shots only feet away.

He tried to move backward using his arms and the remains of his legs. He ground the shards of his exposed shin bones into the earth and pushed, but the stilts provided no leverage or balance and he only managed an inch. He tried to twist himself around but he couldn't sit up, couldn't make his body work. Why? He put his hands to his stomach and found his bowels. A massive piece of frag had sliced open his belly, right below his vest. Mickey started pushing the blue and white tubes back into his gut with his snot dirt pink mist hands. He knew he wasn't supposed to, but he couldn't help it. It was instinct.

He rolled over and began to crawl. He didn't feel his intestines scrape along the gravel. Further down the path he saw his squad mates firing back, up the cliff face, into the valley. They were so far away. Chip was on the ground, lying on his side. Another soldier was working a jam on his machine gun. Sergeant Gabe was missing somehow, nowhere to be seen.

A rough hand rolled him over. Mickey lay on his back and stared up. Two Taliban, eyes rimmed with kohl, their AKs on his chest. Mickey reached for the rifle still slung against him but they pinned it with a foot. He struggled and called for Chip and Sergeant Gabe but he could barely hear his own voice above the gunfire.

Another man approached with a rough hemp rope. They slipped the noose over his head. The rope caught. They stretched his neck. He saw the machete.

A blink.

A break.

A fade.

The Taliban's head explodes. Another reaches for his rifle and takes two in the chest. The third runs. Refreshed pink mist in his eyes and ears. Mickey rolls on his side and sees a dozen men with baseball caps and beards and wraparound sunglasses, running up the path, firing from cover up the hill. Now Mickey can hear the helicopter flap behind him and he tries to turn around and look but the sun overwhelms him and he can't see the bird or the lines the men had used to fast-rope down.

Gusts of light-headed euphoria, and Mickey tries to prop himself up. One of the operators runs up to Mickey, squats in the gore, places his body between Mickey and the incoming Taliban fire, lighting up the ridgeline with his grenade launcher. Another comes on Mickey's left, starts ratcheting tourniquets on his legs. The pink mist dissolves like fog at first light. Mickey's pumping heart floods the path, pools and ponds and a stream over the lip of the cliff face.

"He's going to bleed out," the medic says.

"No, he's not," says a third operator just arriving. He checks the blood type stitched on Mickey's vest, compares it to his own, written in black marker across the top of his boot. "Hook me up."

The medic pulls out two catheters, two tubes, one bag, ties one man to the other. Buddy transfusion. The man takes a breath and balls his fist and flexes and Mickey's brain glows from the hot transfer.

Bullet tracers light the sky and fast-movers thunder over the valley. Mickey's anus lets go. The medic leans over, holds him close, grabs Mickey's hand, looks him right in the eye.

"You're going home," he says.

Mickey's first sight at the hospital is Chip and Sergeant Gabe. They are standing at the end of his bed, in uniform, Chip grinning. Mickey tries to reach for them but can't seem to figure out how. His torso is buried under wraps and blankets, his leg stubs are mummies stuck in shrink-wrap plastic bags.

"Sergeant Gabe," Mickey manages to say. "Where did you go?"

"I was right there, don't worry," Sergeant Gabe says.

"Chip, I thought you got killed."

"No, I'm all right," Chip says. "We had to be here to welcome you home. No way we would miss it."

Mickey feels relief but anxiety starts to creep in.

"But what now?" Mickey asks. He doesn't need to point below his waist to explain what he means.

"Now you get into rehab," Sergeant Gabe says. "You have work to do."

Every day at the gym, Mickey works his stumps, lifting and kicking and straining. He does leg raises with weights hanging from his femurs, crunches and twists that pull the stitches in his abdomen wall taut as guitar strings. As soon as he receives his metal legs, he starts running every day, first one mile, then two, then more, many more. When his stumps are too sore, he bikes. When his belly is too sore, he works chest and arms and gets big, bigger than he's ever been. When he takes off his shirt you can see that the scar stretches completely across his belly, turns up at the ends like a smiley face, his nipples as eyes. Mickey works until his legs look like the tips of two muscled torpedoes jutting from his hips.

Mickey is in the weight room, crushing his bench, kicking his stumps, when the telegram arrives. The telegram says: "We need you back." His eyes fill. Mickey turns to his wife.

"I'm so happy for you, Mickey," she says. "You've worked so hard. You need to go. I'll be here waiting for you."

Mickey arrives at the mustering station walking on his new steel pins. Chip is there, and Sergeant Gabe, and the whole squad.

"Syria," Sergeant Gabe says. "They're sending us all back over."

"But how? It's been so long since I got hurt, you guys should have been reassigned by now," Mickey asks.

"There's a new policy," Sergeant Gabe says. "No more moves. They're keeping the units together. They're never going to break up our squad ever again."

They land at Tartus. The front door of the landing craft drops and Mickey and his squad mates hit the beach. Mortars fall in sheets and enemy strongpoints lay down overlapping machine gun fire but Mickey and Chip and Sergeant Gabe press up the sandy slope and take cover behind a concrete wall. The enemy soldiers are all dressed in uniforms, black man-jams that silhouette sharply against the grey and dusty homes. Mickey and Chip find their marks, move their squad in one block, then two, into the center of the city. The black uniformed men fall in piles and fill the gutters with blood. Children appear in doorways and immediately run to the Americans, take cover behind them, safely out of the way. One boy grabs onto Mickey's leg in fear, but Mickey musses his hair and the boy smiles with his wide dark eyes.

House to house they move and the Syrian Army liquefies before them. A rout becomes a slaughter becomes an extermination. Mickey and Chip reach the center of town to see enemy tanks fleeing. Tartus is free. A woman in a headscarf walks up to Mickey and touches his cheek and puts a flower behind his ear and says thank you. The boy smiles. Their commander, Captain Wodinski, drives up in his Humvee, steps from the armored truck, and addresses his men.

"Keg's on me when we take Damascus! Two kegs for Babylon!"

Chip and Mickey are resting in the shade of the palm trees as Sergeant Gabe walks among the squad and tosses out field rations.

"Chip, what'd you get?" Mickey asks.

"Beef stew and a can of Cope. How about you?"

"Chili Mac and Lucky Strikes."

"Nice."

The vacuum-packed meal pouches are already warm in the desert heat, and Mickey and Chip and the squad dig in. Chip puts in his dip and Mickey smokes and they talk of all the girls they left behind and the enemy that lay before them.

"Chip, can I tell you something? I was always afraid I had made the wrong decision, re-enlisting," Mickey says. "Can you believe that? I thought the war was evil. That maybe what we did was evil."

"Evil?" Chip says, shaking his head. And then Sergeant Gabe is there, standing over them.

"Nothing is evil when it's done for love," he says.

Outside of Tartus the inland hills rise in waves of scrub. Up the dusty paths Mickey and Chip and Sergeant Gabe march, their squad the vanguard of fleets of soldiers and Marines at their backs, until a regrouped enemy battalion counterattacks from above. They dive for cover and artillery shells donate around them. American fighter jets tear the sky and drop bunker-busters on the positions ahead. Chip screams to make himself heard.

"We're pinned down," he says.

"We have to keep moving," Mickey says. "We have a whole Army behind us. Let's go."

"Stop! Don't take that path!" Sergeant Gabe yells and grabs Mickey's arm. His ear is pressed to the radio. "The drones can see the IEDs. That path is mined. This one is clear." And he turns and climbs a new crease in the hillside and the squad follows him into the incoming fire.

Up they go, shooting, bounding, covering. Mickey looks out at the Mediterranean and can see the Navy's battleships turned broadside, firing their sixteen-inch guns at the enemy positions above him. He keeps moving, always moving, up the hill, his metal legs untiring, until a mortar lands between him and Sergeant Gabe and his world turns upside down.

Mickey looks at the sky. He pats down his chest, his thighs, finds his prosthetic legs are nothing but twisted metal.

"Medic!" Chip calls.

"No, no, I just need new legs," Mickey says.

"Medic!" Chip calls again, louder now, and Mickey sits up and sees a lump where Sergeant Gabe once was. Chip is working on him, surrounded by other soldiers. A litter appears, a form is loaded on, far too small to be Sergeant Gabe. They begin to carry him away but now Mickey's view is blocked as an engineer arrives with a package. Two new titanium legs. Mickey is up in a moment.

The artillery comes in. The naval fire goes out. Chip is back, the rest of the squad behind him, and he and Mickey huddle for cover, pinned down by the Syrians, when they hear a new sound, a growing sound. From behind them, a Humvee is barreling up the dusty road, its machine guns clanking and pumping in an unceasing ruckus. The armored truck stops next to Chip and Mickey and they look up at the gunner in disbelief.

Strapped into the turret is a piece of Sergeant Gabe. He looks like a larva of stitches and bandages, and smells like a summer cookout.

"They say I can come back," Sergeant Gabe says and smiles through tears. "They say I can still fight. They say I'm still useful."

And with one hook he spins the wheel and winches the turret around and with the other he works the paddles on the M2, singing softly to himself of mama, Ma Duece, so sweet, she's got everything he will ever need. Sergeant Gabe points his metal hose over the heads of his advancing comrades, the stream of bullets dousing the enemy hill and the men below freshened as if basking in the cooling mist thrown off by the spigot.

Sergeant Gabe suppresses them all. Mickey and Chip fight their way to the top of the first rise, toss a grenade in a machine gun nest, kill every man-jam that stumbles out dazed.

Mickey's mother turns to him and says, "We're so proud of you."

"Thanks, Mom."

"Mickey, look at what you've done for all of us," his father says. The pile of corpses rises to his waist. "All is forgiven. You are welcome home any time."

"Dad, I have things I need to do. My squad needs me," Mickey says.

"Of course. That's the kind of man you are. We understand. Your mother and I love you."

"We've always been proud of you," she says.

Another Syrian hill awaits, and another, and yet more. Mickey and Chip follow Sergeant Gabe in his Humvee as they slowly work their way inland, up the rise, clear the trench, advance again. The Syrians squirm in their holes like maggots in meat, and Mickey throws his grenades, shoots every rifle mag, is down to his pistol, down to the last click, when Chip arrives with reinforcements and clears the trench.

Mickey's grandfather claps him on the shoulder and smiles.

"Good job, Mickey," he says.

"Thanks, Grandpa."

He hands Mickey a new bandolier of rifle magazines.

"Mickey, we can take this hill," his grandfather says.

"You're right, Grandpa."

"I'll stay here. You and Chip out-flank 'em." And they do, his grandfather boiling off his Browning machine gun in an endless belt of covering fire.

"I want to tell you all about the war, Mickey," his grandfather says. "What it was like in France and Germany. Everything you've always wanted to know. Come walk with me."

"Where are we going?" asks Mickey.

"We're marching to the Pacific," he says, and puts his steel pot on his head.

"It's what we should have done to start with, right after 9/11," says Chip.

"It's Manifest Destiny," says Mickey.

"That's right, we're going to wipe 'em out, from the Med all the way to Korea, and then they'll sign the peace treaty, and when we get home, there's going to be a parade."

ABOUT THE
CONTRIBUTORS

ELLIOT ACKERMAN is the author of the critically acclaimed novel *Green on Blue*, and *Dark at the Crossing*. He is a frequent contributor to *The New Yorker*, *The Atlantic*, *The New Republic*, and the *New York Times Magazine*, among others. He served five tours of duty in Iraq and Afghanistan as a Marine and is the recipient of the Silver Star, the Bronze Star for Valor, and the Purple Heart. He currently splits his time between New York and Istanbul where he writes on the Syrian Civil War.

NATE BETHEA served as a US Army infantry officer from 2007 to 2014, during which time he deployed to Afghanistan and Central America. He teaches at Voices From War, a workshop for military veterans and families in the New York City metro area, and is a graduate of Brooklyn College. His writing has appeared in the *New York Times*, the *Guardian*, *McSweeney's Internet Tendency*, *The Iowa Review*, *The Morning News*, *The Daily Beast*, and *Guernica Magazine*.

ADRIAN BONENBERGER wrote *Afghan Post*, an epistolary memoir about his decision to join the military after having protested the Iraq War, and his experiences in Afghanistan over two deployments as an infantry officer. He has a master's in journalism from Columbia, an MFA in creative writing from SUNY Stony Brook Southampton, and helps edit and run *Wrath-Bearing Tree.*

BENJAMIN BUSCH is a writer, filmmaker, actor, and photographer. He served sixteen years as an infantry officer in the United States Marine Corps, deploying to Iraq twice. He is the writer/director of the film *BRIGHT,* was an actor and military consultant on the HBO mini-series *Generation Kill,* and he portrayed Officer Colicchio in the HBO series *The Wire.* He is the author of a memoir, *Dust to Dust* (Ecco) and his essays have appeared in *Harper's, The New York Times Magazine,* and NPR's *All Things Considered.* His poetry has appeared in *North American Review, Prairie Schooner,* and *Michigan Quarterly Review.* He teaches nonfiction at Sierra Nevada College and lives on a farm in Michigan.

BRANDON CARO is a former US Navy corpsman (combat medic) and advisor to the Afghan National Army. He deployed in 2006-2007 to Afghanistan in support of Operation Enduring Freedom. He is the author of the novel *Old Silk Road* and co-author of the Carl Higbie memoir, *Enemies, Foreign and Domestic: A SEAL's Story.* His work has also appeared in the *New York Times, The Daily Beast,* and *WhiteHot Magazine,* among others. He resides in Austin, Texas.

MICHAEL CARSON served as a US Army Infantry officer from 2005 to 2009. He studied history in New England and now lives on the Gulf Coast with his wife and son.

BRIAN CASTNER is the author of *All the Ways We Kill and Die* and the war memoir *The Long Walk,* which was adapted into an opera and named an Amazon Best Book for 2012. A former Explosive Ordnance Disposal officer and veteran of the Iraq War, his writing has appeared at the *New York Times, Wired, Outside,* and on *National Public Radio.* In 2014, he received a grant from the Pulitzer Center on Crisis Reporting to cover the Ebola outbreak in Liberia, filing stories for *VICE, Foreign Policy,* and *The Los Angeles Review of Books.*

MAURICE EMERSON DECAUL, a former Marine, is a poet, essayist, and playwright, whose writing has been featured in the *New York Times, The Daily Beast, Sierra Magazine, Epiphany, Callaloo, Narrative, The Common,* and others. His poems have been translated to French and Arabic. His theater pieces have been produced in the US and Europe and *Holding it Down,* a collaboration with Vijay Iyer and Mike Ladd, was the *Los Angeles Times* Jazz Album of the Year in 2013. Maurice is a graduate of Columbia University [BA] and NYU [MFA], and he is currently at work on the playwriting MFA at Brown.

DAVID F. EISLER served as an officer in the US Army from 2007 to 2012, with assignments in Germany, Iraq, and Afghanistan. In 2014, he earned a master's degree in international affairs from Columbia University. He is also a member of the Board of Directors for the nonprofit literary organization Words After War. His writing has appeared in the *New York Times, The Daily Beast, Collier's, Military Review,* and the *Journal of International Affairs.* He lives with his wife and son in Alexandria, Virginia.

TERESA FAZIO served as a Marine Corps communications officer from 2002 to 2006, deploying once to Iraq. Her writing has been published in the *New York Times, Task and Purpose, Vassar Quarterly, Consequence Magazine,* and *Penthouse.* She is the recipient of the 2015 Consequence Fiction Prize and a fellowship at Yaddo.

PJ FREDERIK deployed to Iraq from 2010 to 2011, graduated from Columbia in 2012, and worked for an NGO in Afghanistan from 2013 to 2015.

THOMAS GIBBONS-NEFF is a former enlisted infantry Marine and current staff writer at the *Washington Post*. He has a BA in English from Georgetown University and a mean widow's peak.

COLIN D. HALLORAN served as an infantryman in Afghanistan with the US Army in 2006. Since his return to civilian life, he has worked as an educator, writer, and visual artist, and his poetry, essays, and photographs have been published internationally. *Shortly Thereafter*, his memoir in verse, was awarded the 2012 Main Street Rag Poetry Book Award and his follow-up collection, *Icarian Flux*, was released to acclaim in 2015. He lives in Boston with his wife, fellow vet-writer LAUREN KAY HALLORAN, where he teaches college writing and literature.

LAUREN KAY HALLORAN is an Afghanistan veteran and former Air Force public affairs officer. She holds an MFA in creative writing from Emerson College in Boston, and her writing has appeared in *Glamour*, *Pleiades*, *Cobalt Review*, *Mason's Road*, *20 Something Magazine*, and the anthology *Proud to Be: Writing by American Warriors* (Southeast Missouri State University Press). Lauren's forthcoming memoir chronicles her coming-of-age against the backdrop of war, beginning with her mother's Army career and later with her own service in Afghanistan.

MATTHEW J. HEFTI is the author of *A Hard and Heavy Thing*. He was born in Canada and grew up in Wisconsin, and then spent twelve years as an Explosive Ordnance Disposal technician, deploying twice to Iraq and twice to Afghanistan. While enlisted, he earned a BA in English and an MFA in creative writing. He is now working, studying, and living in

Madison, Wisconsin, where he is pursuing his Juris Doctor at the University of Wisconsin Law School. He spends most of his time working for the Wisconsin Innocence Project, working to free the wrongfully convicted. His words have been seen in *Pennsylvania English, Blue Moon Literary & Art Review*; Chad Harbach's *MFA v. NYC*; and *War, Literature and the Arts*.

ALEX HORTON served as an Army infantryman in Iraq during the troop surge. His writing has appeared at the *New York Times, The Atlantic, Foreign Policy, Washington Post*, and other publications. His short story "Problem Dogs" won the 2015 Veterans Writing Prize held by Syracuse University's literary journal *Stone Canoe*. Alex is a graduate of Georgetown University, where he also taught journalism.

DAVID JAMES served as a Fire Support Officer in the 173d Airborne in Afghanistan from 2005-2006 and 2007-2008. He now teaches English in Italy where he lives with his wife and twin daughters. His hobbies include reading, writing, and rock climbing. He maintains a personal blog at tigerpapers.net.

After graduating from college in 2002, ERIC NELSON joined the US Army and deployed to Afghanistan as an infantry platoon leader in the 173rd Airborne Brigade. He then served as a company commander in the 101st Airborne Division in Iraq during the surge. His military service also brought him to Germany, Italy, Poland, and Ukraine. He has worked as a screenwriter, and has written essays and articles on topics ranging from international relations to brain hemorrhages. Eric lives in New York City, where he writes and is a medical student and researcher.

SHANNON HUFFMAN POLSON is the author of the memoir *North of Hope: A Daughter's Arctic Journey*. Her essay "Naked: A Triptych" won honorable mention in the 2015 VanderMey Nonfiction Contest, and her work has appeared in the *Utne Reader, River Teeth Journal, High Country News,* and *Ruminate Journal,* among others. Polson served as one of the first women to fly the Apache attack helicopter in the US Army. She holds a BA in English from Duke, an MBA from Dartmouth, and an MFA from Seattle Pacific University. She and her family live in northeast Washington.

MATTHEW ROBINSON's first story collection is *The Horse Latitudes.* His words have appeared in *Word Riot, Nailed Magazine, Clackamas Literary Review,* and *Grist Journal,* and he is co-editor of the literary journal *The Gravity of the Thing.* He earned his MFA from Portland State University and is the recipient of an Oregon Literary Fellowship. Matthew lives, writes, and teaches in Portland, Oregon.

KRISTEN L. ROUSE served in the US Army in Afghanistan in 2006, 2010, and 2012, for a total of thirty-one months in the country. Her essays have appeared in the *New York Times, The Daily Beast, Talking Points Memo, Tampa Bay Times, Salon,* and *River Teeth.* Her blog is trueboots.com. She lives in New York City, where she writes, consults, and advocates for veterans causes.

KAYLA M. WILLIAMS is a former sergeant and Arabic linguist in a Military Intelligence company of the 101st Airborne Division (Air Assault) whose service included a yearlong deployment to Iraq. Kayla is the author of *Love My Rifle More Than You: Young and Female in the U.S. Army,* a memoir about her experiences negotiating the changing demands on today's military. She graduated cum laude with a BA in English literature from Bowling Green State University and earned an MA in international affairs with a focus on the Middle East from American University. She currently lives near Washington DC with her husband, a combat-wounded veteran. Her book *Plenty of Time When*

We Get Home: Love and Recovery in the Aftermath of War, about his injury and their joint path from trauma to healing, was also published by W. W. Norton.

BRANDON WILLITTS enlisted in the US Navy as an intelligence specialist shortly after 9/11, where he was assigned to the Joint Chiefs of Staff and Kandahar, Afghanistan. After leaving the military, Brandon went on to co-found and serve as the executive director for Words After War, a literary organization that brings veterans and civilians together to examine war and conflict through literature. His work with Words After War has been featured in *Vanity Fair*, the *New York Times*, *Narratively*, *PBS NewsHour*, and the Council on Foreign Relations. He holds a BA in literature and writing from Marlboro College. A native of California and Maryland, he now lives in New York City.

CHRISTOPHER PAUL WOLFE, originally from Fayetteville, North Carolina, graduated from West Point in 2000 and spent six years serving as a US Army officer. He subsequently earned a Master of Business Administration degree from Duke University and worked in financial services. Chris now resides in Bedford Stuyvesant, Brooklyn, with his wife and three kids, where he is completing his MFA from Columbia University and working on his debut novel, *The Revival of James Cartwright*. His writing has also appeared in *Veoir Magazine*.